James Jackson

James Jackson has written six previous thrillers, including the acclaimed *Blood Rock*, *Pilgrim* and *Realm*, all published by John Murray. His non-fiction works include *The Counter-Terrorist Handbook*. A former political risk consultant and a postgraduate in military studies, he was called to the Bar and is a member of the Inner Temple. He lives in London.

Praise for James Jackson

'James Jackson has established himself as a fine storyteller . . . *Perdition* keeps the standard flying' *Press Association*

'A real page-turner. Drama and suspense are there in plenty . . . Once started, I could not put it down and highly recommend it' *Historical Novels Review*

'This is history – and terrific history – on every page' Frederick Forsyth

'The history is . . . reliable and convincing' *Times Literary Supplement*

'James Jackson writes with passion and authority in this fast paced, lively historical epic. His vivid writing skills bring both life and death acutely to the reader's sense' www.welovethisbook.com

Perdition

THE CRUSADERS' LAST STAND

JAMES JACKSON

JOHN MURRAY

First published in Great Britain in 2012 by John Murray (Publishers)
An Hachette UK Company

First published in paperback in 2013

1

Map drawn by Rosie Collins

A CIP catalogue record for this title is available from the British Library

ISBN 978-1-84854-006-4
Ebook ISBN 978-1-84854-527-4

Typeset in Monotype Bembo by Servis Filmsetting Ltd, Stockport, Cheshire

Printed and bound by Clays Ltd, St Ives plc

John Murray policy is to use papers that are natural, renewable and recyclable products and
made from wood grown in sustainable forests. The logging and manufacturing processes are
expected to conform to the environmental regulations of the country of origin.

John Murray (Publishers)
338 Euston Road
London NW1 3BH

www.johnmurray.co.uk

For my late father, the most remarkable of men

As a teenager I once climbed the Great Pyramid of Cheops (Khufu) on the Giza Plain in Egypt, sitting on its summit to watch the dawn break across the desert. It was an unforgettable and certainly unsanctioned escapade. That experience, and the visceral draw of walking or clambering (and in the case of a Spitfire, even flying) into the past, has stayed with me ever since. Whether standing in the cramped chapel of Fort St Elmo on Malta, where the doomed Hospitaller defenders took their last Holy Communion, or discovering the abandoned spot on the Obersalzberg mountain from which Adolf Hitler gazed out while planning a war that would eventually devour millions of lives, I have felt the presence and weight of history. I have walked the heights of Masada and visited the Nazi tunnels of Nordhausen; I even 'flipped the bird' to the grim statue of Soviet secret police chief Felix Dzerzhinsky in the heart of Communist-era Moscow. The locations and adventures have been various; a gift and privilege for any writer.

Yet it was in the Israeli coastal town of Akko – known to historians as Acre – that I stumbled across the unexpected. I had journeyed there with friends for background research and spent long hours checking vistas, cross-referencing maps, peering at ruins and immersing myself in the ancient landscape. There is no substitute for touching the stones. The position of the walls and the excavated tunnels, the half-buried Venetian Tower and the Tower of Flies still rising from the sea; all testified to the cataclysmic events of over seven hundred years before. In the gloom of the hall of the Hospitaller Knights of St John, I felt the pillars and scraped dust from the Frankish carvings. This was how all empires ended, with emptiness and dereliction. As my fingers traced the circumference of a high column soon to be encased in supporting concrete, they connected fleetingly with a faded inscription, its lettering barely discernible and scored into the surface. Having observed Crusader graffiti scarring every inch of the rock walls of the Chapel of St Helena in the Church of the Holy Sepulchre in Jerusalem, I should not have been surprised. I picked at it, using a coin to rub away the accumulated dirt. Revealed faint was a ghost, a single name. *Benedict*.

This is his story.

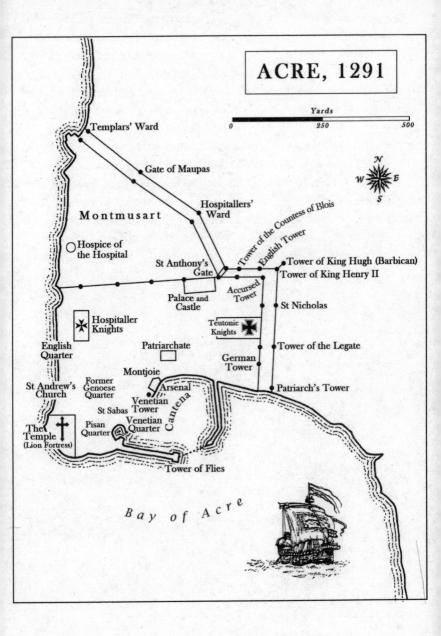

ACRE, 1291

Yards
0   250   500

Templars' Ward

Gate of Maupas

Montmusart

Hospitallers' Ward

Tower of the Countess of Blois

English Tower

Hospice of the Hospital

St Anthony's Gate

Tower of King Hugh (Barbican)

Tower of King Henry II

Palace and Castle

Accursed Tower

St Nicholas

Hospitaller Knights

Teutonic Knights

Patriarchate

Tower of the Legate

English Quarter

German Tower

St Andrew's Church

Former Genoese Quarter

Montjoie

Arsenal

Patriarch's Tower

St Sabas

Venetian Tower

Cantena

The Temple (Lion Fortress)

Pisan Quarter

Venetian Quarter

Tower of Flies

Bay of Acre

✝

Beginning

1289

Tripoli, the Holy Land

There was an age when the Crusader brought fear to the land of the Mohammedan, a time when the Frankish armies first viewed Jerusalem from the Mount of Joy and then fell upon the holy city. From across Europe they had journeyed, princes and nobles, prelates and peasants, pilgrims armed with sword and spear and battle-scythe, all intent on attaining salvation through slaughter. Pope Urban II had called upon them to take the Cross and wrest the sacred sites from the tainted grasp of the heathen. How high those walls had seemed, how great the calling, how fierce the eventual onslaught.

Only some thirteen thousand men, a fragment of the original force, actually reached Jerusalem in the summer of 1099. Yet it was enough. They had paraded in barefoot penance about the crenellated circumference, had stood poised beneath the waving banners of Duke Robert of Normandy and the Count of Flanders, of Bohemond of Taranto and his nephew Tancred, of Godfrey of Bouillon and Baldwin of Boulogne, of Raymond of Toulouse and Adhemar of Le Puy. Legendary names; a thirsting and determined throng. On 15 July 1099 they broke through, breaching the walls on the northern side and wrenching wide the Pilgrim Gate to the west, plunging deep into the alleyways to hack asunder any in their path. The screams were loud and the narrow streets awash in vivid crimson. On Temple Mount, the Saracens had conducted their final and chaotic stand and perished for their effort. In its frenzied aftermath, the exultant conquerors rampaged freely, looting and raping, drinking blood and cooking children on spits to eat their flesh in grisly ritual. All in the name of Christ. When it was done, they left their bloodied footprints on the way to reverence and give thanks at the Church of the Holy Sepulchre on the hill of the skull, the place they knew as Calvary. The kingdom of Jerusalem was saved. A blossoming created from butchery. God had willed it.

'The Saracen takes the south-east wall! He is upon us!'

Almost two hundred years since that opening Crusade and God appeared to be busied elsewhere. Jerusalem was long lost, seized by Saladin over a century before and after only a brief reversal misplaced again. Time had been unkind to the Crusader. The decades had witnessed a loss of fervour and a fighting retreat that saw the Christian invaders forced back to their fortified redoubts beaded along the coast. One by one, those bastions had fallen. The Seljuks, the Fatimids, the Ayyubids, different Moslem clans whose power waxed and waned and whose ambitions eroded the last strongholds of the Latins. Few Europeans still wished to crusade. No king desired to squander treasure and men in fruitless pursuit of a dream. Now it was the Mameluks of Egypt who enjoyed dominion over the Holy Land and their Sultan Qalawun who brought an army to extinguish the remnants of the County of Tripoli. The defenders were right to fear.

'Save us, O Lord! Save us!'

'At the hour of our tribulation, forgive our sins!'

2

'*Almighty God. Be with us now in the shadow of the valley!*'

The citizens of Tripoli were already condemned. They saw the elite spearhead of the *halqa* regiments crest the buckled ramparts, the gilded wave crash with metallic fury upon the defence. Kurds, Turcomans and Arabs came restless on the flow, their battle-cries yipping and keening sharp through the clamour. An unstoppable force.

'*Allahu Akbar! Allahu Akbar! Allahu Akbar!*'

Spears thrust and javelins flew, the sickle-blades of scimitars worked, the flitting darts from recurved bows chased down those in panicked stampede. People tripped and scrambled in aimless desperation. People clung to each other and prayed. People ran or cowered, attempted to hide, jostled and lowed as stricken cattle trapped between a slaughterhouse and the sea. It made no difference.

In a courtyard, a group of French merchants clawed vainly at a wall to gain purchase and height and a means to escape. Through luck and exertion they would reach the flat roof above and cross to the harbour beyond. But fortune did not smile. An arrow took one between his shoulders and he dropped ragged to the ground. His companions turned, their faces pale and mobile. Before them was a vision they had never encountered: a Mameluk hunting pack with the narrowed eyes of killers in plated lamellar breastplates flecked red. Prisoner capture was not the objective. Calmly, an archer plucked a dart from the quiver at his side and fitted it to his bow. Without a word, he raised the weapon, drew fast, aimed and fired. A second Frenchman fell. The rest attempted negotiation, offering money and appealing for mercy, their sob-stained cries swelling high in the confined space. The sound was stifled in a flurry of impacts and a profusion of feathered arrow-flights. The Mameluks moved on.

Few stood to offer a fight. Whether token or concerted,

resistance was swept aside. Outside the palace of the Countess Lucia, a few insanely brave knights had formed up to slow the onslaught. They would go unthanked. The rich nobility had already taken to ships bound for Cyprus; most members of the military orders were withdrawing to their galleys to preserve their strength for future reckoning; the Venetians had simply abandoned the Genoese and stolen vessels and merchandise in vengeful farewell. The small and exhausted band of warriors stood alone.

Yet they had inflicted damage. The area about them was strewn with the heaped corpses of their foe. A battle-axe jutted from the cleaved skull of a Bedouin auxiliary who lay on others shattered in close combat. Here, a broken sword, limp in the hand of an eviscerated Nubian. There, a crossbow quarrel piercing the throat of a gaping Saracen. And every-where, blood. A Templar nudged aside a fresh kill with his foot as a comrade swung his shield to deflect an arrow strike. It was a hopeless situation and becoming more crowded. Three Mameluks hurled javelins and followed through in howling assault, testing for weakness, ceding ground and sacrificing one of their number to the counter-blow. The knights would not easily be dislodged. These high priests of holy war were accustomed to creating piled mounds of dead. At bay, they remained ferocious. But they could not hold back an army.

Benedict stared. Out of sight, his senses almost outside his body, he crouched numb in the lee of the tempest. Somehow he breathed, somewhere his stomach was tight and his bladder loose and his limbs vibrated in the automatic terror of the moment. He was not present, he told himself. He was not hearing the shouts and jeers and the ringing clash of arms, was not choking on the kicked-up dust, was not a twelve-year-old boy and errand-runner sent with a message from Acre

4

and now caught behind the lines. He blinked away the sting of smoke and tears. Maybe he was invisible. Maybe he would succeed as he had on countless occasions in moving swift and low and unnoticed through a bustling or baying multitude. He could walk and talk as the Arab, pass as any Levantine, switch manner and identity with the wit and practised acumen of a spy. Few paid attention to the young. It was why William of Beaujeu, grand master of the Knights Templar, employed him; it was why he had played the fool, the thief, the goatherd, the beggar, the camel-driver, the pilgrim; it was why he conveyed secret missives to Damascus and Jerusalem and to every corner of the Holy Land. And it was why he found himself in Tripoli on this day of 26 April 1289 at the precise hour of its destruction.

Even an orphan half-breed had only a limited number of lives. The knights were down and the crowd surged. Benedict stirred, judging distance and gauging flow, forcing himself to join the direction of travel. Soon he would be discovered; he needed to hurry.

The instant arrived. He slithered into the backwash of converging mobs, a jinxing form scampering, panting, praying, caught and carried in the ecstatic madness of the chase. He fell and tasted earth, shrinking back as the armour-scaled feet of Mameluks tramped by. Then he was up once more, pursued by the grim vibrancy and undulating rhythms, vaulting obstacles and traversing rooftops, ducking into recesses and worming through fissures. The harbour was his goal.

A child wailed. Benedict halted. The boy stood in the shocked misery of his abandonment, a forlorn little figure almost mute and shaking in fright.

'You cannot stay, little brother.' Benedict grasped an arm and squeezed tight. 'You must come.'

'No.'

'I will care for you.'

'No.' The five-year-old drew back. 'They will kill us.'

'Only if we remain. You are safe with me, little brother.' Benedict tugged at the hunched shoulder.

The younger boy resisted. 'No.'

'We have no time.' He squatted and peered closely into the reddened eyes. 'Climb on my back and do not let go. Do so or I leave you.'

Benedict bent down, the boy clambered up and they staggered on. The small boy clung fast. They could do nothing for the wounded or the slain, for those encircled, for the citizens rushing and shrieking and singing hymns. The devil was at their backs.

At the waterfront, the pressure wave of defeat had compacted the populace into an aimless and dehumanised whole. Finales were generally untidy. There were knife fights and frantic transaction and scores to be settled; there was pulsating despair and random hope; there was the sight of galleys pulling for the horizon.

'Marshal Amalric of the Templars gives us passage on board,' Benedict yelled at the terrified face of a customs man. 'Tell me where to find him.'

The functionary pointed past the breakwater. 'There is your Marshal, attended by our other brave defenders.' Bitter sarcasm surmounted the fear.

Benedict lowered his head and thrust on, threading through, clenching tight the hand of the younger boy and tugging him close behind. The last of the longboats and open skiffs were filling and casting off, the haphazard arrangements provoking a clamoured storm of entreaties and a brute response with clubs and blades. In Europe, minstrels sang of chivalry and honour; at the wharves of Tripoli, men and women and children screamed.

A sword blocked his path. 'You have no place here, boy.'

'I do not, yet this young lord does.' Benedict pushed the child before him. 'I would scarce risk my life were his own not of value.'

'What kind of value?' Greed would ever out.

'His father will pay well for his return.' Benedict lied. 'Quick now. He takes up little stowage.'

'His name?'

Without pause and drawing on his own reserves of make-believe, Benedict answered. 'Ralph, son of Raymond, a noble at the Cyprus court of King Henry. It will earn you a chest of golden marks.'

Debate concluded as the Saracens crashed in. With dread inevitability, their lances and plumed helmets and their full-throated roar cascaded on the scene. Benedict propelled his young charge to the well of the boat and turned to run, free of his responsibility. God help them all. There was a dark euphoria to being alive in the midst of death.

A man took an arrow in his temple and disappeared from view, trampled and replaced as the winnowing continued. Such sport. Benedict had reached the harbour limit: perhaps he should do as others did and make his peace and submit to fate. He looked about. An overloaded boat was splashing its way to the bare piece of rock a hundred yards or so offshore. More were following, civilians jumping into the sea with barrels and flotsam and struggling clumsily for the adjacent shore. St Thomas Island provided meagre asylum. Benedict committed himself to the swell.

He might have drowned as many did and vanished without trace or murmur, yet he persevered. He wished to tell his friend Hazzim of these events, to regale Roger de Flor and El Selim and the old Patriarch with tales of his adventure. They were all he had. At some future date he would dive again for

7

shellfish and throw nets with the fishermen in the Bay of Acre to intercept the glittering silver run of shoaling sardine. Heavy limbs and waterlogged lungs would not prevent him.

Retching, weighed with the fatigue of his exertion, he crawled ashore and lay face down and spent upon the sandstone ledge. It was a respite of sorts. The seawater seemed to bleed from him. It was peaceful on this outcrop, an ocean away from the maelstrom behind. He did not care to dwell on the crowding images, on the narrowness of his escape and the fate of the hundreds overtaken. But the reflected horror on nearby faces compelled him to glance back. Instantly, he regretted the act. Across the water, framed against the orange-black backdrop of flame and smoke, the Moslem horde was wholly engaged. Light refracted on sharpened steel and arms flung wide to the next downward stroke.

'Their cavalry make for us.' The voice of a woman trembled no louder than a whisper. 'See, they gather at the shore.'

'They have no means to reach us.'

'Yet their number grows with that intent.'

'Be of faith, sister. They can do us no harm.'

A child screamed. 'The horses enter the water!'

'She is right.' Alarm dragged a voice to higher pitch. 'Riders and mounts set out for us. We are undone.'

So they were. Carefully and efficiently, the horses swam the distance. Mameluk cavalry were rarely inconvenienced or diverted from their purpose.

Half submerged and barely conscious and resting on a plank of wood Benedict floated on the current, a deserter from the field of massacre. The screams receded, the dissonant noise replaced by the slap of waves and the restless emptiness of new surroundings. A chill and lonely place. It allowed him to drift and would permit him to die. *They can do us no harm. They can do us no harm. They can do us no harm.*

Benedict, aged twelve, an overlooked victim of just another war.

Victory contained its own particular scent. Attended by his generals and personal guards, Sultan Qalawun breathed deep as he toured the charred ruins of his most recent prize. Triumph rarely came cheap, yet it was always rewarding. He would embrace success in whatever form it was presented. The corpses blackening in the streets and wallowing in the harbour were as meaningless as crushed scarabs; the buildings that once had housed these infidel Latins would be razed and their stones carried elsewhere. Nothing would remain. To leave it standing would be to offer a future beachhead for the Crusader and an opportunity for return. That was not his plan. He had waited and watched too long to tolerate such things. He had held back his army until King Bohemond was dead and the competing factions of Genoa and Venice were at each other's throats before committing himself to the siege. Timing was critical.

He paused, a martial figure resplendent in jewelled turban and gold-worked armour, his beard greyed and face lined with age and his dark oval eyes betraying the warrior caste of his Mameluk ancestry. His forefathers might once have been slaves, but they were hardy progeny of the Asiatic mountains. Trained in the military schools of Damascus and Cairo, they had risen to rule the Saracen domain with consummate ruthlessness and skill. Not since the mighty Salah ad-Din, uniter of the Moslem worlds, had the True Believer enjoyed such hegemony and keenness of spirit. Everyone paid tribute.

Qalawun stooped above the broken and headless remains of a priest and plucked a wooden crucifix from the stiffened fingers. The Cross had yet again proved itself inadequate. In battle, it was the forces of Islam that would prevail; in a trial of strength, it would be the Sultan of Egypt who would dominate. Saladin had left unfinished business. The great Mameluk leader Baybars had pushed the Christians from Galilee and kept them on the defence. It would be he, Qalawun, who reclaimed the entire Holy Land and brought the sacred quest to a climactic finish. The Latins clung to their hopes and their redoubts, disporting themselves in merry abandon within the royal city of Acre. If only they could see what happened here. He tossed aside the crucifix and walked on. One day, matters would be resolved.

✝

Chapter 1

1290

ACRE, THE HOLY LAND

'B en . . .'

He turned at the familiar voice, happy to escape
bleak memories for the concerned eyes and serious countenance of his friend Hazzim. Up here on the roof of the
Fonda, they could sit and while hours away with the ease and
idle chat of fourteen-year-olds who had the sea before them
and the royal city of Acre at their backs. Hopes could be
shared and fears debated, anecdotes swapped and laughter
exchanged. Benedict, the orphan progeny of a Sicilian whore
and Pisan soldier, the talkative bringer of news and cheer, the
adopted son of this enclave of Outremer that embraced him.
All would smile at the approach of the black-haired and
snub-nosed boy with the racing feet and gleeful spirit. And
with him, Hazzim, a head taller, more cautious and reserved,
the offspring of a local sheikh from a village on the plain. Of
different forebears and separate faiths, yet they were twins
of a kind. That was friendship.

'Sit, brother.' Speaking Arabic, Benedict slapped the flat
roof beside him and waited for his comrade to comply. 'I did
not expect you.'

'Where there are ships, there is trade.' Hazzim nodded to
a weathered merchant galley pulling past the harbour mouth.

'And where there is trade, there are Templars.'

Benedict shielded his eyes against the morning glare and scanned the cluttered vista. Laid out in busy review, the arrayed commerce of the Latin kingdom moved in frenetic flow as though it had always been and forever would remain. Everyone profited. At the narrow mouth to the port, men toiled at a capstan to lock in earnings and raise the chain that restricted access and ensured the paying of imperial duty. Along the breakwater and at the wharves of the Cantena vessels were unloaded and resupplied for homeward passage. In the Customs House, the excise was taken and rendered to the burgeoning account of King Henry of Cyprus. And in the galleried periphery and central square of the Fonda, the international marketplace, goods were bartered and traded, paid for with gold and silver, gems and goodwill, in a tumult of tongues and mutiny of colour. It was how Acre stayed alive, ignored its fragility and pretended at its divine right of permanence. To the left, the Venetian Tower still rose, an eighty-foot statement of commitment and power; to the right, four hundred yards west along the waterfront and looming resolute in kurkar stone, was the moated Temple, the Lion Fortress, the command post of the Knights Templar. From his vantage, Benedict surveyed the whole with a practised and devoted eye. It was his empire; his home.

He clapped his friend on the back. 'How is the fruit harvest, brother?'

'By the grace of Allah, a fine one. And when the cherries ferment, they will be first for the still.'

'You grow rich on the thirst of the Latins, brother.'

Hazzim shrugged. 'Our medicines are good.'

'Roger de Flor swears they cure all but an aching head.' Benedict sank back and stretched out his legs. 'You may be sure he will drink every drop from those flasks.'

'Then no person in Acre is safe.' They shared the joke.

'Eau de vie.' His eyelids shuttered, Benedict softly rolled the words in his mouth. 'Eau de vie.'

'The boiling vats are readied, the collecting vessels too. My father claims he waits for Benedict before he may begin.'

'I will accept his summons, brother.'

He loved the alchemy of the process, the sweet intensity of the odours, the sight of the first pure drops of spirit condensed like dew on the glass lip. Rose petals, apricot, plum, cherry, the focus of the village and the stuff of life. He was part of it, embraced into the family. It meant he could catch a glimpse of Leila, older sister of Hazzim; he would smile shyly as she blushed and was ushered away by the women. It was a pity she no longer played as children played, no longer laughed and ran and held his hand. Thoughts of her often raided his mind, making his pulse quicken and his pores sweat, forcing the pressure in his temples and groin.

'Will things change, Ben?'

The question was delivered with quiet sincerity and caught Benedict unprepared. He cocked an eye. 'Change what, brother? Change how?'

'There are rumours, Ben.'

'We are in the Holy Land. There is always rumour of this, of that, of everything and nothing.'

'Of war.'

Benedict sat upright and rested his arm across the shoulders of his friend. 'You worry, brother. And worry is not for us, nor for the hour when the sun warms our backs and the world rests at our feet.'

'This world may vanish, Ben.'

'See the ships. See the merchants. See the knights strutting proud.' He swept his finger across the scene and pointed to the squat and square-built Tower of Flies. 'Each morning,

13

the same. They change the candles and clean the glass. Every night, the light shines out again.'

'For how long?'

'Until we are old and grey as Abraham himself.'

'Do you believe this, Ben?'

'As we are friends and brothers, I do. As those twin lions atop the gate towers to the Temple are named by us Hazzim and Benedict, I do.'

'Shall it prevent walls collapsing or restrain the wrath of the Sultan of Egypt?'

Benedict cuffed his friend good-naturedly in the chest. 'Your misery will surely prevent me enjoying the day.'

'You are forgetting Tripoli, Ben.' Hazzim felt the grip tighten on his shoulder.

'I forget little.'

Out beyond the Tower of Flies, behind the July moisture clinging as mist above the Bay of Acre, the distant shoreline and rising ground of Mount Carmel were almost obscured. At the base of the escarpment lay the former Christian settlement of Haifa. Like Tripoli, it too was in the hands of the Mameluk.

A shout and the boys jumped to their feet at the hollered news, chasing each other to reach the ground. Selim had arrived at Acre. The old cameleer had been gone these three months and would be seated as was his custom near the spreading mulberry, waiting for reunion. He was both counsel and friend, a fierce and flinty patriarch, a trader whose extended caravans trailed across deserts and mountains to bring goods to eager merchants in Jerusalem and Damascus and the coastal towns of the Levant. Arab or Frank, all did business with Selim.

Benedict led the way, his pace furious and his face keen.

None compared with the grizzled ancient Selim, a man who had survived sandstorms and bandits to travel the earth, a Bedouin legend known to have dispatched by his sword scores of marauding foe. Few dared oppose him; few were as staunch in their love and loyalty as the European orphan boy.

They darted fast through the crowded streets and winding passageways, moving with the fluency of practised denizens. Every roof was their eyrie, every nook and compound well explored. Acre, a city of forty churches and the stench of Hades; Acre, a cramped profusion of dwellings, taverns and brothels girded by high and castellated walls; Acre, a place where some twenty-five thousand souls lived and worshipped, plotted and bickered and scarce could breathe in the fetid atmosphere. A toehold, a strongpoint. The epicentre and summation of remaining Frankish power.

'*Move that donkey.*'

'*Make way! I am on errand!*'

'*You rob me with such prices! You are no better than a thief!*'

'*Insult me at your peril!*'

Murmur and hubbub were punctuated by the sharper tones of altercation, by the cries of sellers and braying protest of mules, by the drunken oaths of harlots and sailors. Anyone who visited the Holy Land was washed up here, and it was in Acre the journey ended. Saracen hostility ensured neither pilgrim nor soldier would reach the interior or were likely ever to return alive. Stalemate and stand-off and the inhabitants clung on.

The two boys pushed through, waving to Theobald the Knight of St John and cheering at the sight of the court dwarf Amethyst perched high in the saddle-basket of an ambling pack horse. St Andrew's Church, the English quarter, the Hospitaller redoubt, the solemn form of the Patriarchate, the Auberge of the Teutonic Knights, were all way points on the teeming route as the youngsters made for the outlying gates. Ahead of them was the inner line of defence dominated by the soaring edifice of the Accursed Tower. Next, a dry moat contained by the outer wall and its key gateway nestled within the protective bulk of the mighty King Henry Tower. Another deep and dry moat, spanned by a drawbridge, and the outer fortification, the barbican known as the Tower of King Hugh, was reached. Comforting features, a series of angled killing zones and cul-de-sacs, portcullises and armoured doors, murder holes and arrow slits. They gave the impression of impregnability and permanence. Benedict joshed with the guards as they lazed at their posts and ushered his companion onwards.

This was his garden, the plain of Acre. There were citrus and olive groves, a profusion of orchards, the blanket spread of fields and plantations that stretched to a brown and more barren horizon. Scattered sparse among them were the fortified farmsteads and villages, the agrarian fiefdoms of the knights, the homes of the Arabs and Jews and others uninvited to live among the Christians. There was hardly an irrigation channel the two friends had not leapt, scarcely a tree they had not climbed. It was only the tanneries and slaughterhouses Benedict avoided. They reeked of death, redolent of a recent past in which he was twelve years old and running through the howling streets of Tripoli. He would not venture back.

They found Selim as they always found him, a tall and still figure watchful and austere at the heart of his clan. His authority was total. After all, he had lived long and was worthy of deference. He had seen the Kush and the Himalyas, he had traded with the Mongol and the Chin. With his sword and camel whip at his side and his retinue in close attendance, he chewed on pistachios and spat the shells and stared out from the shade of a woven and embroidered canopy. His basalt-black eyes missed nothing; his instructions were issued with a nod or an inflection of the hand. People said he was as ancient as the holy texts. People said he was moulded from the weathered dunes. People said he was the greatest cameleer of them all.

The fierce immobility of his countenance dissolved to a grin as he rose to greet his visitors. Hazzim stood back respectfully, but Benedict stepped forwards to the wide embrace.

'Ben, *Waladii*.' Selim kissed him and held his arms, the better to scrutinise. 'You grow towards manhood in my absence.'

'And you still live, *Amm* Selim.'

'Though I wrestle monsters and fight demons, by the grace of Allah the Most Merciful, I do.' He patted the boy on the face. 'I am the younger at seeing you, *Waladii*.'

'Did you visit Egypt?'

'And every town, caravanserai and stretch of desert in between. It is why my caravan is heavy-laden. Gold from Cairo, frankincense from Gaza, silks and myrrh and horses and hunting-birds from a hundred other places.'

'Now you may rest, *Amm* Selim.'

'Not I, for I have business here.' He motioned for the boys to sit. 'Yet all may wait while we talk and eat bread and dates.'

The youngsters accepted happily, squatting on their haunches, settling into a ritual as old as their memories and as comforting as the arrival of the swifts. Selim was here and that was what mattered.

The old man peered towards the walls of Acre. 'What news, *Waladii*? Does your city still stink of shit?'

'What city does not, *Amm* Selim?'

'The truest of words. You know what we Bedu say of such

places and people?' They did, but he continued. 'When Allah created the world, he captured the lightning and from it fashioned the nomad. Then he took the wind and created the horse, plucked a cloud for the camel and a pinch of earth for the donkey. Finally, he selected the dung of the donkey and produced every one of the town-dwellers.'

Benedict feigned offence. 'But I dwell in a town, *Amm* Selim . . .'

'You are a son of the deserts and sea, would never be born of the arse of a donkey.'

'I know some who are.'

Selim nodded. 'How is my great friend, the rogue Roger de Flor?'

'He makes more enemies than friends, *Amm* Selim.'

'An untamed spirit who is true to himself. For it, I respect him. He would die for you, *Waladii*.'

'And I for him.'

'Let us trust it shall not come to that.' The aged caravan master broke bread and turned to the young Arab. 'Greetings to your father and mother, Hazzim.'

'I thank you, *Sidi*.'

'As I am grateful for their elixirs and trade. The village prospers?'

'With the blessing and will of Allah, it does.'

'May He grant you all peace and riches.' Another tear of the bread. 'I bring you both gifts from my travels, bounty you may pick from the smaller packs. First, our game.'

They crouched about the *gul bara* board, the ivory counters ready, each of the three players directed to their contest. Selim always made time. Another rite took place about them, the camels kneeling or standing in rows, their drivers drinking tea or offloading merchandise or patrolling the encampment.

Enthusiastic cries rippled faint from the ramparts, following the trajectory of a stone as it was flung high from a catapult. A training shot. Small figures crowded the walls to witness the display, their interest rewarded with a solid strike and eruption of dirt some several hundred paces out. The applause was deserved.

Selim squinted. 'As boys will throw a pebble, so men will hurl a rock.'

'Is it not fair sport, *Amm* Selim?'

'A sport that leads to bloodshed. A sport that leaves few victors.'

'They are drawing back the arm again.' Benedict peered at the indistinct view. 'It will range further this time.'

'We have a soldier, a sergeant of artillery, in our midst.' The old man contemplated the youth.

'There is dignity in it, *Amm* Selim.'

'Foolhardiness also. You listen too much to Roger de Flor.'

'He speaks with the wisdom of his experience.'

'And with the experience of one who should know more.'

'Have you not killed many, *Amm* Selim?'

'War is different and you have seen it.' His voice gruff, the old camel master concentrated on the board. 'Leave such theatre to others, *Waladii*.'

'I cannot. See, they let fly another boulder.'

Selim left them to it; he would not interrupt. He had witnessed such things on countless occasions, had spied the same martial drills among the warrior caste of Egypt. Black oxen, the Mameluks called their siege catapults. Perhaps they would soon be dragging their way up here, to nod their heads and graze on the plain of Acre. The second shot was taken and a direct hit scored against a thorn bush.

'They do well, *Amm* Selim.'

'Will it suffice? Shall it preserve the safe destiny of Acre?'

'I prefer *gul bara* to riddles.' Benedict reached for the ivory pieces.

His hand was taken and squeezed tight in the roughened palm. 'No riddle, *Waladii*. For you, only a choice. Between boyhood and manhood. Between Frank and Arab, infidel and True Believer. Between remaining and departure. Between light and darkness. Between life and death.'

The boy smiled. 'You fret like Hazzim.'

'I fear for you, *Waladii*. I fear.' The pressure from the enclosing fingers did not ease.

~

'*Felicitas!*'

It was a battle-cry, a favourite of Julius Caesar and now used by a bare-chested man leaping riotously from a first-floor window. He had plainly attempted the feat before. Tumbling expertly on landing, he rolled and recovered, a giant amused and light on his feet, one hand on his sword-grip and the other fumbling to tighten the cord belt about his waist. There was a certain etiquette to cuckolding a rich Venetian merchant and being caught *in flagrante* by his servants. It was a breach of the code, but even as an audience gathered and a motley and avenging band arrived bearing arms, the escapist was unperturbed. He bowed and strolled, danced a few steps, paraded with the confidence of a trickster. Roger de Flor was enjoying himself.

He called out in Italian. 'You may offer me your surrender if you wish.'

'We offer you our blades.' The retort was blunt. 'You defile our hospitality and debase the honour of one of our brethren.'

'I am the captain of a galley. What else would you expect?'

De Flor adjusted his position, his eyes scanning the belligerent faces.

'You will wish you had stayed at sea, you dog.'

'A dog prefers to lift its leg ashore.'

The enemy spokesman scowled. 'Your ready tongue counts for little here, de Flor.'

'Though it wins me audience and affection in the chambers of your women.'

There were hoots and whistles from the expectant throng. Around the circumference of the small square men and women made room for the coming fray. Frank, Arab and Jew were united in their interest, emerging from the alleyways in their hats, keffiyehs and wound liripipe caps.

The Venetian ringleader spat in the dirt. 'You offend the commune, de Flor. You commit infamy and insult to our pride.'

'Would that I might do it more often.'

'Yet you are outnumbered.' At the wave of a dagger the opposition deployed to a wider front.

'I have my friends.'

De Flor grounded his sword and spun to catch a quarterstaff lofted by a sidekick. He still commanded some allegiance, drew followers with his piratical ways. There might be need of them. Yet for the while he was content to calculate and confront the odds, to dominate the space. It was his argument. His problem.

The voice was mocking. 'What consolation a stick, de Flor?'

'It is my solace you will pray without your teeth.' The adventurer whirled the staff in exhibition. 'Have at me, my friends.'

'You will pay.'

'So, come to collect your wage.'

They tried, advancing in a rush, and were outmanoeuvred in a confused circus of raining blows and upended feet as attackers became the attacked. De Flor moved among them, a muscled and dextrous practitioner alone and fast at the centre of the fight. A knifeman took an end of the staff full in his face, his companion the other. Both fell screaming. A studded cosh swung and was parried, its wielder struck and thrown raggedly back; a sailor tried his hand, and was rewarded with a pummelling; a baker, a leather-worker, an infantryman all leapt forwards and each in turn had his nose, knee and clavicle broken. Their target deftly worked his quarterstaff. To the left and right, jabbing and feinting, sweeping and controlling, he let his opponents come on. The next wave descended and was dealt with as summarily as the first. The field of battle was transformed to a groaning catchment of crippled and crawling men.

His chief antagonist glared, uncertain. 'The Doge shall hear of this . . .'

'That is for the good.' Holding the quarterstaff double-handed as a sword, de Flor tapped the weapon rhythmically on the ground. 'Perchance he will send from Venice men and not beardless infants to do his battle.'

'You will regret such action, de Flor.'

'At present, I am enjoying it.' He noted a prone figure reaching for a misplaced knife and stepped to break the fingers with a single pestle stroke.

'Roger!'

Benedict's voice was sharp in its alarm. The fourteen-year-old had sought out his friend and patron and found him. Laughter or trouble were common accompaniments. Slow and deliberate and nonchalant in defiance, de Flor raised his eyes to the new threat. A brace of kneeling crossbowmen had their weapons cocked and levelled at his chest. They awaited the order.

De Flor continued to beat tempo with his quarterstaff. 'No soldier may outrun the flight of an ash quarrel.'

'Nor would we expect it.' The Venetian tried to suppress his own delight. 'Are we to hear word of contrition at the hour of your death? A plea for clemency? A sermon of regret?'

'None of these.'

'Then you are surely damned and deservedly so.' The hand was raised, preparatory to the finale.

It failed to drop. Behind de Flor, in the sightline of the Venetians, an armoured rank of sergeants in jupon jackets and dun-coloured mantles had appeared. They were Templars and they too had crossbows.

Their leader called out. 'By authority of the Temple, you will not harm a servant of our order.'

'Servant?' Dull outrage glowered back from the Venetian. 'He is nothing to God or mortal but a Catalan louse or reptile.'

'A base creature over whose possession you would not care to shed your blood.'

'He is ours, Templar.'

'You will find he is not.' An air of calm authority exuded from the newcomer.

It met and fractured on the thin skin of the Italian. 'We cannot give up our prisoner.'

'Yet your jailers appear ill matched to their task. Deliver him to us.' Crossbows lowered. 'Alive.'

Pride and contest were already lost. Grudgingly, with curses and backwards glances, the Venetians limped away in their retreat. They were poor losers. The crowd applauded and jeered, jubilant or dismayed according to allegiance. But the champion was de Flor.

He shook himself down and collected his sword, donning

the undershirt thrown him by a man-at-arms. For the burly galley captain and chancer, it would prove merely an interlude to further escapade and roving pursuit. He tousled the hair of a beaming Benedict and winked.

'I am a poor exemplar to you, boy.'

'You are the victor.'

'For my sins I am, and they are varied in their number.' He seemed comfortable at the thought. 'I cannot say my foes are much depleted by the action this day.'

'They seem wounded by it.'

De Flor laughed. 'If only the Grand Master of the order would see matters as you do. But he will not. Beaujeu will make me sweat for the honour of his intervention.'

'He saved you, Roger.'

'There is always purpose in his method as there is in mine.' The large man stooped and whispered in his ear. 'When the dust is watered and the throng dispersed, return to the house from whence I jumped and collect from its lady the keepsakes she promised.'

'Gold?'

'What better token of high esteem? Now, I am to the Lion Fortress and you go to your duties.'

Accustomed to running errands or ferrying excuses, Benedict sloped into the multitude. Just another boy dressed in a dusty djellabah. As de Flor watched him, his heart pinched briefly and protectively. Behind him, the Templars stood waiting.

Conflict of a different kind was underway in the great hall of the royal palace in Acre. Altercation and duel might flare on the streets, but it was in this chamber that bitterness and disputation truly showed. There was power at stake, prestige and position to struggle for, the allocation of favours and riches fractiously to debate. Acre was the last great port and presence of the Latin kingdom of Outremer. Crusader nature was to fight, and so here they fought each other.

At the head of the long oaken table, Amalric, Constable of the city and brother to King Henry of Cyprus, sat wearily and kneaded the growing ache behind his brow. This was his fief and his curse. He viewed the men arrayed before him, the most senior knights and influential lords, the grand masters of the military orders, the silk-trimmed dignitaries representing private ambition and city-state interest. A snake-pit. To the guttering glow of oil lamps and tallow, and in the backwashed stink of the exterior, they would continue to pound their fists and vent opinion. Fine tapestries were small recompense for such a posting.

Amalric sighed. 'Am I not *bailli* of this city? Do I not command your fealty and obedience?'

'We answer to the Pope.' William of Beaujeu, grand master of the Templars appraised him with deep-set and calculating eyes. 'Whilst he is aware of coming war and calls for Crusade, you and your courtiers dance and carouse and dream of Camelot.'

'His Reverend Lord the Pope is not in Acre. Nor do I see his fleet arrive.'

'The more reason we prepare our own defence, your highness.'

'And provoke Qalawun?'

'He needs no provocation or excuse.' Beaujeu leant back and addressed the whole. 'It is two hundred years since we took Jerusalem. Two hundred years of futile sallies and fighting retreat. Two hundred years in which we have squandered every gain we made.'

'Your point, Beaujeu?' It was a Pisan who spoke.

'The Sultan of Egypt has waited long enough. Each morsel

he has taken gives him greater appetite. As he seized Tripoli, so will he come to swallow us.'

'Where is your proof?'

'I hear rumours from Cairo, reports from every corner of the Saracen realm.'

'Rumours? Reports?' There was snorted derision from a French noble. 'Is mere gossip to undermine our treaty of peace and truce with the Mameluks?'

With withering civility, Beaujeu surveyed him. 'What is a treaty to the Mameluks? What are peace and truce to one such as Qalawun who is sworn to rid the Holy Land of Christians?'

'Your warmongering will not aid us.'

'Nor your blind ignorance.'

The nobleman struck the table with his fist, his face tight and mottling in ire. 'I am not the one who is blind, Beaujeu. Look about you. See the warehouses fill, the harvests grow tall, the caravan trains from Damascus weighed heavy by their goods.'

'I peer upon a wider distance.'

'No, Grand Master. You Templars consider yourselves and guard your interests, protect your banking and your wealth.'

'None has defended the faith or Holy Land more bravely than we.'

'As you did at Tripoli when your Marshal and his men took flight aboard their galleys?' The sour intervention came from a Burgundian. 'You are not the sole receiver of news, Beaujeu. Some would claim your belligerent sounds and martial fury are linked close to the hostility and censure you suffer in Europe.'

'And what would you suppose?'

'That your much vaunted order is reviled. That your

warrior-priests grow fat and rich and slothful. That you lost Outremer to the Saracen and favour with our princes and thus forfeit your reason to exist.'

'Such spite and venom.'

If he were pricked by criticism, Beaujeu did not show it. He was accustomed to dealing with ingrates and fools, to negotiating the treacherous currents of politics and power-play. Acre must survive. Should it fall, his reputation would follow and the sacred flame and mystery of the Temple would die. He could not let that happen. Too much blood had been shed, too many of his brethren sacrificed. By sleight of hand or force of arms, he would ensure the longevity of his order and avoid the ignominy of failure and the torment of eternal damnation. This was his vow and his objective.

The Constable directed his gaze to the old man quietly listening at the far end. 'What say you of such matters, our beloved Patriarch?'

'I am a man of God and not of war, know little of any rumour or hearsay of coming campaign.' His Beatitude tugged at his robe, a dignified and kindly presence uncomfortable among the quarrelsome brood. 'Yet of this I am aware. I am sufficiently aged to have wept in Gethsemane and bent my head in reverence before the Holy Sepulchre. I recognise that we in Acre are the weakened rump of what was once our Kingdom of Jerusalem. And I understand that as the blessed St Sebastian was pierced by arrows in his chest, so we too may suffer martyrdom for our faith.'

Silence ensued, an interlude that allowed Beaujeu to observe the sadness in the ancient eyes and the shadow of premonition. The moment passed, shattered by the sound of heavy chamber doors being slammed wide. Through the open portal scampered the dwarf Amethyst dressed in the skins of a hound, a comic turn bearing a parchment letter in its jaws and bounding on to the table in frantic quest to reach its master. The mood changed and mirth returned.

Beaujeu nodded to himself. He was not so isolated after all. The Patriarch too had seen the future.

✝

Chapter 2

'Our wayward and unruly beast is penned.'

Roger de Flor did not appear chastened by the words. He sprawled unrepentant on a horsehair couch, feigning disinterest as the grand master entered his cell. Beaujeu was accustomed to his insolence. He carried a ceramic pitcher from which he decanted generous measures of wine into a pair of goblets before handing one to his prisoner. The adventurer took it, drank and returned the vessel for more.

Beaujeu seated himself in a chair opposite and studied his prisoner for a while. 'How many times have you flouted the laws of this order? How many occasions have we plucked you from the jaws of your own destruction?'

'I do not count.'

'Nor do you see much reason to think.' The grand master reached to refill the still proffered cup. 'Are you impervious to the power of the cross affixed there above your head?'

'Our Saviour would forgive me my weakness.'

'There are manifold number in Acre who would not. I brought you here to the Temple as much to preserve them from your depravity as you from their clamorous indignation.'

'Your order must hold me in great esteem.'

'We pay you well, de Flor. You captain our galleys, train our men-at-arms, and are sent where we require an element of brute force.'

'My gifts are forever at your service.'

'Sadly, they are attached to the man.' Beaujeu summoned a thin and unconvincing smile. 'Your wiles are those of the jackal and your strength that of a baited bear. Yet your manners belong to a wild goat.'

'It is why you and not I wear the blood-red Latin cross upon the left shoulder.'

'It is fortunate then that I am a soldier of Christ, and provident too that I believe in your redemption.'

More wine was drunk and the minutes passed in quiet contemplation. They were warriors fashioned of separate cloth. On one side, the groomed slyness of Beaujeu, the noble-born immersed in intrigue and consumed with cold and holy passion; on the other, the wilful intelligence of de Flor, the twenty-three-year-old son of a falconer and a soldier of small fortune, a Catalan-Germanic wanderer drawn by the prospect of women, war and prize. It was an unconventional and often adversarial alliance bred largely of necessity, but from difference could grow a symmetry of purpose.

'I hear that in Sicily they still speak of you with terror, de Flor.'

'It was hard fighting.'

'You gave no quarter, spared no life.'

'Is this your complaint?'

'My observation.' The grand master tapped a finger, marked time and chose his words. 'There is every reason to believe that your prowess once more may be called upon.'

'I see no sign of it.'

'Then you are as blind as the Council, and as gripped by your own reflection as the perfumed young knights and effeminate squires who parade and carouse and dress for the pageant of the Queen of Femenie.'

De Flor grimaced. 'They choose to garb themselves as damsels. I would rather dress in mail.'

'So speaks a true fighter.' Beaujeu leant forwards, his voice dropping to a conspiratorial murmur. 'The auguries are dark for those who seek them. Acre is imperilled, de Flor.'

'I rarely inhabit a place that is not.'

'As He did to Admah and Zeboim, to Sodom and Gomorrah, so the Lord shall rain down brimstone and fire upon our heads. We will be turned to a waste of salt and sulphur–nothing.'

'Then I will be sure to carry my affairs elsewhere.'

'The Knights Templar shall remain to the finish.' Beaujeu kept his gaze fixed. 'As will you.'

'Indeed?' De Flor raised an eyebrow quizzically.

'I am in no doubt Sultan Qalawun plots in Cairo with his emirs and generals to take us.'

'Did we not sign an accord in April in solemn faith with Qalawun?'

'Our faiths are hostile.'

'Yet the treaty remains.'

'It is a truce crafted to last ten years, ten months and a full ten days. An enemy feint intended to lull. I am far from lulled.'

'Are there reinforcements for our cause?'

'None that are of consequence. I sent John of Grailly to Europe to raise men and money and he has inspired nothing but a rabble of Lombardy peasants to flock to the ports.'

De Flor yawned. 'My argument with Italians is well enough known.'

'I have more pressing concerns. The armies of the Saracen will converge from Egypt and Syria. Eighty thousand, ninety, one hundred thousand infidel or more will come with savage intent and engines of war against us.'

'Your *Beauséant* might seem a little paltry against such force.'

That famed *Beauséant*, the banner of the order depicting a red cross charged upon a black and white field, had fluttered over every battlefield in the Holy Land where Crusader met and fought Mohammedan. They might trade and bank and amass a fortune in their coffers, yet the Templars never lost the cutting edge of their swords or forsook their vow of eternal combat. When the trumpet sounded and the great steel helms were donned, carnage was more important than compromise. William of Beaujeu and his prayerful and ruthless brethren of the Temple were not about to yield.

De Flor rested his goblet. 'You inform me for a reason.'

'I am calling upon you to fulfil your duty and abide by our compact.'

'And if I were to choose an alternate course?'

'The protection afforded to you by the Temple will be withdrawn.' Beaujeu delivered the news in the reasoned tones of a consummate bargainer. 'The Venetians are not alone in wanting your head.'

De Flor reclined his head on the rough pillow of rolled blanket. 'I'm listening.'

'There is only one army that might blunt the thrust of the Mameluk.'

'The Mongol.' It was a flat statement of fact.

Beaujeu inclined his head. 'Arghun, their Khan, has pledged to invade Syria with his horde by the end of their Year of the Tiger. This is the year.'

De Flor absorbed the tidings without an obvious glimmer of response. He could shadowbox as well as Beaujeu. But the Mongols? The grand master had surpassed himself. He was throwing the dice with the blind tenacity of a man who believed God and destiny were at his shoulder. Perhaps there was no option. Yet the Mongols, those great warrior-horsemen of the plains, had been defeated by the Saracens in battle some thirty years before, had been driven from Syria and showed no inclination to return. The adventurer was not so foolish as to underestimate or completely trust the Templar.

Beaujeu interrupted his silent musings. 'I hear a rumour that Arghun sickens unto death. Should the Khan not endure and his horde fail to come, we in Acre are doomed.'

'You intend me for a mission?'

The knight stood to replace the burning rushes in their brackets, the fresh illumination catching his features in their yellow glow. He turned back to the soldier.

'I must first have proof that Sultan Qalawun deceives us. I need evidence his troops are readied and his battle plans drawn.'

'I will be cut to pieces if I journey near Damascus.'

'Not if you should travel in disguise with the caravans. Not if you are accompanied by the boy.'

'It is too dangerous for him.'

'He will be eager to go and you will ensure it.' The tip of a bulrush sputtered to flame. 'Was Abraham not willing for the love of God to sacrifice his own son Isaac?'

'I am no Abraham and you are not God.'

'My authority is from the Pope and his direct from heaven above. Discover what I ask for, de Flor.'

'And then?'

'You have my sanction to proceed with haste to the Mongols. Find their Khan. Bring us his army and our salvation.'

~

They were setting fire to the sugar cane, the burning brands spreading the flame and the tall grasses sinking into the deeper and reddening glow. It was the precursor to harvesting. When the smoke was cleared and the dead vegetation gone, the labourers would scythe through with their cane-knives, cutting low and collecting fast and sending the heaped carts to the crushing mills nearby. This was Hospitaller territory. With their five guarded plantations located on the plain of Acre, these Knights of St John of Jerusalem controlled the sugar trade and made their fortune. The Templars might have finance and the sea; the Hospitallers had in their thrall the sweet palate of every court and castle in Europe. Such a concession was worth fighting and crusading for.

Benedict glimpsed the blaze and averted his eyes. With the young knight Theobald of Alzey at his side, he often accompanied the mules as they ferried the crystallised produce to the storerooms of the order. That was a tradition, like tasting the cane juice and stirring the molasses, like scrubbing the boiling-vats and cleansing the condensing cones in the outside troughs. Yet the flames reminded him of St Thomas Island, of the day he looked back to the Tripoli foreshore, of the moment he was pulled from the water scarcely alive and on to a longboat.

'Shall we gallop and stretch the horses, Theo?'

'When our duties here are done and we have toured the sick and needy in the hospice.' Theobald cried an order to the muleteers and resumed his pace. 'There are bones to set and heads to bind since your guardian de Flor put about him with a staff.'

'I saw it for myself, Theo. Not a man could put a wound on him.'

'Then I am glad to be a Hospitaller knight and no mere Venetian brawler.'

The youngster kicked away a stone. 'Do you prefer to fight or to heal and tend?'

'There is time for each and demand for both. It is why I made a sacred oath to bring succour to the Christian and harm to the infidel who threatens. It is why I am as ready to give medicine as I am to wield the lance.'

'Selim is an infidel. Hazzim too. They are yet my friends.'

Theobald laughed. 'Man is imperfect and God mysterious.'

'Saracen or Jew, leper, beggar or thief. All are helped by you, Theo.'

'Did not the Samaritan aid the Pharisee? Are we not bidden to do unto others as they would do to us?' It provoked a nod from the boy. 'My grandfather was Otto of Alzey. He was not much older than you when he came to the Holy Land with the blighted Crusade of Children.'

'He is spoken of in reverence and regard.'

'And he is worthy of his repute, Ben. He cared for many and too, when called, found employ for his sword.'

They paused close to a village on the Turon ridge a mile out from the city walls. An event was taking place, a gathering of citizens and worthies that suggested a sporting contest or execution. It was both. The crack of a whip and the rearing whinny of horses, and two riderless Arab geldings stampeded away on an outward course. The animals knew the circuit and their role. They would cover the ground at furious speed, trampling scrub and thorn, kicking up clods of earth and the pebble spray of limestone. In their wake, tied fast by the ankles and attached by lengths of rope, were dragged a couple of flayed and screaming prisoners. A lap of dishonour, an untidy end to their careers.

The ash-blonde knight and the dark-haired boy stood to let the procession by. They could hear the cheers and observe the ploughing and bounding passage of the bundles towed.

With a gentle hand, Theobald steadied the youngster. 'You should not witness such things, Ben.'

'I have seen worse.'

'We speak of chivalry and honour and commit these acts of baseness.' Disgust clouded the handsome face. 'I vouch they lay wagers on the game and gamble on its detail.'

'As to who shall win?'

A shake of the head. 'As to which miscreant will lose most parts. A nose, an ear, an arm, a scalp.'

Benedict's voice was weak. 'Crime is deserving of punishment, Theo.'

'It will not be wiped clean by committing another.' Theobald scanned the thundering progress of the runners. 'For certain they are sinners. I have yet to find a man in Acre who is not.'

With a whistle and a motion of his hand, he commanded the mule train on. They were covering ground over which Saracen and Frank had attacked and counter-attacked for generations. Here, Saladin had stood to direct his siege; here, the victorious troops of Coeur de Lion had led the captured Moslem garrison and with dagger, sword and axe slain three thousand men. It was a blood-soaked domain. The light sprinkling from the current violence was of no consequence.

To the shouts of the muleteers, the convoy reached and entered the Hospitaller compound. At its centre was a quadrangle girdled by the stone monumentality of the great hall, the refectory, the auberge and the storeroom. Like the Lion Fortress of the Templars, it too provided monastic seclusion and military refuge in the very heart of Acre. And it stood also in the brute shadow of its own fortified keep. Knights could pray or practise for combat, could respond fast to threat and by underground tunnel rally to the city walls, and they could retreat if necessary behind the solid face of their redoubt. Today, at least, it was simply a matter of taking delivery.

As the blocks of raw sugar were unloaded, Benedict wandered from the scene. The cavernous interiors held a fascination for him, the banners and carvings and shadowed spaces drawing his eye and encouraging him to explore. From an etched fleur-de-lis to the melted stub of a tallow candle, there were few details he had not noted. Theobald had once taken him into the Stygian darkness below the donjon, where he had willingly helped to apply salves and bandage the wounds of the Mohammedan prisoners kept in chains. Some of the captives would be ransomed and others would be kept to die. It was the way of things. The youngster had whispered in Arabic to the wretches, trying with the clumsiness of his years to give them hope. The world of grown men was complex.

The great hall was deserted, save for a pair of hunting dogs slumped idle before the unlit hearth. They were of old acquaintance and would not trouble him. He found the stone column set within a row and dragged an oak stool across to it. He might, if discovered, be chastised or scourged, or even thrown in a dungeon to pay for his wrong. He did not care. This was important. It was the leaving of his mark and inscribed proof that he, a fourteen-year-old boy named Benedict, had walked the ground of the knights and lived at the time of the Crusader. The Patriarch had taught him to read and write and he would put it to effect. Carefully, he applied the point of an iron nail to the lettering he had already traced, scraping to widen and deepen the groove. *Benedict*. It was a labour of concentration; a work in progress.

From somewhere a voice called his name. He stopped scraping and got down from the stool. There would be ample opportunity to complete his project.

*

When de Flor delivered his news the boy seemed overjoyed at the chance to engage in the plot and subterfuge of the Templar grand master and accompany his old friends into danger and mischief. A pity, Roger de Flor decided. He had attempted to excuse Benedict from the task. But Beaujeu was the devil and the devil insisted. More importantly, it was the devil who paid.

De Flor swung himself over a shallow balustrade and skirted the pools of candlelight. He did not want to be caught. That would cause embarrassment, which in turn would lead to altercation. He had seen it happen before. So he was careful to tread softly, tiptoeing an indirect path to the private chamber of the lady. There were several farewells of this kind to make, all of them fond and each of them hazardous. A false move and he would be undone; a few steps more and each would be undoing the other.

She was a pretty woman with a bored Saxon countenance that brightened at his arrival. The chestnut hair was coiled and adorned with a fine gold fret, the comely shape of her body defined by a tight-fitted undertunic of scarlet silk. De Flor smiled and studied her. Much could be learnt by listening to tales of grievance, and there was a fortune to be amassed through pleasure and persistence and scratches to his back. With effort and application, even her haughtiness could be sweated out.

'I hear tell you did for the Venetians.' She viewed him through dipped lashes. 'Is a lady now to tumble to your prowess?'

'I bow before your virtue, mistress.'

'To honour or to seize it?'

'It will ever be safe within my charge.'

Her head tilted in feigned disapproval. 'What of the slattern from whose window you escaped?'

'I am a flawed yet chastened man, mistress.'

'We trust not too repentant.' The words were soft and beckoning.

He advanced at her demand, pressing himself against her, allowing her hands to wander and her lips to graze his own. The women of Acre vied for his attention. It was a game of mutual convenience and the way to the treasure-trove was often through the whalebone gores of a fustian skirt. He was born to roam, raised as Rutger von Blum, bred for the sea and for war. In a little over twenty years, he had come a long way and had every intention of going further.

Their kiss was long and the breath held, pressure and passion tightening the lungs and loosening the clothes. She groaned and let his tongue slide inside. It would be worth the fall.

She panted harsh in his ear. 'I would forfeit all rank and position for you, my soldier.'

'As I will submit to whatever position you choose.'

She was shrugging off her garb and encouraging de Flor from his. As her garments dropped, so her resistance gave way.

'Where is your maid, my mistress?'

She sighed and twisted as he licked her breasts. 'Would you again desire the both of us?'

'My hands are full for the present.'

They fell on to the silk-swathed divan, their love-making intense and loud and forgetful of all things. It was what the woman and her rivals craved for.

So far, the leave-taking was going well.

A piebald pony trotted out across the plain, its rider a fourteen-year-old boy and its destination the Arab village some six miles from the city. With charm and persistence,

Benedict had won temporary possession of the mount from the stable of a Pisan knight. He would exercise the animal and clear his own mind along the way. For sure, he had doubts, but in the morning light, when the air warmed and the egrets gathered and the walls of Acre glowed so resolute against the sea, he could slough them off to the excitement of another day. He was to go on a secret expedition with Roger de Flor. He would creep away in the darkness as he had done before, he would find himself as a courier and spy and would crawl over rooftops and loiter in alleyways to spearhead the cause of Beaujeu. No other boy was given such a task. His city depended on him and the grand master relied on his industry and success. The thought filled him with an ecstatic delight.

He encouraged the pony to a canter and felt it surge faster into a gallop. Releasing the reins, he lifted his arms at his sides and charged on in blind stampede. This was the life. There were no bounds and no control, simply the wind on his face and the frantic pounding of hooves. For a moment, nothing else mattered.

The village came into view, a settlement guarded by adobe walls and announced by a gateway of palms. It was ancient and welcoming territory and it was home to Hazzim. There would be the old Arab watchman crouching where he always crouched, the soft bubbling of the irrigation sluice and murmur and chatter of routine, the sweet scent of the orchards and of the boiling-vats behind. Benedict slowed the pony to a walk. They had been spotted.

Cries of greeting tumbled towards him as he got nearer, children and adults crowding to embrace their visiting and adopted own. He was not of their blood, yet they were warm and generous people and he loved them in return. Their pace and ways were as much a part of him as were those of his guardian de Flor or the knight Theobald; these people dwelt in his heart, close as any kin. 'As-Salamu Alaykum,' they cried. 'Wa 'Alaykum as-Salaam,' he responded. And then there was Leila.

Even as he dismounted and was ushered through, he searched for her and smiled and talked. Accompanied by an informal retinue, he paid his respects to the elders and traded news with his friends and worked his way between the drifting groups of donkeys and goats. On open ground, where the women sat to gossip and mould their pots of clay, he glimpsed her. A coloured headscarf and the delicate brown of her forearm as she reached to sprinkle water, the tilt of her head, the brief glance and the coy fondness in her eyes. It would never do, could never be, yet he acknowledged the truth in his affections.

Hazzim approached. 'It is your turn to surprise me with a visit, Ben.'

'I promised I would make the journey.' They hugged as brothers. 'I would never turn my back on my family.'

'Nor I on you.'

Benedict sniffed the air about him. 'You smell of orchard fruit, brother. Mostly apricot.'

'Better than the stench of the Acre sewer.'

'I cannot deny it. Where is your father?'

'He travels to trade with the Druze on Mount Carmel.' Hazzim straightened to stare from his fuller height. 'You may now deal with our new sheikh.'

'Perhaps the new sheikh would care to receive a fist to his head.'

They lapsed into the banter of comradeship, walking on with an arm each about the shoulders of the other. These were always good moments. The Arab boy was proud of his village and took solemn care in describing the events and rituals of its daily life. The gaggle of accompanying children

41

fell behind as they strolled out to a dusty line of pomegranate and persimmon trees marking the edge of a nearby well.

'Selim said you must choose, Ben.' Hazzim gestured in the direction of Acre and back to the village. 'The Frank or the Arab.'

Benedict had plucked a fruit and was pounding and rolling it against a stone. 'I choose both.'

'Is this possible, Ben?'

'It is why I rode a pony and trekked across the plain.' With a wood splinter, he punched a hole in the pomegranate and offered it to Hazzim.

The Arab drank and passed it back. 'When I am grown and the head of this village, you will always be welcome.'

'And when I am grown and as famed a caravan master as Selim, you will have a thousand gifts carried by my camels.'

He lifted his chin and let the sweet juice of the fruit trickle down his throat. Soon he would have to steal away from his friends and all that was familiar. In keeping it from Hazzim, he lied. It created a conflict in loyalties between his Saracen brother and his Crusader master. He wished to serve both.

Hazzim regarded him. 'My father will be saddened he could not receive his son Benedict.'

'There will be the next time and the next, brother.'

'I trust it is so, Ben.' Hazzim had understood. 'You come here to bid goodbye.'

~

'If it is not my prodigal apostle returned.'

The Patriarch looked up and beamed in kindly surprise. Seated in the cooling and fountain-dripped shade of the nymphaeum on his palace rooftop and engaged with a priest in a duel of chess, he rarely turned away a visitor. Benedict was always welcome. Though not of studious bent, he had sat at the old man's feet to learn the Scriptures and absorb the wisdom and to listen to tales of the Holy Land. There was succour and sound counsel to be discovered here. His temporal realm might have shrunk, but the Patriarch maintained his benign watch on Acre and still found time for the game of kings.

He dismissed the priest with a quiet nod and waved Benedict to his place. 'You while your hours away with the sinner de Flor and the infidel Selim. What a misspent youth and what a waste of all that I have taught.'

'I forget nothing, Holy Father.'

'Let it be this ancient cleric who is the judge.' The Patriarch jabbed a finger at the board. 'You will find my force in the ascendant.'

Benedict moved a piece and swooped to take the position of another. 'The elephant crushes the footsoldier.'

'I tutored you well.' The old man stroked his beard and perused. 'Yet it shall not prevent your elephant falling to a trap.'

'I have my horses.'

'While my chariots are in reserve and deployed on to the flanks.'

Benedict rested his chin on his hand and studied the field. His opponent was as fierce in contest as he was benevolent away from it. To live up to his expectation and be worthy as a rival in the play of *shatranj* was a matter of honour. He moved, was countered and sidestepped again.

The Patriarch fingered a rosary and furrowed his brow in concentration. 'You were always deft on your feet, my son.'

'Is that not how we survive?'

'Look to the whole and to the wider surrounding.' A hand reached out and a piece was moved. 'There is vulnerability where we least expect.'

'Refuge may be found.'

'All bastions one day must fall, all mortal flesh corrupt and mountains sink, all kings lose their crowns and find their armies scattered.'

Benedict raised his gaze to the old man. 'What are we to do, Holy Father?'

'Await the Rapture. For the Lord will come to scourge the world and cleanse the sanctuary.'

The fourteen-year-old preferred a game of chess. At Tripoli he had seen a bastion fall and an army scattered and had witnessed the corrupting of mortal flesh. For all its deep ditches and towers, Acre too might be scourged and cleansed. He returned to his diminished band of brothers on the chequerboard.

'Should I concede, Holy Father?'

'Never.'

'And if there is no way out?'

'You shall be true to yourself and stand at your post. It is the mark of a man and true measure of his soul.'

With a methodical flourish, the Patriarch brought the battle to a swift conclusion. Benedict grinned sheepishly and bowed his head. One day, he would prove himself equal to such bouts; one day, he would learn to ignore the distracting worries of departure.

'Can I help you, my son?' The Patriarch's voice was warm.

'I would ask you to bless me, Holy Father.'

As Benedict knelt in reverence, the Patriarch laid his hand upon the head of the youngster and murmured a Latin benediction. On the roof of the Patriarchate, as the sun yawned its shadows towards dusk, a boy sought absolution and a state of grace.

Prayers were done and the blankets furled, the cooking pots collected and the tents stowed. Dawn would soon be washing

44

the horizon. With boots stamping out the last of the dung fires and the groans of heavy-laden camels ghostly in the murk, the caravan was readying. Selim walked among his men, energising by his presence and saying few words. At a glance he would know the weight and safety of a load, at a sound could determine the health of a beast or the mood of his team. It was a practice rehearsed for millennia.

Kneeling animals rose to the upright and the line uncoiled into ordered array. The old camel master strode its length. This was his family, his business, his life. Almost two hundred camel and the riches of the Mediterranean world bundled high, and he was preparing to give the command. Damascus was the destination.

He paused before the twin silhouettes of a tall man and a boy. 'Even in darkness, you are no Arab, Flor *effendi*.'

'It is as well I wear armour quilt beneath my robe.' De Flor kept his voice low and in the native Saracen tongue.

'And it is as well I shall slit the throat of any who pry too close.'

'I thank you for granting us escort, Selim.'

'I would be no friend had I refused.' The cameleer gripped the shoulder of Benedict. 'I would be no uncle had I delivered you for protection to this oafish Frank alone, *Waladii*.'

They laughed softly, sharing the joke and a few seconds before the odyssey began. Wary respect and a history of expedition had created a bond of sorts between de Flor and Selim. Each to his own tradition and trade.

Selim prodded the chest of the Latin. 'It is the heart which beats behind this front that determines the man, Flor *effendi*.'

'You will find it strong as it ever was and my sword hand as keen.'

'Let both be ruled by judgement.' Selim rolled his whip in his hands. 'I have taken you each on many journeys and hold no fondness for the Mameluks and their Sultan. Yet your argument does not belong to the wanderers of the desert.'

'We shall ensure it remains our own, Selim.'

'You may trust my brothers here to guard you.'

'Though I shall ever favour the horse above the camel.' The soldier drew Benedict beneath his arm. 'We are set for a fine adventure, boy.'

To a pink-blushed sky and the soft tread of camel hooves, the exodus began. Somewhere in the moving throng, as the animals swayed and the slow rhythmic pace set in, Benedict glanced back to the shadowed walls of Acre. Things would be all right. *Insha'Allah*. God willing.

Deep within the Lion Fortress and kneeling in prayer before the cross, William of Beaujeu, Grand Master of the Temple, offered up a silent plea of intercession. He was consigning a man and a boy to certain hazard. It was as nothing to the encroaching danger for Acre, his order and Christendom itself. Resolve and purpose were the key. There was no other recourse left.

High above the heads of the camel train, three carrier pigeons circled briefly and found their bearings. At this hour, they would escape the hunting falcons of the Franks; through luck and instinct would reach their destination. They veered east and flew fast, far outpacing the humans below. Attached to the leg of each bird was a receptacle containing a coded message, a warning to be deciphered and read in Damascus. The enemy was on its way.

46

✝

Chapter 3

A pair of Nubian wrestlers faced each other. Their feet spread wide and their stares locked, muscle and sinew taut beneath the oil-burnished skin, they crouched almost motionless and ready for the grapple. In this sandpit arena within a courtyard of the great Mameluk palace of Cairo, they would fight as though their lives depended on it. They had been brought from the eastern Sahara. Their skills were prized, their instincts honed, their ability to please an audience never in doubt. Weight shifted, a shoulder twitched. Then the rush.

Attended by his emirs and his son Ashraf, Sultan Qalawun observed the proceedings from a colonnaded balcony. There was no finer vantage point from which to view the movement of these giant and battling crabs. The black fighters appeared well matched. They were rolling and skittering, grunting and hissing in the ferocity of their effort, their hands slapping and clutching and losing their grip. The men separated and clashed again. In time fatigue would set in and mistakes would be made; a victor and loser declared.

Qalawun watched impassive as a combatant tumbled free from a neck choke and gained the upper hand. He valued the deadly artistry of the game.

'I commend their keenness and spirit.'

Beside him, his son maintained his gaze on the contest.

'Which will snatch the triumph? Ability and daring or brute force alone?'

'It is the combination of such things.' The sultan paused as the wrestlers clinched and circled in furious scuffle. 'At the outset, they both stand. By the finish, only one.'

'Like the True Believer and the infidel.'

'That is so. Yet we must be ever vigilant of feint and treachery, of the capacity for the heathen to cause us woe.'

'Their ambassadors abase themselves before you.'

'It is not the act of friendship. Rather, it is the recourse of desperate and weak men who seek time and believe flattery and gesture will spare them from our wrath.'

'They will find we are deaf to their blandishment.'

'As I trust in Allah they are blind to our intent.'

Below them, the sparring duo was reaching for conclusion in a flurry of sand and violent manoeuvre. One wrestler dropped and was turned and pinned and held on his belly, his mouth and eyes widening to the pressure on his throat. It did not take long. With a knee to the back and a single elbow wrench of the head, his neck was quickly broken. His body shivered reflexively and then stilled. The duel was over.

Qalawun turned away and his retinue followed. The spectacle had provided a welcome interlude to his deliberations. Here, protected by the walls of the Citadel and set amidst the graceful splendour on this lofty spur of Muqattam Hill, where caged birds sang and scented roses bloomed and where pools and fountains created an earthly paradise among the domes and minarets, he could plan. War was never far from his thoughts.

They passed between the house of gold and the marbled hall of justice, moving through gardens and along pathways flanked by the royal guard and brushed with a cooling breeze. Salah ad-Din himself had once walked this hallowed ground, and his successors would not forget it. With eunuchs and courtiers bowing low and fan-bearers and spearsmen standing rigid in salute, the assembled hierarchs processed to a chamber picked out in gemstones and richly hung with cloth of precious thread. Conference was in session.

'My faithful brothers.' From the dais-throne on which he was now seated, Qalawun eyed his court. 'The hour is soon upon us when our regiments march and our lands are retaken.'

The emirs replied with clamorous zeal, hailing him and praising God. Their loyalty was not a given. While he won them battles and granted them favour, they were obedient and docile. But tribes could be fickle, clans could plot and a palace coup could leap from any corner. It had happened on countless occasions. The dagger, the poison, the bowstring, the overthrow. Treason prowled even in the heart and eye of a man who offered fealty. Qalawun would rip out both if circumstance demanded it.

He waited for the enthused murmurings to subside. 'From every corner, the infidel Latins send their ambassadors to treaty and prostrate themselves at my feet. From Greece and Armenia, from Germany and Genoa, these fools come to parley.'

An emir spoke up. 'My Sultan, does their religious head, the Pope, not call for holy war against us?'

'And is not our faith the stronger and our God the only One and True?' The sultan listened to the swelling sound of agreement.

The emir persisted. 'My Sultan, some of their armed Crusaders might yet journey for the Levant.'

'What of it?' An imperious wave of the hand signalled disdain. 'A few galleys sent from Venice? A few thousand mercenaries paid in tainted gold?'

'Perhaps we misjudge their spirit and fight, my Sultan.'

'Or perchance I misunderstand your own.'

'I have always done as you command, my Sultan.'

'Then do so again. Find the courage of Salah ad-Din at Hattin when he laid waste the infidel host and later took Jerusalem.'

Another and more fawning courtier ventured his opinion. 'We are unafraid of such a challenge, my Sultan.'

'There is little challenge to be found. The princes of Europe are divided and the Crusader King Edward of England is directed elsewhere.'

'Still there is the law, Qalawun.' It was an elderly scholar sitting cross-legged on silk cushions whose frail voice intruded. 'We break our covenant with the Latins of Acre should we embark with force against them.'

'Our sole covenant is with our faith and people to take what is rightfully ours.'

'While our terms of treaty would forbid it.'

'You would doubt me?' Qalawun stared, his question issued as a threat. 'Was I not the general once entrusted by the great Baybars with his vengeful armies? Am I not your ruler who has led you before to victory, who rent the walls of Tripoli and put the enemy to the sword and to flight?'

The scholar lowered his eyes. 'Forgive my foolish insolence.'

'I am the law.' The words came slow and precise and the bearded chin of the sultan jutted in forceful persuasion.

Obediently, his closest subjects prostrated themselves. They had become well versed in reading his mood.

Beside him, his son and heir Ashraf stepped to address the muted throng. 'You have heard my father and of his dearest wish. Trust in his wisdom. You shall be given your just cause for venturing to war.'

A further member of the assembled cleared his throat in nervous diplomacy. 'If we are to walk before Allah in our military duty, I would ask to know the day or week or month.'

'It shall be when you are sated with all your dainties and sweetmeats, al-Fakhri.' The martial offspring of the sultan paused at the laughter. 'And it will be when the infidels of Acre breach the treaty as they must.'

Qalawun rubbed the pearls seeding the embroidered edge of his pelisse. 'To these ends, and in the name of sacred war, we send message to the Governor of Damascus to prepare. I vow this to you, my brothers. The mightiest army in Arabia is to be raised and directed to its task. Like rotten fruit that has fallen from the tree, the last outposts of the Crusader kingdom will finally be crushed.'

The audience was over and the emirs dispersed, yet the business of the day was far from complete. Three individuals had been ushered to the chamber and stood before the throne, their dress modest and their demeanour unafraid, a trio of men in possession of secrets and skills upon which the sultan often drew. Where once their lethal sect had resided in hilltop forts in Persia and Syria and brought terror to Moslem and Christian alike, slaughter and subjugation by the Mongols and the Mameluks had brought it to vassal status. Its power was broken and the legend and murderous ways of the Old Man of the Mountains almost forgotten. Yet the descendants stayed true to their faith and their art. For they were Ismaili *hashshashin*, hashish-eaters. The Assassins.

'You summon us, my Sultan.'

Qalawun nodded. 'I do.'

'It is a brave ruler who admits us to his presence without recourse to a regiment of bodyguards.'

'Would it alter fate? Would it preserve my life had you decided to end it?'

'You honour us by your insight.'

'I recognise you for what you are.'

One ruthless leader surveyed the other, each appreciating the moment and the trembling balance of their power. Saladin himself had once called in his personal guard prior to a meeting with the Assassins and had been informed by these most loyal of his servants they too would kill him if the *hashshashin* demanded. None were beyond their reach and allegiance could be fluid. It was best to keep them paid and occupied.

The ageing sultan would reveal his tactics and target at a pace of his choosing. 'Your men performed well for me in Aleppo and Homs.'

'Criticism of our Sultan is less apparent since our visit.'

'For it, I am grateful.' Qalawun watched the sunlight flickering on the mosaics. 'There remain further matters to address, areas to which your craft may be applied.'

'We will go wheresoever you command and commit to whatever you decree.'

'This shall be the greatest of tests. Honour and empire rest on it.'

'As you in turn may depend on us.'

'There exists a remaining jewel in the battered eastern crown of the Crusader. It is preserved by high walls and the ferocious faith of the military orders, comforted by the treaty to which I have placed my name.'

'You speak of Acre.'

'The very same. The thorn that pierces the flesh of all believers. The wound to our pride and the curse upon our land. The insult to the One True Faith.'

'There are other Latin ports.'

'None so vital. Should Acre fall, the rest will follow. Their knights, their rule, their spirit are there.'

The Assassins considered the words. 'You intend us to kill the *bailli*? Or the grand masters of the Temple and Hospital?'

'They may be replaced and the Constable Amalric would go unlamented.' Qalawun rested his hand on his scimitar hilt. 'I desire you to provoke and incite, to shatter the peace and cause incident that provides us excuse to send our forces.'

'And when our act is done?'

'Remain behind in Acre. Should you be alive, I will find later use for you.'

The instructions were delivered and accepted with little ceremony or emotion. The terms of the agreement were fully understood. In the sultan, the Assassins had a reliable patron; in the Assassins, the sultan possessed a strategic instrument of terror and control. Qalawun was confident his tame Shia killers would perform their task as arranged. Acre was closer to being his. There were plenty of ways to deliver up a Christian city.

In the crocodile pool of the palace, the torso of a dead Nubian wrestler was already partially devoured. Perhaps the victim had been fortunate. The creatures were more accustomed to human prey they could first drown.

He was as nervous as any traitor should be, sweating as he made his way in the airless heat for the teeming Nile waterfront. The emir al-Fakhri carried a message. It was possible that the watchers of the sultan followed him, that informants manned every felucca and barge or were posted at the wharves. He must calm himself. Yet the information he carried was beyond value and could alter an outcome. It would earn him either the eternal thanks of his paymaster William of Beaujeu or the savage retribution meted by a

Mameluk torturer. It was worth the risk. Not everyone loved the tyrant Qalawun.

In a dusty Cairo alleyway he found the vendor tending to his stall of amphorae and clay pots. There was nothing to cause alarm. Pausing only to inspect the wares, to haggle and to shake his head, the emir broke contact and walked on. Possession of his letter had passed. On its single folded papyrus sheet he had written every remembered detail of that conference with the sultan, had recorded the royal ambition to dismantle peace and embark on military expedition. Within the hour, the captain of a small trading vessel would arrive to purchase a wine container. The man would carry it back to his boat and set sail for the mouth of the Nile and the port of Damietta some one hundred and twenty-five miles north. There the jar would be transferred to a fishing-dhow for onward journey and rendezvous with the Templars. A circuitous route and a deadly game. Espionage in these parts could be cruel and unforgiving.

~

At a wayside *han* in Galilee another agent of William of Beaujeu waited. He too had information for the grand master of the Templars. As an Arab and a trader, he could roam as he wished, counting and observing as he stood with his donkey watching imperial messengers ride by and troops on manoeuvre. It was both a lowly and a privileged position. Six hundred miles between Cairo and Damascus, a route along the ancient Roman Via Mares that would take a royal courier changing horses at every way point and riding at full gallop a mere day and a half to complete. He had seen more of them of late. Without word or pause, they leapt from one saddle and into the next, whipping and spurring their horses to the charge. Around their waists were wrapped silken bands and within those were the encrypted and urgent dispatch. The spy could only look and wonder.

He had seen and heard of other things too. It was not for him to interpret, support conjecture or divine significance but to relay news and rumour to the generous Latins. Certainly, he had gathered intelligence. The governor of Damascus was acquiring weapons in the arms bazaars of Mosul and Baghdad; he was importing iron from the mines near Beirut and from eastern Anatolia for the foundries in his city. If that were not enough, camel trains bearing iron ingots from India had been sighted journeying inland from the Red Sea coast. A stockpiling of weapons was underway.

The agent spat in the dust. He was eager to wander on, to keep a step ahead of any who might hunt him. Staying in one place for too long served only to attract questions and attention. But he would bide awhile. He expected his own caravan to arrive shortly and for the Frankish boy sent by William of Beaujeu to seek him out. It was how intelligence had been relayed before. Just a ragged traveller with a forgettable face meeting an easily overlooked youngster. The most successful networks had been built on less.

'*Marhabbah* . . .'

The greeting in Arabic carried a sentence of death. The word was whispered softly and the voice was close in his ear. He did not turn to see, had no need to ask or negotiate or plead. Whoever stood behind was surely armed and already decided on his fate. The Latins of Acre would go uninformed of what he had to tell.

'*Here are good figs! The best dates!*'

'*See the quality of this leather!*'

'*Gold from Armenia! Glass beads from Venice!*'

'*We carry silks of the Orient and spices of Persia!*'

Merchants and middlemen vied for attention and space in

the loose encampments surrounding the *han*. The crossroads and meeting posts of the Holy Land were forever colonised by those seeking advantage or reward. They were places where deals could be struck and bargains hunted, where camel trains passed and rumour flowed. A lawless site of pilgrimage.

Benedict caught an orange thrown to him by a friendly trader and peeled it as he walked. He was going in blind, tracing the contact he knew would be waiting. While Roger de Flor tended to other matters and sat out in the parched scrabble landscape, it was an anonymous fourteen-year-old who went forwards in his place. He had performed such tasks a hundred times and would not disappoint: he could move with the confidence of a veteran, his wits and senses tuned. Selim had deployed a number of his trusted henchmen in case of trouble. Their care and their knives provided some defence. Nothing to it.

'What brings you to this *han*, boy?'

He smiled in response. 'Money and trade, uncle.'

'Then may you find both.'

'God willing, I shall.'

It was the brotherly banter of the road and the warm cama-raderie of the Arabs. He wondered if it would last had they inkling of his motive. However comfortable and unafraid at carrying a secret, he was yet a Christian intruding on hostile ground. The Mameluks would flay him alive. They would do worse to those suspected of apostasy or collaboration.

There was still no sign of the traveller and his donkey. Benedict repeated his circuit, traversing the walled com-pounds, climbing to gain height, straining to search countenances and actions. Unease needled his consciousness. It was not fear, but the sharp jab of dissatisfaction at his own apparent failure. The reason existed somewhere. He tried again, blinking out the sunlight and peering into the shadows.

A face swayed into focus and steadied in his field of view. He ignored it, trawled on and returned. *Ahdath*, without a doubt. The eyes were still in an environment inviting movement, the hands without calluses, the stance too contrived. Benedict had seen such men before in Jerusalem and Damascus and Aleppo. Each one a militiaman with the role of enforcing security and policing the streets and all presenting a threat. They almost gave off a scent.

With care, he perused the man. There was a thrill to being so close. The stranger was loitering, observing without wishing to be observed, was plainly no trader, craftsman or cameleer. An intriguing situation. A shemagh clean and pulled tight and a pair of unscuffed sandals. To the practised eye, they jarred. The man distractedly swatted aside a fly, the sleeve of his long shirt slipping to show his forearm and the deep stain of a birthmark. Another thing to record. Benedict crouched beside a pile of dyed blankets, his instincts competing to pull him back and send him near, his pulse edging to a faster beat. His target would not be alone. Somewhere behind, disguised and hidden, was a troop aiming for the capture or the kill. That was how the *Ahdath* worked.

Maybe they sought him. The boy cuffed away the sweat from his brow and narrowed his focus. In the place of an agent and a swift rendezvous was the understated menace of an enemy presence. It would not do. He must report to de Flor and Selim. His foe was maintaining the pretence, the face blank and the gaze vigilant, flitting random glances to items of interest. His attention alighted on Benedict. It did not last or settle. But in the darting instant it trapped him, squeezing his gut and shutting down his breath and holding him in rigid fright. He was back in Tripoli with the armour-scaled foot of a Mameluk soldier only inches from his nose. So naked and so frail. Concentration switched and he gulped for air, a demi-second of his life expended. He felt no relief. For in the frozen look of his adversary, he had detected awareness and a casual probing. The man knew.

'Should any one of you perish, it is a loss we may accept.'

The grand master of the Templars was unmoved by the exhaustion of his men. It was the third time this morning he had commanded them to don their chain mail hauberks and seize their weapons and run the length of the city walls. A gruelling undertaking in the furnace heat. For six hundred yards they had lumbered north from the waterfront to the King Henry Tower, clattering through its darkened passageways to vector on to the east–west stretch of Montmusart. William of Beaujeu stood with his marshal at the finish. About them, knights and sergeants knelt or lay in varied stages of collapse, some retching and others with their heads immersed in pails of water, a few barely conscious. There was always a price to be paid for readiness.

Beaujeu spoke to the marshal as he tossed a soaked sponge to a prone underling. 'I do not believe they will thank me for their exercise.'

'In time they shall, your grace.'

'The Constable and his courtiers deem me mad.'

'Yet they will be first to hide behind us when the cry goes up and battle comes.' The marshal leant on the pommel of his sword. 'You seem certain it will do so, your grace.'

'Would I order these manoeuvres were I not? Why else would I direct the dismantling of three of our finest galleys for the purpose of building mangonels and trebuchets? Why else would I send our knavish hireling to find proof and then seek out the Mongol Khan?'

'I see no others but ourselves who are convinced.'

'They will be when the trumpet sounds. Let us hope it is not too late.'

The marshal grunted. 'As my name is Peter of Sevrey, I swear Acre is the more quiet for the absence of de Flor.'

'Then we may be thankful for our threatened state.' Beaujeu scanned east along the ramparts. 'One day, the sound of crashing drums and cymbals will roll from the distance to our ears. And one day, the massed ranks of the heathen will enfilade these walls.'

'We will put our faith in God, your grace.'

'What privilege if He should place His trust in us.'

'There is no brother here who will fail Him.' The marshal looked on at the slumped and recovering men. 'Without feat of arms, we grow lacklustre and spiritless, your grace.'

'With it, we may be crushed.'

'All of us would cherish occasion to fall with a sword in our grasp, a prayer to our lips and a heaped mound of the Saracen dead about us. It is the highest of all callings.'

'When Qalawun marches it might presage the end to our order. While I have breath and strength, I will strive to prevent it.'

They stood side by side, the grandees of a military order under threat. Perhaps the Knights Templar would become no more than a footnote to the chronicles, an entity that would pass in a glorious blaze to myth and legend. If it were ordained, it would take place on this parapet.

A head emerged over the brow of a stone flight of steps and the dwarf Amethyst clambered into view. It had been quite a climb. He wheezed a little, his cheeks blown and his mouth contorted before it settled for a grin.

'Our saviours. Our gallant knights.' He doffed his cap in greeting. 'I see you are already fallen at the ramparts.'

Beaujeu was courteous in reply. 'We will be ready when the hour comes.'

'As will I, my esteemed lord. For though I am the height of a dwarf, within me beats the heart of a giant.'

'Most in Acre have the hearts of dwarves.'

Amethyst grimaced in comic disdain. 'That is the truth, my lord. And the truth may vex and hurt and arrive on the point of a Mameluk lance.'

'Even garbed as a hound, you bring more sense to the Council than most.'

'It is the plight of little Amethyst and his reason to serve.'

'Regard well, dwarf.' The marshal swept his longsword in a broad arc. 'The next instance you set foot upon these battlements, they will be scourged by wildfire and the arrow shot of the Saracen.'

'I am glad, then, to be short in stature.'

'And we shall be thankful to have you beside us.'

The grand master cast a final glance about him and with a perfunctory nod took his leave. There were other matters deserving of his thought, the logistics of defence and the pressing call of worship to wear into his hours. Acre would show him gratitude one day or might no longer exist. He thought of his tame emir in the court of Qalawun and of the adventurer and the boy he had sent to Damascus. Fate could be determined by the most unlikely of allies.

It was the end of day after long furlongs walked in the solemn company of camels. As slowly the light drained and greyed the rockscape, fires were built and men clustered to boil water and cook their stew. Progress was always leisurely with a heavily laden train. The need was to reach a destination rather than for hurry, to cover ten miles a day in the sapping heat of summer. Besides, there were tribal chiefs to meet and commanders of forts to bribe, a parade of friendships and acquaintances to renew or reinforce. Selim was an old hand with ancient skills.

In the lee of a tight grouping of camels and watched by Benedict, de Flor busied himself applying extract of gypsy-wort and walnut husks to stain his face and hands. With his blue eyes and cropped brown hair, his Frankish build and soldierly ways, he made for an unconvincing Arab. Yet even this Crusader could blend at a distance and when occasion demanded.

'How do I appear, boy?'

'As a Saxon who has dyed his face and hands.'

'We will make a jester of you yet.' De Flor dabbed at Benedict with his cloth. 'But I wager you are right. It is why I keep my sword and Persian bow close.'

'Would they change our fate?'

'They have done so before, even deep behind the enemy line.'

'What if the Mameluks suspect our coming? What if they are looking for us?'

De Flor rested from his pastime. 'Fear not, boy. We will slip through as wraiths, will never be caught.'

'That stranger at the *han*. He was *Ahdath*, Roger.'

'I care not if he were an army.'

'He spied me.'

'And what did he see? A roguish boy in a crowded scene, another face amidst a hundred.'

Benedict lowered his eyes, momentarily ashamed at his concern. 'There was no friend to greet me.'

'A man and his donkey will vanish for any reason.'

'Such reason may be bad.'

'Look at me, boy.' De Flor reached and gently tugged at the chin of the youngster. 'Put aside doubt, for there will be moment and challenge ahead. Be strong in yourself and trust in me.'

'I do.'

'A fool as well as a jester.' De Flor snorted a laugh. 'Yet you were blessed by the Patriarch himself. It will afford you better shield than this infernal dye will do for me.'

'Acre shall hang you as a foreign infidel, Roger.'

'Our beloved city requires no excuse to punish me. It is possible William of Beaujeu sent me out here for my safety.'

Benedict smiled. 'Now it is you who must trust in me.'

They turned to the sight of Selim striding their way, the old cameleer ever inspecting his caravan. De Flor raised his hand in greeting.

'The boy tells me I am unpersuasive as a nomad, Selim.'

'We shall know it only when reckoning is upon us, Flor *effendi*.' The ancient face was impassive. 'Until that moment, the camels walk and you use them as your shelter.'

'Have you news from any fort or village?'

'Little that concerns. If Qalawun prepares, he is keeping his counsel and hiding his intention well to the east of the Jordan.'

'It is why we go in search of it, Selim.'

'My camels, my trade, my brothers, my *Waladii* here. These are my true consideration.'

'I honour each, Selim.'

'Thus our friendship is secure.'

A low whistle interrupted, its sound travelling almost at random through the camp. But men stirred from the lethargic calm, their attention focused in a new direction, the tension sharpening as the note died. A lookout had given the alert. Gesturing for his companions to stay low, Selim walked stiff and neutral to observe the nature of the hazard.

Horsemen were approaching. They came at a trot, armed

62

Turcomans with spears held at the vertical or with bows slung on their backs and arrow quivers dancing at their sides. It could put the fear of God into any and often had. They might be a patrol or *razzia*, a raiding party, could come with hostile intent or none at all, were capable of killing without mercy and at the gallop. Saladin had used them to effect; the Mameluks still employed them. Their reputation was deserved.

Selim stood firm and understated and waved in austere salutation as the cavalcade swept by. Somewhere behind him, de Flor had rolled into a prone position and crawled to watch from cover.

He hissed back to Benedict. 'They are the Turk, tribesmen of the Diyarbakr. Each one of them a venomous serpent.'

'Why are they here?' The boy slithered alongside and was pushed flat by a restraining hand. 'What does it mean, Roger?'

'It means they are no accidental infiltrators or members of a Bedouin *lisus*. It means that the regular force of the Mameluk is preparing. It means that Sultan Qalawun is set in his course.'

The horses trailed over a ridge line in an ebbing vibration of hooves and steel, and the dust then settled to the ground. It took longer for the encampment to return to its state of repose.

~

From the roof of the Fonda, Hazzim looked down upon the Acre waterfront and trembled. His fears were undefined. Yet he could not help himself or share in the happy communion of the crowd as it welcomed the arriving vessels, could not shed the pricking doubts conjured by the banners and shouts of those on board and disembarking. Benedict would have shaken him from his thoughts. Had he been present, his friend would make him laugh, would slap him on the back and steer him to fresh diversion. The Arab boy wondered where his comrade was and how he would react. He stared out on the ships disgorging their raucous load, heard the snatches of song and psalm and the threats that echoed with them. His senses did not lie. Below him, an army of Italian peasants was making for shore. And, Hazzim comprehended without truly knowing why, these pilgrims would bring no joy to anyone.

✝

Chapter 4

Enthusiasm for the newcomers had already palled. These men wanted to fight, while the citizens of Acre wished to prosper; the locals were willing to trade and coexist with the Arab and the peasants from Tuscany and Lombardy intended for Crusade. It was an uneasy state that could ignite to uglier incident. Disputes flared and fights broke out and drinking bouts descended to riotous affray. The singing of hymns had been forgotten. In its place were thieving, whoring and gaming, the sport of finding and beating senseless the infidels, the rising aggression of a rabble that had no pay and obeyed no order. The Constable was right to have increased patrolling of the streets.

Hazzim tried to ignore the change in mood. He saw the tension in the faces of his erstwhile friends, experienced the hurried interchange and the averted eyes. Lines were being drawn and barriers erected that he could not truly perceive. Matters would resolve and calm prevail, he reassured himself. Acre and its Latins were not immune to the occasional unexplained spasm. His village and people had lived through much; they would surely endure whatever fate decreed. He would continue as he always did.

Late afternoon found him walking purposefully from the Venetian quarter, a purse of coins hung on a cord about his neck and tucked inside his robe. Collecting payment for his father was rarely an onerous task. Outside the walls, he would untether his donkey and ride across the plain in time for evening prayer. The habit of daily life.

A hand reached and pulled him roughly to the side, the sour breath of liquor hostile on his face and intruding on his nostrils. Frightened, he stayed mute, uncertain how to respond and unwilling to provoke. There was danger here. He gazed at his assailant, felt the tightness of the grip, knew that Benedict would by now have thrown a punch or delivered a kick and would be scampering on his way. Maybe not. There were others surrounding and moving close, sealing off all exits.

'You do not like us? You have no time for conversation, little heathen?'

He shied as the bristled chin scraped against his, as a kiss was planted long and intimidating on his cheek. The man smelt bad. It was the stench of Europe and of an unwashed body, the sweat and mouth decay of a carnivore. Hazzim heard laughter. He did not understand the foreign tongue, the thick accent of these base Italian low-borns. Yet he grasped the nature of their meaning.

'Regard me when I speak, Saracen boy.'

The unyielding pressure of a hand forced his head to turn. He would not blink or shut his eyes but it was a vicious and extraordinary sight. Gaping enquiringly at him, the face was weathered and scarred and enlarged by the baldness of the pate, the features obtrusive and ill defined, the eyes dull and appraising with the relaxation of one who liked inflicting hurt. There was a restless intelligence behind the brute stare. All the more perilous.

'Should we skin you as a calf, Saracen? Or slit you as a pig?' The Arab had no answer and the Italian pressed on. 'I discover a full purse.'

Hazzim resisted as the hand patted him down, tried to defend his takings as the bag was ripped from his neck. He felt the bite of the cord and the blood trickle on his back. At least the Latins might let him go.

Their leader weighed the windfall in his palm, held it up for his followers to enjoy. It would allow them to carouse for a while, give them a chance to swill wine and ale and plan for future escapade. Gratitude would have to wait, for they still had a captive.

The man peered at Hazzim. 'I come from an Umbrian village called Norcia. It means the place of butchery, for there we kill pigs. Are we to bleed you like a pig, heathen? Are we to cut you open, slice off your balls?' It was said with a grin and the dangling of the leather pouch.

'*What happens here?*'

Feigning innocence, the Italian swung to face the challenge. A foot-patrol had stumbled on the scene, its sergeant wary and perplexed at what he had uncovered. He wavered. After all, it was best to turn away and let matters take their obvious or unnatural course.

Holding out the purse, the peasant leader allowed a minion to select a silver piece and toss it to the soldier. With a nod of recognition, the squad was led away.

'We will suffer no more interruption.' Attention returned to Hazzim, a finger tracing hard from his forehead to his chin. 'You will give us play of many kinds, Saracen. Play to make you scream and worthy of your bestial nature. Play that will forever remind you of my name.'

If Hazzim whimpered, he did not hear it. He was unaware of any sound but for the single and repeated word. *Spada*. The name was spat in his face, was being shaken into him.

Distraction again arrived and was less likely to fade away. Theobald of Alzey was impervious to bribery or threat.

Wearing his mantle with its eight-pointed cross, his frame dominating one end of the alley, the young Hospitaller tapped his sword against a stone and slowly gained attention.

Spada glared. 'We tend to our concerns. You stay with yours.'

'I cannot.'

'You risk ending in your own hospice, fair one.'

'Whilst you have greater chance of ending in the ground.' Theobald sloped the blade across his chest. 'Set the boy free.'

'It is not our wish.'

'Yet you will know it is mine.'

'A Hospitaller knight defends a worthless infidel? Outremer is truly in need of our steel.'

'There is no place for your kind or for your provocation.'

'Provocation?' The Italian raised a sullen eyebrow. 'We perform a sacred duty in cleansing holy soil of the plague.'

'Let him go or suffer the consequence.'

Drawing a knife, the peasant edged behind Hazzim and put its cutting edge to his throat. Spada smiled. 'One sword against another. *La spada* to *la pada*. What say you, knight?'

'Your time runs short. Harm him and you shall be harmed. Kill him and you shall be killed.'

'The Saracen defiles this city.'

'No more than you.' Theobald took a step forwards. 'I have seen filth as you slop in and flow out. I have witnessed the desolation your kind bring.'

'Such passion from a Crusader so young.'

A further step. 'Release him or die.'

Spada glanced at his cohorts. There seemed little appetite for armed response, a general wariness at the approach of a knight who plainly would not compromise. The Italian released his hold on Hazzim and the boy slipped away.

Theobald halted and rested his sword. 'A wise judgement.'

'Not so for you, knight.'

Backing away, the peasant leader gestured to his men to follow. Easier pickings lay elsewhere. Theobald did not flinch as the Italian swivelled on his heel and bared his teeth to offer a hissed farewell. Out of sight, Hazzim still ran. He would not stop until he was beyond the walls, would not be safe until back in his village. The name raided his thoughts and robbed him of breath. *Spada*. The devil himself had arrived in Acre.

~

When the music swelled and the stars were bright, Benedict could forget himself and put aside all else. This was happiness and perfection. It was the moment that counted, the stamping of feet and the clapping of hands, the sharing of friendship and the freedom of movement. He whooped and shouted and spun in the dust. As the beat of the tablah drummers climbed and the plaintive call of nays mingled and chased each other to the night, the youngster could let himself dance as the camel drivers danced.

Selim looked on, de Flor at his side, a leader of his clan content to watch and break bread and take pleasure in the spectacle. His men knew both how to fight and play. Their swords and spears were never far from their grasp. Wherever they travelled, their wake was often populated by a light scattering of corpses, the blackened remains of brigands, pilferers and hostile tribesmen. Few dared confront them. But the old caravan master did not seek out trouble. He rested among these low and barren hills for a purpose, would not push through for the marshlands at the head of the Jordan until reports from ahead had improved. Several merchants had given warning of occasional skirmishes and attacks. It was sufficient to merit a pause. So they created music and drank their tea, offered up prayers and tended their camels. The desert journeymen would be staying awhile.

'You grow restless, Flor *effendi*?' Selim tapped his hand rhythmically on a knee.

'I am not celebrated for my patience, old friend.'

'Yet I am respected for my wisdom.' There was humour in the eye of the Arab. 'If we wait, we bring less attention on ourselves. If we are zealous and urgent, trouble will come in search of us.'

'Perchance it does already.'

Selim shook his head. 'Neither the absence of your spy at the *han* nor the presence of Turcoman cavalry shows there is a plot to catch you.'

'The boy swears he saw *Ahdath*.'

'It concerns you?'

'I told the boy it does not.' The adventurer waved to Benedict as the youngster turned and saluted him with a tambourine held high. 'There is no benefit in burdening him with doubt.'

'You and your Frankish masters already send him to danger.'

'Whilst it is you who carries him there.'

'Then I am not so wise a desert creature after all.'

Their conversation ceded to the undulating wail of the pipes and the hypnotic patter of the drums. De Flor swayed, a man as easily seduced by pleasure as he was by the prospect of clashing steel. It was not he who dictated the pace of the mission; it was circumstance and the artful ancient who commanded the train.

Selim sat back. 'Even should my *Waladii* be right and the man he crept up on be in service of the Mameluks. There is no pressing danger for us.'

'Unless they have been informed of our intention.'

'Your imagination is strong, Flor *effendi*.'

'My instinct is greater.'

'We shall discover soon enough on approach to Damascus.' Selim was as sanguine as ever. 'They will not attack my caravan.'

Flushed with exertion, Benedict essayed towards them and beamed. 'Will neither of you dance? Roger? *Amm* Selim?'

'Selim is too aged and I as clumsy as a hobbled camel.' De Flor patted the stone beside him. 'But fetch the 'ud, boy. I will pluck some notes and conjure tales of King Sharyar and his Queen Scheherazade and of One Thousand and One Nights.'

Dutifully, Benedict left on his quest, returning shortly with the Arab lute clutched tight. Aside from his sword and bow, it was one of the more cherished possessions of de Flor. The Crusader would spend long hours cosseting and oiling it, protecting it from the ravages of heat and sand. A challenging endeavour. Rarely did he leave the instrument behind.

He took it and ran his fingers across its frame and neck, picking tentatively at its four strings and summoning a plectrum of trimmed eagle-feather from his sleeve. Whether as soldier or balladeer, there was always showmanship. Benedict settled to listen and Selim silenced his men. Then the soft and mellow tone of the lute flickered and seemed to shiver in the air and the fine voice of de Flor followed it in song. His audience did not stir. They were lost to the stories, absorbed in the sagas of heroism and cowardice, of love and loss and betrayal. He was an Unbeliever, yet could still embrace the sensibilities of the Arab. The Frankish adventurer was at home in whatever landscape he chose.

Once the entertainment was over and the oil lamps snuffed, the group returned among the hobbled camels to find their sleeping berths. Some would rest in tents, some wrap themselves in blankets against the open chill of the wilderness, some patrol. The sound and light faded. Occasionally a camel groaned and a jackal yipped in distant greeting, but the camp slumbered.

Benedict and de Flor had cleared their ground, removing stones that might give scorpions cover, preparing their bedding on wicker pallets and creating shelter close by the herd. A comfortable position after the most rewarding of evenings. To the heavy snores of his guardian, Benedict fell asleep.

Abruptly, pulled confused from his dreams to a semiconscious state, he awoke. He thought he heard a noise. It was nothing, he thought at first; the backwash of his mind or a discordant part of the wider whole. He grasped once more for the depths, but whatever had alerted him had not left. There was a presence close, a shadow that lingered and hunched low and crept forwards. Benedict raised himself on an elbow.

'Who goes there?' He whispered it loud, his words designed to ward off threat and bolster his nerve. They succeeded in reinforcing his isolation.

He sat upright. 'I see you.'

It was a lie, faltering even as it left his lips, cracking with the fear that now gripped him. For seconds there was a pause, as though the hidden or imagined foe considered whether discovery mattered. Reaching for his knife, Benedict waited. The breathing of de Flor was more regular than his own. Slowly, the silent and intimidating field of energy retreated. And the boy lay back and kept his eyes open and his ears tuned for a return, his body cold and shocked. He did not sleep again that night.

'Ignore these peasant Italians and we shall rue the day.'

There was no doubting the ire in the voice of the grand master of the Hospital. John of Villiers was apt to forcefully state his case and had little time for either fools or diplomatic nicety. If there was a problem, it needed to be met; should there be disagreement, the weakest would be coerced through vehement weight of argument to submit. The grand master glowered accusingly at his colleagues.

'Is our Council not called to emergency order because there is emergency?'

'We in the Temple must agree with our Hospitaller brother.' William of Beaujeu spoke, emollient and supportive. 'There is little but discord since the cursed Italians came.'

The Hospitaller jabbed a finger at the Bishop of Tripoli. 'What say you, my lord bishop? Was it not you who was granted command and brought them here on ships?'

'I did as my reverend lord the Pope decreed.'

Amalric, the Constable, offered a sour laugh. 'Did he decree a rabble be disgorged upon my city? Did he decree lawlessness and insult? Did he decree drunken riot and lasciviousness?'

'I thought it was already the reputation of Acre, your highness.'

'Do not jibe so lightly, my lord bishop.'

'What would you have me do?' The prelate searched the faces of the delegates. 'Neither prince nor noble would take the Cross. Only peasants and humble townsfolk answered the call.'

The grand master of the Hospital scowled. 'Acre suffers for it.'

'Your coffers are more full than mine. Perchance his grace would care to embrace these Italians in his pay.'

'I would readily place their necks within a noose.'

'They come to the Holy Land for Crusade. They seek glory and merit and salvation.'

'Through robbery and drink? With debauchery and

disorder?' Amalric rested his arms on the gilded wings of his chair. 'Their instinct is for booty and not for service.'

'With my own eyes I witness them prey on the local and peace-loving Arab.' A Frankish worthy felt impelled to comment.

Another replied. 'Is there such thing as a peace-loving infidel?'

William of Beaujeu scarcely heard the debate. There was too much chatter as the menace grew and too much ignorance while he alone sought the truth. Nero merely played the harp while Rome burned. These blind and pampered nobles flew their hawks and coursed their hounds, pretending their lives and positions were secure. Such great folly. He had yet to hear from his spies, and waited for information from every corner of the Mameluk realm. When it reached him, it would confirm his fears and prove how prescient he had been. Meanwhile, the squabbling continued.

He stifled a yawn and rejoined the exchange. 'I recall how when last we convened, my warning of Saracen threat was rejected.'

'It does not deter you from your own martial plans and scaremongering and scheming.' Amalric let a flash of antipathy show. 'In spite of my entreaty, you beat the drum of war and quicken the tempo of your training, tear apart your galleys and form them into catapults.'

If only you knew how I plan, Beaujeu mused. 'What if I am right, your highness?'

'And what if you are wrong?'

'Then at the least my order is prepared for whatever danger is presented.' Beaujeu swept the assembled with his gaze. 'Am I like the prophetess Cassandra to forever go ignored?'

The Constable shifted discomforted in his seat. 'Your views will be considered as will any others in this chamber.'

'So hark to my words. You believe I may provoke Qalawun if I don chausses and chain mail and choose to clench an armoured fist. The Sultan is already provoked and inclined to march on Acre. Not the Templars, nor the Hospitallers and Teutons, will provide him the excuse he craves.'

'Our Cassandra will tell us who then.' A Pisan was blunt in his disdain.

'Stand at the window and look down. It is the Italian mob that disturbs all peace. If it is not brought to heel, it will kill. Should it kill, it will be an Arab that dies. When report reaches Cairo, it shall be war.'

'Prettily spoken.' The Pisan would not give up. 'But arrest these men and they will riot the more.'

'Squander your time in timidity and trance and you will face worse things than riot.'

His admonition was shrugged off. Other nobles joined in the debate, agreeing or contradicting in a petulant chorus of tongues. It was always the way of the Council. They would go to their Maker still quarrelling, Beaujeu supposed. Few had ever met the Saracens in combat. Because of it, they were complacent and self-regarding; they talked as Crusaders and yet were possessed by the robust naivety of dullards. An encounter with a Mameluk arrow might bring some changes.

The grand master peered towards the doorway. Amethyst the dwarf kept his distance today. There would be no light relief or madcap tumbling or the lewd telling of a joke. It promised to be a long and bruising session.

An arrow pierced the leather hide of the gourd and a second quickly followed, each striking true, their heads and flights projecting eccentrically from the sides. It earned some applause and de Flor reached for a third dart. He had put aside musicianship in favour of weapons practice, erecting a temporary butt to refine his skills before the caravan progressed. It was the final evening in the camp. Tomorrow they would cross the Jordan at Jacob's Ford and climb the Syrian Heights. Better an indirect approach than inquisitive eyes and roving patrols along the valley passes to Damascus.

From the background came a cheer and pounding feet and the gleeful features of Benedict as he ran to report his triumph.

'I leapt an entire camel, Roger! Without touching by hand or foot, I vaulted the kneeling beast!'

De Flor lowered his recurved bow. 'I commend you, boy. Many crack their bones in such an attempt.'

'Not I.' Benedict jigged on the spot as proof.

'God might not smile should you tempt chance again.' The soldier pressed his thumb against the arrow tip. 'I do not care to return you home broken.'

'There are greater dangers than a camel.'

'Then spare your energies for them. The camel is too surly and unworthy to risk your neck on. Come, I will tutor you in more soldierly skills than jumping.'

He beckoned the boy to his side and placed the bow in his hands, turning him to face the aim-point and positioning him for the drill.

'Steadiness is all, boy. Keep your feet wide and your breath easy. Hold your shoulders back and your head high.'

'I'm trying, Roger.' The bow quivered as the youngster struggled to draw.

De Flor added his grip. 'Less strength and more constancy is needed. Now to it, boy. Raise. Pluck. And release.'

The arrow flew to its mark. Without pausing, de Flor took

the weapon, selected a shaft and fired it from the hip to chase its predecessor.

'That is the art of bowmanship, boy.'

'I am no archer. I could hardly draw the string.'

'Your eye is keen and your spirit sound. In time you may challenge any.'

Benedict grinned. If de Flor detected in him a warrior instinct, it must be present. He would prove himself worthy of the belief. No weakness would undermine him, no night dread and flight of fancy distract or disturb him. He was a warrior, an imagined knight on errand for the grand master of the Temple.

Later, as the sun set in a deepening glow across Galilee, they retired to their quarters. Departure would be early and their wits would need to be sharp. Benedict stared up at the inked sky, attempted to recall the names of the constellations and soon remembered nothing. The camp was once more at rest and he could permit himself to slide with the day into the deepest of sleep.

He woke to a spasm of movement and a cry of pain. Before he had blinked to consciousness, a hand was clamped across his mouth and a voice was in his ear.

'No sound, boy. We need not wake the rest. You under-stand?' Benedict nodded through the muzzling palm and the pressure eased.

'What is it, Roger?'

'The attack I suspected would come tonight. You thought I dozed and dreamt last night and roused the dead with my cacophony.'

'You kept watch?'

'I was vigilant all the while.' Even in the darkness Benedict could see that de Flor was smiling. 'Even when you believed yourself alone.'

'Why did you not act?'

'I wished for our murderer to return, to gauge if he had an accomplice.'

'Murderer?'

The adventurer sounded unconcerned. 'He plotted to kill either one of us and to spoil our entry to Damascus.'

'Yet you let him go.'

The flat of a hand pushed the boy flat and ended the questions. 'For certain, he runs and shall not be back. But he leaves his dagger and I placed on him a bruise with the stone I threw. Sleep as you must, boy. At dawn we rise to a new test.'

Maybe he was not quite ready for the world of adults, Benedict concluded. Their games were rarely straightforward. He was glad though for the presence of de Flor. None could match him. Yet the familiarity of home seemed many miles behind. Acre was where true security lay.

~

That security was already breached. Arab horses were renowned for their feats of endurance, a prize stallion being able to cover a hundred miles in six hours or so. Three steeds had brought the Assassins across the desert to Gaza and on to Caesarea. There the men had changed to fresh mounts before journeying north along the coast towards their chosen target. Then it was a simple matter of arriving in Acre with something to sell. The trio merged easily with the crowd. Few bothered to glance or ask questions, none thought it remarkable for anonymous Levantines in indistinguishable clothes to sit in taverns or wander in the streets. That gave ample opportunity for reconnaissance and the time would not be wasted. The killers had trained hard and made their vow of obedience; they had committed themselves to the path of self-sacrifice and death. Sultan Qalawun of the Mameluks expected it.

Seated in the drinking den, the leader of the group thought of paradise and of what he must achieve. This next task he would perform alone. He was to be the spark that would ignite the fire, the catalyst that would bring catastrophe upon the whole. How fortunate the Italians were here to play. In Caesarea, he had walked through the shattered Crusader fort that had been in the hands of the Mohammedan these twenty-five years; on his short northward trek, he had passed the walled farmsteads of the Unbelievers abandoned during their retreat. All roads led to Acre.

Spada rattled the dice in his cup and threw again. 'A coin, Saracen. My number betters yours.'

'Luck smiles on you, Christian.' The Assassin spoke in the tongue of the Umbrian as he paid. 'It will not last.'

'How so?' The peasant was drunk and in belligerent mood.

'Chance may disappoint. You come to Palestine for prize and glory and end dicing and earning pennies.' He prepared to make his throw.

A hand reached and grasped his wrist. 'Is what I do not blessed?'

'It is scarce a Crusade.' The Assassin pulled free his hand and shook and tipped the cup. 'A five. A four. A six. That is fifteen, Christian. Your turn to pay.'

'Thus speaks a heathen.'

'One who scores a higher count.'

'You would command me?' The Italian waited for the laughter from his men. 'Do you know with whom you game?'

'A man soon to be the poorer. A sword that shows its limpness.'

'I have taken the Cross, heathen.'

79

'As I intend to take your money.' The Assassin met and held the aggressive gaze.

'I do not see your friends present.'

'Then you do not look outside these walls. The land is held by the Believer.'

'We shall seize it back and put your kind to the spear. We will march to the trumpet and restore the Holy Land.'

'Yet for now you are content to drink and gamble.'

Spada narrowed his eyes and gulped from his wine bowl. 'You mock me, heathen?'

'I enlighten you, infidel.' The Assassin sat back an inch on the wooden stool. 'Over years, I listen to loud talk of this and that, to crowing intent and grand promise of slaughter.'

'Will you doubt me?' The voice of Spada had lowered.

'Where is your courage, infidel? Where is your army?'

'It surrounds me.'

'Peasants who would shit their tunics at the sight of a Mameluk regiment.' The Assassin dropped the dice into the cup. 'Now pay.'

'Never, heathen.'

'So you lie and cheat as any Frank. It is no wonder the women of Acre prefer a True Believer to mount them.'

It splintered the peace as he knew it would, summoned a roar of outrage and the onrush of angry men. But he was quick and well rehearsed. As they made their move he responded, a lone artiste against a lumbering herd. A knife in his hand, he was light on his feet and leaps ahead. One Italian thrust at him with a blade and found his own throat cut. Another attempted to crown him with a studded cosh, and was gutted from pelvis to sternum for his effort. A third sank groundward and screamed all the way.

Numbers would eventually tell. In the constricted melee, the Assassin was unlikely to leave unscathed. He did not plan to. *Allah, Allah, Allah.* Even as he scored a hit on a fourth victim, he staggered to a blow. His guard dropped and his knife fell and he looked down for a moment at the crude handle of a shank jutting from his ribs. It was the cue for others. They fell on him, a frenzied and howling throng wanting to erase, intent on spreading brains and viscera about the room. The calm enveloped and the mist settled and the Assassin was satisfied his work was done.

'*To the streets! To the streets!*'

'*Kill every heathen!*'

'*Show no mercy! Avenge our loss! Grind the Saracen to the dust!*'

'*Cut off their heads! Slit their bellies! Any with a long beard must die!*'

Seized with an ecstatic rage, the Italians disgorged to the open. They were gathering pace, spreading terror and harnessing support, their cries and bloodlust climbing. At their centre, his sword raised high, Spada drove them on. He and his peasant army were at the start of their campaign. The Crusade had finally arrived.

Close to the mouth of the River Nile, where Egyptian fishermen from Damietta cast their nets for the evening catch, a body was found floating. Badly mutilated and decomposed, it would go forgotten and unidentified and left to wallow in the water. Yet the corpse was that of a felucca captain who had brought a clandestine message from a traitorous emir in the court of Qalawun. It was a communiqué that would not reach a waiting dhow or a Templar galley off the Levantine coast, that would never be passed to William of Beaujeu. Another intelligence source had been closed down.

Chapter 5

'Now will the lamb make war upon the dragon! Now shall we kill the accursed heathen for Christ!'

In the tumult, few needed to be encouraged. With gathering energy the storm broke across the city, the gangs channelling through the narrow streets and spreading out in restless quest. Butchery was their aim and none could withstand it or pull the rabble back. It was why they had travelled this far, why they carried knives and swords and scythes and why no Moslem who was cornered or outpaced ever stood a chance. The good citizens of Acre knew what to do. They would neither offer protest nor put up resistance. Mohammedans were scarcely worth the bother and probably deserved their fate. Doors were barricaded and windows shuttered, people scattering and scurrying from the path of rampage. The field was clear.

It sounded like a murmur that grew into a roar and spilled through in a lava flow of festive hatred. An old Arab was wrenched from his donkey and his head crushed beneath a welter of blows. He was quickly dismembered and his body parts born away as keepsakes. Axes were taken to a door and three young men dragged outside and beheaded on a limestone mounting block. Others were found nearby, their screams rising brief and shrill before the blades descended. More souvenirs and celebration. Howling in fright, a trader tore loose from his captors and raced naked before the chase. The Italians were grateful for the sport. Their prey was an imaginative creature, made hollering sounds as he blundered and leapt and considered his escape. There was none to be found. He was eventually brought down by a javelin and castrated before he died.

Hazzim prayed. He should never have returned to Acre; he should have remained in the village as his father had advised. But pride had brought him back. He was not about to be scared from the city by a single encounter with a mannerless and foul-smelling Umbrian. Besides, trade demanded the village maintain contact with the Latins. It would be dishonourable to let his uncles or brothers risk the journey. He had enough friends to guard his back. Yet those allies seemed absent, the streets now pulsing not with commerce but with the blazing ferment of a pogrom. He smelt burning, heard the screams, caught the searing flash of an image of Arab men and women rolling and stampeding with their hands tied and their robes alight. The crowd was delighted with its inventive use of naphtha. Hazzim recognised some of the faces. Expressions were changed, yet he had once conversed with persecutors and victims alike. May Allah forgive him for his cowardice.

'*There is another! See how the heathen skulks!*'

'*Put him to the torch!*'

'*He is mine! I have him!*'

'*Slay the devil!*'

Hazzim did not wait for capture or the stabbing pain of a sword thrust. Ten paces, twenty, the quickest and the dead. He told himself the enemy were slow, that Benedict had escaped in Tripoli and he would do the same. These infidel savages were unfamiliar with the terrain, with the rooftops and the cut-throughs, with the tricks of an Arab youngster who wanted to live. No drunken and clumsy peasant would claim his scalp. He headed for the Hospitaller compound.

It was the correct decision. In full armour, with their swords drawn and their shields presented, the Knights of St John sallied out. They offered a formidable front. Marching in close order, they swept the streets before them, pushing back the Italians and dragging Arabs to safe haven. Like the Templars, the order distrusted anarchy and preferred the status quo. Its grand master understood what was at stake. If his knights could save a single heathen, it might placate Sultan Qalawun; if his men could restore a semblance of control, perhaps the effects of the madness would be short-lived.

Resentful of interference, the Italians renewed their efforts to break through. Spada urged his forces on to their holy duty. A peasant was cut down, a second had his face removed with the strike of a mailed fist, a third folded to the impact of a crossbow quarrel that exited to pierce a fourth. Gradually, with enraged shouts of discontent, the peasants drew back. The standoff was unstable.

'Quick, Hazzim.' The voice was familiar, although Theobald's face was disguised by the helmet and nose-guard. 'Make haste for the compound and take shelter there.'

Hazzim was shaking, unable to move. 'I cannot do so.'

'Your life depends on it.'

'I am a Believer, a Mohammedan.'

'One who is soon to be torn apart by these dogs,' Theobald said fiercely. 'Do as I command, Hazzim.'

'My people are hated by your brother knights.'

'You prefer to face the wrath of a thousand blades?' Theobald pointed to the baying crowd.

And Hazzim saw Spada, identified the squat shape and brutish features, remembered the breath on his face and the

84

knife to his throat. The ogre would not let him flee from his grasp a second time. Acre had changed. It had become a city of rage and of faces contorted by emotions he had never encountered; it had been transformed into a place engulfed in loathing. If it were the Knights Hospitallers who offered him sanctuary, then the danger was absolute.

'We are friends, Hazzim.' The hand in its mitten of linked mail clamped hard on his shoulder. 'You have my vow of safe passage. Retreat to our territory before the multitude breaks through.'

To the aggressive chants and screamed defiance of the swarm, the Arabs staggered shocked to the redoubt. Their path was guarded by lines of knights, their withdrawal ensured by Theobald and his men-at-arms. These too fell back. From behind the protecting walls and studded door of their domain, the Hospitallers would nurse the wounded and give succour to the refugees they had saved. It was all they could do for the Arabs. Outside, the hunting packs roamed. In time, the frenzy would abate and the uprising burn out, the authorities would step timidly to impose control. Unnecessary woe might be caused by putting down an agitation that would pass. The peasants needed to believe they had productively wet their blades.

It was not over. While most butchered and made merry inside the city, Spada and his cohorts had more ambitious plans. A Crusade could take several forms. With over two hundred men, the Umbrian switched his attention to the heathen villages dotted temptingly on the plain. The target was easy, the journey short, the lure of money and killing and liquor stills strong in the minds of the armed pilgrims. There would be no tiresome intervention by the military orders to deflect them from their purpose and prevent their implementation of the divine will. The Arabs possessed orchards and the secrets of eau de vie, the sweet nectar and essence of life. Spada gave the order.

So they issued from the gates, lighting torches in the soft gloaming and commandeering wagons and horses and mules. Behind them, the disturbance continued; before them was a peaceful landscape and the prospect of disorder to come. Small wonder they were elated. They sang the same songs that had brought them ashore, bristled with the motley arsenal they had brought from their towns and villages in Italy. An instrument designed for the fields could always reap a different whirlwind.

Such a slow procession would hardly pose a threat. The old watchman leant on his spear and watched the trickle of flame seep in a winding column from the distant city. It certainly could draw the eye. Others joined him to gape at the unusual display. These infidels had practices all their own. Yet the government of Acre and the foreign merchants were willing partners in trade, who rarely allowed religious difference to interrupt their business. Whatever the spectacle, it meant nothing and would surely go away.

Instead, it continued in its progress. Marching east along the trail the peasant force came on, a vengeful band crossing the fields of cracked earth and aiming for the village. It took a while for the inhabitants to comprehend. They were a peaceful breed, masters in the medicinal and spirit-making arts, knew little in the way of mounting a concerted defence. They were slow to respond and by then it was too late. The villagers heard chanting; the villagers saw hostile faces and the glint of steel reflected in the glow of firebrands. Spada had arrived.

As though in a seamless dream of threaded event and endless screaming, the theatre began. Holding his spear in determined challenge, the watchman confronted the first wave and was slit open for his effort. A rearguard action of sorts was mounted, but it too was torn to pieces. At the entrance to the village, the timber gate was being barred by men and women with fumbling hands and terrified eyes. They need not have bothered. The crashing impact of a battering-ram splintered the barrier before it was fully closed, and the Crusaders waded in.

'Each one of them must die! Every heathen slain is a tribute to God and recompense for your soul!'

Spada roared his commands and plunged through with his sword. He would lead by example. As a man of faith, he could carve wide a human and raze a dwelling without compunction or fear of contradiction. Armed superiority gave him the privilege. Figures appeared before him and vanished beneath the blows; mouths opened and babbled and were silenced; all ran this way and that and were finally brought down. The compacted earth of the compounds was softening to the tread.

She was still alive when he found her, a girl grown to early womanhood and fetchingly mute in the midst of horror. Her family were already dead, of course. Somewhere in the piles of the dismembered were her kinsfolk, people surprised and overwhelmed by the ferocity of the assault. The headman was now without his head. From upheaval could dawn a new understanding. Spada wiped his sword on a sleeve and saw her flinch, gauged the passive fury in her look. She was hardly in a position to show him disrespect. That was akin to blasphemy. He and his compatriots had done Christendom a favour and demonstrated to the timid fools of Acre how believers should conduct themselves. God would not deny him a few additional pleasures. Firewater and female company would aid the celebration. He intended to spare the Saracen girl, at least until the close.

*

Besieged within the quadrangle of the Hospitaller compound in Acre, Hazzim lay dazed against a stone flight of steps. It was strangely discomforting to be a Mohammedan guest at the military heart of the Latin kingdom. He thought of his family and village and of how worried they would be. Few Arabs in the city would have lived as he to see the sunset. Allah had shown great mercy to him. He would not forget it, nor fail to recall the images of the day and the baseness of the Franks. The invaders hated him. In the darkness he made a vow that tomorrow he would return to his own kind, that he would show his back to the place he once embraced and never again walk in friendship through its streets.

There was a quietness to the aftermath, a stillness colonised only by the busy hum of flies and the hiss and crackle of smouldering trees. Both village life and the village itself were ended. Scattered about were the corpses, the casual litterings of rampage. Each cluster held a tale, every cleaved skull and arm thrown wide expressed desperation in the face of death. None had withstood the onslaught. Possessions too were strewn, the artefacts of a simple existence discarded or trampled among the fallen. Yet the visitors lived. Oblivious to the warming stench, they slumbered off their labours, blood-caked worshippers sprawled in drunken fatigue and unresponsive to the snores of their own. Peace of a kind had settled.

Theobald of Alzey dismounted close to the line of smoking palms and waved to his troop to follow. It was a matter of pursuing the trail and stepping over bodies at the open gateway, of proceeding from one site of atrocity to the next. Behind him, his sergeant retched and spat a ball of vomit and his men crossed themselves and muttered prayers. They had already seen what the Italian peasants could do. Even hardened warriors eschewed such things. They were far from the holy war to which by oath they were pledged.

'*Stand*.' Theobald delivered a kick to the side of the prone Italian. 'Stand or I will ensure you never shall.'

The man groaned. 'Let me be.'

'I would sooner let you die.'

'Find others to yap and scratch at, you dog. I wish to sleep.'

Grasping the peasant by his hair, the young knight hauled him protesting to the ballooned stomach and entrails of a cadaver and forced his face inside. Immersion seemed to have its effect. Shrieking, clutching at his streaming head, the Italian staggered to his feet.

The Hospitallers were unrelenting in their task. There were plenty of spilled remains from which to choose, scores of drowsy killers to waken with booted feet and threats and beatings. Some of the Italians had been blinded by the quantities of eau de vie consumed; some still straddled the bodies of victims they had raped; some were as dead as the Arabs they had butchered.

Sullen and complaining, the Italians were corralled and escorted in ragged pageant from the scene. Their return to Acre was not to be as ecstatic as the outward journey. The Italians grumbled amongst themselves. They were being blamed for the weakness in others, persecuted for the prim inertia of the noble classes and the squeamishness of these knights. What they alone had achieved was immense. They might be prisoners now, but the results mouldering behind them made it all worthwhile.

~

The caravan of Selim wended its way up the ancient track-way until it reached the plateau of the Syrian Heights above.

From here it was some sixty miles to Damascus, a route across heat-shimmered undulations scarred with cinder cones and dormant craters and sporadically marked with sunburnt scrub. It was starkly beautiful terrain. The camels would traverse it with unvarying tread, their drivers steering them on.

Yet the old caravan master had called a halt. There were matters to address. Lined up in a snaking row, his men stood and waited, their glances concerned and their mutterings suspicious. There was a natural order to things. Never before had Selim found reason to pause here or change arrangement at so late a stage. It must be important.

His pace deliberate and slow, Roger de Flor moved along the front. He would not rush the process. As Selim and Benedict looked on, the adventurer confronted each nomad in turn and engaged in quiet exchange. He was searching for something, seeking out the truth. Few would have the courage to resist. In his hand he held a dagger, a theatrical prop for his investigation to be dangled before each face. A turncoat was present and he would discover him.

'This is yours, brother?' The knife swayed.

'No, I swear it.' The Arab gestured to his own. 'See, my dagger is carried with me.'

'Then who might have lost such a blade?'

'I know not.'

As each interview was terminated de Flor progressed up the rank, pursued by the flickering gaze of the cameleers. Honour was at stake. It was unconscionable that one of their number might have betrayed the word of Selim and offended a guest and brother, and they were unnerved to see the Latin giant bearing down. One moment he had been the lute player and the next a stern and calculating figure inspecting them on parade.

'You.'

A single word that conveyed so much. De Flor had travelled over five hundred paces before he turned to retrace his steps and reveal his find. The man he faced registered no guilt. He was as proud and unyielding as the rest.

The soldier waved the knife. 'Your dagger falls to my possession, brother.'

'You are mistaken.'

'Am I?' De Flor leant forwards, his words sinking to a murmur. 'Your relief when I walked by would tell me otherwise.'

'I have my dagger.'

'Whilst I have certainty. You approached by night with stealthy intent to kill, had orders to prevent myself or the boy from ever reaching Damascus.'

'This is untrue.'

'Sayeth a spy. Sayeth a serpent. Sayeth a camel driver who pretends as a brother and takes the pay of the Mameluk.'

'My love and loyalties are for Selim.'

'He would laugh to hear it. As I put bruise upon you are you tainted by treachery.'

De Flor jabbed with his finger into a shoulder. The man yelped. It must have been a painful blow from the hurled rock the previous night, an injury difficult to hide when tending camels and manoeuvring heavy load. The Latin narrowed his eyes, riding the seconds, willing the move. There was indecision in the face of his opponent. A hot breeze tugged at the sleeve of the Arab and blew up the dust about his feet. Each party regarded the other from close quarter. Tension quivered. No parley, entreaty or way out.

It was the camel driver who blinked and broke first, heading for a shallow escarpment and scrambling to gain height and purchase. He did well. But in bolting he had provided his confession and brought down upon himself a sentence of death. De Flor unslung the bow on his back and reached to fit an arrow.

'Lower your weapon, Flor *effendi*.' Selim called out from his temporary vantage. 'Draw the blood of our brother and you must fight us all.'

'My argument is with but one.'

'It will turn to a quarrel with many. That is our custom.'

'Justice will speak, Selim.'

'With my voice and to my hand.' The old Arab pointed and a pair of volunteers ran to outflank their errant comrade. 'Neither the nature of the man nor the character of this plateau will permit him to voyage far.'

'You intend to capture him, Selim?'

'I mean to kill him.'

The ancient caravaneer would rather perish than break his word. His reputation had been challenged and his code of hospitality insulted by the incident. It demanded retribution. On this arid high ground east of Lake Tiberias, blood-honour would be restored. Selim drew his sword and began to march up the hill. He needed no assistance, save for the flushing tactics of his cohorts on the wing. His quarry had disappeared into a rock defilade and without pause Selim climbed after him. Below, the men and camels waited on. The outcome was not in doubt. Age would never weary Selim or diminish his appetite to close and kill.

From the hidden amphitheatre came a sharp cry that was swallowed in an instant. Within minutes the caravan master reappeared, holding high a severed hand as trophy before tossing it aside. Benedict felt the supporting grip of de Flor on his shoulder. There was a great deal to commend the unchanging tranquillity of life enjoyed by Hazzim and his sister Leila.

*

He did not weep. He simply could not absorb the magnitude of his loss. Hazzim walked the blistered ruins with a dull and uniform tread, trying to recall how things once had been. It was not a village he remembered; it was not a village at all. Everything was gone. He had travelled to Acre and been delayed, had returned to a blackened void. Maybe it was the mad conjurings of a mind exhausted by the turbulent experience of the city. Reason told him otherwise. The stench reinforced it.

His life, his family, his fault. He should have been present to help protect his people. He should have escaped the chaos in Acre to cross the plain and warn. But he had not done so. About him lay the result of his cowardice and inaction, the accusing silence that deafened his ears. He saw the pyre. How conscientious of the Hospitallers to pile the dead into a mound and clear away the evidence. They could not hide it all.

Flames still lapped at the charred remains and smoke wreathed and thinned as it coiled skyward. Hazzim stooped and retrieved a discarded sandal to put it to the fire. His offering. For several minutes he circumnavigated the glowing mound, searching for the familiar and committing each detail to a recess of his mind. He owed his loved ones that much. Yet he would discover no answer from this site; he would not pull alive his father or mother or siblings from the furnace. Atrocities occurred and Arab hamlets vanished. It was the way of men and the will of Allah.

A sulphurous puff of haze belched putrid from the core. Like so much burning livestock, Hazzim mused. Once he had believed in friendship and peace. His innocence had brought him to the foot of a charnel mountain. There could never be concord between Believer and infidel. So long as they existed the Latins were a threat; so long as they remained on the soil of Palestine they would enslave and cow the Arab. Benedict had allied himself to the tyrants based in Acre. That was his choice and his world, but it made him no better than the slayers of the village. He had once been a brother; now their fraternity was void. Hazzim owed it to his family and the fallen of the village. This was all that was left.

Emissaries from Cairo had arrived demanding apology and eager to inflict reparation upon the hateful Latins. It had created friction within the Christian camp. No true Crusader would bend the knee to a heathen ruler; no prince or noble-man of faith could admit responsibility or accept mistake on the part of his kind. So the Italians had overreached them-selves in their eagerness. It had been an unfortunate episode. Yet it was already in the past and the ringleaders jailed, the rabble calmed and its violence checked. The Mohammedans should be thankful for that. Their sultan had scant need for concern and little reason to offer threats or claim a breach of the accord. Peace could still reign between Saracen and Frank.

In an antechamber to the great hall the Constable was not overjoyed at the approach of the Templar grand master.

'We have discussed all matters, Beaujeu.' Amalric made to continue for the door. 'The debate is over and our position agreed.'

'Heed my warning, your highness.'

'For a holy knight, you are easily frightened.'

The Templar did not rise to the insult. 'I am aware of what Qalawun may do.'

'And what is that? Curse and fret and rail against us? Send his ambassadors to entreat? Threaten us with clash of drums and cymbals?'

'We have given him the excuse he seeks. And with stubbornness and pride, we deny him the recompense he is owed.'

'He is owed nothing, Beaujeu.'

'Yet he will take all.'

Antagonised, the Constable rounded on Beaujeu. 'Would you have me hand to him our fellow Christians? Would you permit our own to be sent in chains to the heathen lair?'

'It is no less than they deserve. Spada and his vile brood have wronged.'

'What of it?' Amalric reddened with irritation. 'They are not the first Crusaders to cut assunder the Saracen. I will not be the first ruler to throw them on Saracen justice.'

'Acre will suffer.'

'It is I who would suffer should I bend to your petition. The people would not forgive me.'

'Such are the perils of your leadership and our predicament.'

Beaujeu appraised the Constable with a cool contempt. For all his finery and station, Amalric sat on a crumbling throne in a condemned and dissipated city. Qalawun would not let the matter lie. He had waited too long and schemed too hard. He had prepared each move with the skilled patience of a master. The grand master of the Templars could scarcely fault the strategy.

Amalric glowered at him. 'Beyond this portal are the five emissaries of the Sultan. I will bow to no demands of the heathen.'

'Then you are played as any Egyptian harp.'

'We shall see what music comes.'

He swept through into the great hall and mounted the dais, giving assent for the introduction of the envoys. The Mameluk ruler was not the only potentate who could muster pomp and show off majesty. It was a gold Frankish circlet that sat on the head of Amalric, the symbol of authority and of vestigial Christian power. Lest the ambassadors in their silks and turbans should forget.

They entered and bent their heads in strict formality, grave men with quiet ways and watchful eyes. The Latins were no strangers to them and they would not go fooled by cant or bluster.

Amalric sat regal on the throne. 'My greetings to you.'

'And to you, highness.' Their leader spoke in perfect French.

'I know for what you look and why you travel from the court of Qalawun.'

'We ask solely for justice.'

'No.' The Constable leant forwards from his seat. 'You come in gaggle to threaten and cajole, to ask of me the impossible.'

'Our brethren are dead. Peaceful Arabs, women and children, villagers and traders.'

'Regrettable things.'

'Events that cannot be dismissed.'

'It is we in Acre who are offended. It is we, the Christian kingdom, whose patience was tested and trust betrayed.'

'How so, highness?' The ambassador was inexpressive in his disbelief.

'The riot was incited by Mohammedans and grievous insult given.'

'Yet it appears to be their bodies that were strewn about the streets.'

'We can brook no affray.'

'Nor shall our Sultan accept a reply that does not satisfy honour.'

The Constable fell silent, studying the men as though gauging their intent. They were hard to read. Yet he was not prepared to be embarrassed before his court. Spread about the hall, nobles and knights looked on. They expected kingship and he would prove worthy.

'Deliver to Qalawun our word of regret and our desire for continued accord.'

'The Sultan would hope for more.'

'Is a mere ambassador to dictate my course? Is the gesture of amity by a ruler not sufficient?'

'Gesture is simple, highness.' The envoy dismissively waved his hand. 'Qalawun will measure you by deed.'

'We have done all that we may.'

'Then peace is threatened.'

'Our resolve stands.'

'Your city may fall.'

Perspiration beaded around the circlet, the residue of fear or fury. Amalric was stubborn when confronted. From beside a pillar, William of Beaujeu stood in silent witness. No Italians would be handed over and no dues paid. The *bailli* and his acolytes would believe they had somehow wrung some victory and instead they had buried themselves. Their triumph promised to be short and hollow, founded on the groundless optimism of conceit. The grand master would remember this moment and the image of a Christian ruler abandoning the last true remnant of Outremer. Pride always came before a war.

~

'Damascus.' Selim peered from the high ground and drew the boy to his side. 'The Prophet Mohammed himself called it an earthly paradise.'

Benedict nodded, temporarily speechless at the beauty of the scene and the thrill of return. He had done the bidding of Beaujeu before and travelled through its ancient heart a myriad times. But the mesmeric impact of its first sighting never left him. Against the sand glow of the eastern desert it sat like a jewel in its own oasis, its walls rising elegant from the green and fertile setting and the shimmering water of the Barada River curling past. There was no place on earth so rare. To the west, the grandeur of Mount Hermon and the mountains of the Anti-Lebanon, dispensing their melt-water to irrigate the plain; to the north, the massive rock outcrop of Jebel Qassioun with its sloping escarpment adorned with gardens and orchards. He imagined he could smell the roses and jasmine and citrus flower; he was already scurrying in his thoughts through the gates and down alleyways and going on his errand. This was life and it filled him with joy.

✝

Chapter 6

Arrayed along the grassland banks of the Barada were the tents of the traders and cameleers. It was where they always gathered, a place to water their animals and to rest, a site at which camaraderie abounded and information flowed. Damascus was the hub; Damascus was where the spice routes met the Silk Road and the ancient races of Araby and Asia mingled. If Qalawun had a plan afoot and an army mustering, the evidence would be uncovered here.

Selim had arranged a camel roast. It was typical of his hospitality, a chance to announce his arrival and reacquaint himself with old friends. Fanfare often provided the optimum disguise. So they came, the travellers and the merchants, eager to pay their respects to the great leader of the caravan. Wine flowed and hashish was taken and the blackened seeds of opium by the handful were consumed. A happy reunion. And at its centre, listening and watchful, the old man played host.

'Observe well the scene, boy.' Away from the light and with Benedict beside him, de Flor studied the proceedings. 'They believe they are entertained and do not recognise that the old thief removes their purses and their balls.'

'I have never seen such revels.'

'The more they eat and drink, the more they talk. The more they talk, the more intelligence we acquire.'

'Grand Master Beaujeu will be pleased.'

'Or his mood darkened by what we may find.'

Against the sparking glow thrown by campfires and the whirling brands of fire-eaters and dancers, the feast was well underway. None would notice the Frankish interloper or pay attention to those beyond the circle. Music played and Sufi mystics called. Few would remember what they did or said that night.

De Flor laughed quietly. 'Every part of my soul is drawn to the carousing.'

'Your painted skin would not save you.'

'Though it might fetch a handsome price. Let us hope your own guise will be more convincing.'

'It has not failed me yet.'

'Damascus will put it to the test. There are sentinels at the gates and spies in every quarter.'

'They are no match.'

'Until the moment they give cry and chase and pride unseats you. Until the hour you are killed or captured.'

'The Grand Master has faith in me.'

'I too, boy.' The adventurer clamped a hand on his shoulder. 'Had I no trust, you would be left in Acre.'

'I am glad I was not.'

'And I too, boy. What is it I teach you?'

Benedict recited the mantra. 'Never to drop my guard. Never to catch a glance or draw the eye. Never to believe myself safe.'

'When challenged, who are you?'

'A True Believer loyal to the Mameluk.'

'For whom do you run errands?'

'My imagined master from Lattakia.'

De Flor nodded in the darkness. He should not worry. The boy had the guile of a desert fox and the slipperiness of a river snake. He was a match for any opponent and the equal to himself.

'You have the makings of a spy, boy.'

'Whilst you should keep with singing.'

Joshing helped pass the time and avoid thoughts of danger. Saracens were not kind to those they captured. A man without noble blood or a family to raise ransom could face the torment of being impaled on a stake or skinned alive; a boy might end with a choice of execution or religious conversion and a short life as a slave. The wiser course was to outpace the pursuit.

A cough and a shadow and Selim was in their midst. The old man brought camel flesh wrapped in bread and proffered the morsels to the onlookers of his feast.

'What news, Selim?' The soldier already had a mouthful of his food. 'There must be gossip and boasting and rumour among your raucous throng.'

'They talk as much as they drink. The merchants, the camel men, the officers of state. Most is of no consequence.'

'The rest?'

Selim paused. 'It is said that secrecy is everywhere, that armouries are being emptied and formations of *rajjalah* infantry are called in from every point to encampments beyond the cities.'

'Foot soldiers are despised and mistrusted and forever kept deep in the country.'

'Never in such number and with the attending banners of their generals.'

'Convince me of it.'

'A great army musters and prepares, Flor *effendi*. Camel drivers speak of a force massed along the road north to Homs, of how it grows in size each day, of the mounted rehearsal by Mameluk and Turcoman and the tents spread to the horizon.'

'Is the purpose known?'

'None are told of it. Yet tunnellers and fire-troops have been brought from Aleppo.'

De Flor grunted in recognition. 'It is proof enough that a city is their goal. I warrant Acre is that city.'

'I deliver what I hear.'

'We are thankful. Return to your revels, old friend. This Frank and his boy are set upon a different expedition.'

'Whatever is required, I shall provide.'

'A camel and its driver should suffice.' The adventurer patted Selim on the arm. 'I will make close pass and study this migration for myself.'

'My *Waladii*?' Selim directed his grizzled concern to Benedict.

The boy replied for himself. 'Each one of us has his task, *Amm* Selim. You, to the gathered here. Roger, to hunt an army. I, to scour the Damascus streets, to spy on the Governor and find our agent.'

'Take care, *Waladii*.'

Benedict would do that. He revelled in the chance to prove himself. It was a mission reserved for him alone. He wondered how long-lasting his blessing from the Patriarch was.

'We are fed and informed.' De Flor licked his fingers clean. 'Now we go to work.'

In the changing shadows along the riverbank, the drugged chants and easy chatter faded against the louder rhythms of the music. Selim, master of ceremonies and creator of the spell, returned to his guests as though he had never left.

There were nine gates to the walled city of Damascus on which to gamble life and luck. Benedict would select one. He thought of Acre only a hundred miles behind, of the blue waters of the Mediterranean and of an existence so different to the present. The citizens there relied on his daring; the citizens here would wish him dead. It was fortunate they could not read his thoughts and ignored him as he passed. The invisibility afforded by youth was his keenest weapon. He was the spy of Joshua heading into Jericho, an instrument of salvation and the point of the Crusader lance. Be purposeful and unhurried, he reminded himself.

It was through the Bab al-Faraj that he entered, a boy with his head down and a look of concentration on his face. Among families returning from the cemetery, he barely merited a glance. He waited for the shout, hunched his shoulders and offered up a prayer. *Give me strength, O Lord. Be at my shoulder. Walk with me now.* If challenge came it would be at this point, where the populace was channelled and the well-guarded entrance lay close by the Citadel. He kept moving. In Galilee, an informer had not shown and a camel driver had sought to kill him. On the plateau of the Syrian Heights, that same camel driver had met his fate. The Saracens wished to keep their secrets. Perhaps they expected him. The blades of their swords had flashed so bright at Tripoli.

He shivered. Whatever the ending, he would put up a fight. The gateway pressed in about him and then he was through.

For soldiers on the brink of campaign, they appeared relaxed. But protectors of a governor and his fortress often had little to do. Ruqn ad-Din Toqsu was in residence. His Mameluk standard flew from the ramparts, his bejewelled entourage paraded by, his supplicants queued with their petitions for redress and pleas of clemency for entry to his court. Justice and existence was decided on a nod.

'*Make way! Find room! Stand aside for the royal messenger!*'

Benedict was flung against a wall and his face pressed into its stone, a flurry of hooves and movement announcing the departure of another courier. The boy caught a glimpse. There was no doubting the urgency or sparing of the whip. Even as he recovered his breath and brushed the dust from his shirt, the rider and steed were gone.

'You react quickly, young one.' The soldier was amicable and unthreatening and held his spear with a relaxed grip.

Benedict rewound his headcloth. 'Not quick enough, friend. They demand we all of us eat dirt.'

'Day or night, they will not rest. To Cairo and Aleppo and back, to every known and distant corner. Necessity drives them.'

'I see it for myself.'

The infantryman laughed. 'Neither injury nor death could bring a pause. We each of us may fall victim to what comes.'

'It is nobler to die in battle than be stampeded by a herald.'

'A soldier takes whatever is ordained.' The man twisted the spear in his grasp. 'The war draws close, young one. The Sultan decrees it.'

'Then the infidel must perish.'

'By the grace of Allah, he shall. Never have I witnessed so great an army or so many trees felled to build its catapults.'

The youth seemed impressed. 'All this you have seen for yourself?'

'Wherever the Governor journeys, I am with him.'

Boredom and boastfulness could encourage indiscretion. Guards were a useful source. Benedict listened and smiled wide-eyed with attention and eventually took his leave. There were other places to visit. Ahead of him were the alleyways and souks, the narrow vistas and the wide expanse and soaring dome of the great Umayyad Mosque. Everywhere was the imprint and presence of the mighty Qalawun. The

Mongols might have sacked the city, but the feared Sultan of the Mameluks had rebuilt and graced it with his favour and his wealth, restoring it to prominence as the eastern jewel of his Moslem realm. Such benevolence demanded obedience; such patronage and protection ensured troops were available when occasion required.

~

'Tremble and bow low in the presence of Qalawun.'

The command was superfluous. Most who were ushered in to audience with the sultan prostrated themselves without instruction. Those who ignored either instinct were generally dealt with in the cruellest fashion. Even the two Templars felt compelled to kneel. Their grand master had ordered it and as envoys of peace from Acre they would swallow pride and endure humiliation and do what needed to be done.

From his marble plinth and golden throne, Qalawun considered them. These creatures were brave to come. Of all his enemies they were the most pernicious and zealous, the representatives of Satan on earth, the order whose disciples Saladin had put to the sword in the aftermath of the legendary Battle of Hattin. It would take every measure of imperious self-control to avoid sending their heads back in a basket to William of Beaujeu. The grand master believed he could put off the reckoning. How remote and insignificant he was in his Lion Fortress abutting the sea. His ambassadors negotiated from a position of abject weakness. The sultan spoke in Arabic. 'Your names, Christians?'

'Olivier of Mauny and Jean of Sagozan.' One of the pair assumed the lead. 'We venture here in good faith to offer parley, majesty.'

'Yet you are infidel warriors committed to the act of war.'

'Thus have we cause to know when conflict would be folly. Thus have you reason to accept our word as the truth.'

'There is only deception from the lips of an Unbeliever.'

The Templar persisted. 'Our Grand Master is anxious to live in sympathy with your people and to pursue the path of common brotherhood. He bears you no malice and bids us bring you his pledge.'

'Sympathy? Brotherhood? Pledge?' Qalawun slowly repeated the words. 'Such a vow is simple when atrocity is already done.'

'We took no part in the slaughter of innocents, majesty. We threw our gates wide to offer refuge, our men-at-arms sortied to bring order to the streets.'

'Yet foul deed was done and the dead piled high.'

'No blame is affixed to us, majesty. Peasants from Italy committed the crimes. They are not men of honour.'

'Your own creed is Crusade. Hence a Christian is a Christian and a corpse is a corpse.'

'None are so committed to peace and trade as we.'

'It is why Olivier of Mauny and Jean of Sagozan come to offer terms.' The sultan was leisurely in his appraisal. 'Are you then these men of honour?'

'Our vow is to God and our Grand Master.'

'Your Grand Master builds catapults from the timber of his galleys. Your Grand Master prepares his men to fight.'

'Such is the nature of a military order.'

So it was, Qalawun mused. And it was in his nature as supreme ruler of the Moslem world to smite his foes and drive them from the Holy Land. He considered for a while the red crosses emblazoned on the left breast of the Templar surcoats. Each one an insult; each one he intended to replace in future with a crimson wound inflicted by a scimitar.

He stroked his beard, his eyes fierce and his expression

unforgiving. 'You speak for Beaujeu and not for the sovereign ruler of your kingdom.'

'Our concerns extend beyond those of Amalric and his brother King Henry of Cyprus.'

'It seems I must confer with you.' Qalawun narrowed his gaze. 'Deliver to me what I ask and we shall dismiss the outrage, ignore past barbarism and transgression of the law.'

'We await your terms, majesty.'

'Venetian sequins and glass beads, one for every life in Acre I will spare. A modest price.'

The Templar blanched. 'You demand too much, majesty.'

'I expect no less than is my due.'

'Who may raise such an amount, an impossible trove of a thousand upon a thousand treasures?'

'Any Grand Master or Constable with deep coffers. Any caring to survive.'

They undoubtedly cared and yet would not survive. Qalawun had plans. Within two months he would be leading his army from Egypt; his army in Syria was preparing to march. Their convergence on Acre was imminent. However William of Beaujeu manoeuvred and whatever the argument presented by his knightly envoys, the Christian city was doomed. The conditions he suggested were indeed unfeasible. He wondered if the grand master would sicken as visibly as his representatives here.

A counsellor whispered in his ear and he banished the Latins with a distracted tilt of his head. In the outer ward an exhausted and travel-stained rider had dismounted and brought word from Damascus. He was ushered through, bowing deep before offering up his scroll. The sultan read. His armed forces were stirring.

Retiring to eat and rest, the messenger could be satisfied with a task completed and ridden at full gallop. He was the same horseman who had charged from the Citadel in Damascus and sent a dark-haired boy tumbling to the side.

Isolated in a splendid antechamber, the two Templar knights conversed in a low and anxious murmur. Their grand master had consigned them to a thankless errand with little chance of success. Now it was time to be escorted from Egypt by a Mameluk cavalcade and report grim tidings to the waiting figure in the Temple. Beaujeu would not be surprised. He had always suspected that diplomacy was merely a precursor to war, that the future of Acre was already decided. Yet even in failure there was opportunity. Trained eyes could see, ears listen, instinct read the nuance of the heathen. Beaujeu had deployed his most experienced knights for a reason.

They barely acknowledged the hurrying approach of the Arab. His eyes were nervous and his countenance troubled, a portly form richly dressed in the court robes of a senior emir. Precisely as they expected. Al-Fakhri, the intelligence source and traitor in the enemy camp, had finally made contact.

The emir drew them to the side. 'We have not much time.'

'Of that we are certain.' Olivier of Mauny was dry in his response. 'It affords us the true meeting for which we visit.'

'You are either heroes or fools to come.'

'As you are to stay. Yet we are Templars and must do as our faith and duty command.'

'They will count for nothing when Acre falls.' A solitary nerve twitched in the cheek of the courtier. 'Does Beaujeu obtain my report?'

'He pays you well and receives only silence.'

Another slight tic and a quiver of the lip. 'Then Qalawun and his spies are closing in and I will not escape.'

'For these brief minutes here we all of us live. Tell us what you have learnt.'

'I speak of warlike intent and plans for battle. The Sultan will wipe free these lands of the infidel.'

'He has chosen his moment?'

Al-Fakhri nodded. 'It is within a heartbeat. Already the army in Syria is formed and foregathered and ordered to invest Palestine for Caesarea on the coast.'

'A short step to Acre.'

'And a convenient ruse.' The emir toyed distractedly with a string of worry beads. 'He will tell your *bailli* not to concern himself because his campaign is aimed for Africa.'

'They will not believe him.'

'The condemned grasp for whatever they are given.'

Jean of Sagozan, the second knight, spoke. 'You mention the army in Syria. What of the gathering force in Egypt?'

'When the harvest is reaped and martial practice done, Qalawun will then march.'

'How long have we in Acre?'

'He will lead his troops from Cairo in two months hence.'

Two months. If there was despair in the thoughts of the knights, they kept it hidden behind the ordered facade of their rigour and discipline. The greater the challenge, the more they welcomed the test; the more dismal the odds, the worthier their sacrifice in the eyes of God.

Mauny regarded the emir. 'Is there any chance to divert the Sultan?'

'None.'

'There is ever the blade of an Assassin or the skill of a poisoner.'

'His food is tasted and his person guarded both night and day.' Al-Fakhri shuddered at the implication. 'I provide your

Grand Master with information and am not trained for the task of killing.'

'We are all called upon to forfeit comfort and commit ourselves.'

'Not to squander ourselves in madness and futile gesture.'

'Is there any chance of insurrection? Of nurturing attack from Nubia or revolt among the emirs? Of causing over-throw within the palace?'

Al-Fakhri offered a hollow laugh. 'Had you encountered Ashraf, the favoured son of Qalawun, you would not suggest such remedies. He is more deadly and ruthless than his father.'

'So we are left with destiny unchanged and our kingdom poised at the abyss.'

For a few seconds the three men stood in silent commu-nion, a clandestine grouping thrown together by circumstance and the machination of the high priest of a military order. Beaujeu alone was unlikely to save Acre.

'It seems the month of November will be full of incident and event,' the senior of the Templars commented without emotion. 'God be with every one of us.'

~

Caution was the key. For two days since his last incursion, Benedict had sat on the banks of the Barada. It was a pleasant spot. Occasionally he would walk through the gardens and orchards or climb the slopes to Saliheye before looking back upon the city. There was little to suggest that war was immi-nent. Yet the vibration was changed: there was a smell of sweat among the spices and strain in the chatter and bustle betraying what lay beneath. By the hour, news reached Selim. Now Roger de Flor had gone to investigate and the young accomplice left to complete his own enquiry. Within

Damascus was a long-term agent of Beaujeu and in his grasp the careful notes and detail of a thousand observations. Even the Constable of Acre would be persuaded by the facts revealed. It merited another trip.

His keffiyeh wrapped tight about his head and pulled low on his brow, Benedict entered through St Thomas Gate and ducked out of the busy thoroughfare and into the seclusion of the back streets. On enemy terrain they were the nearest he would come to finding sanctuary. This was the Christian quarter, the remnants of Byzantium secreted behind high walls and preserved in hidden churches. There was a sense of precariousness to the place, a prayerful solitude that told of a community withdrawn and aware of future trouble. Tenancy was not a given and pogrom always possible. The Mameluks were less understanding overlords than their illustrious predecessor Salah ad-Din.

He smelt frankincense and thought of the Patriarchate in Acre. Neither Latin nor Eastern churches were secure in the land of Qalawun. He wondered if the old Patriarch was sitting in the shade of his nymphaeum playing chess, if William of Beaujeu knelt in prayer, if Hazzim was up on the roof of the Fonda, watching the last of the galleys arrive before the autumn storms. Already it was September and the grand master had warned that the Saracen would campaign when the ground cooled and provisioning was complete. The aged priest in Damascus would know. He had reported to the Templars these fifty years or more, surviving Mongol invasion and Mameluk hegemony to smuggle messages to the Latins. A brave and resilient soul.

Benedict searched the shuttered windows and scanned the roof lines, listened for a stray footfall that might indicate pursuit. Everything was as he remembered. Chickens scratched and a handcart rumbled and a nightingale flitted in its cage. No need to worry. He circled back and found the courtyard, saw the ladder positioned as it always was leading to the upper door of a vine-clad house. The only way in. Nearby, men sat and played dice, too engrossed to notice visitors or the passing of the day.

Swiftly he ascended, ignoring the random outcomes rehearsing in his head, focusing on the moment and what lay above. The next step and another. It would only take a moment. Within seconds he would be through the opening again, as though the rendezvous had never been. Beaujeu had insisted on the meeting. Only the spoken word was sufficient proof.

'You are come.' The voice was weak in the startling gloom.

'It is my duty, father.' Benedict replied in French and peered towards the labouring breath. 'Do you sicken?'

'I am old and wearied, that is all.'

'There are pressing matters, father. I bring you greeting from Acre and the Grand Master of the Temple.'

'His greetings commonly bear a price.'

The youngster tried to discern the dark outline of the ancient. 'No cost exists if we are quick. Have you news?'

'Plenty.'

'Share it and I will be gone, father. I am commanded not to tarry.'

'Tell me first of Acre.' Speech drifted and recovered. 'Are the cityfolk of cheer? Are they strong?'

'They possess stout hearts, father.'

'And they shall need them. For they shall soon be consigned to the bottomless pit.'

'By the Mameluks, father?'

There was a delay as the priest struggled for air. In the stillness of waiting Benedict attempted to uncouple the real from his imagination as he listened to the rise and fall of the toiling lungs. He sensed a stronger energy than that of the ailing priest. A third presence was in the room.

Backing away, the youngster glanced to the window and back into the chamber. Outside, the ladder had vanished; inside, the spectres were emerging into flesh.

Frantically, he shouted to the priest. 'Is it a trap?'

'We are each of us bound in chains.'

'Not I, father.'

Seizing a wooden stool, Benedict flung it hard at the figure rushing him from the shadows and swung himself into a shallow dive from the ledge. The sharp cry behind indicated a lucky strike. It would delay rather than prevent. With a prayer and the impetus of desperation he scrambled for purchase on the vine and fell in a tangled collapse of foliage to the ground. The drop had not killed him, but as he kicked and rolled free, he sighted the dice players moving to intercept and spring the secondary ambush. They had plainly not anticipated such a dramatic retreat. He would yet surprise them again. Bending low, he slithered and ran across the courtyard, reaching the alleyway as a hand fastened on his robe. Any moment, he might be pinned fast.

Not while he still had feet to spring and hands to drive a calloused twig direct into the eye. The man staggered, a disfigured demon feeling for the wood shaft protruding from his face, before he screamed. Benedict twisted and threw himself into running flight. There were cries and shouts, the dancing vignettes of baskets dropped and jars toppling in the bow-wave of his exodus. Chaos engendered a certain thrill. He had outpaced the Saracen in previous encounters and would summon those skills again for Damascus. The grand master relied on him.

'*Where is the young infidel?*'

'I see him! He goes that way!'

'You are wrong!'

'There he is! He runs hard!'

'A boy! Stop him! He heads south!'

And though he limped and panted and his body ached, Benedict smiled. It was the pace he enjoyed and the adventure he craved. His guardian de Flor also thrived in such conditions. To treat it as a game helped ease the nerves; to slow and walk as an ordinary denizen of the city removed the sense of being hunted.

Then the twin strands of a lasso flew and coiled about his legs and tripped him to the ground. He fought with the indignant rage of one cheated. A trick had brought him low. Bucking and rolling, he clawed at the bindings, fighting to disentangle and drag himself free. It was no use. Yelling his fury, he pushed himself up and collapsed once more. He stared at the sky, wincing through angry tears as the shadow of his captor fell across him.

'A noose tightens and they do not feel it.'

William of Beaujeu contemplated his returned envoys with the cool fatalism that came with his office. He had no doubt of what the Sultan of the Mameluks intended. Word from the emir al-Fakhri simply confirmed existing supposition. Yet Acre and its people remained unable to accept what they had brought upon themselves and the actuality of the hour. The moats and high walls would save them, or the princes of Europe, or the military orders. After all, this was the land of Jesus and He was on their side.

The grand master turned his face towards the light glancing through the arrow slit of the chamber. 'We convene where in two months hence our order is fated to make its final stand.'

'Where better to die than in defence of the Temple?' Olivier of Mauny managed to smile through the fatigue of his travel. 'It will be an honour, your grace.'

'Qalawun demands Venetian sequins for the lives of our citizens. Yet scarcely a man in Acre is worth a grain of salt.'

'We are committed to protect all Christians, your grace.'

'While in return they despise us and would prefer to release the Italian peasants from the dungeons and imprison us instead.'

'They are misled and confused.'

'And they will be the more so when I inform the Council of our secret mission of peace to Cairo. In their eyes, we are the cowards and appeasers; Spada and his rabble the sainted and courageous.'

'We shall see how they acquit themselves against the steel ranks of the Mameluk.'

'That we shall, my brother.'

Amalric would be calling a meeting and Beaujeu was obliged to attend. It would make no difference. The same avoidance of the truth, the same politics and power play, the same pettiness and posturing. Ignorance was their downfall. For all of that, the grand master could comfort himself with prayer and the knowledge that his knights were the finest warriors on earth. Diplomacy continued and defensive preparations never slowed. It was not over until the final lance was broken and the last arrow spent. Or until the dark horde of the Mongol rode in.

In another part of Acre, a Pisan storeman was entering a cellar with his oil-lamp to conduct a routine examination of the stock. He would not re-emerge. One of the remaining Assassins had claimed a further victim.

✝

Chapter 7

He should have expected such a reception. Serene amidst the condemnation, the grand master stood in the great hall and listened to their complaints. They did not much care for the Templars. In the febrile atmosphere of Acre, friends could turn and enemies gloat and all the while the Constable sat with a barely concealed sneer of satisfaction on his face. Amalric had been persuaded to dissolve the Council and convene the high court to call Beaujeu to account before his peers and judges. It was a futile exercise. Yet it would allow the leader of the military order to peer into their eyes and read their souls. They were weak and the weak liked to make a noise.

A Venetian stood and pointed his finger. 'You are a traitor, Beaujeu.'

'How so, my lord?' Beaujeu met the accusation with calm indifference. 'Is it treachery to seek to broker peace? To preserve the lives of the many thousands here? To serve as we have always done the greater cause of Christ?'

'You strive in the cause of your Temple alone, Beaujeu.'

'The Knights Templar guard you all.'

His words drew protest and howls of disbelief, knights and nobles clamouring to vent their ire and outshow the rest. They were easily pricked, Beaujeu reflected. He could do little about their bruised opinions and self-esteem. These were courtiers who had not heeded his counsel on the coming danger; they would dismiss his argument now. Baiting and vengeance were their game.

The hall quietened as Amalric spoke. 'I ask again, Beaujeu. Why did you send envoys in secret to the Sultan of the Mameluks?'

'To prevent the Sultan bringing those Mameluks here.'

'We gave our reply to his ambassadors. Our mind was set and our position resolved.'

'Your position will be shattered by the first Saracen boulder to strike our walls.'

'That is our prerogative and not yours.' Amalric looked about him at the heads nodding in assent. 'Whilst we showed ourselves to be resolute, you sent a craven message of defeat. Whilst we were unbending, your minions skulked back from Cairo with terms crafted to ridicule and punish.'

'This court creates its own absurdity.'

'We are not the ones accused, Beaujeu.'

The grand master stared. 'A Templar must follow his conscience.'

'And a Grand Master must take the consequence.'

'I discovered the true intent of Qalawun.'

'You reveal nothing save your pride and the imaginings of your mind.'

'No imagination is required for what will befall us, highness.'

'A Templar runs scared. It is a sight for all.'

Beaujeu waited out the jeers before he answered. 'His highness believes he is strong and stands fast. He considers himself immortal and secure. Yet in that perceived strength lies illusion and in the security is foolishness.'

'It is not we who are misled, who have in turn dissembled and ventured beyond their task. Nor we who suffer the wrath and censure of the people.'

'Indeed it is not, your highness.' The grand master surveyed the court. 'It is Acre that faces judgement. Acre that shall feel the fire. Acre that will be consumed.'

Amalric rose from his seat. 'Who are you to so presume?'

'A poor fellow soldier of Christ. A knight whose earlier brethren stood against Saladin on the slopes of Hattin. A Grand Master of an order sworn to defend all pilgrims and what is left of Outremer.'

'Defend?' The Constable shook with indignation. 'You plot and conspire.'

'As you in turn dance and feast and throw dainties to your hunting dogs.'

Mutual animosity flared, accelerated by the jealousy of Amalric and the goading disdain of Beaujeu. The more pressing the external threat, the pettier the antics of the nobles became. Yet the Templars would not be distracted. They obeyed their own calling and operated to their own laws and custom. It was why the grand master had sent for reinforcements to his commanderies throughout Europe; it was why the several thousand clerks and bookkeepers in the Paris Temple toiled to direct funds to his military project.

He cast a pitying glance at the assembled. 'You call me to this place to condemn a brotherhood that would shed its blood for you.' They were silent. 'I stand accused. Yet it is the Saracen who is your enemy, the Saracen that will scale these walls with intent to kill.'

'Qalawun would let us in peace if it were not for you.' An ageing noble cried out his accusation.

'Is this so, my lord? Is it not because he has long held an ambition to hurl us from our rock? Is it not because Italian peasants breached the peace and slaughtered the Mohammedans in our midst?'

'Those Italians performed the deed and duties of all good Christians.'

'They shall not be the ones who face the result. They shall not be the faithful warriors who side by side will hold the rampart against the encroaching foe.'

Amalric had not finished. 'Hear the shouts of the crowd beyond these bounds, Beaujeu. It is your head they demand.'

'I have never sought their friendship.'

'A strange twist you should be hated by those you avow to defend.'

'Was Jesus not taunted and despised and brought before Caiaphas?' Beaujeu folded his hands. 'As His penitent and humble servant, I embrace whatever is my lot.'

The Constable scoffed. 'A Grand Master humble and a Templar penitent? Legend records Coeur de Lion jested on his deathbed the vice he bequeathed your order was his pride.'

'He did not fault our fighting spirit.'

Let them have their moment of gratification, Beaujeu mused. They should be permitted their sport. He was unmoved by the naked attempt to make him a scapegoat: it served as a portent of things to come. This quarrel was merely the rehearsal. He noted the leering faces, the diplomatic silence of the Hospitallers, the manner in which the false charge was laid. The carrion birds gathered. He knew that the day would come when a court would convene and a grand master dragged in chains before it; a day when the privilege and power of the Templars would finally cause the envious masters of Europe to wreak terror on the knights. Perhaps for a while he could stave off catastrophe. Not if Acre fell.

It was boisterous outside, the populace looking for any excuse to vent its confused anger. News had spread fast that

Beaujeu had entreated in secret with the dread Antichrist Qalawun. There could be no reason for it or greater contempt shown for the views of the citizens. The grand master was plainly a cringing fool and traitor, hiding inside the white mantle of his order. So they would jostle and spit and yell their insults without restraint. The great hall was for noble words and idle rhetoric. Out here among the common herd, Beaujeu and his ilk would receive the rougher welcome they deserved.

'*Friend to the heathen!*'

'*Sail home to your treasures and estates!*'

'*You are no knight! We have no need of you!*'

'*Discard your surcoat for the robe of the Saracen! You are no different to they!*'

Guarded by a phalanx of his knights and men-at-arms, Beaujeu progressed south through the streets towards the Lion Fortress. It was an uncomfortable parade. His men forced a passage, shouldering away protesters and brushing aside complaint. Occasionally a sword pommel or the flat of a blade would dislodge the most vociferous and persistent. But it was hard going.

'Provocation will not harm you.' Beaujeu rested a hand upon the arm of a sergeant. 'Do not allow your eagerness to any more than bruise them.'

At his side, his marshal scowled. 'Would that we had not taken a vow to abstain from killing Christians.'

'We will count on their number when the Mameluk arrives.'

'I doubt they will be any use in battle. Sneering and affray are more to their liking.'

'Our cause is to protect them all the same.'

'A thankless task, your grace.'

'Reward will come later in heaven.'

The marshal threw a man from his path. 'I am certain it will not be found here.'

'They will learn.' Beaujeu calmly saluted a wild-eyed gaggle hurling invective. 'Even Peter the Rock denied Christ and abandoned Him in the hour of darkness.'

A missile flew, an overripe fruit that forced them to shy. There was a cheer from the crowd. People liked to see dignity tripped.

'*The Grand Master pledges war upon the Saracen and flinches at an orange!*'

'*Little wonder he crawls to Qalawun!*'

'*Release the Italians! They will show how to strike fear in the Saracen!*'

If he were stung by the words, Beaujeu feigned uncon-cern. He was above such matters. Yet he heard the name oppressive and repeated. *Spada. Spada. Spada. Spada.* An Umbrian peasant, a murderous criminal, a worthless and unschooled Barabbas elevated to the status of a saint. They were calling for his release.

He paused and nodded his command. 'Hold that knave.'

His target was overpowered and wrestled to the ground, the drunken objections temporarily silenced by a well-directed blow. Beaujeu considered the man. He was a sorry and insignificant sight. Cut from his companions, the miscreant had lost some of his spirit.

The grand master stepped closer. 'Our hero of the city. Quite the duellist with a jibe and insult.'

'I mean no offence.'

'My men would disagree.' A tilt of the head. 'Why do you give such acclaim to the beast Spada?'

'He cleanses our streets of the heathen.'

'You will find he brings Mohammedans as stirred and vengeful hornets to our door.'

'We are ready.'

'Is this so?' Beaujeu was aloof in his disdain. 'Have you faith in God and strength in faith?'

'I do.'

'And a will rendered of steel?'

'That besides.'

'Are you trained in the use of the sword or battle-axe? The javelin and spear? The crossbow?'

'My instruction is from the Holy Scriptures.'

'Your bluster is from the nearest cask of wine.' The Templar gestured to his men. 'Throw our rotten catch back to the sea.'

They hauled away the drunk and the grand master and his lieutenants continued on their way. Eventually the storm would abate. The populace was no more stupid than the leaders and no less ready to live and die as fools. They did not share his premonition. They could not see what his spies observed.

~

One of those spies lay flat and motionless, surveying the sprawling vista from the cover of the rock scree. The rumours had been true. Below was a military city of pitched tents and wagon parks, of regiments etched out in lines and dust plumes kicked up and tracing the restless journeys of horse squadrons and driven oxen. De Flor congratulated himself on the find. It was the rarest of events and the most beautiful of sights. To the one side, the readied batteries of siege catapults; to the other, the headquarters of the generals.

He let his gaze wander the field. The grand master had entrusted him with a task no holy knight would undertake. Obedience, poverty and chastity were never to his taste. Better by far to escape the fetid confines of Acre for chance encounter and the open road. No rancorous and cheated husbands could reach him; he was at liberty to do as he wished. There would be reward from Beaujeu for every detail he reported and profitable accolade from Amalric should he bring rescue to the Latin kingdom. Not a poor achievement for a base mercenary.

'Brother, see.' His Arab accomplice tugged urgent at his sleeve. 'Horsemen come near.'

De Flor squinted, tracking the mounted troop of Mameluks as it crossed the dried bed of a stream and advanced on their position. It posed no threat. Cavalry would keep to the well-worn tracks and the valley floor. This formation would have a more pressing occupation than to scout for the improbable presence of infidels.

The Frank blinked as the solid form of men and horses sharpened to a clearer image. 'Who attends them?'

'Infantry, brother.'

'I see no pikes or spears, no discipline in their movement.'

'They are skirmishers, brother. Bedouin maybe.'

'Skirmishers are not herded.'

The pair watched the expedition as the cavalry crossed to and fro and forced the rest before them. It was not a conventional outing. Those on foot were prisoners being marched and chased in scrambling array towards a stretch of barren ground.

The adventurer rubbed his eyes. 'How many do you count?'

'Twenty on horseback, brother. Over twice that number on foot.'

'They are guards and prisoners. And Mameluks rarely treat their prisoners well.'

'It is a harsh life, brother.'

'We shall witness how unforgiving it may be.'

On countless occasion he had stumbled across the aftermath of atrocity, had found cadavers tied out or buried up to their necks in sand. Crusaders put out eyes and cut off lips, noses, ears and balls; Saracens hollowed out corpses and filled them with straw, setting them on rocks as welcoming scarecrows. Terror was the aim and arbitrary violence the method. The dialects might have differed, but the motives were the same.

De Flor whispered low. 'Keep still and hold your nerve.'

They could hear the yips and keening cries of the horsemen and distinguish the strained faces and large-eyed fear of the ragged band pushed on at the fore. Certainly it was a harsh life, thought de Flor. Yet, as ever, his pity was mixed with interest. He was exposed to dangers of his own and could not intervene. That was his destiny and theirs. Good fortune to them all.

Huddled forlorn, the mass of prisoners had reached the end of their forced transit. Some were old and others young; some carried scars and were stiff and almost lame from their cruel incarceration. A sorrowful sight. They would fetch little in the slave markets, perhaps had been bought for a pittance or were the offcuts for the day. They showed no enthusiasm as the cavalry retreated, but they probably had a notion of what was to come.

With a shrieking battle-cry, the Mameluks abruptly wheeled and changed direction and dashed in at their targets, a formidable and thundering formation. The prisoners stood no chance. There seemed to be a collective sigh at the rip of bowstrings and the silken rush of arrows. It was a meticulous and bloody execution. In a single instant, opposing fronts brushed and divided and the mounted troop turned on a wider arc to repeat its skilled display. The dead and wounded lay collapsed behind, the first cull of the session. Gradually, the living would be whittled down, stripped away in the storm of darts that arrived with every pass.

A second rush and curving strike, and the screams mingled with the beat of hooves and the pattering slap of steel. The billowed dust added a smoked filter to the scene. The bodies appeared to have grown feathers. In crazed panic, several prisoners broke from the pack and blundered free aimlessly. Designated horsemen rode them down, chasing them with drawn swords or couched spear, gliding to dispatch them with a twist in the saddle and a flick of the wrist. One of the captives staggered on.

De Flor shrank lower. 'He heads for us.'

'What must we do?'

'Pray he is taken before he reaches sanctuary.'

De Flor's prayer was answered. They heard the double impact of the wood quarrels and the sound of a body falling. Earth and rock fragments travelled with it. Then stillness. The Mameluks withdrew, their departure marked by howls of triumph and a calm that settled on the debris. Later there might be another batch and further slaying. For the while, the blood could dry and the dead blacken.

The Arab glanced at de Flor. 'We must see if any live, brother.'

'It is not our duty.' The adventurer was edging back. 'Men will come from the camp to gather the arrows. We shall not be caught idling.'

Retracing their route, they found the camel and prepared for departure. Among the ceaseless flow of commerce and provision that attended the encamped army, two more strangers leading their beast would go unnoticed. They were goatherds or armourers, cameleers or farmers, homeward-bound having made a delivery. Commanders and men should be grateful for their effort.

'*Horsemen* . . .' The hissed warning reached de Flor as he laboured to tighten a saddlebag.

He did not turn. 'How many?'

'There are only two of them, brother. With spears held proud and no urgency in their trot.'

'An excellent start to discourse. Show no concern and give no reason for alarm.'

'They are closing on us, brother.'

De Flor loosened one of the packs, to all intent and idle scrutiny an unhurried local without a care. His fingers were nimble and his eyes alert, even as he worked around the kneeling camel and the patrolling soldiers drew to a halt. They called in greeting and he replied. Their tone suggested this was a routine sweep and nothing more.

As a cavalryman dismounted unhurried from his steed, his associate remained in the saddle. Maybe they could bully these solitary Arabs into making a trade or emptying their purses. Few were immune to armed blandishment and the threat of being pressed into the service of the sultan. Things would go badly for these creatures should they fail to please or share. It explained the certain swagger in the horseman as he ignored the younger and smiling Arab squatting on his haunches and advanced upon de Flor.

'You.' A word that carried a challenge. 'What business have you here, giant?' He tried again. 'Are you too busy to speak?'

Silence could provoke or intrigue, entice another close. De Flor spurned the attempt at conversation. He was content to wait, to judge distance and timing and gauge the moment. His discourtesy was having an effect. De Flor tugged at the blanket.

'Stand to your front, giant.' Impatience had entered the voice of the horseman.

His colleague called from his mount. 'Put a whip across his shoulders.'

'I would rather plant my blade.' The man was a pace nearer and his words harsh. 'Would you then learn respect?'

Answer came. 'I doubt it.'

The action was too quick to dodge or parry. What the horseman saw was fleeting, the blurred and startling image of a Latin with cold blue eyes and darkened skin presenting with a sword. And that was all. With a single downward blow, de Flor split his opponent from his crown to his sternum and kicked the dead weight away. Before him, the second horseman was reaching for a weapon and struggling to control his rearing steed. He lost critical seconds. It gave de Flor the advantage. There was a nonchalant deftness born of experience in his movement as he unfurled his bow and fitted an arrow. Although he spied the hazard and urged his horse into the gallop, the second horseman could not outpace the lethal radius of the dart. It struck him in the lower back. A difficult shot on a travelling line. The man swayed drunkenly for a few moments, clutching to stay upright and keep alive, and then fell.

De Flor rewrapped the bow and gave orders to his companion wrestling to steady the Arab gelding of his first victim.

'Pursue the other mount and return.' He was already studying the ground for shallow excavation. 'It seems we must become horse-thieves and grave-diggers.'

Those grave-diggers had earned a prize for Selim and gleaned intelligence for Beaujeu. The adventurer had discovered the evidence of an enemy force prepared, sufficient reason to cross the desert and hold the Mongol khan to his pledge. He needed to hurry, to fetch Benedict, to act with the daring of a madman and the diplomacy of a statesman. Without powerful assistance, Acre was lost.

*

Occasionally a scream wakened Benedict from a surface sleep, reminded him of the blackness he had entered. He knew the sounds and their meaning. There were the groans of starvation and the mumbling of the insane, the faint prayers of the desperate and the colourless whimpers of the dying. Only when the guards beat or tortured did the pitch change and the walls reverberate. It was a truly terrible place. But he consoled himself that in being captured and thrown to the dungeon he was the equal of other men. He counted for something and it mattered. But they had yet to come for him.

In spite of the airless heat, he shivered a little. The bruises hurt and the pain of failure lingered. Whatever fate and the Mameluks decreed, he would be brave and strong and would not break. That was how any warrior was expected to conduct himself. Roger de Flor would have laughed or scoffed or shrugged at the circumstance. A pity the hunger clawed at the stomach and left room only for uncertainty. To think of happier times was to mourn their loss; to dwell on the present was to admit fear. He preferred to ignore everything. Thank God he had scratched his name into a pillar of the Hospitallers. Somewhere he existed.

Footsteps and a glimmering light announced the presence of a visitor. He heard no accompanying tread to signify he too was destined for a courtyard execution or brutalisation in a deeper cellar. Imagination and hope grasped at anything in such conditions.

'You ran fast and put out one of my men's eyes.' The words came in French and the lamp was placed down. 'Our military schools would embrace such a boy for his pluck and daring.'

Benedict stayed silent. He would not behave as though he understood. He had already identified the stranger from the birthmark on his forearm. It was the man he had seen standing at the *han* in Galilee. A killer and an agent of the feared *Ahdath*.

The man appraised him from the gloom and switched to Arabic. 'You were right to suspect me when last we met. I am your sworn enemy.'

'Those who are innocent have no enemies.'

'A Latin spy is ever guilty.'

'I come to trade and nothing more.' Benedict shook his head, transferred the trembling from his body. 'My master is from Lattakia. A good man. He would show no disloyalty to the Sultan.'

'But it is from Acre that you journey.'

'You are mistaken.'

'Whilst you are wrong to consider me dull-witted, to believe it is possible to creep unobserved into Damascus and seek a rendezvous with a Christian priest.'

'I was lost and forgetful in my wandering.'

'Now you are found and a new path decided.'

They regarded each other, the youngster crouched on the bare floor and his captor seated on a stone bench. It was no conference of equals. *A new path decided*. The words resonated uncomfortably in his mind and Benedict sought to quell them. He reminded himself that all exploit was part of adventure and adventure was part of his life, but the rule was becoming harder to accept.

The stranger spoke. 'Your wounds heal?'

'Bruising is no true injury.'

'Our slavers will be glad. They will want you sound and your skin unbroken when they bring you to the market.'

'I am to be sold?' The question came with little breath.

'Be pleased. It will earn you food. It has saved you from the bite of the lash here and the appetites of other prisoners.'

'Set me loose.' The youngster began to shout. 'I must be freed.'

'To spy? To plot against the word and law of Qalawun?'

'I bear no hatred for the Mameluks. Let me go.'

'Your price dissuades me.'

'A camel boy bears no price.'

'A simple driver or herder would not find himself here. A common criminal would be sent to sharpen the aim of a javelin and bow.'

'I visit Damascus in peace and faith.'

'You shall depart the city in chains.'

The boy quivered. 'You do me wrong. You waste effort on a loyal servant.'

'Of Beaujeu.'

The boy insisted. 'Qalawun is my master.'

'There are those who would bid for you whatever is demanded. Ambitious governors who like to flaunt their Latin trophies and rich emirs with particular needs and tastes.'

Benedict sank his face into his hands, his defiance overridden. He would rather a quick death, but the choice was gone and hope had fled with it. Acre might fall and one of its sons was already condemned.

~

Sitting tranquil, another prisoner in a different location allowed himself the small luxury of a smile. Temporary incarceration in a Hospitaller cell was no great hardship and suited him well and added lustre to his reputation. Spada was the name they mentioned on the streets. Not William of Beaujeu or Amalric the Constable, not any knight or noble. Peasants had been the ones to cleanse Acre of its Saracen filth. For years the citizens had suffered and compromised, had sullied their hands with heathen silver, had taken their lead from the craven and weak. No more – because he and his fellow Italians had answered the papal call and taken the Cross and arrived on this shore to renew and inspire with Crusader zeal. Blood was shed and there was no return.

Using his free hand, the Umbrian kneaded circulation back into his leg. Manacles were an uncomfortable manifestation of his vocation. Yet he wore them lightly as would a martyr and with a certain satisfaction. His followers were imprisoned in varied pens, having been rounded up for the sake of public order and flung into the dungeons of the military orders and beneath the palace keep. Let them be patient and bide their time; let stories circulate and reputation grow of how the mighty Spada led out his men in conflict with the Mohammedan and razed a pestilential village to the ground. Only he had the strength and courage and will.

From humble beginnings, great events could flow. He had dreamt of such things and seen visions of Christ in golden armour and St Michael with his sword. While his father had lent him a fierce temper and brutish bent, from his mother he had inherited sly purpose. Control of others was everything. A low-born maybe, but one who could inspire dread and alter outcome, out-politick all rivals and turn misfortune to his gain. His was a rare and dangerous breed.

For a brief moment he thought he could hear the mutterings of an Arab. The Hospitallers maintained hostages to enhance the balance of their treasury. So much for the purity of their calling. Spada grunted. He did not care to share space with the Unbeliever. It reminded him of why he had travelled from Europe, of what he had accomplished and might yet achieve. May the forces of Qalawun arrive and Christendom be tested. He was chosen and he was blessed. Sacred work was never through.

✝

Chapter 8

'Have you come to wash my feet, knight?'

It was a taunt that Theobald of Alzey chose to ignore. The young Hospitaller had grown accustomed to the boastful and malevolent ways of Spada and also to bringing gruel each day to the prisoners. Humility was next to godliness and menial duty was part of a true calling. Yet it rankled to serve these murderers and thieves, to seek a state of grace when surrounded by brute peasants with the blood of innocents on their hands. He decanted water to a wooden bowl and proffered it to an inmate, saying a prayer and moving on.

'Bring me water, knight,' Spada called again from his straw pallet in the corner. 'It is the task of the Hospitaller to give succour to a pilgrim.'

Theobald turned. 'You are no meek and gentle pilgrim.'

'I took the Cross and reached the Holy Land.'

'A land you defile and a Cross you desecrate.'

'It is you who has failed in your holy obligation, knight. It is your order and Grand Master who has betrayed their vow to battle the heathen, who place the worthless lives of Saracens above the calling of the Lord.'

'We choose our enemies.'

'As you are foolish in your choice of friends.' The Italian eyed the anger he had roused with approval. 'We Crusade where you most fear to tread, knight.'

Theobald crossed the flagstones and crouched level with the peasant. 'You are trying to goad me.'

'I tell the truth.'

'Here is the truth, Spada. I witnessed with my own eyes the slaughter you vested on our streets and brought to an Arab village.'

'Unbelievers must die.'

'And an unschooled peasant is to be the arbiter and judge?' Theobald grimaced in contempt. 'What did you bring to Acre save bloodlust and misplaced pride?'

'A spirit that was lacking and ferocity that had faded.'

'People have suffered for it.'

'I recall how Christ suffered for us.' The Umbrian smirked. 'Before I set foot ashore, I had heard tell of the decline of this city. It was timid and weak and walked in the shadow of doubt. I and my men have given it glory.'

'You and your kind will reduce it to dust.'

'Who then is the Crusader? A fair and pretty noble who feeds the prisoners and tends the sick? Or a toiling man of the fields who elects to take up arms?'

Theobald was calm before the baleful presence. He sensed the power of the man, his desire to influence and control. Even in chains, Spada behaved like an upstart king. The Hospitallers were wise to have imprisoned him.

The peasant took and drank from the vessel, his eyes vicious and watchful. 'It is my name they call out, knight. My name they reverence. My name they will remember.'

'Your arrogance deceives you.'

'In time you shall learn. We have only started in our quest and on a journey to salvation.'

'Through the slaying of women and children?'

'Whatever is demanded. There is no finer preparation for the campaign ahead.'

133

'Wait until it is their own blood your men see, their own entrails that hang from their bellies. Wait until your enemies are not the defenceless, but the fearsome ranks of the Mameluk.'

'We are equal to any.'

'Your scythes against a flurry of arrows? Your pitchforks against a host of racing javelins?'

'Jesus is with us.'

'I have heard similar boasts on the lips of the dying.'

Spada nodded. 'Are you afraid of death, knight?'

'Only of ignominy and shame.' The young Hospitaller stared unflinching at the peasant. 'Only of shirking my duty and slipping to the base depth of a murderous demon.'

'You will not join me in my cause?'

'My preference would be eternal damnation.'

The knight continued his rounds and the peasant chief from Norcia settled in patient contemplation. There might be weeks or months yet to while away, a period for the government of Acre to panic more and keep stoppered the unrest he had released. It was no great hardship. His men would not forget him. Nor would the Saracen. Perhaps the Pope himself would come to hear.

'Tender cuts from the high table of the court . . .'

A face grinned at him, the short and ambling form of Amethyst emerging from the gloom. The dwarf bore a cauldron from which, with mischievous glee, he ladled potage for the prisoners.

Spada scowled. 'What brings you here, dwarf?'

'Boredom and a benevolent soul.' He deposited some slop on the slate platter. 'Prince or commoner, Templar or Hospitaller, to all I offer my humble service.'

'I have no need for your gibbering wit.'

'Nor I much reason to visit a sty. Yet feeding a pig may nourish the soul.'

'Take care, dwarf. Little people are stepped upon.'

'Is it not better to be small of stature than have the standing of a tyrant?'

'Your riddles weary me.'

'So let me speak plain.' Amethyst leant on his ladle as though it were a staff. 'One month in Acre does not make you its King. A single affray does not render you a champion.'

'I could have you cooked on a griddle, dwarf.'

'What a rare and magic dish. A dwarf grows listless at forever leaping for his master from a pie.'

Spada grabbed for him and was caught by his manacle, the dwarf jovial and secure beyond the radius of the chain. The peasant tugged furiously as Amethyst stood and baited with his presence. There was as much humorous diversion in a dungeon as could be found at the palace.

Amethyst cocked his head. 'Do you lose your hunger, Umbrian?'

'Come closer and I will pick clean your bones.'

'Very well.' The dwarf hopped lightly within the area of threat. 'Give thanks for what you are about to receive.'

'Pray I dismember you quick.'

More words might have been intended, but the ladle swung fast, striking the peasant between the eyes in a ringing impact that sent him sprawling. It took seconds for him to return to groggy consciousness. By then, Amethyst sat astride his chest and had him pinned with a hand clamped about his throat.

'Vanquished by a dwarf.' Amethyst tutted. 'What would your brute apostles think?'

'I cannot breathe.' Speech filtered slurred from the constricted larynx.

'Then you must die and all will rejoice.'

'Have mercy . . .'

135

'Do I hear a voice?' The dwarf looked about him and shook his head. 'It seems I imagine and am a fool.'

'I mean you no ill.' The tongue was thick and the face mottled dark.

'A pity I am no goodly knight moved by code and scruple.'

'I beg you.'

'Speak it with conviction.' Amethyst pressed harder.

'For the love of God . . .'

With a single bound, the dwarf sprang into a reverse tumble and recovered to his feet. He bowed slowly to the writhing figure on the ground. Not every audience could be pleased. Amethyst sighed. He was plainly losing his touch.

Theobald appeared beside him to view the spectacle. 'I trust you avoid meting such treatment to Amalric and his court.'

'In truth it is an act I continue to refine.'

The veneer of a frown dissolved to a smile. 'Leave soon for the palace or the Templars, brother. The Hospital is undermined enough.'

'So true.' The dwarf shrugged. 'I am better suited to somersault and juggling.'

'And you, Spada. You are no cock of the farmyard. No emperor. No lord. Behave as other prisoners and we shall treat you well.'

'Or Amethyst shall return.' It was a threat made with glee.

The only response was short and painful gasps. Spada had calmed. *Behave as other prisoners*. He lay still and unanswering in the straw, a manacled captive with plans.

~

Slave markets were wretched and yet rarely dull. The pens were crowded and the traders busy, the bids and counterbids and argument and haggling flowing in ceaseless noise about the carts and stands. On trestles and flat-topped boulders, silver and gold were weighed and counted; in public view, the merchandise was examined, prodded and discussed. Many races were represented. There were Chins and Persians offered by Mongol merchants and Nubians brought from Egypt, the occasional Maghrebi and forlorn Levantine, the old and young taken in a hundred raids along the Red Sea. Human flesh and sinew carried value, were commodities to be shifted. Most highly prized of all was Frankish stock.

'Their eyes are on you, young one.' An Anatolian kept his face averted and whispered to Benedict through the latticed palisade. 'Lift your head and straighten your spine. Seem bold and proud. It will raise your price and guard your life.'

'How do you know?'

'I have witnessed what happens to those too sick or weak to be sold.'

'And if I should not wish to live?'

'While you breathe there is hope. As there is hope, so fate may turn on an instant.'

Benedict swallowed the despair in his throat. 'Look about you, friend. The crowd shows no pity.'

'Yet it may offer payment.' The words in broken Arabic were calm and accepting. 'A home and certainty are what we seek.'

'My home is not here.'

'Nor mine, young one. But it will remove us from this sorry place.'

The youngster sagged disconsolate in his stall, his spirits low and his limbs heavy. For over a week he had mouldered in the dungeon twilight and now swapped the shrieks of the condemned for the clamorous transactions of the bazaar. Each contained its own terrors. The invisible stranger was wrong: this offered no hope, only dust, excitability, the shouts of the handlers and the crack of their whips. All represented a further step away from his guardians and friends. They would go their way and he would go another.

The thick accent again drifted through the barrier. 'Do not surrender to your fears, young one.'

'What else do I have?'

'Your feet and your hands, your heart and your head.'

'They have brought me here.'

'And they shall be with you when you leave. This is only part of the journey, young one.'

'If you are so wise, why too are you a slave?'

'Even the Mameluks started as slaves. They are now our rulers.'

Benedict pondered the words. Perhaps fortune could change, whatever the circumstance; perhaps the Templars would ride in force to save him. They would expect him to be stoic and brave. Out there, Selim and de Flor would have their spies. They would follow his progress, at least remember him in their thoughts.

From the adjacent pen came the sound of movement as men slid wide the gate and dragged the Anatolian from his refuge. His lot had been called. Benedict tried to peer through, glimpsed fleetingly a pair of eyes fierce in their conviction.

'Be always strong, young one.'

'You also, friend.'

Then the foreigner was vanished to the noise. The fourteen-year-old closed his eyes and rested his head against the rough-hewn wood, inert and numb to his surroundings. He would not provide the grim officer of the *Ahdath* a single hint of his trepidation or a reason to crow.

Eventually they arrived for him, the commotion crashing in and the hands reaching to pluck him from his rest. Overwhelmed by the abruptness of the change, Benedict was funnelled through the throng and manhandled to a platform, the prize exhibit and the object of a bidding frenzy. He shook a little, shy at his status, his mind remote and his eyes straining for the familiar. Faces gazed back in fascination as calculations were made and the abacuses engaged. The dark-haired Crusader boy was in demand.

'How much do you bid for the heathen boy? Ten silver dirham? Twenty?'

It had drawn the interest of the chamberlains and the agents to the senior governors and viziers. They had deep purses and an experienced eye.

'Turn him to the side so we may view him.'

'What is his age?'

'His weight?'

'He is well muscled for his size.'

'Does he speak our tongue? Has he tongue at all?'

'Are there scars or injury he bears?'

'Throw in a pair of Russians and we shall bargain.'

The price rose briskly, the bids cried from every quarter and climbing from dirham to gold ashrafi. Benedict remembered the advice of the Anatolian and drew back his shoulders and raised his chin. There was no escape, no Selim or de Flor present to effect a rescue. Few things were lonelier than to stand as a slave at the point of sale.

Financial duelling continued for a while, participants falling away until the competition rested in the hands of rival households. The repute and honour of Aleppo and Homs were in the balance and measured out in coinage. It was Aleppo that triumphed, a brilliant game of bluff and out-manoeuvre concluding with an extravagant flourish. None could compete and the next lot was called. The boy of the Latins had been sold.

*

Acre held many secrets and hid a multitude of tunnels, its foundations excavated over centuries to provide a labyrinth of cellars, crypts and subterranean passageways. Some were well used and others near forgotten; some were created for military purposes and others employed for nefarious ends. It was said a man could be lost forever in these parts. Most avoided them. They were left to the rats and occasional fugitive, to myth and story of witchcraft and ghouls. A prime location for those who sought to avoid capture or discovery.

Olivier of Mauny had his own reasons for journeying to the gloom. As a senior Templar and trusted confidant of Beaujeu, as a knight commissioned by his order to parley with the great Sultan of Egypt, he was a model of probity and discretion. He knew about secrets. His brethren believed him upstanding and the nobles saluted his intelligence and integrity. All were duped. They should glimpse him now as he hurried cowled through the shadowed alleyways of the city towards his destination. No one would identify him as a denizen of the Temple or wearer of the white mantle with its blood-red cross.

He had fought to control his compulsion. He had fasted and prayed and mortified his flesh to drive the demons from his corrupted soul. Still they remained to taunt and lure and plant echoing whispers in his head. Nothing quelled the craving. It had driven him to the very edge of madness and despair, yet lust always won.

He glanced about him and descended a rough flight of steps cut close to the wall of Montmusart. Thought of pleasure for the moment outweighed the risk and guilt. He had pronounced sternly on the sins of others so many times. He had sneered at the excesses of the citizenry and at the licentiousness of the hireling de Flor. Hypocrisy and sacred oath provided him his cover, yet it would not save him should he be caught. There were few worse crimes than sodomy and no excuse that would lessen the severity of sentence. Even the grand master would be forced to commit his friend to the scaffold. For unnatural acts were contagious and an affront to God and ordered decency, a canker that might spread within the brotherhood if leniency were shown. Perhaps the threat added frisson.

The knight found the lantern lit and ready and slipped a tinted pane of rose-pink glass into the groove on its side. It would act as a signal. One backwards look, a pause to listen for footsteps or danger, and he entered through a worn oak door he bolted fast behind. A religious world exchanged for something darker and more ecstatic. Naturally it was a pity the Arabs had been butchered or expelled; their boys were pliant and offered charming company. Yet others were willing to provide favours for money or to sate their own desires. With the sure tread of a regular visitor, he went deeper into the warren.

A light glimmered pale blue in the blackness, its faint illumination drawing him on. The cares of Acre belonged outside. In these sepulchral caverns he could forget himself, abandon his habit and acquire another. Faith and dignity were strangers here. What mattered were passion and the meeting of bodies and like minds. Two coloured lanterns were what it took.

Nearing the source, he peered into the surrounding shadow to identify his catch. A surprise could delight. Bashfulness was clearly part of the play, and he preferred it that way. He would persuade the man to open up.

He stopped. 'Show yourself to me.'

There was no response, not a flicker of sound or movement from the dark beyond. In a heartbeat he understood that he was to die and had walked to his grave, that time remained only to make his peace and offer up prayer. Except a Templar was forged to give fight. He turned to confront the danger, unhooking his belt as an improvised weapon. The lead weight kept in its buckle would damage any assailant. Not this one. With a scream of religious fury and a curved knife extended, the Assassin leapt for Mauny. It took several blows to bring the knight to his knees, the grunts laboured and the blade plunging fast, the coarse-spun robe weeping blood from ragged tears. It was a well-rehearsed execution. In a final gesture, whether in a defensive reflex or as a plea to God, the knight clasped his hands and raised them high. The knife slipped in beneath. May Christ forgive his abominations. The Templar sighed and bubbled air and toppled on his face. Not quite the climax he had sought.

Another jolt of the cart and Benedict marked it as a further step from Acre. He had tried to put the city from his thoughts, but the more it receded the sharper became its image in his mind. A few of its citizens might think of him. He was the boy who had run their errands and made them laugh, who had done them kindness and relied on their largesse. From here on he would depend on himself. He glanced at his fellow captives. He could determine which were former soldiers and which were learned scribes, which would be put to tilling the fields and which were destined for a more cosseted life. There were boys and girls of his age too, the future handmaidens and warriors of tomorrow. The Mameluks had come from such a caste and their kingdom was built of slaves. He would learn to adapt and be as ruthless as they, would as their sultan grow to conquer.

It was morning and a September dew was evaporating from the higher ground. Leila would be picking herbs or selecting fruit and Hazzim would be loading his donkey to cross the Acre plain. All things led to the city and the sea. Yet he was condemned to a different course by dint of circumstance and his mistake. Around him, Bedouin spearsmen sat watchful on camels and a cavalry troop guarded the train. The wealthy of Aleppo had paid handsomely for their purchases and would resent any damage or loss en route. At the head of the column rode the chamberlain to the house of the governor, his bearing proud and status confirmed by a fluttering standard and silken umbrellas and the gold-clad peacock feather adorning his turban. They were heading north.

From the caged confines of the wagon, Benedict joined the prisoners in staring at the dust trail behind. None wished to look forwards. At intervals, a company of soldiers or mounted archers would pass by in urgent quest for the gathering army elsewhere. Their purpose was clear. In time they would hurl themselves against the walls of Acre and turn their weapons on the last remaining Christians of Outremer. It was strange to sit behind the lines and traverse the scenes of preparation. The youngster noted everything. He was still a spy for Beaujeu.

In the van of the formation, the chamberlain raised his hand and the transports behind shuddered to a rolling halt. Something had unsettled him. There was a single individual blocking his progress. The visitor was either insane or foolhardy. Yet it deserved brief investigation.

'Move from our path.'

'I will not.' The stranger stood his ground, his eyes alone visible through the wrapped keffiyeh.

'Then you choose death over living.'

'Some may reach it sooner.'

'Are you a shepherd? A holy man? A dog driven from the city?'

'None of these things.'

'Or are you an enemy host come to give us battle?' The chamberlain laughed at his own jibe and leant forwards in his saddle. 'As a merciful man, I shall grant you swift ending by spear or arrow.'

'You are indeed merciful. But not wise.'

'What manner of threat is this against an armed force of soldiers?'

'One that will surprise.'

If the chamberlain was perplexed, his confusion deepened as the mounted officers to each side were unseated by a volley of crossbow bolts. He shouted for the cavalry to advance and meet the hazard. But they were turning and drawing back, their weapons and bridles jangling in retreat. They had performed their duty and delivered him to a trap.

Stripped of his retinue, the chamberlain swung desperate in his saddle. 'What is the meaning of such challenge?'

'A lesson in humility and a sudden change of fortune.'

'My master is the lord of Aleppo. Harm me and you will find no place of hiding.'

'I would offer you the spear or arrow as you offered them me.' The stranger seemed sympathetic. 'Yet I will leave such judgement to your prisoners.'

His face still shrouded, the visitor strode along the line. He released the catches and wagon bindings as he went, throwing wide the cages and setting free the slaves. They shouted with relief, mobbing his progress and giving their thanks, jumping down in euphoric trepidation. Freedom was an uncertain place. At one of the carts, the stranger helped a boy leap to the ground and then embraced him tight. De Flor was reunited with his charge.

'You came for me.' Bewildered yet ecstatic, the youngster hugged his guardian.

'I would no more discard my lute than abandon you to enslavement.'

Benedict buried his face against the broad shoulder. 'Never did I show them fear, Roger.'

'You are the young lion I expected.'

'But the soldiers?' The boy glanced in wonderment at the dust cloud of departing horsemen. 'Why did they not resist?'

'It is a long tale of many parts, most involving payment. We will speak of it as we journey.'

'There is danger everywhere.'

'Put your trust in me, boy.' De Flor placed an arm about his shoulders. 'Let us walk a little way away.'

They strolled from the jubilant pandemonium and climbed the thorn-lined track that crested and dropped to a dry wadi. Benedict recoiled, poised to run and yet stalled by shock.

The hand of de Flor steadied him. 'You seem troubled, boy.'

'He will kill you, Roger.' The voice had hoarsened to a whisper. 'He will kill us both.'

'I have learnt that outcome is rarely so simple.'

As Benedict maintained a wary and distant oversight, the adventurer moved to greet his accomplice. Templar gold could purchase the loyalty of almost anyone.

'You have my pay?' The man from the *Ahdath* was measured in his enquiry.

De Flor tossed him the purse. 'Count it. The gold is as you asked.'

'Then for the while we are brothers.' Oblong coins were tipped glittering into an open palm. 'Your Grand Master is the most generous of patrons.'

'He demands assistance in return.'

'Did I not save the cub and return him to you? Did I not call off the jackals here and leave the chamberlain undefended?'

'I thank you, as would Beaujeu.'

'We are each of us his hired men. We are both of us the same.'

The Arab returned the money to his purse, the birthmark on his forearm revealed as the sleeve slid back. Benedict continued to watch from his safer radius as the two men talked and the sentries stood guard with crossbows cocked and loaded.

De Flor looked over his shoulder and winked at the youngster. 'How did the boy fare in your dungeon?'

'With the courage of a soldier. He bears himself well for an Unbeliever.'

'I am glad, for there are further trials ahead.'

'So be away.' The *Ahdath* officer gestured with his hand. 'Time runs and the army marches.'

There was no expression of friendship or farewell. Relations were built on common currency instead of common cause. In killing or capturing the intelligence assets of Beaujeu, the double agent had secured his position among the Mameluks and established himself as an irreplaceable conduit for information to the Franks. One side played off against the other. It was a dangerous pastime, but he was a ruthless player.

He called after de Flor. 'Our fates may be written. That of the boy is in your hands.'

In the adjacent valley, the freed prisoners were exacting their revenge on the captured chamberlain. Against the backdrop of a coming war, it was an ugly incident likely to be forgotten.

~

On the plain of Acre, Hazzim surveyed the distant city walls and thought of nothing in particular. Every tower and castellation he knew and yet the image was become unfamiliar, a place haunted by the screams of ghosts and inhabited by the enemy. The foe occasionally sortied out, the knights of the military orders cantering in martial array to exercise their mounts and refine their prowess in the charge. It was an impressive sight. Once, he had thrilled to it as he and Benedict had stood to wave and marvel at the show. Now he hid behind a rock. They were Christian and he was a Mohammedan; they still lived while his family and village were gone. Neither lance nor sword would save these people.

He watched the waning light shed by a deepening sun as it bottomed towards the sea. Tranquillity reigned. Only the gliding and beak-nosed shape of a galley or the feathering motion of a spear on the rampart gave a hint of darker things. He was not fooled and yet the Franks were. They believed in their invincibility and right and considered themselves forever part of the destiny of Palestine. But by night they left the plain to the Arab, drew up their bridges and lowered their portcullises and sat out the dark with their backs to the sea. Hardly the actions of a conqueror.

Among the True Believers there were rumours of the coming Mameluk, whisper of a call to arms. Neutrality was not an option. To hope for the best was to invite another raid by the merciless Franks; to lie passive and mute was to encourage from Qalawun a charge of treachery. Loyalties had hardened. Hazzim owed it to his protectors and cousins on the plain and to the sacred memory of his family and the blessed name of Allah. He must fight against the infidel. Leila would have teased him for his new-found purpose, but his sister was a mound of ash and he was a volunteer for duty.

In the gloaming, the horseman picked his way with care along the track. The Crusaders would not give chase. They were corralled behind their walls, immersed in their whoring and drinking and ungodly ways. Nor would the Hospitaller villages send forth a troop to offer pursuit. The Christians had few allies available after dark and needed to conserve their resources. So the rider was comfortable in skirting the bounds of Acre and crossing the open fields, in visiting the hamlets and meeting the tribes. There were preparations to make and agents to recruit. Survivors of atrocity were often willing hands.

Saluting Hazzim with his whip, the rider halted. 'You will join the cause of Qalawun?'

The Arab boy nodded. He would show who was the outsider and help erase the foreigners from the Holy Land.

✝

✝

Chapter 9

Carefully, William of Beaujeu lifted the gem-set lid to the reliquary and gazed in rapture on the object within. It never failed to bring him to his knees. A simple and unembellished item rendered in wood, an artefact that would go unnoticed in any other setting. Yet it had the power to command the hearts of men and rally the armies of Christ, to make the grand master of the Knights Templar bow his head and tremble. The holy grail. With quaking fingers he lifted it from the casket and felt the energy of contact, pressed the modest drinking bowl briefly to his lips. There were times before when he had fainted from the moment. It was a direct connection with the Crucifixion and the Lamb of God, and no man alive but he was blessed with such responsibility.

He raised the vessel between his hands as it must have been held to catch the blood of the dying Messiah. Over a thousand years later, this cup had been discovered buried beneath the ruins of the Temple of Apollo in Caesarea as the foundations of the new Crusader church were laid. That holy site was adjacent to the summer palace of the Roman governor of Judaea; that governor was Pontius Pilate. And so the ownership of the relic had passed.

Beaujeu gently returned it to the gilded case and with a final prayer locked it from view. It was useful to remind himself why he fought and what was at stake. He was custodian of the Christian presence in the Holy Land. His knights were the last and fabled line of its defence and in that they would surely be tested. Only a day before, the camel master Selim had returned from Damascus with news from de Flor of a great military host assembled and ready to venture from Syria. He already knew of the preparations in Egypt. The renegade emir al-Fakhri had not lied. He had predicted every step. Acre was the target and Acre was unready.

The grand master rose from his knees and moved to an arched window to survey the harbour, dull-lit by a chill autumn dawn. Still no reply or relief from Europe. Its princes would rue the day that Acre fell, thinking themselves as safe across the water as Amalric the Constable believed himself secure behind the city walls. Nowhere was safe from the rapacious grasp of the heathen.

Another thought disturbed his musings. Individuals had vanished from the heated confines of the city, disappearances beyond the usual. Now Olivier of Mauny had gone missing. His friend and fellow Templar was a stickler for protocol and pursued a daily regimen marked by vigil and prayer. Something was wrong. The grand master had learnt to trust his instinct, and it told him the Templar and the other missing were dead. The enemy was operating with guile and stealth about the streets below. Qalawun was softening up Acre. The sultan should be applauded for his endeavour. But Beaujeu was not about to let his strategy go unchecked.

Hunger could bring a man from his hiding place. The Assassin knew that his mission was suicidal, but he needed to eat to sustain himself and continue his task for as long as he was able. There would come a moment when a patrol gave chase and the swords of the infidel cut him down. That was the customary path of the martyr and he would not shirk his calling, would go happily and without complaint. After all, his forebears had for centuries gone to their deaths with a dagger in their hand and a holy chant on their lips. He would neither betray their memory nor the command of the sultan.

At this hour, most of the citizens of Acre still slumbered; at this hour, he had succeeded in the silent execution of random victims. Soldiers were seldom alert to the danger. A hand over the mouth and a blade slipped through the abdomen or beneath the ribs, a warm body dragged away and a blood smear left behind. He crouched to listen and sniff the rank city air, his senses freed from the confines of below-ground existence. The Christians were so direct and obvious in their approach to warfare. Their way was to charge headlong with lances couched and horses in full cry. They did not appreciate nuance and artistry, would never grasp the skills employed against them. Even the grand master and devil-serpent Beaujeu would be confounded.

The Assassin ran forwards and flattened himself against the building, edging round with his head turned towards the likely travel of threat. From inside the structure came the murmur of life and the smell of baking dough. He paused. There was no harsh timbre to the ambient noise, no suggestion of alarm or anything more than the early ritual of firing up the ovens. They would not miss a loaf or two or even know that he had visited. Surviving on a crust and at the margins was what he had been trained for. Creeping on, he traced his way with care and pressed in closer to the target. At short range, the warmth could comfort and the sweet aroma of flour and yeast overwhelm the judgement of a famished man. He must resist the temptation to hurry.

The sounds disentangled themselves into individual voices. There was a snatch of song and the clatter of a tray, the sharp delivery of an oath and general grumbling from beside the kneading-trough. No one was aware of the eavesdropper. The Assassin marked time. There was always the option of murder should he be confronted, yet he preferred to steal in and out without fuss or incident. Now was his chance.

'Fingers which thieve may often be lost.'

The words were hostile and uttered by a man in possession of the sharpest of pastry-knives. Mouton was his name, a character large in build and renowned both for his baking and his temper. There were few things he enjoyed more than inflicting hurt on those he found pilfering or offensive. With the ragged subject before him, he could give full vent to his hobby.

'Speak or you will lose your nose and ears.' The knife moved from palm to palm. 'Do you not believe me?'

'I believe you.' The Assassin dipped his gaze in temporary submission.

'What are you? A Levantine? A Jew?'

'A humble beggar with no home or crust.'

'So you come to me. To take what is not yours.' Mouton nodded. 'The last ball of shit to venture here had his face held to the hot oven stones. The one before was forced to eat raw dough. Each was cured of his greed.'

The Assassin feigned terror and maintained his jabbering French. 'It is not greed, but hunger that brings me.'

'What am I to do? Set you free? Permit you to escape your beating?'

'I do no harm.'

'You offend me and that alone demands redress.'

'I beg you, brother.'

'A beggar who begs. You waste your effort.'

Mouton whistled and his comrades joined him, a fraternity intent on inflicting pain. The Assassin cowered and coldly assessed them, measuring the distance and reviewing each move, reading the faces and the readiness to act. Confidence could blind or kill a man and death arrive before he had instant to blink or pray or utter a protest. Cooks and bakers should stay with tending the ovens.

The pastry-knife glanced near. 'We will pattern you well for your trespass.'

'I plead forgiveness.'

'You offer us nothing.' A large apprentice rolled his sleeve and weighed the cudgel in his hand. 'Nothing, save fine and bloody sport.'

They intended some diversion and he would provide it. Naturally, he could eviscerate them in seconds and quickly carve his exit. But he would adapt to the circumstance. On any battlefield, it was often the wounded that slowed the enemy and sowed confusion, the cries and screams of bleeding men that undermined morale. He wondered how his small group of adversaries might accommodate the unexpected.

With one last whimper and a coiled shrinking from their presence, he sprang forwards to attack. They were too slow and blundering in response and too crowded properly to engage. It was his gain. With total precision he addressed each objective, his own blade directed to creating attrition and distress. A face was slashed and a shoulder punctured, a wrist broken and a tendon sliced clean through. Rapidly, he reversed the haft and brought it down on a clavicle. Another opponent was removed from the fray. The hollering was loud. Without pause, the Assassin dropped and rolled and severed a proffered hamstring on the way out. He was clear.

Alerted by the noise, citizens came late and stumbling to the scene. They in turn became part of the unfocused agitation. Everyone was agreed that dark forces were loosed among the city; everyone concurred the Mohammedans were out to gain vengeance for the earlier losses they had suffered. It was an unsettling thought and few believed it was the end to the affair. Meanwhile, the screams and groans of the wounded did not abate. There would be some hiatus in the provision of fresh loaves that morning.

~

'Like pilgrims on the road, we are once more together.'

They watched the darkness ripple across the desert and the sand and rock fade to its cooling touch. It was the end of another day. Standing beside the adventurer, Benedict could forget his recent privation. After all, he had survived capture and imprisonment and the early stage of slavery: anything was possible. Yet to be engaged in a wild trek some three hundred miles across the Syrian wilderness seemed to challenge the bounds of luck and reason. The terrain was searing and inhospitable, the wandering tribes probably hostile, the wells often dry. Little remained but to put his trust in de Flor.

'Look.' The Frank spat the stone of a date and lifted his sword to trace the horizon. 'Behind us is the Mameluk and before us the Mongol. Our direction is already set for us.'

'Why should the Mongol ride to save Acre?'

The sword lowered. 'For the plain fact that the Khan detests the Saracen and desires blood for the previous loss of Syria. For the opportunity presented by Qalawun in bringing his armies to bear on the one anvil of Acre.'

'Is the Mongol Khan our friend?'

'He is enemy to our enemy and that will suffice.'

'What if you fail to persuade him?' The youngster looked up at his guardian.

'Then conditions in Acre will be poor for future trade and I must remove myself elsewhere.'

'Why do you strive for a city you care little for?'

There was no answer, but even aged fourteen, Benedict sensed the truth. His mentor was neither pious nor sentimental and held no great fondness for any part of Outremer. He adopted and abandoned towns and accepted tasks as way points to exploit or for enrichment. Religious war was for those who cared.

De Flor drew air deep into his lungs and exhaled slowly, the image of contentment. 'Breathe in the desert, boy. It is the smell of freedom.'

'Selim speaks of similar things.'

'A cameleer should know.' The adventurer shaded his eyes and pointed. 'The North Star appears. What once directed wise men and magi now guides us.'

'You think they followed these same paths to find the Blessed Virgin and holy infant?'

'Ask the Patriarch when you next see him.' De Flor rummaged for dried fruit in the pouch at his belt. 'In days past, Christendom relied on good and learned men. Strange its survival should now rest with us.'

'Will we ever reach the Euphrates?'

Another date was flipped upwards and caught in the open mouth. 'Fortune smiles on those who dare.'

'I was taught fate will punish those who are reckless.'

De Flor chewed and pondered and eventually nodded. 'We are not reckless, boy. We take risks because we must. We travel from oasis to oasis as any humble nomad.'

'They are strong in number.'

'While we have strength in purpose and a sword and bow to hand.'

Benedict turned his head away in the gathering shadow. 'I have no wish to be a prisoner again.'

'It shall not happen. I have more tricks in my saddlebag

than turning myself to a deeper hue or an *Ahdath* into a loyal ally.'

The youngster smiled. 'You fool no one with your disguise.'

'Mockery will earn you a beating.'

'I am equal to your threat.'

Man and boy scuffled in amicable combat, de Flor the ogre and Benedict his baiting rival. Later they would sit and talk and the young charge would listen to tales of skirmish and expedition and of galley raids upon the foe. Then the Frank would play his 'ud and sing and his companion drift to sleep.

It was the screaming of the horses that broke through and forced a pause. Panting, Benedict rested his hands upon his knees as de Flor hissed a warning and loped blind in the direction of the sound. The youngster had never before heard a beast cry so much in terror. He crept in the wake of his guardian, ready to lend assistance, urging his stuttering heart and faltering legs to push him on. Bandits must have pounced as darkness fell. From the noise of the animals, the savagery was extreme.

'Rest where you are, boy. Not one move if you value your life.'

De Flor's voice was taut and cracked with an unfamiliar tension. Benedict peered towards the glimmer of the camp-fire. In the subdued glow he could just discern the writhing of the horses and the still form of the Frank. There were no robbers or armed Mameluks, no hostiles lurking with intent. Only pervasive fear.

Obediently, Benedict balanced atop a boulder. He was dimly aware that the thrashing limbs of the tethered steeds had subsided to final convulsion, that the adventurer was delicately reaching with his sword to pluck a knapsack from its temporary perch. Every move was considered and controlled. It meant death was close and even de Flor was scared.

Benedict shivered involuntarily. 'What is it, Roger? Where is the threat?'

'Can you not hear them?' De Flor was bent above his sword, binding it with cloth tow. 'Snakes.'

He reached and swept the weapon close to the orange embers of the fire, letting the naphtha-soaked rags catch before withdrawing the blazing steel and putting it to the bulrushes in his fist. The night brightened and the vision cleared. All about, the ground was alive with the coiling shapes of desert vipers, their brown and spreading mass in seething flux and their scale-clad heads darting and probing towards the source of the heat. The presence of warmth drew them from their nest. Their eye-pits detected the invisible energy of strangers and their tongues tasted the air for sweat particles and indications of animal stress. They homed in.

Isolated and immobile, the youngster stared at the enveloping prospect. 'They are at my feet, Roger. They climb to strike me.'

'I will deliver you fire to hold them. Sweep it like a scythe in front of you and ward them back.'

A bulrush fell short into the boiling formation, the patterns reconfiguring about it. The second landed close on the rock and Benedict stooped to snatch it to his grasp. The torch revealed the extent of his predicament. He jabbed at the marauding leaders, driving them back, meeting their progress with a scorching reply. Some retreated; others reared aggressively and unyielding. In the background, the thrashing limbs of the horses had faded to twitching throes and their screams had been overtaken by a dry rustling as though from a blanket of dropped leaves.

A serpent curled angrily from the spitting firebrand, its

markings faint on the dun-hued skin. It would try again. The nose bobbed and the horns inched forwards.

Benedict called out. 'The flame dies and the beasts press in. I cannot fight them.'

'I, however, may.'

De Flor crossed the distance at speed, cursing loudly and hacking aside the venomous creatures in a flaming rampage with his sword. It might have been the devil himself. Without pause, he leapt on to the rock and swept the boy to his shoulder, ferrying him in a random dash to safety. Behind them, the vipers clustered about the dead horses and moved cautiously among a field littered with their burnt and beheaded number. Carried high, Benedict hung limp and felt the striding rhythm of the Frank. His friend and rescuer had not lied. Fortune did indeed favour those who dared.

Elsewhere too, firebrands were being used. In the tunnels of Acre a manhunt was in progress for the Saracen assailant who had so grievously harmed loyal servants of the city and audaciously escaped the retribution of the mob. If there was one, there might be several; should they be found, there would be blood. Doors were kicked open and recesses searched, squads of soldiers and citizens tramping armed to the airless underworld and driven by pride and thought of reward. Gold had been put on the life of the unknown criminal.

At the head of a troop of Hospitallers, Theobald of Alzey entered the labyrinth. It was important to the grand master that their order should trounce Beaujeu and his Templars. Rivalry often provided an incentive and informed relations between the pair. Yet Theobald was concerned more with duty and the enforcement of justice, with pursuing his knightly vocation to protect brother Christians, to battle the forces of infidel darkness and to act as his grandfather Otto would have done. He had every intention of bringing the fight down to the depths of the enemy.

Holding his sword at low guard, he whispered back to his men. 'Listen well and keep your eyes averted from the light. Our foe is more reptile than man.'

'While we are from the Hospital and not of the bakery.'

The young knight smiled in the wavering gloom. His sergeants were afraid of little and had proved themselves in countless skirmishes with the Saracen. A lone killer was no match for them. He inched forwards, the chain mail hauberk heavy on his shoulders and the sweat pooling beneath the leather coif that protected his head from the linked steel rings. Crusader armour was designed for the open field rather than the confines of an underground chamber, but there was work to do.

He sniffed the fetid atmosphere, smelt the burrow staleness of dereliction and abandonment. On the bare rock walls he glimpsed the marks scratched hastily by previous generations, by tunnellers and thieves and a varied host of stockmen. Few would have wished to remain for long. Theobald raised his hand and stayed the advance. A different odour had reached his nostrils, a dry sweetness that alerted the brain and pricked the skin and wafted from an unseen distance. He had encountered it often enough in the hospital morgue.

'We have found the hiding place, brothers.'

An older sergeant tried not to disagree. 'Any head may be tricked by these surroundings.'

'Not mine.' Theobald adjusted the grip on his sword and held out his hand for a flaming torch. 'If we do not have surprise, we at least have brute strength.'

'Your command?'

'To enter with fury and a shout on your lips. Make ready and wait on my word.'

There was scarcely room for three abreast, yet Hospitallers were renowned for their combative spirit. They rushed forwards, their clamour and battle-cries multiplied and their assault channelled through the reaching hollows. Sharpened steel and not manoeuvre would win the fight. They arrived, erupting into the space and spreading fast to dominate and confront. Whoever faced them would quickly submit.

'What in the name of Our Lord . . .'

The expression of horror was shared by them all as men balled their fists to retching mouths or made the sign of the cross. Before them were human remains, the pale cadavers of Christians drained of blood and arrayed seated or hung about the walls. The murderer had been industrious. His prize exhibit was a Templar, the senior knight Olivier of Mauny, still recognisable and laid prayerful and like an effigy on a slab of stone. If the Assassin were showing his hand or humour, the joke was not quite finished.

'Move back! Retreat for your lives!'

Even as Theobald screamed his warning, the ignited fumes of naphtha scorched his throat. He should have suspected a trap. Pitch on the floor and oil-dipped rags draped from the ceiling had been placed to transmit an unguarded spark from the lit brands of intruders to the fire pits around. The inferno was rapid. Through the conflagration and the pressure wave that removed his breath and propelled him back down the tunnel, Theobald saw the outline of his men running against a world transformed to brilliance. Not everyone would emerge alive.

Outside, the Assassin was engaged in his own game of chase. He had been sighted and a crowd mustered for the pursuit, its direction overseen by Amethyst, whose instinct had led to the discovery. Perched atop a castellation, the dwarf now waved his cap and encouraged the hounds. Their quarry was flushed from its hideout and would not this time get away. For a man who had caused such death and injury, the Assassin seemed insignificant before the ferocity of the mob. A handler slipped his hunting dog from its leash and cheered it as it raced to overhaul. Joy was short-lived when the stranger turned and summarily gutted it with a single knife thrust. The next canine was flicked aside and cartwheeled to break its back. Soldiers who rushed to intercept fared no better, were sent bloodied and tumbling in steep descent. On his pedestal, Amethyst folded his arms and whistled a merry tune.

The Assassin gulped for air and leapt to a further flight of steps. He had done well. The vengeful squeals of the heathen were testimony alone. He scurried along a narrow overhang and vaulted on to a steeper incline, dodging beneath an arrow shot and switching direction before making for a turret. These Latins believed they had him cornered. They rarely recognised the longer narrative or identified the deeper truth. He had sown the seeds and spread dismay, had undermined the self-belief of the rump kingdom of Outremer. Naturally he would be martyred; another would take his place. Thus would the cycle continue. He could abandon all earthly cares. Golden pavilions awaited him in paradise, where he would be attended by virginal handmaidens as he sat beside rivers of honey and milk. Allah be praised and may the great ambition of Qalawun be met. He reached the highest point and jumped.

Perhaps it had once been an oasis. But its waters were long dried and its palms dead and reduced to fossilised stumps, the place covered in the drifting sands of the surrounding desert. A parched and inhospitable location. Benedict and de Flor had trudged there, the adventurer laden with weapons and saddlebags and his apprentice keeping pace with their meagre provisions tied in a canvas sack. Their water would not last and their fortunes had evaporated with the agonised demise of their horses. In time, by turn, they too would succumb. As his guardian scanned the boundless horizon, the youngster watched through blistered eyes. Maybe snakes would come again, or even scorpions; maybe their dry bones and hollowed skulls would be discovered by future wanderers.

'Be of faith, boy,' de Flor called back from his lookout. 'We escaped the serpents and there will yet be more adventure.'

'Without horses? Without water? Without food or shelter?'

'They will come if we are but patient.' The adventurer grinned with the confidence of a man at ease. 'I would not have carried my lute these miles if I imagined we were to perish.'

'There is a chance that you are mistaken.'

De Flor strode across and seated himself beside his charge. 'I will permit no doubts, boy. We are warriors both, agents of Beaujeu and saviours of our city.'

'I do not feel like a saviour.'

'Few heroes ever do.'

'What if the Saracen army you saw has marched? If it is already encamped at the gates of Acre?'

'Then it will stay there until Qalawun moves up from Egypt.' The Frank thumped Benedict heartily on the back. 'We are still actors in this pageant.'

'October advances and we sit in a desert.'

'Not for long, I vouch.'

The youngster stared ahead and did not reply. He had always delighted in expeditions and in those moments in which he was alone with de Flor. He yearned to emulate the twenty-three-year-old Crusader, for few either forgot or ignored the man. Yet part of Benedict longed also for the familiar, for the rabble noise of home and a seat beside Hazzim on the roof of the Fonda. A rock somewhere in the eastern desert was a poor substitute.

'Speak your thoughts, boy.'

He tried. 'I wonder how war will change us. I wonder if Hazzim will remain my friend.'

'A friendship may fade for any reason or none. For love or hate. For blood or betrayal.'

'Hazzim is like my brother.'

'I have seen brothers brawl to the death.' De Flor unstoppered a leather gourd and put it to his lips. 'Should a brother be of separate faith and armed conflict set it against your own, you too may end in such a brawl.'

'It shall not happen.'

'Those are words I ceased to utter a full score years ago.'

Putting down the flask, de Flor rose slowly to his feet and unsheathed his sword. His attention was directed to the measureless reaches of sand and rock and the wavering vista of overheated air. He shaded his eyes. It was either a suggestion of travelling dust or the echo of imagination. Something disturbed the grim tranquillity.

Benedict clambered up beside him. 'What is it, Roger?'

'Our relief or our damnation.'

To wait might be to invite a challenge; to run might only encourage pursuit. The spectres developed shape and form and the hands of de Flor tightened on his longsword. He and the boy faced an entire cavalry formation.

The adventurer was calm. 'They are riding Arabs and carrying spears. They are irregulars but not Bedu.'

His summary brought no comfort to the youngster. The opposing assembly had spread wide across an attacking front and seemed to be intent on encirclement. Benedict began to count the mounted figures, his gaze darting and his mind churning possibilities. He was out of one incident and cast headlong into the next.

These were weathered Arabs a hundred strong, outlaws of a kind, rough men with dark and territorial eyes and immobile faces. Only a paltry Latin blade came between them and their projected victims. Their leader was different: he had adopted the airs and apparel of a sheikh. He sat astride a white stallion and silently studied the Europeans. Benedict stood close to de Flor and readied to pull his knife. If the Frank so commanded, he would commit himself to a short and furious defence. In front of them horses' tails twitched and heads nodded impatient in their bridles as the scrutiny and stand-off lengthened.

Without a word, the commander swung himself from his saddle and moved unhurriedly towards the trespassers. His men looked on. He had yet to draw his sword. But it was the Crusader who responded, planting his sword in the earth and stepping forwards to greet with a fraternal embrace. An old alliance had been restored. Marzouca had arrived.

~

There was less cause for relief in the castle palace of Acre. Cloistered in a privy chamber with the aged Patriarch, Amalric vented his annoyance with the choleric complaint of a weak ruler growing weaker. The old man listened and nodded and said few words. He was accustomed to acting as confessor, to hearing the litany of woe and peevishness that tripped fretfully off the tongue of the Constable. Prayer and gentle counsel no longer had any effect. People were scared and people argued; people suspected conspiracy and expected the worst. What Acre needed and Amalric demanded were the certainties of security and the continuation of peace.

'A fever takes hold upon this city.' Amalric paced morosely on the flagstones. 'We find *hashshashin* in our midst who kill our citizens and leap without fear to their deaths. We have a Grand Master of the Temple who contents himself with spreading panic and rumour of infidel advance.'

'Perhaps there is truth in what William of Beaujeu claims.'

'He is a Templar. Deceit and falsehood are in their nature.'

An eyebrow was raised in mild rebuke. 'They have defended Outremer on numberless occasions.'

'And undermined it with the rest.'

'You dismiss their sacrifice, highness?'

'Such sacrifice is to their gain and always with an eye to power.' The Constable again turned and retraced his steps. 'Meantime, I am left with a kingdom whose inhabitants grow nervous and jostle to depart, whose trade slackens and wealth diminishes each wretched day that passes.'

'Will you allow in ships to bear away the fearful?'

'I will not.' Amalric punched a fist into his palm.

'Would you wish to be surrounded by women and children and those unfit to fight?'

'Remember it is I who grapples with affairs of state and you who deals in matters of God.' It was a cheap and petulant jibe. 'If I permit a flight from our shore, it will begin a stampede. If we display timidity, it will encourage Qalawun to pounce.'

'What then of our preparedness?'

'Our walls are lofty and our defences strong. Where the will exists, we shall prevail.'

'I pray on my knees and for the sake of Christendom it is so.'

Resentment flared in the features of the Constable. He preferred gentle flattery to chafing truth, the fawning company of nobles and knights over the subversive wisdom of older heads. Too much was expected of him; too little reward came with his office. He was obliged to milk the land and gather resources for the benefit of his brother King Henry in Cyprus. It did not win him respect and had not earned him the love of a fractious populace over whom he ruled as proxy. The military orders despised him and the leaders of Europe ignored him. Sovereign reign had ceased to be a happy undertaking.

He stared accusingly at the Patriarch. 'Is it that you deem me the last Crusader? The final Christian ruler of our realm?'

'Heaven forbid it, highness.'

'Yet many think it.' Amalric glowered. 'I shall prove them wrong and show the mettle of which I am cast.'

Doors crashed wide and a herald stumbled in to offer an apology and explain the disturbance and announce the intruders who were already entered. Behind him stalked William of Beaujeu and a pair of Templar men-at-arms supporting an injured turcopole. Diplomatic pleasantry was for another time.

The grand master took his cue from the silence. 'Regard well this man. For he sees the future. I send out patrols for proof of the Saracen and nearing Caesarea they find it.' He nodded to the dazed and bleeding scout.

'We were ambushed by a patrol of enemy *Saqa*. My brothers were killed and I alone escaped.' In broken French and with laboured breath the story came. 'The great army of Syria has marched in strength and lies not forty miles south.'

'Tell his highness how numerous is the foe.'

'I counted tens of thousands and tens of thousands more.'

Beaujeu fixed the Constable with a narrowed gaze. 'Now will you believe war is close and Qalawun means to finish us?'

✝

Chapter 10

'Give praise to the mighty Qalawun and rejoice!'

Another army was almost ready to depart. Beneath the heat haze of October and attended by his Mameluk praetorians, the sultan had come in pomp from his Citadel to review his troops assembled on the plain. It was an auspicious moment; a landscape in which the ancient pharaohs had once hunted lion and the young Saladin fought his first military campaigns. There would be blood spilt again. From his dais above the serried multitude, the old man considered the spectacle and let his attention flit from his nearest generals to the furthest and most humble *qufl* infantrymen. All were present and imbued with the spirit of sacred war.

Leaning stiffly on the gold pommel of his sword, he rose from his throne to acknowledge his men. His battle-criers would relay his words; his presence alone conveyed his purpose. The bristling ranks of spears and the rippling tips of cavalry lances, the glittering swords of Turcomans and black and bare-chested regiments of Nubia were the physical manifestation of his dearest wish and the earthly form of the will of Allah. Soon would they be hurled against the walls of Acre.

It felt good to stand here among the banners and the pageant, to invoke the past and imbibe the promised glory. How easy it was to forget that age wearied him and in private he walked with the aid of a sturdy reed cane. And how simple it was to remember his earlier time as a ruthless commander of armies for Sultan Baybars. Far-off days and distant places, and now the Crusader was again the foe. From the ancient period when the Sunni slew the Shia apostates in the house of the Prophet and three of the four righteous caliphs had been murdered, the instinct for war flowed in the veins of the True Believer.

'My brothers. My subjects. My loyal servants.' The sultan raised his hand. 'You know why we are gathered anew and what is to be done. Already our army of Syria has reached the coast and waits at Caesarea. Now it is your turn. Together our force will press down upon the enemy and rip from the heathen his beating heart.'

He could sense the muscles of his troops tautening as they stood tall to his address. The sultan drew his sword and held it high. 'Each one of you must redden his blade with the blood of the unrighteous. Each one of you must be willing to sacrifice his life. Each one of you must perform his holy duty.' He paused. 'Fail me and you betray the one God and your own people. Show weakness and you will perish for the shame you bring.'

They roared in loyal unison, thousands of throats opening to give swelling cry to the euphoria of the moment. Banners waved and trumpets sounded and still the sultan stood with his sword lifted to the heavens. He brought it sharply down and the noise was quelled. Yet more needed to be said.

'Purify your souls and harden your hearts. Pray that you may achieve greatness of renown amongst other martyrs. The hour is come.' He waited as his words were spread. 'Yet there are those who doubt and bring a canker to our midst, those who ally themselves with the demonic forces of the Latins.'

Anger replaced the ecstasy, a consternation that flared in the faces and showed in the unease of officers and men. A squad of religious *muttawiyah* were engaged in pulling a senior emir from the crowd and dragging him before their master. In a ritualised show, they threw him down. The spy had been unmasked.

'You believed you could deflect our aim? Defy our cause? Escape our wrath and punishment?' Qalawun was unpitying in his enquiry.

A rivulet of blood from a cut above the eye ran down the face of al-Fakhri. It mingled with his tears as he grovelled and abased himself at the feet of his sultan. It was an undignified sight. All in the court of the Mameluks understood the consequences of causing displeasure or suffering a fall from grace. The portly little emir had reason to near faint in his distress and to wrestle in the dust with his terror at what would come.

'I ask for clemency from my lord Qalawun.' The voice emerged spittle-laced on quivering lips. 'I beseech his majesty as one who has served him well.'

'You serve our avowed enemy, the Templars.'

'I meant no harm, my Sultan. I sought merely to learn their ways and intent, to have closer bond so that we may gain insight to their souls. None knows the infidel better than I.'

'For none other receives his pay.' Qalawun stared coldly at the man. 'You are condemned by us as a traitor, al-Fakhri.'

'As Allah is my witness, I bear only love for his majesty and our people.'

'Then you will accept the judgement that is meted.'

An example was necessary for the sake of military discipline and political control and for reinforcing values. Soldiers fought more bravely when their fear of superiors outmatched their dread of the adversary in front; sheikhs and emirs displayed less inclination to rebel in the aftermath of a public execution.

At a single command, the guards seized al-Fakhri and bore him in ramshackle parade towards the end of his journey. A grand finale had been decided. Against the sky, wooden siege towers jutted some seventy feet in height, edifices constructed to train joiners and engineers and ready the troops for campaign. One had been adapted for a different practice. With its ladders and platforms removed to its exterior, the hollow structure was open at its base and seemed only partially complete. Screaming now, his body almost rigid in fright, the emir was encouraged to climb. He was neither agile nor committed, his reluctant progress driven on by the sharp prod of daggers and the enthused yell of troops. Qalawun knew how to please his forces.

At the summit al-Fakhri halted, a man bemused at sudden infamy and diminished by the method chosen for his death. He rolled his eyes heavenward, searching for an answer or salvation, muttering in the tongue of those for whom reason and hope had fled. His body swayed. He gazed about him and looked down, flinched at what he saw. There was no alternative or retreat. Louder and insistent the clamour rose, was joined by a drumbeat and the clashing rattle of swords and spears on shields. Everyone wanted a conclusion. The emir tottered forwards and instantly dropped from view.

His shriek was short-lived and echoed abrupt from the interior, his fall staggered by what lay within. Fixed horizontally throughout were a series of sharpened blades, one hundred swords positioned to exact a toll on whoever was descending. Al-Fakhri was being reconstituted. His remains emerged in a wet cascade, the head and a foot and a loop of gut joining the heap in tardy afterthought. There could be no doubting the thoroughness of the process.

Qalawun spoke. 'Behold the fate of our enemies. Observe the inglorious end to those who falter in their task. Be proud and true and as merciless as your ruler in visiting woe upon Satan.'

Assisted on to his horse and with his son Ashraf riding at his side, the warrior-sultan paraded resplendent among his divisions. Flies were already collecting at the base of the execution tower. Yet the focus of the military had switched elsewhere. They hailed Qalawun as he processed, throwing themselves down to kiss the earth or pumping their spears to give salute. He rewarded them with the dark benevolence of his gaze, a figure in gilded armour and a cloak of gold and silver thread, a grizzled bringer of swift justice. A master of the Holy Land.

William of Beaujeu had other plans. Accompanied by his marshal, he walked the outer bounds of his Lion Fortress and studied its defences. There were always improvements to be made, weaknesses to resolve, contingencies to consider. But no longer was the grand master the villain. His predictions had been proved correct and his warnings more than justified; his Templars were now the guardians and champions of a city likely to face siege. Everywhere was alarm. Letters again had been dispatched to Europe and a frantic call to arms sounded, and in all quarters of the city the menfolk were undergoing training. By the day they improved; by the evening, they were exhausted. And by each hour the threat grew and its reality pressed in.

'Sharpen them well,' Beaujeu called out to a labourer fashioning wood spikes at the bottom of the dry moat. 'Should the infidel breach the city walls, your barbs and thorns may prove the best defence of our Temple.'

His marshal grunted. 'How long will we endure if the city falls about us?'

'Long enough to earn our place in legend and to honour the name of Christ. Long enough to ensure our enemies at home have no reason to condemn us.'

'They are circling, nevertheless.'

'Allow them their envy and their greed. They are not the ones sharpening their stakes and blades and preparing to give battle.'

The grand master glanced about him with a practised eye, his ear cocked to the sound of ringing blows hammered from nearby forges. Every blacksmith worked at a furious pace, their furnaces bright and their bellows pumping and their mallets tempering mail and swords. It was the orchestration of panic.

'At least they find the urgency they once lacked.' Beaujeu seemed to muse out loud.

'What use is urgency when it is ill-directed, your grace?'

'We shall welcome their new-found zeal with grace and charity.' The grand master resumed his walk. 'I would rather men came late to skill-at-arms than to sit and wallow in despair.'

'Many will die.'

'A fate we all must share. Yet to wield a sword or pike will bring them comfort at that hour.'

The marshal grimaced in contempt. 'Most of them will drop their weapons when the moment comes.'

'A few will show stalwart.'

'Not the Constable, I vouch. His royal galley sits manned and ready for flight to Cyprus.'

'His feebleness will add lustre to our steadfastness.' Beaujeu was sanguine. 'The world will look to our knights. The world will honour and remember us.'

'All I recall is that a dwarf named Amethyst offers us his loyal service.'

Beaujeu might have smiled. 'That too will shame the nobles.'

Their spears shouldered, a platoon of infantry stumbled by at a quick pace. Mouths panting, their faces betrayed nervous shock at such an unfamiliar role. Beaujeu could read their fraying thoughts. They were civilians, accustomed to excess, comfortable with the notion of prayer or fornication and not with the exigencies of combat. In short order they would be transformed. He imagined them hollow-eyed and drenched in blood, hardened by the first few clashes. They would certainly fight, for their backs were to the sea and their spine was provided by the Lion Fortress.

~

The thieves were on the move, a cavalcade in which Benedict had found a new mount and rode at the head with Marzouca and de Flor. The two men were of a kind, the brigand a former *Shihna*, a police chief turned rogue, and the Frankish adventurer a profiteer and chancer by nature and his trade. They were much alike and old friends. The youngster listened rapt to their stories.

'I am to this infidel rascal as he is to you.' Marzouca spoke to the boy and cast a provoking glance at de Flor. 'A guide and counsellor, an uncle and friend. An older and wiser head.'

'Ignore his words, boy. There is little wise within his skull and precious few truths from out his mouth.'

Marzouca shrugged away the insult. 'I prick his temper.'

'Better than to be pricked by my sword.' De Flor loosened the shemagh about his face.

'Hear his threats, Ben. You would suppose he had the army and I none.'

'Marzouca has an army?' The adventurer looked over his shoulder and scoffed. 'I have never heard it described thus.'

'Yet it found you staggering through the desert like a leprous hermit.'

De Flor bellowed a hearty laugh. 'Take care who you offend, heathen.'

'Or you will wrestle me? Cross swords? Crown my head with a mace?'

'I may even pick up the lute.'

'Then let us engage in less hazardous pursuits.' The Arab pointed. 'For honour we will race to the heights of the dune and back.'

'I am equal to it.'

Without warning and to the cheers of his men, the bandit chief slapped the reins and urged his horse into the charge. His guest gave chase in a storm of dust and a tattoo of hooves, his oaths and insult flowing loud and his mount straining in pursuit. Marzouca enjoyed a distinct advantage. Yet de Flor could eke heroic effort from even a lame or dying beast. The distance was closing.

Among the frenzied band of onlookers Benedict shouted with the rest, emotion and excitement raw in his throat. The sliding ascent of the horsemen had started. They were no different to himself and Hazzim, he thought; neither religion nor war need divide a brotherhood.

'They are equal in the lead!' He stood in the saddle. 'Only a nose comes between them!'

The contestants pounded back, horses and riders jostling for position. It was an aggressive race well run, a competition that ended with equine whinnying and foaming bridles and the back-slapping of equals. Reputation was maintained and calm restored.

Marzouca panted. 'You are the devil, brother.'

'And you a fiend.' De Flor wiped a sleeve across his brow. 'Had I my own horse, you would even now be trailing in.'

'Had I my wits, you would have been left for dead in this wilderness.'

'There is the possibility the Mongol will exact such a price on all of us.'

Benedict sensed a seriousness behind the jest. He had heard tell of the vicious and marauding riders of the east, of the dark horde, of the Asiatic plainsmen who worshipped the eternal sky and with a single pass could put a thousand arrows in a victim. These were the feared legends with whom de Flor had come to parley.

Marzouca leant and lifted the chin of the youngster. 'We are the match for any, nephew.'

'A horde of Mongol?'

'They trust and trade with us as we trust them.' The thin face of the brigand was stern and encouraging. 'We warn them of Mameluk presence and they defend our rear. We mount raids upon the Baghdad road and they share our spoils.'

'Yet the Sultan is a Believer as you.'

'He is not of my tribe or people. He rules his empire and leaves the desert to others.'

'You served him once.'

'It was before I recognised I was born to rob.'

The boy wrinkled his face in puzzlement. 'Now you lead many men.'

'Some of them are soldiers and some farmers exiled by the rapacious grasp of Mameluk lords. Some are poor and some rich. Some were officers in my command and some the criminals we took prisoner.' He eyed his brood with paternal pride. 'All are my children. In these lands, we are the law and also the lawless.'

*

For miles they rode as they had done for days, always heading north-east, the sun harsh and the ground unvarying. The contest had provided the briefest of interludes. But the horses had picked up pace and the scrub thickets grew more abundant in the arid landscape. Marzouca said it was because the Euphrates lay ahead.

And then came the stampede. It arrived as suddenly as any tempest, a howling force that shredded the air and grazed their front in a charging torrent. Somewhere, there was purpose and formation; somewhere, atop their sturdy mounts, warriors plucked bowstrings and released waves of arrows. A blurred and formidable sight. In perfect order the darts struck, peppering the ground with black-feathered flights. A declaration had been made.

'We are here, my friends.'

It would not do to show nerves. Marzouca stayed in position and signalled his retinue to keep their weapons lowered and fully sheathed. Like any desert creature, he reserved his strength for trials he could win. Few would best the Mongol.

The bandit chief nodded approvingly at the arrow tails patterning the earth to his front. This was true marksmanship. A single misunderstanding and the next volley would be redirected.

He lifted his eyes and watched as a lone Mongol horseman and his mount trotted towards them. Garbed in a riding coat of vivid colours and protected by a round shield and painted helmet, the rider clutched a war banner in his hand. There was no hint of his intent.

Marzouca whispered to his side. 'A *bahadur*, a senior knight and hero of their army.'

'He is brave to visit.' De Flor viewed the ritual with lazy interest.

'They would claim the same of us.' The bandit raised his

176

hand in polite salutation. 'We bring you greetings and gifts, brother.'

'Are these white *ch'agua* man and boy to be given to us as slaves?' Enquiry came in Arabic.

'The Frankish lord William of Beaujeu and his Christians of the west send them to parley with the great gurkhan.'

'Arghun is dead and his successor unchosen.'

'What of the clan chiefs? What of the Council? What of the warriors and restless spirits that seek vengeance upon the Mameluks for the insults heaped upon you?'

Tension flickered as the man considered such brazen reply. The Mongols were a superstitious race and Marzouca had invoked the name of the ancestors. It could not go ignored.

The oval eyes stayed inexpressive. 'We received earlier word borne by your horseman.'

'He carried a message of goodwill and our reason to journey here.'

'Then come and we shall see if Mongke, the Eternal Blue Sky, and Tengri, our Sacred Mother Earth, should smile on your endeavour.'

Having motioned to Marzouca, de Flor and Benedict, the Mongol wheeled his horse and paced away. His three guests were compelled to follow. Detached from the security of their own, they maintained their poise and showed no fear as a mounted host fell in about them. Benedict felt the weight of the multitude and held his reins tight as he was swept along in the pressure wave of the advance.

De Flor directed a muttered question to the bandit. 'Is it good they ask guidance from their Eternal Blue Sky?'

'Give thanks they do not call upon Erlik Khan.'

'Who may he be?'

'Ruler of their underworld.'

The earth shuddered to the thudding tread of hooves and

the Mongols swept on for the Euphrates and the Mesopotamian plain beyond.

'What is the duty of all Believers?'
    'To praise and obey the word of Allah.'
    'How may we obey?'
    'By slaying without mercy the enemies of Islam.'
    'Who are these enemies?'
    'The wicked. The unrighteous. The heathen.'
    'Where do they reside?'
    'Behind the walls of Acre.'

Hazzim stared into the fire and gave his answers without emotion. Repetition helped ease the pain of loss endured since the destruction of his village. The slaughter of his family had branded his soul and religion and rage provided the salve. His mentor had been patient and kind. He had talked gently and listened to his distress and had taken him to meet other youths committed to the fight. Each had his role and all were prepared for the rigours ahead; none wished to betray the cause or be excluded from the glory. The sultan expected much of his young soldiers.

'You have witnessed those scouts of the infidel, the treacherous turcopoles, sent fleeing back to Acre.' The Mameluk agent gazed across the flames at him. 'Does it not feel good?'

'It does.'

'And it is merely the beginning of greater event, a sign of the wider and concluding battle to come.'

'I should head south for Caesarea to join the army there.'

'Let the army come to you. I have more pressing use for you here.'

'Sitting on the plain of Acre? Speaking and eating while others train?'

'Be less impetuous, Hazzim.'

'I cannot punish the Latins with my bare hands. I cannot go to war without a sword or spear.'

'Strength may rest in guile and cunning and wars depend on many fronts.'

'One front alone will see Qalawun at the head of his forces.'

'Am I at his side arrayed with armour and weapons?'

'Matters take you elsewhere. There is no mission for me.'

'Yet you have eyes to see and a head to think.' The voice was soft and persuasive.

'Watch the enemy outposts and settlements. Spy on their routines and weakness. Hold in your heart the belief that as your home was razed, so too will these places of iniquity be wiped from the earth.'

Hazzim would not fail his new masters. Qalawun made demands of him. No more was he the quiet boy who led a carefree life; no more did he respect the heathen or hold friends among their number. Hazzim had completed the crossing.

On a mud-baked field close by the walled encampment, Mongol horsemen charged their steeds back and forth in a brutal game of buzkashi. There were few rules and little restraint. With luck, a player might survive the savage intervention of opponents and run the gauntlet of their whips to gain possession of the headless carcass of a sheep; without it, he might die. There was no better way to harden fighters or rehearse the ancient arts of horsemanship and war. At any moment, the alarm might sound and the regiments be called. Day or night, the gers could be dismantled and their contents stowed aboard oxen carts rolling for a new horizon. So the women and children whistled and shouted and the men cursed and sweated and bled.

Attention drifted to a returning patrol and the clutch of strangers riding in their midst. The newcomers had arrived from the west and been carried by boat across the great dividing river. They were making for the grand central tent, its rounded sides protected by wattle slats and its importance signified by the command flags planted near its entrance. Whoever they were, these creatures were esteemed guests of the hierarchs. In the background, a buzkashi player was unseated from his mount. Dead or alive, the match continued at a furious pace.

Inside the imposing ger, Benedict studied the alien sights and tracked the light thrown by bronze lamps from the bright lacquerwork of the benches to the oculus gaping high above his head. There was the sweet smell of juniper and the sour stench from the fermented milk of mares, the aromas of dung and sweat and oiled saddle leather. Everything that made these tribespeople the feared Mongol lay in the horse. It was how the peoples of the late Genghis Khan survived and how they fought, how they manoeuvred and how they conquered.

Attended by a group of elders, a *Darughachi* entered dressed in a richly embroidered del coat and carrying an ornate whip. He gave no flicker of warmth or welcome. A local governor could not afford to lower his guard.

He seated himself and indicated his visitors should do the same. Beside him, the senior warrior who had been first to intercept their progress provided translation.

'You journey to offer or to beg?'

'To rekindle friendship and reforge alliance.' De Flor was courteous in reply. 'We bring you gifts as is custom for sworn brothers.'

'In return you seek our help.'

'Your Khan Arghun once pledged to us the might of the dark horde. Now is the moment it should ride.'

'We hear of how the Arab musters and how Qalawun sends his forces in attack.'

De Flor nodded. 'It is a time of menace in which all lands may be taken by our common foe.'

'What would you have us do?'

'Send your horse armies west across Syria and into Palestine. Divert the infidel Mameluks from their task and drive them back to Egypt.'

'Yet your own princes and the holy man in Rome refuse to grant you succour.' Appraising eyes rested behind heavy lids. 'Why is it we should commit to saving a city for which they do not care?'

'If Acre falls, the Sultan will be strengthened and his name glorified.'

'Let him enjoy the praise and titles.'

'That will fuel his ambition and direct his eye to territories new. If Qalawun has unfinished work with the Latins, he also has business with the Mongol.'

'You attempt to sow unease in our hearts.'

The adventurer held his gaze. 'I point out that once the Christians in Palestine are no more, a triumphant Mameluk will have only one true enemy remaining.'

'We are far from his cities and his grasp.'

'Dreams have no limit and conquest few boundaries.' De Flor was solemn. 'Did Alexander the Great rest when he had taken lands? Did the mighty Genghis decide to halt and graze his oxen?'

'The situation has changed.'

'The threat by Qalawun is ceaseless.'

The Mongol lord turned to confer in a low voice with his council. There appeared to be consensus. Benedict heard their muttered tones, remembering similar debate amongst the court of Acre. Power forever obliged men to talk behind their hands.

With no announcement, the governor turned again to his guests.

'Denied authority of a khan, we may not call for war or summon hither the clans. Your demand is refused.'

'Thus are the famed Mongols cowed and content to graze sheep and goats and pull a carcass about a field.'

'Beware it is not your corpse we toy with.' Anger flamed in the rigid countenance.

De Flor ignored the threat. 'Strike fast against Qalawun and you defend yourselves.'

'Your city is condemned and we will not squander our warriors for it.' The governor beckoned to a guard. 'Yet you bring gold and come in faith. For it, we shall repay in kind.'

A portal was opened and a small and wiry figure ushered in. He was a prisoner, a Buddhist monk with shaven head and attired in saffron robes, a watchful creature light on his feet and entirely composed.

De Flor hesitated. 'You offer to us a jester? A sorcerer? A priest?'

'He is a Chin, a wise and learned man taken by the forces of Kubla Khan near his home of Shaolin.'

'William of Beaujeu will be surprised.'

'I have no doubt. For this captive is versed in magic and martial practice. He is a master of *Chu'an Fa*, the fighting arts, will confront a regiment with his hands and feet alone. We believe him a demon.'

'Has this demon other skills?'

'A talent to conjure flame and thunder from a gourd of blackest powder.'

'Then he at least will entertain our court as the walls of Acre fall.'

Heading back for the river to rendezvous with the bandits, the group was silent. Their arduous trek had been for nothing. Riding alongside, the Shaolin monk sat calmly astride a horse. He showed no regret or fear in his abrupt change of circumstance.

'What is the meaning to these events?' Benedict looked enquiringly at de Flor.

The adventurer sniffed. 'No meaning, but that Acre is lost.'

~

With the crash of cymbals and to the clarion-blast of trumpets, the vast army of Egypt began to march. It was a pageant without compare. As Qalawun and his son al-Ashraf took the salute, their forces tramped past in armoured array and flowed into the desert. Behind them was Cairo and before them the Sinai. They had been imbued with holy zeal. Now they would be sent to do the bidding of Islam. From North Africa and the Levant and from every quarter of Araby, their brothers would unite to expel the heathen Crusader. The fourth of November 1290. It was an auspicious occasion.

Crowds had flocked from the city both to bear witness and to voice their support. They marvelled at the spectacle, applauding the pennants and standards and crying out joyously as the catapults and mangonels rumbled by. Each of the siege engines bore a name. Furious, Victory, Revenge, Executioner. And each had scrawled upon its frame a line of sacred text. It would serve to remind all why war was declared and what the inhabitants of Acre would soon endure. There would be no deflection from the task and no sparing of a single heathen life.

A slave fell and was crushed beneath the travelling wheels of an ordnance wagon. No one stopped to aid the man or drag the body free. The crimson smear was quickly dispersed. Through the fanfares and the fervent shouts of thousands, the crack of whips and bellow of oxen and the groaning protest of over-laden carts sounded faint. This was an unstoppable momentum.

✝

†

Chapter 11

Winter set in and the expedition stalled. Some five miles from Cairo, at a place known as Marjat at-Tin, the aged Qalawun was brought low by sickness and shortly after died. Malaria or the flux, none knew the cause. Yet even as the body of the ruler was borne to the Citadel and interred in its gilded mausoleum, his son Ashraf was assuming control. Succession could be a bewildering and bloody affair and the new ruler had acted swiftly to contain the threat. Scores of officers and courtiers had been arrested, many of them sent to the torturer before meeting their varied and agonised ends in crocodile pools or the cages of Egyptian cobras. There could be no doubting who was in command.

Others too believed that a sudden change in leadership afforded hope and opportunity for reprieve. From behind the cover of a mosaic screen, Ashraf observed the envoys sent by the infidel Christians of Acre. They had come to sue for peace. How little they understood. Perhaps they would have kept their distance had they known of his pledge to a dying father to finish what had been started. He had promised to slay every living Frank and to prove himself a worthy son to the fabled father he revered. Qalawun had never doubted his ability.

He peered closer at the four Europeans gathered in the anteroom. A Templar and Hospitaller, a scholar and a scribe, a quartet of fools not long for this world. Their very presence testified to the weakness of their masters. His spies had informed him of the absence of reinforcements and the paltry trickle of knights assembled by the military orders and the city fathers. Even at this late hour, few Latins wished to commit or sacrifice their lives in the rescue of their jewel of Outremer. It existed for the taking. He could afford to wait, to let the winter pass and the Crusaders sweat. Storms would be breaking across the Bay of Acre and swells of over forty feet sent crashing against the seaward walls of the Temple. They had good cause to cower and pray. It was already February 1291, the year in which Acre would vanish and a month before he renewed the campaign. The Frankish ambassadors would provide diversion and sport for a Mameluk.

~

Under sullen skies, Benedict trudged his way from the gates of Acre. Both he and the city seemed changed, the rhythms and charm of everyday life gone. Heaviness and dread sat everywhere. It showed in the strained faces of knights and citizens, in the ceaseless patrolling by squadrons of horse, in the skeletal outlines of catapults erected on the towers. War was imminent. Yet Benedict thought only of Hazzim and the beautiful girl Leila. It was why he was crossing the short miles across the plain to a village that existed no more; it was why he carried food for his friend and why he dragged his feet with the shame of complicity. His kind had casually spilt the blood of innocents, of comrades, of his surrogate family.

He paused at the sight of the palms, their fronds stripped away and their trunks blackened and shrunk by fire. Theobald of Alzey had warned him against venturing near the place, but he had ignored him. He had to come to see for himself that the rumours were no lie, to bear witness and to atone. Grief welled solid in his throat and forced out a guttural sob. He had endured privation and danger, he had been imprisoned and rescued, he had encountered serpent, brigand and Mongol, but these experiences paled against the horror of the present. This was the end of his childhood, here where Leila and her family were butchered and their village razed. And Benedict, who had once cherished them as his own, had abandoned them to the knives of the Italians.

Suddenly weak, he dropped to his knees and bowed his head in supplication. He was not sure for what to pray or from whom to ask forgiveness, it was simply a reflex. He had dreamt of returning to Acre, of a shy Arab girl with retiring eyes and silken smile, but savagery had visited in his absence. There was no reason and no God that would have permitted destruction of this kind. Benedict clenched his eyes and fists tight shut and repeated a Latin psalm the Patriarch had taught him. It brought scant comfort.

For a while he wandered, remote in his own anguish. Here were the displaced stones and crumbled adobe, the shredded rags of what had once been clothing, the scorched ruin where there had been life; here too was silence. His memories were choked off by what he saw.

'You have come to gloat?'

There was a hardness in Hazzim's voice that abruptly halted Benedict. He stared at his friend.

He stammered an answer. 'I bring you food.'

'We once grew our own.'

'There are things you may want.'

'As recompense? As alms to an orphan?' Bitterness swelled.

'It is what any brother would do.'

'I have no brothers remaining, nor sisters nor cousins nor father nor mother.'

'I grieve for it and my heart breaks.' Benedict heard the timid earnestness of his words and watched the jaw of Hazzim tighten. 'I know of the grim deeds of the Italians.'

'Then you will know too that they showed no mercy. They raped and killed and left the dead unburied.'

'We are still brothers, Hazzim.'

'Never speak such blasphemy again. Never bring me your treacherous gifts.' Hazzim's delivery was cold and his body rigid. 'We are enemies by blood and birthright.'

'I love you as I loved your family.'

'See where my family now lies, infidel.'

Benedict faltered. He deserved the condemnation. It was his punishment for betraying the people whose existence he had shared. The loss and misery clung to him. He wanted to step forwards and embrace his friend, to lend support and beg absolution, to be again the confidant and companion who ran in the fields and tasted the fiery eau de vie. Instead, he was just another Unbeliever.

Hazzim, the stranger, tilted his head. 'Should you trespass once more on these lands, you will suffer the fate of any foe.'

'Does our past mean nothing?'

'Truth matters more. The truth that we may never live in peace with the Christian invader. The truth that the murderous Franks will lose their kingdom and soon will be gone.'

'Ships will arrive and soldiers with them.'

The laugh of the Arab boy was short. 'They are no match for the armies of the sultan. From every quarter he draws the followers of the Faith to send into battle against your walls. Not a stone of Acre will be left to stand.'

'You are wrong.'

'Will de Flor save you? Or your Patriarch or William of Beaujeu? Or his highness Amalric in all his fine robes?'

'Once you thought us your friends.'

'It led to the grave and to my eyes becoming open.'

Benedict shook his head. 'What of Theobald of Alzey? What of his Hospitallers who offered you sanctuary from the raging mob?'

'They fear the Mameluk as you should fear.'

'Would your father have wanted enmity between us? Would Leila have smiled upon our distance?'

'Enough, Ben.' Pain had entered Hazzim's eyes. He spoke as if his throat was constricted. 'Spada did this. Spada has turned our kinship to dust. Spada is the true face of your kind.'

'You believe this?'

'Look about you and tell me I am imagining it.'

They faced each other in a charged and awkward stand-off, tears beginning to flow down both their faces. Benedict wanted to console and plead his case with the ferocity of the wronged, but he was ill equipped for advocacy and Hazzim was a brother too estranged. The Arab boy had been transformed; no one would ever reach him now.

Yet Benedict tried. 'I will find you justice, brother.'

'Justice and judgement are gained by the sword.'

'With more innocents dead? With more pyres and headstones?'

'Do you not comprehend, infidel?' A chilly self-control had returned to Hazzim. 'Not one innocent dwells among the Christians. You have the blood of my people on your hands.'

The Latin boy opened his palm. 'I see no blood. I see only the hand that took yours in friendship, that helped you over walls and pulled you laughing to the roofs of buildings.'

'Laughter is ended.'

So too was the meeting. Benedict unslung the canvas bag of provisions and dropped it at Hazzim's feet. It seemed an unworthy gesture, but it gave him excuse for retreat.

Hazzim stood, a clan chief among the ruins. 'Return to Acre, infidel. Tell them you have witnessed your own future.'

As he left, Benedict glanced back only once. The Arab continued to watch him, a tall boy unyielding. It would be futile to raise an arm to bid farewell. He turned quickly away lest Hazzim should see his weakness. In his ears was the silence that had travelled with him and in his head the words: '*Spada did this. Spada has turned our kinship to dust. Spada is the true face of your kind.*' He hunched his shoulders and walked on.

'A giant I wager will bring all others low.'

With mock solemnity, the dwarf Amethyst bowed low and doffed his cap to Roger de Flor as the adventurer pulled a leather coif tight upon his head. A grand melee had been declared and the Frank was not about to absent himself from the fray. It was a serious matter, an opportunity to win acclaim and show prowess, to garner booty and hone fighting skills. Through seizing as a hostage a wealthy knight in tournament combat, a high ransom could be earned and de Flor was keen to profit. He was not high born, but his enterprise and adeptness with the sword had won him a place in the promised entertainment. The coming war was a natural leveller.

He donned a hood of chain mail and squinted at the dwarf. 'Who should be my target, dwarf?'

'Those who are richest or have recently come to Acre.' Amethyst twinkled with the gleam of conspiracy. 'They have much to prove and most to lose.'

'And fewer allies to rush to their side.'

'They come to Palestine for war and you no doubt will provide.'

'That I shall.' The adventurer was pulling mail mittens over his gloved hands and flexing his fingers inside. 'Name the unfortunates I shall be hunting.'

'They say the Swiss knight Otto of Grandson is one to bring down. He is wealthy and respected.'

'Can he skirmish?'

'I hear he is unmatched with the lance.'

'Then it is just as well we are confined to the sword and mace, the cudgel and hammer.' De Flor gazed about him in anticipation. 'On the field, each of us is as noble or low born as the next. Who else deserves my favour?'

'Christopher of Lona, an Englishman, has been sent out by his sovereign.'

'How generous of King Edward to direct payment straight to my coffers.'

Amethyst chortled. 'You boast, de Flor.'

'Would that I did. It is their helmets that will be dented and names and honour bruised.'

'I trust it is so, de Flor.'

'Depend on it, dwarf.'

'You return to Acre and already the peace is shattered.'

'Such is the nature of a brute and a brawler and a cheat.' De Flor was fully dressed for combat, the chausses armouring his thighs and espaliers fitted on his shoulders.

The dwarf clambered on to a low wall and stood to review the enveloping scene. It might have been a pageant instead of a precursor to a feat of arms. There were strutting squires and scurrying cadets, the humanity of the city mingling among colourful tents and awaiting the start of battle. Caparisoned horses neighed and stamped fretfully as grooms checked their harnesses and fitted war saddles; heralds carried messages between ladies and champions; knights splashed their faces from water butts and drank wine and talked in low voices of tactics and threat. Death and serious injury were abiding hazards of these events.

'They do not know what they face in you, de Flor.' William of Beaujeu had wandered understated and white-mantled to their side. 'I can already sense the calculation in your countenance.'

'Who am I to escape your scrutiny, your grace?'

'I will not ask you to play fair or by any written law. It is each man for himself and according to his skill.'

'Your blessing honours me.'

'It is not a blessing, de Flor. It is the mere acceptance of a certainty. So I have instructed our more pliant friends to guard your flank and add weight to your charge.'

'A Grand Master resorts to such devious device.' There was no surprise in the voice of de Flor.

'Would I be a Grand Master without sly ruse and clever practice?' The Templar remained unruffled. 'You will earn a prize and the Temple will benefit. As you revel in bringing to earth the mighty and the vain, so shall we give praise to God and thanks for His reward.'

'Ever the priest and the banker, your grace.'

'All is in the service of the Lord and our order. The Mongol will not come to our aid and the new Sultan of Egypt is as committed as his father to our destruction. If Acre is to be saved, the Knights Templar will provide.'

'What of diplomacy?'

'A dream. A tableau. A dance without meaning.' Beaujeu nodded to a passing notable. 'Acre can muster some four-teen thousand drafted men. Ashraf will bring against us over sixty thousand warriors.'

De Flor pointed to a band of longbowmen. 'We have archers from England.'

'We also have royal troops from Cyprus and a breeze

from the Mediterranean. They will not hold back the enemy.'

'It is an unwelcome prospect.'

'It is the very prospect that causes Amalric the Constable to weep and panic. He is even demanding the release of all prisoners for military duty.'

'Will that include the Italians?'

Beaujeu studied the middle distance. 'We have agreed to loose our captives and the Hospitallers theirs. Spada and his peasants will soon be freed.'

'Then Acre is truly burdened.'

A trumpet sounded the call to mount up and take to the field. Almost two hundred souls had volunteered for the fight. They were brave men. As they crossed themselves and kissed their swords, heaved themselves from stepping blocks to sit astride their mounts, their servants clustered in attendance. Shields were gripped and steel helms placed and weapons lifted in salute. It was a moment of tension and plumed display and wheeling for advantage.

Another call and the melee began. Knights circled to cut weaker brethren from the throng, the whole mass splintering into a myriad chasing encounters. Swords and maces rose and fell with a clattering impact, the effort feverish and the results brutal. Within the armoured vortex, de Flor cantered his steed in a leisurely circuit. He had found his mark.

Pausing to check to his side and rear, he leant forwards on his pommel and plunged into a thicket of Franks. His adversaries appeared off-guard. They had intended to be the aggressors, an elite and marauding pack rather than the hunted. It left them unprepared for the rushing and ferocious dervish intruding in their midst. Battering his way through, his horse foaming at the mouth, its leather poitrels taut, the adventurer reached his first objective. The man put up a valiant defence, jockeying to escape capture and land a blow and locking blades to drive away incursion. He was quickly overpowered, de Flor shouldering him from balance and curling an arm about his waist to wrench him from the saddle. The knight struggled and was coshed into submission, the body hanging passive and carried off as trophy. One down and so many more to go. Behind them, an accomplice of de Flor seized the reins of the riderless horse as his colleagues crushed a furious counterstrike. Otto of Grandson had been removed from the field. He would fetch a handsome price when the sensitive business of ransom was discussed.

De Flor was already sallying to a fresh skirmish over at the site where Christopher of Lona fought against a trio of Pisans. The Englishman refused to yield to those he considered his inferiors and was taking a beating for his stubbornness. After all, he had won his spurs and the admiration of his king in oppressing the wild and loathsome Scots. Today, both he and his opponents were confounded by the galloping cavalry line that enclosed and unseated them. Further points and monies won.

Through the sallow haze of dust, bodies tumbled and horses raced liberated of their cargo. Knightly ways had come down to earth, men clawing and scuffling in anthill tumult without dignity or swords. In one corner, a victim was assailed with a heavy shield; in another, two men slugged bloodily at each other until they fell together and unconscious. It delighted the crowd.

'Our miscreant adventurer sweeps all before him, your grace.' Amethyst performed a congratulatory flip on his wall.

The grand master continued to watch the tournament. 'Enjoy it while you may. The next time we hear such din, it will be the rasp of heathen scimitar on Christian longsword.'

The grand melee was done and its participants were carried

or limped away themselves. Wounds would be bound and oil of clove applied to broken teeth, steel reforged and chain mail repaired. None had forgotten the day was practice and pretence.

Five months of incarceration had not cowed Spada or curbed his tongue. In the dungeon beneath the Hospitaller compound, the Umbrian had sat out the autumn and winter with the peasant doggedness of his kind. He was still the undisputed chief and would one day be released. It helped that the Constable of Acre had forbidden any mass exodus from the city, helped too that his defending forces were small and the Mameluks threatened. If not a pardon for the prisoners, at least there would be a welcome.

'Our fair and perfect knight returns.' Spada called out to the approaching Theobald. 'What has kept our pretty maid from these parts?'

The young Hospitaller was cool in his response. 'There are wounds to tend and limbs to set. The grand melee caused many hurts.'

'Now he comes to Spada with his kindness.'

'By command of the Grand Master, you and your men are to be released.'

'Such soft and sweet words.'

'You are bound for training immediately. You will be equipped for war and posted to the ramparts. Emergency is come. Now will you see the face of the enemy.'

Spada sat back in the straw and gazed amused at the messenger. 'Hostility remains in your eye and distance in your voice.'

'I obey my orders according to my vow.'

'Then delight for me, child. For we henceforth are comrades in arms.'

'Your cropped ears suggest you are little more than a thief.'

'It is not the full measure of me.' A dark warning had crept into his voice.

Theobald ignored it. 'A man will earn respect by his bearing and his deeds.'

'Spada wins repute through the violence of his ways.' The Italian raised a manacled hand. 'Break me from my bindings and I will show you how I lead.'

With a sharp whistle, the Hospitaller summoned the waiting prison blacksmith. There was a deft technique in removing a captive from his chains without injuring the man. It took several blows and the straining twist of pliers to free him.

Slowly, the peasant rose, shaking his limbs and easing circulation back into his dormant frame. Acclimatisation would not take him long. His natural aggression and the perverse charisma of his inner certainty ensured he was already back in charge.

He breathed deeply and exhaled with ironic satisfaction. 'I like to remember where I have been, knight.'

'Never forget from whence you come.'

Spada peered at the young man. 'We all reach for the light, do we not?'

'Some dwell more content in darkness.'

'Acre needs what I and my people bring. Not the preening vanity of nobles. Nor the feeble timidity of merchants and traders. But the iron and sinew of devout and simple peasants.'

'Then direct your devotion to our defence.'

They emerged through the gateway to an ecstatic reception from the Italians gathered there. Spada acknowledged their joy with a clenched fist raised and the defiance of the wronged. He was a martyr and a hero, a seer and a saint. He had cleansed the city of Saracens who so clearly wished them ill. Old rivalries could be discarded and common cause discovered. The Mameluk threatened and Spada and his army offered hope.

Not everyone was convinced. In a burst of sudden fury, a boy with a knife darted low from the crowd. He was too quick to catch, but Theobald of Alzey was as well trained as a soldier. His foot caught the youngster hard on the shin, his punch knocking the travelling aim wide of its mark. But rage and momentum carried Benedict on. He slashed with the blade and Spada screeched, his hands clamped to a face that was leaking blood. His peons lunged for the boy, but he was hauled beyond their reach.

His clothing spattered and his beard glistening red, Spada glowered venomously at his foe. 'Any one of my followers would kill you for such insult.'

'I would gladly try a thousand times.' Benedict panted and trembled in the aftershock. 'You shall pay for your crimes.'

'As you will pay for yours.'

Theobald had drawn his sword. 'Redress is done and no further harm will be committed.'

'Do not swear by it, knight.' Spada motioned to his men to step forwards.

They were intercepted by Hospitallers, a disciplined troop presenting an armed and impervious wall. Behind, two sergeants held Benedict and prized the knife from his grasp.

'He should hang, Theo.' His face creased in rage and wretchedness, Benedict bucked against restraint. 'He murdered the villagers, the family of Hazzim. They were my friends, my cousins, my brothers and sisters. All are gone.'

'Would you create justice by committing a wrong?'

'It is not justice to set him loose. It is not justice to see his face unashamed on our streets.'

Theobald fixed the youngster with a steady eye. 'Be still, Ben. There are mysteries none of us may fathom.'

'What of my wound and its consequence? What of recompense?' Spada held a cloth to his gaping cheek to staunch the flow. 'Our matter here is unresolved.'

'Make sure it is through or I shall drag you back inside.'

'I am the injured.'

'So wear your wound and be on your way.' The young Hospitaller kept his sword raised. 'I have saved your life this day. I have no desire to take it.'

The Umbrian appraised the situation. 'You once pulled a Saracen boy to safety from our grasp. Again you interrupt us. There is no nobility in folly, knight.'

'As there is no purpose in your defiance and debate. Apply your labours to the rampart and avoid darkening the path of our order.'

There was little point in extending the confrontation and more to be gained from tapping the rough exuberance of the celebrating throng. The Hospitallers could keep to their prayers and rigid ways within the confines of their brotherhood. Spada enjoyed a wider constituency of support.

He glanced at Theobald and then to the youngster. 'I shall choose when and where.'

The peasant leader was wrong, of course. From here on, it was the Sultan of Egypt who would dictate events.

~

Diplomacy was stuck fast in the sand. Buried to their necks and viewed from the surrounding elevation by the sultan and his court, the four men sent from Acre were in no position to negotiate. They had once enjoyed the respect of their fellow Unbelievers, not that that counted much any more. There was Bartholomew Pisan, the Templar knight, the

Hospitaller grandee Henri of Falletans, the noted scholar Philip Mainboeuf, and a secretary to complete their number. They were arrayed in a neat row facing to the east, awaiting an unknown fate. To inform them would be to ruin the sport.

Ashraf listened to their prayers and mutterings and studied the blank terror of their eyes. Such a setting would test the faith of any man. They had been naive to come, but the Christians had always been reckless and foolhardy and on alien terrain they were completely at a loss. Even with their heads poking from the ground and the moments counting down to certain death, they appeared perplexed by the sequence of events. Most of them wept.

The sultan felt the sharp tug of emotion, the recent memory of having stood beside his father to observe a pair of Nubians wrestling on the site. Power had passed and conditions had changed. Today, there would be no survivors of the show.

'My Sultan.' An officer bowed and was rewarded with a neutral stare. 'As commanded, I bring you news from the camp.'

'We are ready?'

'From general to common foot soldier, each awaits your orders and your presence at our head.'

'They shall not wait long. Take word I will join them on the morrow and complete the sacred task my father set.'

'It is an honour to serve both his memory and yourself, my Sultan.'

'While it is our duty to bring the infidels low.' Ashraf indicated the scene below. 'Stay and witness how the foreign usurpers are dealt with.'

Obediently the officer assumed his station. In the stillness of expectation, the plaintive groans and Latin phrases filtered louder from the prisoners and were joined by other faint and discordant sounds.

Imagination was a terrible thing. The captives were yelling before they caught glimpse of the wild dogs, writhing to escape as the ravenous and feral pack descended through the opening. Evolution had honed the instincts of the canines; starvation compelled them to follow a scent. They did not pause in their advance. In snarling fury they slunk in fast, powerful jaws tearing at faces and clamping on skulls. Heads were demolished and the pieces snatched, the ragged morsels consumed in a running bout of tag and fight. Finders were not necessarily keepers. Later, the creatures would be whipped away, but for the while could enjoy their prize. The sultan was content. A key rule of parley was to judge when to walk away.

On 6 March 1291, Sultan Ashraf, favoured son of the late Qalawun, led his forces out of Egypt.

✝

Chapter 12

'It is time, *Waladii*.'
And Benedict knew it to be true. He had rehearsed in his mind a hundred times the departure of Selim, but no imagination could simulate the pain. In the misted half-light of dawn, the old Arab stood beside the tree that always acted as a way point to his journeying. It was here that he sat in conference and played his backgammon, from here that he would send word to the youngster the convoy was arrived. As regular in appearing as the seasons and as constant as the waves, Selim and his camels would trek to Acre. No more. The coming war had displaced trade and the nomad and his drivers were moving on.

He held the boy by his shoulders and gently kissed his cheek and forehead. 'Like a son, you will stay in my heart.'

'Will we again meet, *Amm* Selim?'

'God willing, we shall.' The old man patted his face. 'I took you to Damascus and was later there to bring you home. You will ever be my little nephew, my laughing Frank, my *Waladii*.'

'As you forever will be my Selim.'

'Tell Flor *effendi* I entrust to his charge this precious thing named Benedict and will hold him to account should he lose or let harm befall it.'

'I will take care of myself, *Amm* Selim.'

'Even a boy with courage and wiles is not immune to fate.'

'We have ditches and walls and Hospitallers and Templars.'

'Whilst the Mameluk has siege engines and an army tens of thousands strong. Rumour burns everywhere that Ashraf departs Egypt and sends his harem to Damascus. It will not be long before his banners emerge from the horizon.'

'He will be greeted with steel and fire.'

'What he will wreak on the Latins will be worse. It is no place for a boy.'

Benedict was stung. 'Have I not crossed deserts and encountered danger? Have I not met the Mongol?'

'You have not faced war.'

'I will show strength and courage, *Amm* Selim.'

'That you live is my only wish.' The camel master tightened his grip on an arm. 'Did I not once warn you there would one day be dark choice between Frank and Arab, between life and death?'

'You also told of choice between being a boy and becoming a man.'

'No man should look forward to slaughter, *Waladii*.'

'Is this why you flee?'

His own harshness took Benedict by surprise. He regretted it in the instant, but would fumble in apology. Selim understood. A modest outburst was permitted. He nodded at the youngster, his presence commanding and his face still shaded by the darkness.

'My duty is to my men and camels, *Waladii*. I must go where the trade takes me, head for regions untouched by hint of combat.' He reached and plucked up his camel whip that jutted from the ground. 'In caution there is wisdom rather than dishonour.'

'Caution is gone, *Amm* Selim. All are committed to the fight.'

'I grieve for it. A camel spider may fight a scorpion and Selim will not step close. There is still a chance for you. Walk from here at my side.'

The offer was made, but the answer was already known. Silence was an eloquent reply. Benedict had been born and raised in Acre, had grown to love its very stones. Whatever its stench, its politics and depravity, it served as his refuge and his home. He was no wanderer like Selim or rootless adventurer like de Flor; he was a boy whose being was forged in the streets and on the rooftops of the last great Crusader enclave. If its ending meant his own, he would stand fast to greet it.

Finally, he spoke. 'My name is scored on a pillar in the great hall of the Hospitallers, *Amm* Selim.'

'Neither they nor the city own you.'

'Yet I own part of them.'

'Such insight from one so young.' The voice of the camel master seemed gritted with rare emotion. 'Do you betray me or I you, *Waladii*?'

'We could never betray the other.'

'That is so.'

They embraced and Benedict broke free and ran. There was nothing more to be said. The youngster had lost Hazzim and now Selim was leaving. It felt like the stripping away of his skin and the layers that had made him whole.

In a dark recess he found seclusion and sat with his head in his hands. He had no desire to talk or think or recall, no impulse to witness Selim's departure and compound his anguish. He was a Frank and that was how it was intended. This was his decision, his tribe, his future. Let the Mohammedans keep to their own and may God prevent them drawing near.

Somewhere out on the plain, a long trading caravan snaked away into the flickering sunrise. Selim was gone.

*

Roger de Flor was also engaged in preparations for departure. His commitment was of a different nature, his exertions loud and actions directed as he pumped his hips between the straining thighs of a willing lady. There was no more conducive way to conduct a transaction. He could drive a hard bargain with sweet promise and the urgent thrust of his pelvis. Not that she complained as she lay shuddering and moaning and lost to rapture. She would forgive anything and forget all for the sake of this young adventurer taking her for himself.

'You are a brute and a knave.'

'And you a harlot.' He kissed her deep and gave her air to squeal. 'Yet I honour you as a queen.'

'A queen would have your head.'

'As you have mine.'

'Is this honour? Respect? Dignity?' Her words issued in short gasps.

'There is no finer means to show regard.'

'I am a mere sacrifice to your appetites, a woman fallen in your path.'

'Fortunate then that you fall upon your back.' He nipped at her neck and felt the panting laughter and the belly rise and the give and take beneath him.

'You will discard me as with other women.'

'Never, my pretty, my lady, my countess, my desire.' He rocked her back and slid in with reply, his lips butterfly-flitting across her. 'You shall come with me.'

Her fingernails scored him. 'Do I not always?'

With renewed vigour they grappled and writhed, their noise descending to the inelegant grunt of the rut. He was on top and opening the bid.

Carefully, he eased the pace, caressed her hair, her cheek, her mouth. 'These minutes may see our last embrace.'

'Swear it is not so, my lord,' she sighed.

'In the same breath, you would dub me a knave.'

'I have no breath.'

'You have your reason and hearing. War is with us and we may die. In weeks or days the Sultan and his armies will breach our walls and show no mercy.'

'There is still salvation in your arms.'

'Greater safety lies at sea. I command a Templar galley. I have a loyal crew and room aboard for those who favour me with pay.'

'What price for me?' Her eyes stared glistening to the ceiling.

'Half the contents of your treasure chest. Your husband will be butchered by the Mameluk. Yet you will live, will be carried beyond the arrow and shot, will be at my side and in my bed.'

'Such heartlessness and calculation.' Her protest was contrived and stifled with a further kiss.

'Would you prefer enslavement by the Saracen or being left to dwell among the slain? Do you want to see your gold snatched by the heathen and carried off to Egypt?'

'Persuade me with your counsel.'

'As you demand, my lady.'

He applied himself with ruthless energy, ever focused and always willing, feeling his way as her back arced and her body trembled. She was no innocent, she knew his purpose was to transport her to another place for a fee. And so the exercise proceeded to plan.

~

Running errands allowed Benedict to fill the hollowness left by the departure of Selim. There were windlasses to turn and handcarts to manoeuvre, messages to bear and countless duties to perform. On occasions he still sat with the old Patriarch to play their customary game of chess. Or he would pause in his hurrying to glimpse the refugees tramping in from outlying villages to seek the protection of the walls and the Druze soldiers with their shaven heads and black pantaloons arriving to proffer their service. Everyone seemed on the move.

This day in March 1291 was as any other. More rumour and half-truth, more drilling of the troops, more anxious scrutiny of the far-flung skyline. Pressure was building within the city and the patrols and lookouts had been doubled in number. No one knew what to expect and yet every citizen knew Ashraf was close. It was in the air, in the stench of the alleyways that thickened with the heat and served as augury of things to come. A lot of prayer was said.

The youngster still maintained his stoic cheer. Part of him was contemptuous of the fear in others as he attempted to suppress it in himself. If his earlier mission had offered adventure, surely much more would be found in the battle ahead. At Hattin, Saladin had annihilated the Christian forces and moved to take Jerusalem; at Acre, the Sultan Ashraf would attempt to end the story of the Crusade. Only fourteen years old, offspring of a deceased whore and a long-forgotten mercenary, Benedict had privileged vantage. He would not squander the moment.

He was happy to accompany the mute Shaolin monk, intrigued by the calm and birdlike qualities of the man dressed in saffron robes. There was no one else of his kind in all of Christendom, and people crossed themselves and stared as they passed. The youngster was proud to explain that the Chin visitor beside him was no less than a warrior-mystic sent as a gift from the Mongols. Perhaps they did not believe him. Yet there were more pressing concerns, the gathering of wood for charcoal and the collection of sulphur and saltpetre. On the roof of a tower in the Lion Fortress and with the blessing of William of Beaujeu, the monk had established his temporary home and workshop. It was here that he was creating his black powder, the stuff of myth and secret of the emperors, and with lightning flash and roll of thunder conjured explosion in the air. The Templar grand master favoured any such trickery in his struggle against the heathens, and Benedict had found himself fresh employment.

They were close by the eastern wall and loading a barrow for transportation to the Temple when the monk paused. He held up his hand to silence query. There was trouble. Spada and his men had intruded on their day.

The Umbrian grinned, the malice carried in his bonhomie. 'Why, it is my little Benedict. What fortune we should meet.'

A sutured wound was slashed vivid across the face of the peasant chief, a totem of matters to be resolved. Benedict waited, aware of the numbness creeping in his spine and the tightness in his belly. The Italians came armed with cudgels and knives. He would not yield. He was determined to acquit himself with ferocity and honour. They might laugh, dismiss him as a child, consider him easy prey for a band that sought revenge. Their instincts were flawed.

'Are you frightened, boy?'

'Never.'

'Your trembling speaks otherwise.' Spada waited for the ingratiating laughter of his troop to subside. 'You know why we accost you and what we intend to do?'

'Discourse and parley.' The youngster spoke without conviction.

Spada scarcely moved. 'That is not our way. We parade to offer respect to one who will shortly die.'

'I am engaged in business of my own.'

'It can wait.' The eyes flitted briefly to the Chinese monk and back. 'I see no presence of de Flor or the young Hospitaller. I detect no patrol or knight hastening to your defence.'

'William of Beaujeu will not stand idle or suffer a wrong.'

'It is our luck, then, that the Grand Master is elsewhere.'

Benedict's insides shrank. 'Did not Theobald command you to the ramparts?'

'And did I not threaten my return?' Spada touched the scarring on his cheek. 'It is my own command that I follow. You attempted murder and I shall complete it.'

The youngster backed behind his barrow and reached slowly for his knife. 'Step close and you will suffer.'

Mirth rippled through the group as it spread wide to encircle. This child might be beloved of the city, but he had made a fool of Spada. It was an ill-advised move.

The Umbrian leered, basking in his moment. 'You have the heart of a young and cornered cub. Put up your blade.'

'Call back your men.'

'They are too committed in their task.' Spada nodded a wordless order and tutted to the boy. 'Such a pity to snap your neck and stamp your head to a thousand pieces.'

'I shall make this dagger count.' Benedict pointed the blade, fought the dryness in his mouth and the paralysis of his feet.

'We have already practised on the heathens and will butcher you clean.'

'Then have at me and we shall see.'

Spada spat on the ground. 'At least your monk will perform his pagan rites above your broken corpse.'

He had misjudged the holy man. While the attention of the Italians was diverted, the visitor from Shaolin had extracted twin sticks from the barrow. He now loitered unobtrusively forwards of the youngster. Rough and uneducated peasants as they were, these peasants were unlikely to have heard of *Ch'uan Fa* and the Eighteen Hands of Lohan, would never have encountered a master of the ancient oriental fighting arts.

Their induction was swift and unexpected. Before they had chance to deliver a blow, the Shaolin monk had sprung among them with a blurred welter of kicks and strikes. Men did not simply crumple. They were projected, catapulting in broken array, their bodies impacting in a scattered tangle of splintered teeth and joints. A confident force had been blunted by one more powerful.

Enraged and disbelieving, Spada glanced at the extravagant carnage and turned for reinforcements. Those left standing were escaping for their lives. He saw the boy standing astonished and unharmed and the monk poised taut and ready with his sticks. Beside him, the pained groans of his men amplified in his ear. The tactical situation had changed.

'I pledged we would finish things.' He unsheathed his short-sword and held it low. 'And we shall.'

His charge was ferocious, his rampaging stride accompanied by a bellowed roar. Few could have withstood the attack. Yet his blow failed to land, his progress intercepted by a circling kick that propelled him straight into a wall. His nose left a blood and mucus trail as he slid unconscious to the earth. Silently, the Shaolin monk replaced his improvised weapons, grasped the barrow poles and lifted them for onward journey. At his side, picking his way among the injured and still bewildered, Benedict joined the exodus. The peasant leader would not be waking for a while.

'How many vigils remain for us? How many dawns are left for us to greet?'

As rivals they had lived and as brothers they might yet find cause to die. Around the rough-hewn table, the three grand masters of the military orders sat, drawn together in these hours of darkness to break bread and to talk and pray. There was a chance to abandon past competition and rededicate themselves to the shared values of their warrior caste. William of Beaujeu contemplated his brother guests with cool benevolence. He was glad they had come. The Latin cross of the Knights Templar, the eight-pointed cross of the Hospitaller Knights of St John of Jerusalem, the German cross of the Teutonic Knights. This trio represented the mailed fist of Christendom. And Christendom needed them.

Conrad of Feuchtwangen chewed on a morsel of bread. 'My Teutons are ready for the Saracen, my brothers.'

'My Hospitallers also,' John of Villiers growled in accord.

'I have no doubt of it.' Beaujeu was gracious in reply. 'Each one of us guards not merely Acre and the remnants of Outremer, but the survival and soul of his order.'

Villiers nodded. 'You speak with bleak honesty, brother. It may prove our finest hour or our last.'

'Or both.'

'As a pious knight, I welcome death in battle. As Grand Master of the Hospital, I fear for my loyal brethren and successors.'

'Let us first await the course of war.'

Conrad of Feuchtwangen tore off another piece of bread. 'Perhaps the day of the Crusader is gone. Perhaps we are the last of our kind, ghosts who once donned hauberks and sallied forth against the heathen.'

'For the moment we live and that gives hope.' Beaujeu poured himself water from a pitcher. 'Our orders are powerful and rich. No king or prince of Europe has the authority or will to challenge us.'

The eyes of the Hospitaller narrowed. 'You think you are immune to the covetousness of men and the greed and jealousy of monarchs? You believe they do not eye with avarice your fifteen hundred French commanderies and estates and your treasure house in Paris?'

'In God we trust.'

They pondered in silence, allies thrown together by faith and common threat, leaders burdened by the present and the future. The magnitude of their troubles was almost too great to consider. If Acre was vanquished, pilgrimage and Crusade would end and the banking and commercial lifeblood of the military orders cease. They were nothing without their bastions in the East. There were sound commercial reasons to rehearse their knights and men-at-arms, to dig deep their moats and build high their walls and secure their compounds for the siege ahead.

John of Villiers gazed towards the darkened window. 'Even as we sit here, my men are evacuating in secret our sugar mills and estates on the plain.'

'It is a wise precaution.' Beaujeu did not smile at the news, though the withdrawal would strike the prosperity of the Hospitallers hard. He would never forget their studied silence as he was pilloried in the high court for sending emissaries to Cairo. 'Ashraf may raid your outposts at any moment.'

'Already the Arab workers flee, have deserted their station and daily toil in the cane. It is like an ebbing tide before the turn and forward rush.'

'We shall have it all safe within our walls before the Mameluk appears.'

'And you, brother?' Conrad of Feuchtwangen cast a long and sarcastic glance at the Templar. 'I hear you give shelter to a sorcerer, a strange monk of magic and devilish practice.'

'Are we not to look to any means in these forbidding times?'

Old suspicion flared briefly in the Teuton. 'Some might accuse you of witchcraft.'

'Others would embrace the word of a penitent brother soldier of Christ.'

'I count myself among them.' The grand master of the Teutons bowed his head in subtle capitulation.

Beaujeu reached and took his hand and that of the Hospitaller. 'My brothers. In equal measure, honour and trial befall and bind us. We are blessed with mounting the ramparts in defence of this city and yet cursed with the insight of our mortality and fate. Unlike the apostle Thomas, we cannot doubt. Unlike Peter, we cannot turn away.'

'We shall reach the Gates with our swords sharp and a psalm on our lips.' John of Villiers gripped the proffered hand in mutual resolve.

Feuchtwangen did the same. 'Each of us vying to outsing the other.'

The three smiled, comrades set apart from the citizens they protected and relied upon by a Constable of Acre whom they despised. Amalric was not worth the life of a single holy warrior. Yet the fellowship of arms and the sacred vow to protect all adherents to the faith determined how they acted. They would never turn their backs. A sly Templar grasped hands with a gruff Hospitaller and a chill Teuton. There were worse alliances.

Beaujeu rose and crossed to retrieve a small piece of black basalt mounted on a gilt plinth and displayed in a lacquered cabinet. He brought it to the table and set it down.

'Regard it well, my brothers. It is the very rock taken from among our fallen at Hattin and given as a token by Saladin to the Templar Grand Master Gerard of Ridefort.'

Villiers took and examined it. 'For what purpose?'

'As a memento and a warning. As a reminder of our fate should we stand with force against the Saracen.' Beaujeu rested his palms on the table edge. 'To the Knights Templar it is a symbol of battles to be yet fought.'

'Did Gerard of Ridefort not surrender?' The Teuton had to ask.

Beaujeu was steady in his gaze. 'None of us here this night enjoys such a choice.'

Faint to the ear across the city, a single bell was tolling. It was too early for Matins and beyond the hour-stroke to mark the change of any watch. A sentry had observed strange happenings outside the walls and had rushed to inform the Captain of the Guard. What pealed out was the alarm.

In abandoning their fortified plantations, the Hospitallers had employed both a mounted force and a ruse. The plain could be a dangerous place. By day, the eyes of Arab scouts would observe their activity and a roving formation could be quickly assembled to attack. There was no doubt that the agents of Ashraf and the forward elements of his army operated in these parts, but they would have seen nothing unusual as they counted the carts in and out and followed the plodding trains of mule. The grand master of the Hospital permitted himself a degree of satisfaction at the sight of each convoy rolling in, commended his men for the skilled evacuation of vats and condensers and the labourers who worked them. Even the buildings had been dismantled and their stones ferried back. The retreat was proceeding according to schedule.

Little else needed to be done. Only a skeleton guard remained and would be fetched tonight and delivered to Acre. Already, the four outlying stations were deserted and their garrison remnants gathered at the fifth. Wells had been spoilt with hemp, dead animals and bitter herbs and the remains of pigs and dogs strewn about to defile and deter. It was a pity to leave the walls intact, but there was reason to keep the enemy outside and guessing. From here, under the escort of Theobald of Alzey and his troop, the refugees would ride to safety. Moonlight alone would guide their path. Steady nerve and the presence of knights would hold the line.

His ash-blonde hair almost luminous in the gloom, Theobald addressed his following with calm assurance. 'At my command, you will douse your torches and take to the saddle. To my single word, you will depart these gates.'

'What if the heathen should attack?'

'Ride hard for the city.' The young Hospitaller surveyed his charges. 'We must hope that chaos in our ranks will sow confusion in their own.'

Nervous laughter eddied through the group. They had high regard for the cavalry of the foe and were accustomed to tales of barbarism and revenge. Not far distant on the plain lay the charred debris of a former Arab village. It served to remind them of the stakes and the merciless nature of any future armed encounter.

Theobald understood. 'We have the cloak of night about us and St John the Baptist at our side. In no time we shall cross safely to the St Anthony Gate.'

'I would prefer to make the journey without a Saracen spear at my back.' Men murmured in agreement.

'So let us make speed, brothers. We will retreat for the present from this corner of Palestine.'

In tight and silent formation, they exited the plantation, some sixty men travelling on terrain the Franks had once considered their own. No trumpet or signal fire accompanied the withdrawal, yet they were the last of the Crusaders, the stragglers at the finish of two hundred years returning to a threatened redoubt.

A whisper sounded harsh from among the travellers. 'To our left! A light appears!'

'Ignore it and proceed.'

'It is a trap! We are discovered!'

'Hold! Be steadfast and keep your silence! They cannot see us!'

Consternation rippled through the group, its pace gathering. Out in the deep shadow a lit firebrand waved, signalling and directing the enemy pursuit into the chase. The horse archers had come from Mount Tabor some forty miles distant, alerted by dispatch. It had been a hard ride, a rolling advance along the Jezreel Valley to loop north around the wooded slopes of Mount Carmel and on to the Plain of Acre. The communiqué had not lied. Before them, a mass of infidel were picked out in black by the bone-cold moonlight. No Saracen *razzia* would turn from such an offering. Its commander yelled the order and his battle line spread and hurried from trot to canter and pushed through to the headlong charge.

Theobald heard them. 'Now is your moment! Spare yourselves and race for your lives!'

His words were already lost in the torrent of shouts and oaths and the driving thud of hooves. Hunters and prey were in full cry. It was better to die than be captured, better still to dodge the feathered arrows coursing through the tumult and disintegration. In the centre of the chasing wave were the bowmen; to the flanks were the mounted auxiliaries armed with spears and tasked with corralling and shaping the fleeing formation and bringing down its laggards. A practised team, the raiders knew precisely what to do.

Alone within the keening uproar, Theobald of Alzey found serenity and offered up a quiet prayer. Close to the beginning of the century his grandfather Otto had come with hope to Palestine. Near to its end, his descendant was leading a hasty retreat before a marauding pack of heathen. Much could change in the short lifespan of men. He hoped the Crusades had not been in vain and all his labours wasted, that the Hospitallers would survive and Acre might yet stand. With renewed effort, he urged on his horse. God was unlikely to grant everything he demanded.

Away to the rear, Hazzim ground the burning torch in the dust and extinguished its flame. He listened to the receding echo of the fray and trusted in Allah the infidels would suffer. It was an honour to have played his part. The Christians might forfeit through this excursion a few of their number, but it was a foreshadowing of something greater. They would soon grow to appreciate they stood to lose the whole.

As the warning bell continued its solitary dirge, a figure slipped from the upper window of a dwelling in Acre and slithered discreetly to the ground. De Flor too was executing his escape. He was making good with aplomb the season lost to his absence and reacquainting himself with the pining ladies of the city.

He moved towards the harbour front where he would stow his evening's winnings aboard the galley he commanded. Some of the richest women of Acre had paid handsomely for a guaranteed berth on board and many more would follow. Fear could persuade where lovemaking alone would not. In the meantime there was a siege to be fought and his participation was demanded. He whistled a soft and casual tune and leapt on to the jetty. When the wind blew gentle off the sea and the vile stench subsided, the place acquired a rare and melancholic beauty. Tomorrow might bring him fresh gold or the Mameluks and a spear point through the heart. It was a balance of reward and risk that he relished.

~

Had it not been for the troops running for the walls, the constant peal of bells from all forty churches might have announced celebration instead of the onset of peril and pure dread. At this fateful hour, scarcely a man or woman or child did not wish to see the future that confronted them. Through the grey mist of dawn, the armies of Egypt and Syria converged, their size blanketing the landscape and their advance led by camel-borne kettledrummers some hundreds strong whose timpani beat shook the air.

On the ramparts, soldiers and citizens wept and embraced, prayed and vomited, crouched to empty bowels and bladders loosened by fear. None had ever witnessed an armed multitude so great. The hordes and drumbeat of hell, a few muttered. Most simply stared, dumbstruck and trembling. From the south and east, the ceaseless flow colonised the ground and crept forwards towards the city. With it came the siege engines, their shape unmistakeable and their purpose clear.

Garbed in vestments of cloth of gold and accompanied by the Constable and the knightly grand masters, the old Patriarch appeared on the summit of the Accursed Tower. Looking down upon his Christian flock, he raised high a gilded cross and addressed them in an unflinching voice.

'Jerusalem for us is lost, yet we as men are not. Our world might end, yet we of faith are saved. Lift up your eyes to heaven and sing out hymns of praise. For you are the sons of light, the army of Christ, the chosen at this appointed hour.

Ready yourselves and devote your heart and soul to battle. As God commanded Joshua, be strong and courageous. Neither fear nor be disheartened. The Lord be with you when you die. For if Christ suffered for us on Golgotha, we should now happily give sacrifice to him.'

He traced the air with his crucifix in sacred benediction. '*Hallelujah! Hallelujah! Hallelujah!*' they cried. It was 5 April, 1291. The siege of Acre had begun.

✝
Chapter 13

Day and night the mangonels and catapults worked, hurling stones against the walls or lofting wildfire pots high above the ramparts to burst within the city. Everywhere was din and all about the restless and dust-blown scene of war. There were moments when Acre seemed lost behind its pall, other times when the shroud slipped and the castellations were revealed defiant over the fury raging at their base. The Saracens were methodical in their approach. Earth berms had been thrown up to protect the siege machines and give cover to the miners and fire-troops who were already digging shafts to begin tunnelling beneath the Franks. Sultan Ashraf had directed a thousand engineers to each and every tower. From above ground and below, the city would be dismantled.

Benedict crouched as a volley of arrow darts ripped dense and swarming overhead. They were close enough to be audible with their strange passing sigh, close enough for the sweeping feathers on their tails to be seen, close enough to strike a pikeman in the chest. The youngster watched the man vault backwards to the triple blow. There was nothing to be done. He averted his eyes from the dead soldier and scurried on.

This was life on the edge of a parapet. In spite of the fear and the pressing threat, he had needed no persuading to run constant errands for Beaujeu. No knight in mail could duck and dodge as freely as he; no citizen in Acre could move with his speed to bear tidings or an urgent command. Not for him the meek cowering of the women and children or the bowl-shaped eyes of those mute and shaking in terror. He was a youngster who had stepped up to join the world of men.

The ramparts were softening and already littered with the debris and scorch marks of combat. Manning the northern wall of Montmusart, stretching its length to the strategic juncture of St Anthony's Gate, were the Templars and Hospitallers. At this nexus, atop the massive form of the King Henry Tower and in the King Hugh barbican to its fore were to be found the royal troops of Cyprus and the personal guard of Amalric. Here was the portal to the city where the defensive lines met, the point at which the Mameluks would concentrate their force. For that reason, the Teutonic Knights were stationed on the Accursed Tower behind to act as a reserve and last resort. It was critical the position held. Angling southward from it, facing east and reaching to the Bay of Acre, were the six hundred crenellated yards occupied by the French and English knights, the Venetians, the Pisans and the Commune of Acre. A total front measuring about half a mile and a route traced by a fourteen-year-old boy.

Screams erupted in a billow of blood and stone fragments. The casualties had been caught by a catapult strike. One man lay broken and disfigured; one stood dazed with an arm missing; one wept crimson between his fingers.

'For the love of Jesus, help me.'

'I must have water . . . I must have water.'

'I am dying. Pray for me now.'

Appalled, the youngster muttered Latin words he had learnt and pressed onward in his task. Others were at hand to aid the injured and clear the dead. His instruction was to keep moving to shuttle the decrees of the grand master along the powdering heights. He felt the naphtha flash of wildfire hot on his cheek, heard the torsion-thrown bolt from a *qams ziyar* slam near on the stonework, smelt and tasted the molten energy of the conflict. Ahead were barrels of vinegar and water and the troughs of sand, the pikes and poleaxes stationed ready to resist assault. Benedict weaved between the obstacles and darted low across the embrasures. Nothing would halt his progress. Not the Saracen or his aching lungs or the blood and faeces clinging to his canvas soles.

He tripped and fell, cursing at his glancing collision with an unseen soldier. Either he or the man had been clumsy, though in the random flow of siege the occasional stumble was expected. A brief thought flared that he had entered a trap set by Spada and his cohorts, but they would not have been content with such a chance encounter. He sprang upright and slapped the dust from his knees and palms, observing the stranger who snatched hurriedly to retrieve a toppled *chapel de fer* and replace it on his head. There was no response as the youngster smiled and mouthed encouragement through the clamour, no meeting of their gaze as the unfamiliar figure shrank back into the shadow. Another one shocked by close encounter with the enemy, the boy supposed. He nodded in sympathy and turned to race away.

In his wake, the third and surviving Assassin viewed with a certain admiration his leaping and jinxing progress. It would have been too easy to stick a knife in him and bring to a premature close the life of this energetic young courier. Such matters could bide awhile. Other priorities engaged him: the need to infiltrate and examine the surrounding defences and to blend with the citizens drafted to the ramparts. From here he could prepare his next course of action. If he were not killed, he would most certainly ensure that numerous about him were.

~

Even in the council chamber, the flickering light and percussive thunder of battle intruded. Grim fatigue and prevailing tension affected every hierarch at the table. Acre was short on manpower and ordnance and bereft of any hope, a city encircled and inexorably squeezed. These men were present as much to commiserate with each other as confer, for there seemed little left to be done.

William of Beaujeu rose from his seat, his eyes unyielding and his diplomacy hard-edged. 'We sit with our souls corroded by fear and our sword arms paralysed by inaction. We bring shame and dishonour upon the very name of our ancestors.'

A Pisan knight flinched to the gusting crescendo of the fray beyond. 'Our ancestors are not here.'

'Yet they were at Jerusalem when we seized it from the Saracen, stood alongside Coeur de Lion when he sought to break the grip of Saladin.'

'Let us dwell instead in the present, Beaujeu.' The face of Amalric was sweat-grey in the candlelight. 'It is a matter of time and numbers, and we have scarcity in both.'

'So do we fold our arms and wait like effigies to die?' For several beats the question hung and was not answered.

The brow of Amalric furrowed deeper. 'What would you and your Temple have us do?'

'Fight, your highness.'

'And squander our resource? Throw precious troops to the heathen blade?'

'At the least it may inspire.' It was an insult directed full in the face of the Constable.

Amalric acquired a temporary colour that drained away to pallid rage. He would not suffer criticism from a Templar or the cruel asides of his court. William of Beaujeu was forever goading and provoking and playing him for a fool. Maybe it would be the grand master and his vaunted knights who failed the test and fell the hardest.

He leant on his elbows and stared up at the Templar. 'Your views are noted, Beaujeu. Yet I ask you to consider the fate of this city and not that of your order alone.'

'This city?' The grand master waved to the window. 'This city is being pulled down about us, razed stone by stone, undermined by the Saracens whose tunnels claw towards us.'

'Your solution is merely to rebuke us and scold.' A Venetian noble glared defensively from the far end. 'Do you offer us magic or some black spell that will stay the violent heathen?'

'I hold out an example of fire and resolve.'

'What we need is relief. What we desire is a thousand sail appearing off our shore and bringing to us a Christian army.'

Beaujeu looked pityingly on the man. 'Search first within yourselves for power and salvation.'

Amalric intervened with a sweep of his hand, a Constable whose authority was being eroded as rapidly as his walls. It was an uncomfortable position. Yet he could still cling to the trappings of office and make grand gesture. If it served to prick the effortless supremacy of the Templar, so much the better.

He laid his hands flat along the carved rests of his chair and surveyed the assembled, waiting as Beaujeu resettled himself at the table. They could not be allowed to fracture and divide while the enemy was at the gate.

'I give you tidings from Cyprus.' He was right to assume it would win back the initiative and earn him a reprieve. 'My brother, the King, pledges to come in person to our side and bring with him the finest of troops.'

Hope and questions sprang. 'When will Henry join us?'

'How large is his force?'

'Are there further knights among them? Do the princes of Europe at last commit?'

'Is this the beginning of our rescue?'

'Have our cries been heard? Has our plight moved men to act?'

The Constable shifted uneasily beneath the weight of query. There was a balance between offering encouragement and promoting a lie and he teetered dangerously at the join. He recited the lines he had earlier rehearsed.

'Henry bids you be patient and of strong and determined heart. He commands that his city hold fast in the face of the storm. He intends to make land within three weeks.'

'Weeks?' A noble roared in disbelief. 'We may have only days.'

'As Constable, I say we shall endure.' Amalric spoke as though attempting to convince himself. 'Between ourselves and the Saracen lies the forward bastion of King Hugh and to its rear the great King Henry and Accursed Towers. Each throws up a mighty barrier to the foe and each is manned by my royal guards.'

'When they falter in the breach, it will be the brethren of the Templars, the Hospitallers and the Teutons who stand firm.' Beaujeu could not resist the jibe.

It provoked as was intended. 'You are not the sole guardians of our domain, Beaujeu.'

'Yet we are the most proven.' The grand master reeled authority back to himself. 'As I recall, you once dismissed my warnings of the Mameluk and had me brought before the high court on the grounds of treason.'

'The circumstances have changed.'

'Leadership has not.'

Amalric stood and Beaujeu followed, their face-off constrained by event and location. 'Let us see how your Templars fare and fight, Beaujeu.'

'We will battle to the last, even as you take to your galley and your palace turns to sand.'

'Beware it is not your precious order that is buried.'

Beside the grand master, his Hospitaller and Teutonic associates rose as one to proffer support and an indivisible challenge. The fault line was laid bare and Amalric was left motionless on the other side. Today, neither the emollient words of the Patriarch would calm the fractiousness nor the capering antics of a dwarf distract with vulgar levity. Enmity pulsed in the silence.

It was given voice by the doughty Hospitaller. 'Each of you is called to serve and yet sits remote from the ramparts. You talk of fight and know nothing of it. You wring your hands and not the neck of the vile heathen. Our place is elsewhere, for it is where war is decided.'

The three grand masters stalked from the chamber, the tread of their nailed boots martial and heavy on the flagstones. In the antechamber they would don their hauberks and mantles, would once more take up their swords and head for their forward posts. The conference was over. From henceforth, it was each grand master to his order and every Crusader for himself.

Back in the main chamber, Amalric remained standing and had yet to utter a word.

'Any would think the Saracen your friend. Put your heart and shoulder to it.'

The voice of de Flor hissed low through clenched teeth as

he hefted another timber and encouraged his crew to their task. He had laboured hard aboard his galley and spent long hours overseeing its adaptation for a new theatre of war. William of Beaujeu had asked for something different. It was a challenge the adventurer was happy to accept, and one that would lead to reward and goodwill and to some surprise for Latin and Mohammedan alike. Carpenters had been brought in and armourers employed, the decks strengthened and fighting platforms cleared, the enslaved oarsmen reminded that a tardy response to specific command might result in painful death and watery plunge in a weighted sack. Much depended on the venture.

A figure ghost-lit in the evening gloom clambered up the deck ladder to join him. 'You are nearly ready?'

'When Templar messengers cease to harry and pester, then shall I be ready.'

'His grace is anxious matters should proceed.'

'Do you find me idle? Drinking? Playing the lute or carousing in a tavern?'

The messenger knight faltered. 'It is my duty to observe and report.'

'And mine to enact the pledge I made and to bring misery to your life.' De Flor clapped the man on his shoulder. 'Our Grand Master plainly believes I would kick to the sea a lesser herald than yourself.'

'He does.'

'Tell Beaujeu he has little to fear, for his loyal servant toils.'

'We have instructed the winchmen of the Cantena to lower the chain at your call.'

'Is the ordnance coming?'

'We are bringing it now from the Temple. You will have as much shot as you can stow.'

'So we are set fair to even this battle.'

He leapt down to the main deck and was cautiously followed by the knight as he strode aft. Even in a storm or the depth of night, de Flor could negotiate his way blind about his vessel. From below, the animal stench of the shackled slaves seeped and clung to the upper works. The prisoners would need careful handling for the mission. They would be expected to show flair and finesse and the skills acquired through years of voyage. No drum would beat out rhythm, for stealth was of the essence. Any sound could mean discovery and any error would be punished. De Flor was an uncompromising commander.

The messenger caught up with him at the stern. 'Your oar benches seem quiet.'

'I will demand much from them later. They deserve their slumber and sheepskin berths.'

'There is little enough comfort for us on the rampart.'

'Are not Templars born to suffer for their salvation?' De Flor ran his hand over a furled lateen sail. 'I would rather be a freeman on the battlements than sit as a slave on the benches of a Frankish galley.'

'Such tenderness for your Saracens.'

'They labour so I may win. My true affection is for war and profit.'

While the Latins prostrated themselves before their altars and their statues of the Blessed Virgin, de Flor was pursuing a more aggressive course. He had rarely attended a church where he was not conducting a close reconnaissance of its wealth and treasured artefacts. Convenience instead of calling had brought him to the Templars.

He mounted the step to the mast and gazed south, sniffing the air and gauging the weather. 'A smooth sea and a light breeze and the heathen believes we cower passive and afraid.'

'His grace would wish it other.'

'Then his grace is fortunate to find me. Bring him to the eastern wall for a late evening stroll. I will deliver him a spectacle uncommon in these parts.'

'May God go with you, de Flor.'

'He has the sense to keep away.'

As though in afterthought, the adventurer conjured a leather flask from its hidden bracket and unstoppered it before putting it to his lips. He would drink to his crew and command, to his good fortune and his future.

What the messenger knight returning to the Lion Fortress could not know was that he had been aboard a vessel whose holds were heavy-ballasted with a trove of precious gems and gold.

Outside his grand complex of pavilions and tents set opposite the Tower of the Legate, Ashraf considered the evening spectacle of campaign. There were few things as rewarding as to watch a city of infidels in its final throes. They might posture and bark and strut a little on their paltry walls, but time and pressure and inexorable weight of siege would do for them in the end. He would allow them a lingering finale. It was better a monster be bled to death and spill its entrails across the plain. That was how legend grew and his own power and fame would multiply. Ashraf, slayer of the Franks and destroyer of Acre. Ashraf, supreme ruler without compare. Ashraf, worthy successor to his father.

For a while, he was transported by thought and the delicate beauty of the scene. Light and shadow and the murmuring wail of horns and voices played and rebounded from the glimmering walls and washed across a landscape dressed with campfires. Allah must have created war so mortals could glimpse through a dark glass to paradise.

'My Sultan.' A Mameluk general had dismounted from his horse and was summoned forwards to report.

'You have completed inspection of our positions?'

'I have, my Sultan.' The officer spoke in short and military tones. 'Not one of our black oxen fails to strike the enemy rampart. Not one of our men is found wanting.'

Ashraf noted the flame-red reflection on the lamellar armour and the gold tracing of the steel helmet. He trusted the general as Qalawun had done. He had relied on his sword and judgement in moving against the palace conspirators. In the field, he was equally of use.

The sultan indicated the edifice rising spectral from its man-made cloud. 'A daunting sight, is it not?'

'Fissures grow wider each day, will soon create a breach.'

'Our tunnels?'

'Already they make progress. Night and day, the fire-troops dig and excavate towards the moat. It will not take long for them to reach the foundations.'

'I will offer them bounty for the first tower to fall.'

'Thus is contest and impulse the fiercer.' The general jabbed his finger at the target. 'The King Hugh barbican to the front, the St Nicholas Tower, the English Tower and the Tower of the Countess of Blois. Each will find itself tumbling to the earth.'

'They must do so before the Christians inspire fellow infidels with their courage, before an enemy fleet appears off our shore.'

'Is there any danger of it, my Sultan?'

'None.'

The sultan delivered his verdict with the flatness of total certainty. True, the fiery King Henry of Cyprus was agitating to bring in person additional troops to his besieged brother

Amalric; for sure, the remote and disinclined European princes spoke of their regard for Acre and love of the Holy Land. But these were meaningless things. No Lionheart existed and no Crusade was planned. The city would slip into the grasp of the Mameluk.

Ashraf tilted his head, distracted by a further thought. 'What of the Templars on the north wall?'

'They are quiet, my Sultan. Like the rest, they shrink and quiver behind their crumbling stone.'

'William of Beaujeu is never to be trusted. He is a scorpion, a viper, the deadliest of foes.'

'It shall not save him.'

'When he is silent, he plots. Where he is unseen, he appears elsewhere. Increase the night guard before the Maupas Gate.'

'As you command, my Sultan.' The general growled orders to an underling and returned attention to his master. 'We will bring you the head of the Grand Master before this siege is through.'

'It is the sole cure to their poisoned zeal. These warrior priests would sooner suffer a thousand torments than submit to the True Faith.'

The general concurred. 'Saladin was wise to kill them in the aftermath of Hattin.'

'Yet the orders recovered and their knights again thrived. At Acre, there will be no rising from the dead.'

He turned and entered the richly woven portal to his tent. A few steps, but myriad leagues from battle. Here, there was the soothing glow of lamps and the sweet smell of incense, the soft playing of the lute and the sensual lure of hand-maidens. Another tent and he had passed into a cavernous hall bedecked in silk and strewn with priceless rugs, a chamber set for feasting and attended by his emirs. There would be dancers and musicians, fire-eaters and acrobats. War could still be comfortable.

As he assumed his place, they praised and applauded as he knew they would. The leader of an historic campaign, he demanded and received the unstinting support and acclaim of others. Perhaps they remembered the shrieking fall from grace of the traitorous and unlamented emir al-Fakhri. He accepted a sherbert and sampled its nectared taste, surveyed his fawning coterie of officers and clan chiefs. All had gathered to partake in his triumph.

But suddenly new and discordant sounds leaked into the interior, at first ignored and then swelling to intrusion. The music faltered and the conversation dried and the mood sputtered from merriment to concern. Something terrible was underway. Already the sultan was pushing his way through, scattering minions and brushing aside the laden platters, leading his lieutenants out in their raucous confusion. Outside, the view had changed.

A giant catapult installed aboard a Christian galley was roving invisible and close to shore and loosing off its salvoes. The Mohammedans had been staring in the wrong direction. Unprepared for such an act, their camp lay exposed, its tents and men and animals shredded by the curving throw and bound of multiple rocks. A seventh, an eighth, a ninth. They crashed through, volleying bloody trail and trauma direct into the lines. A shot cascaded into a cookhouse and sent flame to the stores, the combustion carried on a flickering stream of resins and nut oil and burning a course to an ordnance cache. Naphtha and wildire went up. In dazzling ignition the shoreline turned white, a train of mule silhouetted bright before it vanished and a mining troop was carbonised where it stood.

'Fall back from the sea!' Ashraf shied from a ball of heat

and covered his eyes. 'Withdraw in order from the range of these devils!'

His authority and orders were lost in the panic as soldiers and labourers, dazed, rushed in heedless flight. A man blundered into his supreme commander and recoiled before he dropped. The smouldering corpse had no face. Ashraf looked away. From somewhere he heard cheering and directed his senses to follow the sound. It came from the castellated walls of Acre, the citizen-soldiers roaring approval and giving vent to their delight at each facet of the turmoil. Their future nemesis quelled the anger climbing jagged in his throat. Let the Unbelievers celebrate and crow. Tomorrow they would reflect on their bleak destiny and the futility of their defiance. This temporary reprieve would not save them. Yet beneath his contrived mantle of calm and with a clarity as illuminating as the surrounding light, it occurred to the Mameluk that only the grand master of the Knights Templar could have arranged so irksome a counterstrike.

~

A firepot arced lazily across the ramparts and descended to explode on the lip of the inner wall. From their eyrie on the Accursed Tower, Benedict and the Patriarch watched the trajectory and its blazing impact. The old man murmured a prayer for deliverance and gazed to other sights, a Methuselah and his young accomplice stranded in a sea of constant movement. Below them, the terrain writhed to the strain of battle and the shifting patterns of the attacking force. And all the while, the arrows flew and the boulders fell and the incendiaries drifted in like burning leaves.

'Where once we played chess, we now address a bloodier game.' The Patriarch held the youngster close to his side and nodded sadly. 'From horizon to horizon, all I see is death.'

'Will we hold against them, Holy Father?'

'That I cannot say. Yet it is no doubt the final battle of our age and the true contest between heaven and hell. We must repent and look to God.'

'There is still hope. People talk of a mighty Christian army setting sail for Palestine and our relief.'

The old man shook his head. 'Despair will always foster rumour. There is no such rescue from abroad.'

'Do you not see how our catapults give reply to the enemy? Did you not witness how Roger de Flor took his galley and brought havoc to their camp?'

'It is scarcely enough to alter fate.'

'What of St Michael?' Benedict searched the aged face for reassurance. 'Will he not come with fiery sword to stand with his faithful Crusaders?'

'I fail yet to spy him.'

They stood in quiet meditation as the air sang and the walls quaked. The youngster felt the energy course through his frame, carrying his mind high above the fury. There was a serenity here, a calm exhilaration that removed all fear of death and imbued the soul with belief in invincibility. Benedict laughed.

'You are not as safe as you may think.' The voice of the Patriarch pulled him back.

Benedict bit his lip, ashamed. 'Forgive me, Holy Father. I am foolish in my ways.'

'Not foolish, but young. War is a cruel and potent siren. She can caress the heart and tempt the spirit, be enlivening and capricious and demanding, may lure boys and men to an early grave.'

'You blessed our soldiers from this same tower.'

'I would again a hundred times. For our struggle is just and pure and the conflict holy. Yet I am not blind to the horror or the bestial and wicked acts committed for our cause.'

'I will heed your words, Holy Father.'

'Then most surely you are no knight or burgher of this city.' The Patriarch smiled.'Now go from here. Run fast on errand and make your report.'

'I do not want to leave you.'

Eyes again creased in warmth and humour. 'You deserted me before in favour of the Mongol. Moreover, I am content to stay alone and dwell upon the proceedings.'

The boy hurried away, making dutiful haste along the inner ramparts to rejoin the Templar grand master who had sortied to the eastern wall. Few but Beaujeu could interpret the signal pennants flying proud from the command flagstaff of the Mameluk sultan; few but Beaujeu had the right to savour the damage inflicted on the heathen encampment by one of his marauding galleys. Benedict was eager to find him.

It was close by the St Nicholas Tower that the snub nose of a crossbow quarrel collided with limestone near to his head and showered him in splinters. He threw himself forwards and rolled, staying low and crawling, counting the seconds and rehearsing the reload. A foot would be in the cocking stirrup and the string drawn back and a second bolt placed in the groove for the lift, aim and release. His shoulders hunched and his thoughts narrowing to the route ahead and the speed of flight behind, he clambered to his feet and sprinted. Whatever else he had learnt this morning, he comprehended that Spada was of an unforgiving bent.

'My errant herald is arrived.' William of Beaujeu greeted the panting youngster with an appraising glance. 'How seems the boy to you, de Flor?'

'As vigorous and fine as any soldier.' In rare attendance,

234

the adventurer stood apart from the grand master and his retinue.

'A soldier indeed.' Beaujeu continued to study the boy, his voice free of irony or tone.

Benedict looked from one to the other, aware of decision and alert to jest. Anticipating the question, the Templar raised his hand.

'Beyond these walls you will see the effect of our assault upon the Saracen. We of the Temple shall not rest or quit. Now we prepare to strike once more.'

'I wish you good fortune, your grace.'

It was de Flor who replied. 'Listen well, boy. He means you for the fight.'

✝

Chapter 14

The Saracens could be forgiven their complacency. They had the Christians trapped and assailed on the landward aspect, were reducing the walls and tunnelling below. All was proceeding to schedule and plan. Ashraf allowed the nights to be given to sleep and the vast military camp to fall silent. There were no horns blown or battle-cries raised, no whir of the catapults or juddering shock of impact. Both sides slumbered. The sultan understood that the infidels were determined, that they might yet stand in the breach and the remnants of their towers and fight until the last one of them was dead. His father had always cautioned against underestimating the eternal foe.

Lessons, however, could be forgotten and the details of past campaigns go ignored. Had the Mameluks reflected upon the fall to Sultan Baybars of the Frankish castle at Caesarea in 1265, they might have recalled that aside from its main gates the fortification contained three secret entrances served by hidden passageways and built into the walls. Acre too enjoyed its share of protected and covert access routes.

It was adjacent to one of these that William of Beaujeu had assembled some one hundred of his Templar knights and several hundred more turcopoles and men-at-arms. After ten days of enduring siege the grand master was unwilling to sit passive as the city crumbled. He intended to pursue a different course. If attack by seaborne catapult had temporarily disrupted the army of Egypt, the foray he proposed from the northern wall of Montmusart would bring utter disarray to the forces of Syria. Stealth and surprise were the critical weapons and overweening confidence the chief weakness of the Mameluk. The knights had swords, the sergeants crossbows and maces, the turcopoles spears. They waited in anticipation.

'We have God and moonlight to guide us, my brothers.' The voice of Beaujeu was quiet yet strong. 'Be savage and merciless and spare no life. Spread terror and death to every corner of the heathen camp.'

A knight responded. 'It is good to fight once more, your grace.'

'Then do so with alacrity and in the knowledge you are blessed. It is why we took our sacred oath and committed to wage war upon the heathen. Should you die, you will have earned your place in heaven.'

'We embrace it with joy, your grace.'

'Each enemy slain is one less to mount a scaling ladder or enter the breach. Every corpse seen strewn on the plain will promote a hardened resolve upon our ramparts.'

'Even with the Constable?' The jest provoked short and whispered mirth.

'Our trade is butchery and not wasteful merriment.' Beaujeu was calm in his admonition. 'We will be silent and fleet-footed and quick in our pursuit. Target emirs and officers and harry and kill every tunneller you may find. Do not become surrounded or extend too far. And listen for the recall.'

'Our blood will be up, your grace.'

'Any mistake will cost you your own.' Beaujeu raised his

steel-mittened hand to still further questions. 'Speak your prayers and make ready. Let this fifteenth night of April 1291 forever be recounted as a time when the Templars entered legend.'

'*It would thus be churlish of me to keep away . . .*'

De Flor was not to be ignored or dismissed from the event. Uninvited and accompanied by the fiercer elements of his crew, he had slipped into the gathering ready-armed and clad in mail.

The grand master seemed unsurprised. 'State the meaning of your presence, de Flor.'

'It has no meaning save I am loath to be parted from the flock.'

'You acquitted yourself aboard your galley. Now is your time to rest.'

'It has given me a new appetite for war.'

Beaujeu rested a hand on the pommel of his sword. 'We are manned enough.'

'Manned, your grace?' There was chiding and insolent challenge in the words. 'Beyond the wall is a boy you sent forward as your scout. As his guardian, I am bound to fetch him back.'

'Yet as my servant and hireling, you are commanded by my word.'

'So command me to sally forth.'

Agreement echoed in the group. Whether rogue or champion, viewed with admiration or disdain, the adventurer could not be overlooked. Beaujeu might have authority, but de Flor possessed a nonchalant aggression and prowess few could ever match.

The grand master peered at the darkened silhouette. 'I am expected to bow to mischief and impudent demand?'

'Merely to welcome those who would serve, your grace.'

'Is our noble order to be inhabited by miscreants and vaga-bonds?'

'This vagabond has crawled over rock to spy out the Syrian force you now set out to confront. This miscreant has struck more blows against the heathen than any one of your pious brethren.'

'Your case is stated well.' Beaujeu paused, judging the moment. 'Follow and do not lead. Obey and do not counter-mand. I am persuaded.'

They filed through to their start points, silent men pensive at the waiting and eager to be set loose. Out in the field was a solitary scout, flitting among the mineheads and earthworks and preparing the ground for the ensuing advance. He would be noting sentries and mapping obstructions, gliding past tents and ghosting through the serried ranks of siege machines, an Arab speaker with the wit and wiles to appear as anyone but a Frank. Benedict was roaming among the enemy.

He had halted at the spoken challenge, imagined the heavy lids and dulled instincts of the tired guard. The man wanted to sleep and was irked by the scampering presence of a youngster passing near. Yawned objection was all he could muster.

'Men sleep and you awake them.'

'Forgive me, uncle. It was not my intent.' The whispered reply came apologetic and submissive.

'Our forward posts are no place for you.'

'Officers demand their figs and dates and emirs their rosewater.'

'So be off and soundless on your errand before you greet the flat of my spear.'

'That I shall, uncle.' The tone stayed respectful. 'May your dreams be deep and in peace.'

Grunting in response, his fatigue replacing interest, the

watch pulled a blanket close about his shoulders and returned to his fitful repose. There was nothing to report and insufficient focus to recollect the password for the night.

Benedict was already slithering back across the dry moat, worming his way by reckoning and ambient light to the base of the wall and the ladder leading to the hidden aperture. His heart still shuddered fast and the sweat shrank the canvas jerkin tight around his back, yet the touch of the stone and the wooden steps brought him instant comfort. He returned among friends. Quickly he climbed, finding the hand that reached to grasp his own, allowing himself to be pulled through and describing in haste to a Templar ear all that he had discerned. The news was relayed to a grateful Beaujeu.

Figures emerged, sliding down ropes or clambering ungainly on their slatted descent, their companions passing through weapons and marshalling the flow. Not a word was spoken or a lantern lit. The swarm was departing. It spread in a widening formation, culling lookouts in easy dispatch and threshing its way into the dormant throng. The spearhead of the Crusades was back. There was no impulse to show mercy or take prisoners, only the intent to carry out with methodical skill the butchery for which each Templar had been raised. They approached their task with ruthless alacrity and in a lumbering rush, their exhortations growing loud and their blood-fury taking hold. All were consumed in the pursuit. Guy-ropes were cut and swords plunged in, brands snatched from sputtering fires and put to tents and stores, and the timid or the slow or the brave hacked to pieces where they lay or stood. A sergeant had dashed out the brains of several men before a Saracen arrow took him in the chest; the bowman was brought down in the same instant with a javelin launched by a turcopole. Screams ricocheted and confusion squalled.

Stampeding animals had joined the battle, terrified oxen bellowing and crowding in their frenzied efforts to escape. They trampled many underhoof. Catapults toppled and ignited and cast their glow, and tunnel shafts collapsed to entomb their labourers within. And everywhere the ceaseless motion and endless noise and countless vignettes of mayhem.

'Lay low, boy.'

A soldier pushed Benedict flat and knelt to fire his cross-bow. At fifty paces and framed by the contagious inferno, an Arab snapped forwards to the impact and clutched reflexively at the black stain welling on his robe. The youngster viewed the scene with remote involvement, too distant to feel much and too close to feel nothing. He saw de Flor carve his way through a herd of enemy, a titan impervious to threat, his sword rising and sweeping and scattering reflections. He disappeared into shadow and another scene burst to vivid life, the flames lapping as they had once done in the fields of cane. Benedict blinked at the memory.

He had rolled to the side and avoided the knife before his senses and sight were fully engaged. At last he was involved. His assailant had crept forwards in the artificial dusk, selecting him as prone and diverted prey and leaping with his dagger raised. Benedict kicked him and closed, grappling and tumbling, raking at the eyes and scrabbling for dominance. He beat the knife free and elbowed the face. The Arab would regret choosing to attack a seasoned traveller of the desert and a survivor of Tripoli. There would be only one contestant limping from the aftermath. With furious strength, the youngster clenched the throat and began to squeeze, but found his hold broken and his body turned. Gain for the heathen. Benedict punched upwards and bit the hand that pinned him. Maybe the foe had a second blade or a strangling cord, perhaps searched for the discarded weapon. The youngster moved again. He tasted his own sweat and tears, felt the scraped skin and the blood smear on his face. Then he knew.

'Hazzim . . .' The choke loosened and he wrestled the Arab aside. 'It is you.'

'Ben?' It was a question spat with a tooth and accompanied by a blow to the abdomen.

The youngster wheezed. 'You would fight me?'

'I will kill any infidel.' Violence was in the words and movement. 'You join in the attack on my people.'

'The Mameluks invade my city.'

'It is not your city. It is not your land. It is not your place.'

Dust enveloped them as their brawl revived to a spasm of ragged blows and yelled invective. Past hurt fed every exertion. The Arab boy was taller, yet his rival was more adept in the brute arts of combat.

'You wish for death, Hazzim?'

'It is better to die than betray.'

'I'm giving you a chance.' Benedict reached for his knife and drew it from its sheath. 'Submit to me and make your escape.'

'Never.'

'You are crazed, Hazzim.'

'And you are an Unbeliever and my foe.'

The blade pressed close to his throat. 'This is the knife with which I struck Spada. I did so for you, Hazzim, for your loss and our friendship.'

'There is nothing left but war.' Both boys shook with rage and tension.

They had not heard the recall, failed to notice the Latins retreat through the cascading smoke and cries. The Templars had performed as their grand master decreed. Yet their withdrawal was encumbered by confusion and challenge and littered with the burning debris of earlier success. Knights became entangled in ropes and fallen canvas; blind skirmish developed between the maddened and the lost. The Saracens had regrouped and were starting to give chase.

'Stay still, Hazzim.' As feet trampled near, Benedict pushed the Arab down.

'Your Templars are put to flight.'

'They may yet place a sword through your ribs.' The Frankish youngster lay flat across the heaving form and pinned the shoulders with his weight. 'Do you wish to tempt their rage? To give yourself away?'

'I take no counsel from a Latin.'

'Move and I shall cut you deep.'

His warning came urgently, reinforced with the pressure of his body and the presence of sharpened steel. Enmity instead of friendship brought them here; coldness resided where warmth had once been. They were not running or hunting, roaming the coast or exploring caves, or paralysed with mirth as the donkey bucked the other boy when a peppercorn was lodged in its rear. Everything had changed.

Through the clamour, the questing shouts of de Flor flurried powerful and close. He was searching for Benedict. The youngster turned the haft of the knife and prodded it into Hazzim, ensuring the danger and message were understood. Clemency was a virtue alien to rampaging Crusaders.

'What have you found, boy?' The adventurer was mired in blood and unravelling a turban to wipe his sword.

'A corpse and no treasure.'

'Neither of which has much purpose for us.' De Flor was striding fast. 'Keep pace at my side and do not crawl behind. Our friends are giving chase as we retire the field.'

Eager to depart and distract the eye, Benedict leapt nimbly to join him. Behind him he left matters unresolved and an Arab boy alive.

~

Cauterised flesh created its own particular odour. As assistants held down the straining man and the mouth gaped behind its leather strap, Theobald of Alzey deftly plucked a heated sword from the flame and applied its blade flat to the open wound. Eyes bulged and the groan was loud and the patient was carried limp from the slab. It took a while for the smoke to clear. By then, another of the wounded had been deposited for inspection, his prayerful whimpers soft and his blood colouring the scattered straw below. There was a pause as the shallow breathing caught and held, as the body slumped and the spirit fled, as the face shaded to a whiter grey. Gently, the young Hospitaller bent to listen, whispered in holy rite and stilled the flickering lips and eyes with a movement of his hand. The corpse was lifted away.

'I cannot save them all, Ben.' Theobald answered the enquiring gaze with a tired and regretful shrug. 'Each one of us goes where the Lord ordains.'

'Many live because of you.'

'Is that not the duty of the Hospital and its brethren?'

Benedict nodded, was content to crouch and watch or scurry about and wait upon the injured on their litters and palliasses. He had long ago learnt how to staunch blood flow and wind a bandage, fix a splint and bind in maggots or poultice. When asked to rake away the soiled overlay, he would do so; when required to feed the sick or read them psalms or bring water to their gasping mouths, he hurried to obey. It was calmer than the heat of battle or being in close-quarter scuffle with Hazzim.

The young Hospitaller peered at him. 'How are your wounds?'

'As well as yours, Theo.'

'We each arrive bruised and cut from encounters on the plain.' Theobald touched the dressing wound about his head. 'Which of us is the more foolish for seeking out such danger?'

'We all must be fools from the number of us here.'

'No truer word was spoken by our youngest physic and philosopher.'

Whether mocked or flattered, Benedict did not care. He was drawn by the company of the knight and warmed by his benign authority. While de Flor might create wars and level mountains, mesmerise with giant frame and noisy boldness, it was the caring Hospitaller who earned respect. He was the manifestation of truth and decency, of kindness and nobility.

'Fetch warmed water for me, Ben.' Theobald spoke as he motioned his readiness to receive a further patient. 'I fear the work will test us.'

'Will he be saved?'

'I am a Hospitaller, not a sorcerer.'

Little could be done for the man. He was curled around his belly wound, his face and torso scored with the jagged chippings of a mangonel shot. It was typical of those brought from the King Hugh barbican. They were having a savage time of it, their position exposed and their ramparts and platforms enduring bombardment unlike all other. Gradually, the royal guard was being winnowed. Their men provided the outer screen and the obvious target, were daily beset with catapult storms and showers of arrow. If they could move past them, the Saracen could reach the drawbridge and St Anthony Gate and access the city.

Surcoat and cuirie had been removed and the body delivered prone and naked. As Theobald sluiced away the coagulations, the scale of the damage became ever more revealed. They had been such proud soldiers, so meticulous in their drill and martial in their bearing, troops dressed splendidly and vaunted in rank above the common military. Reduced to this.

Instinctively, Benedict took his hand and tried to transmit warmth, murmuring encouragement and willing back life. The eyes alone communicated with him, spoke from a distance of helplessness and despair and of sorrow and farewell.

'Stay with us, brother. You must try.' Benedict clenched the hand between his palms. 'I will pray with you and beseech the saints.'

Another one was gone. The youngster knelt and bowed his head as the cadaver was taken and the table cleared for whoever next was brought. He had seen the limepits freshly excavated and the corpses tumbled in, had heard the splash of weighted bundles dumped nightly beyond the breakwater. How much worse it might become. There were faces in the Hospital he knew, faces that had changed, faces that were gone. Hazzim and his kind were responsible. In this place of suffering was the summation of war, the courage and the folly and the fervour. He had yet to find its meaning.

Theobald interrupted and returned him from his thoughts. 'Neither dwell in your head nor too long at this table. Go now on your rounds.'

Grateful to oblige, the boy slid into the cavernous shadows and moved among the alcoves and columns to tend any who needed or called. Mixing a bowl of water and wine, he ferried it carefully to a Templar stretched out on a pallet.

'May God bless you.'

'And you, brother.'

The sergeant drank greedily. 'You performed well as our scout.'

246

'I paid a lesser price than you.'

'And so you are become my nurse.' The man fell back exhausted on his pillow. 'Be sure to care also for yourself.'

A hand beckoned feebly from across the parade, the swathed entity almost shorn of human features. He had been the victim of wildfire. Benedict approached with a tentative step and stooped to proffer the wooden vessel. His forearm was gripped and the pressure tightened.

'You believe you are safe from Spada?' The French was broken and Italian-accented. 'He will find and kill you wherever you are.'

The threat caused the bowl to tilt and its contents to spill free.

'Fate is unkind to you, infidel.'

Ashraf was no kindly visitor to the tent. His prisoner was Jean of Sagozan, the Templar who had once journeyed to Cairo in secret entreaty for peace and in later guise participated in the night raid upon the Moslem camp. His situation had altered. Trussed by his hands and feet and liberated of his armour and sword, the knight had lost his power to bargain. Yet resistance still glowed in his eye and battered face and his demeanour remained uncowed.

The sultan perched on a nearby stool. 'Where once we parleyed beneath a flag of truce, here we meet under banners of war.'

'Truth is eternal, whatever the circumstance.' Parched words filtered through his lips. 'You will never defeat the Word of God.'

'Though I have the Latins cornered and at bay? Though I have a feared Templar bound and at my feet?'

'An Egyptian pharaoh once believed he held enslaved the Children of Israel.'

'There shall be no exodus for the Christians of Acre.'

Sagozan did not reply. A brave soldier, the sultan reflected, a holy warrior without the doubt or frailties of common men. He would need his courage. Naturally, he had no expectation of survival, would doubtless greet death with the same arrogance of conviction with which his kind confronted life. Small wonder the infidels had relied on them to cling to their last possessions in Palestine; little surprise they crept out in darkness to wage battle against his sleeping army. The man was pious and learned and spoke the Arab tongue. He would have been as comfortable in a library of sacred texts as he was on the bloodiest field of combat. Such a pity he was not a True Believer.

'Your Grand Master lost many knights in his foolish sortie.' In the soft lamplight, the sultan observed the countenance for any fear. 'What cost for so little gain.'

'Have you not seen the destruction we wrought? Or the landscape we dressed with your dead?'

'Your success was brief and order is maintained.'

'Yet we delivered a blow against you, Mameluk. Proof we are unvanquished.' Sagozan struggled to sit upright, his haggard features suffused with defiance.

Ashraf nodded. 'It was your Templars who were driven back and you and others of your brethren held captive as my prisoners.'

'We stand as symbols of fire and resolve.'

'I am certain you shall yet provide a fine example.'

No Templar would plead for clemency or offer to convert. They were the backbone of Acre that required to be broken. Where they might have once rallied the spirits of the defence, they now might find employ in crushing them.

The sultan stood and looked down at the captive. 'Ready yourself for death, knight.'

'As a Templar, I am prepared and grateful to meet my Saviour.'

'You will go ahead of the rest of your kind.'

'For the faithful, there is no higher honour.'

It had been a strangely unrewarding encounter for the sultan and he left in pensive mood. These people were the very devil, were unafraid of all Mameluks and their armies. He would put an end to their complacency.

Alone in his twilight, the Templar saw a shadow and called out. 'I ask for little, stranger. But bring me water.'

The young Arab hung back, unwilling to venture close and yet wanting to view the prisoner. His face was illuminated cold and distant.

'I know you, Saracen.' Sagozan stared at the silent form. 'You are friend to the boy Benedict.'

Hazzim turned and walked soundless from the tent.

She was a beautiful woman and it puzzled de Flor how she remained unpersuaded by his charm. A rare jewel indeed. Not even the background din of war seemed to lend weight to his argument or bring panic and pleading to her eyes. So different to the moneyed females who leapt to his arms and bed and scrambled for the promised sanctuary of his galley. The Lady Charlotte simply smiled graciously and spoke in quiet tones as she stood in her sober dress and with her hands folded, countering his remarks with wit and warmth and velvet-clad refusal. It infuriated and entranced the adventurer.

'You must heed me, my lady.'

'Must I?' She peered from beneath lowered eyelids. 'I am neither one of your slatterns nor a knight you have vanquished in the grand melee.'

'I have come to warn, my lady.'

'Which makes you a herald and little more. It is not often I take counsel from one lower born.'

De Flor persisted. 'Listen to the battle, my lady. All about is hazard and death.'

'I shall take my chance, monsieur.'

'What hope is there for those who stay?' He assumed a more pressing and earnest air. 'You would be wise to gain passage on my ship.'

'An argument no doubt you have deployed against a hundred wailing women.'

'Think of yourself, my lady.'

'I think of the children.'

De Flor sighed, powerless in debate and resisted by one entirely irresistible. The young widow of a pious Burgundian knight who had made pilgrimage to the Holy Land and died in a shipwreck while en route, she had made a later journey and established an orphanage in his memory. For five years she had devoted herself to caring for the young and abandoned who arrived at her door. She and her helpers turned none away. It was said she might take holy orders and enter a convent on her return to Europe. But she was clearly in no hurry.

The adventurer spread his hands in innocent acceptance. 'Your fears for the children are my own, my lady.'

'I see no proof, monsieur.'

'Have I not cared for Benedict? Do I not guard the boy as though he were my son?'

'You take him on expeditions, you send him on perilous quests, and you allow him to do the bidding of Beaujeu.'

'Our Grand Master makes demands, my lady.'

'As do I.' She turned her head, her attraction and stubbornness rendered in profile. 'Not one silver coin of mine will travel aboard your vessel, not I nor a nurse from this house will sail beneath your pennant until every child here is first landed safe and well in Cyprus.'

'Authority does not reside in me, my lady.'

'So purchase it and persuade.'

He laughed, disconcerted at the challenge. 'Amalric has given orders that no ship may leave Acre until all is lost.'

'Such a bitter blow that it is the Constable who thwarts the famed de Flor.' Lady Charlotte was gentle in her scorn. 'So we have no agreement and your visit here is wasted.'

'Our business is not through, my lady.'

'For the while, you shall find it done.'

Still disbelieving, the adventurer left the premises perplexed. He had always recognised she would prove defiant, but he had believed she would bend if the situation worsened. There was no treasure in orphans. They were of more value to the Saracens. They could fetch a price in the slave markets with their fair skin and innocent blue eyes. Lady Charlotte was a dilemma, a puzzle, a challenge.

In the street, he glanced back to her window and then headed for war.

~

Standing in an open yard behind the Accursed Tower, the Assassin too was preparing to venture closer to the fighting. Volunteers had been sought to reinforce the depleted troops manning the forward barbican and the brave and foolhardy had reported. He was content to be among them. As he watched the stretcher parties work to bear the dead and injured from the scene, it occurred to him that the misfortune of some provided him with an advantage. No one would question his motive or his presence. He was dark enough to be a Cypriot or Levantine and sufficiently anonymous to go unnoticed. That he was courageous and willing to venture out to an exposed and crumbling front beyond the city walls would banish any doubt. The Assassin had become part of the loyal Christian host.

'If you are to be a martyr, take the heathen with you.' The sergeant rested a crossbow on his shoulder. 'It is the truest way to enter heaven.'

'What shall we earn?'

'Praise from your brothers and a place in legend.'

'Is there no gold?'

'One extra piece for any who crosses the bridge. The barbican of King Hugh is the island in a storm and we are the guardians posted on its cliffs.'

'We shall not fail you.'

The sergeant lifted his bow. 'Nor will you betray each other. What say you?'

'Amen!'

'Will you stand with me?'

'With all our hearts!'

'Commit yourselves and make the journey.'

Of all the gathered souls, the Assassin was perhaps the most eager in giving voice.

✝

Chapter 15

E ven Templars could scream. Arrayed on crucifixes set opposite the northern wall, the Frankish captives held in the night raid blossomed in macabre and troubling spectacle. Nothing could be done for them. As the sun rose and the defenders clustered on the ramparts to witness the grim event, the cries of suffering and slow death floated thin in the air. The sultan needed no herald to convey his meaning. These prisoners spoke eloquently enough, their groans and shrieks and agonised prayers foretelling the future for the rest of their kind. In silence, their brethren stared back. They were being tested and mocked, their faith assailed and the very sacrifice of their Saviour held up in dreadful parody. Pleading and contorted faces gaped up from across the divide and the forest of planed timber.

Upon his cross, Jean of Sagozan gasped his defiance. 'Remember Isaiah, my brothers. Though we grow weary the Lord does not. For He is everlasting.'

'It is noble to die as Jesus.' His chest heaving, another repeated a panted mantra. 'It is noble to die as Jesus.'

'For the Temple and the Sepulchre we rejoice and pass away.'

'Receive us now, O Lord. Remember your humble servants.'

'Forgive us our trespasses as we forgive those who trespass

against us.' A Templar was reciting the Lord's Prayer, his arms outstretched and his wrists pierced, the blood coursing down his naked form.

Yet forgiveness was not among the thoughts of Sagozan. He called out for vengeance against the Saracen, for pestilence and hellfire to rain and the heathen to be scoured from the face of the earth. For the dying complement it was a chance to show the meaning of courage and the strength of their faith. Ashraf had assumed they would weaken in the hour of their dread torment. He had misjudged the nature of those who donned the white mantle with its crimson cross. Two centuries had hardened them, imbued them with a will and zeal impending death would not break. Their grand master could be proud.

Beaujeu regarded them without visible emotion. With a coterie of senior knights, he had ascended the ramparts at dawn to bear witness and keep vigil and lend spiritual succour to the comrades who endured on the plain. Each one of the Templars at his side might too have ended nailed on a cross; each one of them would have stepped out to take the place of his brothers below. God had decided.

'Would that I could ease their plight.' Beaujeu let his gaze traverse the front. 'It is a reminder to us of the base and bestial ways of the heathen.'

His marshal grimaced. 'I would gladly flay every Saracen and cure their skins for public display.'

'A sentiment shared by all in Acre. The barbarism before us shows why we fight and raises us up before the Lord.'

'I see no merit in this piteous scene, your grace.'

'For you are the soldier and I the strategist.' The grand master threw a calculating glance at his lieutenant. 'I weep for our brethren as the Blessed Virgin did for her son. Yet if our men are to perish, we will use their agonies for our gain.'

'Should I not give order to our catapults to let fly? Should we not seek to cut short the woe of the dying with shot and wildfire?'

Beaujeu was calm in his refusal. 'It would play to the vanity of the Sultan and inform him of our weakness.'

'Our Christian duty bids us act, your grace.'

'Whilst our Templar calling is to hold fast and take no part in the killing of a Christian soul.'

'So we bide and we watch?'

'With sorrow and fortitude and acceptance, we do.' Beaujeu looked with patient understanding at his friend.

The marshal shook his head. 'May God forgive us.'

'He shall be with us at the appointed hour. Have no doubt the enemy will come.'

Another piece of the plan was revealed and it did not surprise the marshal. Beaujeu had intended to provoke the sultan. Through his bravado night-time raid, he had set out to incite an enraged response that would rebound on the Mameluk. Crossbeams festooned in Templar martyrs were merely part of the psychological and incidental play to the conflict. William of Beaujeu concerned himself with a longer game.

'See there, your grace.' A knight pointed.

Shrill cries faint to the ear had already alerted the grand master to the next bleak phase. At a distance figures could be seen bearing lit palm fronds and putting them to the crucified men. The enemy were intent on pursuing their sport. Their victims writhed and shrieked, the muftis chanted and the flickering brands moved to scorch feet and faces. On the walls of Montmusart, the prayer became more fervent.

Beaujeu gestured to his men. 'Take strength in their strength and courage from their own.'

'We must attack, your grace.' One of his knights leant on the parapet and railed in impotent rage.

'Be calm and still, my brother. We are called in reverence to bear witness at this hour.'

'Are we not turning our backs as Peter did to the Lord?'

'Yet he is since called the Rock.' The grand master raised his voice so that others might hear. 'It matters not how we die, save that we do so with valour and the name of Jesus on our lips. It matters not the hour of our passing, but the manner of our bearing and the light in our hearts.'

The marshal clenched a mailed fist. 'Heed his grace and show no frailty. The *Oriflamme* still shines and the Holy Spirit guides us.'

'Kneel with me and pray, my brethren.'

It was theatre that played out on both the battlements and the plain, a test of wills set against the backdrop of great horror. Nailed on their sparse pieces of wood, the brave souls below held out or hung limp.

Close to death, his heart stuttering and the darkness drawing in, Jean of Sagozan viewed the Arab youngster as though he were a friend. It counted little he was a sworn foe and carried evil in his soul. Amongst the thousands so melded and remote, to identify a mourner brought comfort of a sort. How pleasing to see the boy again.

He motioned with his eyes and groaned what he believed was the sound of words. 'Where once you denied me water, now you bring me fire.'

To cheers and ululation, Hazzim thrust the burning palm leaf upwards.

Not to be outshone by the Templars, the grand master of the Hospital had also decreed a night raid. In spite of their new-found avowal of common cause, pique and jealousy were bound to flare between the orders. Indeed, Beaujeu counted on it. So it was that John of Villiers commanded forwards his Knights of St John on a moonless night and the small and blundering force was roundly beaten. The Saracens had been alert to the danger and prepared for the perfidious antics of the infidel. From henceforth, the Christians would reserve their energy and refrain from venturing beyond the walls. The savage incident had cost the defenders, but its investment was for a purpose.

The reprisal came as violently as the Templar grand master had hoped. In the streaming shadows of pre-dawn, thousands of Saracen moved forwards and slipped across the dry moat. Not a single challenge was shouted or a signal arrow launched. More troops hurried low to the lip of the ditch and slid down, joining their comrades in the solid spearhead of an advance and placing their ladders and escalades for the ascent. Nothing would stop them. They would seek out every weakness, overwhelm the sleeping and the dazed, exploit the lack of readiness among the sorrowing knights. It was customary to wait until a breach had been forced. Ashraf preferred the tactics of shock.

His adversary Beaujeu also favoured an element of confusion and surprise. As the Mohammedans converged, they at first were unaware of the shower of cotton parachutes opening and floating from above and the clay pots with sputtering fuses that they bore. A man did look up and shout a warning, his eyes widening at the caped swarm of fireflies scattering overhead. By then, the ordnance was exploding. Detonations bit into the ranks, flame and shards of metal spilling across the heaving scene to claw randomly at heads and stomachs and limbs. More eruptions followed, the murderous infestation crackling and shimmering among the troops. Some men began to climb while others tried to flee, the momentum of the assault and promise of success unravelling to untidy terror. The hectic and the dead, the maimed and the bewildered, all were caught in the frenzy.

Other things were falling, curving high and plummeting fast with lethal reach amidst the throng. From behind the battlements, one hundred English longbowmen were drawing back strings and bending yew and sending arrows far into the air. Within a minute, one thousand flights had plunged earthwards or were still in travel, punching through armour and flesh and striking the reserves crowding forwards and the vanguard driven back. Frankish catapults joined in, flinging out wildfire and adding to the chaos, propelling the Saracens in burning retreat.

'We blacken their skins as dark as their souls.' Against the flamed illumination and columns of smoke, de Flor hauled a Druze corpse from an embrasure and surveyed the developing rout. 'Our gifts appear to find no favour with them.'

In reply, three men-at-arms put tapers to fuse matches and launched their bomblets over the wall. The drogues filled and snatched the vessels away, the handlers slick with sweat and already turning to the subsequent batch. The Chinese monk had been diligent atop his tower. Working alone, he had fashioned fireworks and filled pots with his black powder, had cut and sewn strips of cloth and crafted his devices. Now they rained upon the Saracen. In the lee of the battle, the boy Benedict and the holy man in saffron robes shuttled the armaments to the front. William of Beaujeu had been right to trust his instinct and find employment for the human gift from the Mongols. Whatever the black magic or secret practices involved, the Chin was earning his keep.

De Flor roared a laugh as he hurled a brace of the grenades. 'I declare their very tails are smoking as they run.'

'Yet you do not permit me to see for myself.' Benedict shouted his disappointment against the searing noise.

'I cherish you, boy.' The adventurer casually lit a powder jar and tossed it over his shoulder. 'It would not do to have your smile split in twain by an arrow or our talisman dismembered.'

'There is scarce a danger I have not faced.'

'Let me be the judge in choosing them.'

A piercing yell cut the din as defenders stepped back and the blackened carcass of a man pulled itself above the parapet. Burnt and barely alive and yet committed to the fight, the Mameluk had groped his way each painful rung of the ascent and emerged disfigured at the summit. It was hardly worth the effort. The blow from a poleaxe opened wide his head and he tumbled to oblivion.

The figure of Beaujeu materialised in the haze. 'Their zeal is admirable if their method is not.'

'We butcher them well.' De Flor spat a ball of phlegm after the departed. 'A fair exchange for those who perished on the cross.'

'However the numbers of the heathen slain, it is no recompense for our dead brothers.'

'Though it offers us rare sport, your grace.' With a flourish, a further volley was sent on its way.

The grand master was understated in his reaction. 'Most of my men apply themselves with a psalm or prayer, de Flor. You would side instead with merry blasphemy.'

'Such is the thrust and cut of combat, your grace.'

'It is more your nature.'

They stood together for a while, observers to the mayhem. For the Christians it was a rewarding night, one lit by arbitrary iridescence and invested with the high-pitched song of mortal fear and dying. And for the grand master of the Knights Templar it was a scene more calming than evening vespers and more reassuring than papal indulgence. Acre could take pride in the manner of its defiance.

Noticing Benedict, the grand master cast him a measured glance. 'Should you not be learning Greek and Latin with the Patriarch?'

'He is indisposed and I am busy, your grace.'

'War is no excuse for ignorance. You will not always be my scout and runner.'

'I have been fetching provision for our defence, your grace.'

'So now we are provided for and our defence secured. Be away with you and find rest. Take up the stylus and the holy books and wait till you are called.'

With a cursory nod and his retinue trailing, the grand master continued on his way. Abandoned in his wake and temporarily dismissed, the youngster stood somewhat crest-fallen. The Templars were hard to please.

'His grace is both sly and wise, boy.' De Flor flashed his charge a supportive grin. 'Leave us to our games and find a nook to doze. Hell will still be here when you awake.'

Sulphurous flames of oil and pitch were flickering from below and the cries of the Saracen were unabated.

～

The mood had changed and the alleyways that had once rung to curses and laughter seemed drained of the life-force Benedict had known. All struggle and energy was now directed to the ramparts. Here was the backwash, the listless unease of helplessness; here was a silence pervaded by the echoed uproar of reported combat. It was easier to man the walls and behold the enemy than mark the hours in reserve.

A few soldiers idled at a tavern, passing the time before their recall. They appeared to take little pleasure in their drink and recuperation, engaged in conversation without real jest or inclination. The youngster understood. He climbed the steps to the orphanage and struck the bell, waiting for the door to open and the children to rush forwards in clamorous greeting. Lady Charlotte was always kind. Though it chafed against his free and adolescent spirit, he was grateful to be welcomed and mothered and accepted in a home that was never his. Briefly, he thought of Hazzim and the village to which he had once been linked. At least these friends showed constancy and would not attack him with a knife.

'You come to see us, Ben!' A little girl ran to his embrace.

She was joined by a small boy clutching for attention. 'Have you fought battles, Ben? Do you use a sword against the Saracen?'

The next. 'Are you hungry?'

'Will you stay?' Another child.

'How many do you kill?'

More clustered around, their delight obvious and their questions loud, as they escorted their hero and prodigal brother towards the interior. He tried to answer, to meet their hopes and allay their fears, to settle and distract them. They were persistent in their devotion. The women looked on in benign resignation.

One of them whispered in his ear. 'Lady Charlotte wishes to speak with you, Benedict.'

The youngster felt his nerves constrict with mild trepidation. He was summoned before a chatelaine of selfless hue and rare benevolence, to stammer and redden in discomforting audience. Lady Charlotte was as virtuous and noble as he was dishevelled and unworthy.

She remained seated as he entered her room and smiled sympathetically. 'Fighting keeps you from us, Master Benedict.'

'I have many errands, my lady.'

'None so well greeted as your visits to our children.' She

beckoned him to sit. 'From the city ramparts to the Hospital of St John, I hear report of your steadfastness and valour.'

'I am no soldier, my lady.'

'Yet you have assumed the tasks and bearing of a man in these past terrible weeks. We fear and pray for you, Benedict.'

'Saracens lie at the gate, my lady. I cannot sit idle while my friends give battle.'

'Your friends are armed and wear hauberks of steel. They are versed in every manner of war.' She gently reached and took his hand and pressed it between her palms. 'Whatever the destiny of others and the grim lure for you of the fray, you are still only a boy.'

'A boy may defend his home and put aside his childish things.'

She raised an eyebrow. 'Are the words and teaching of the Patriarch to be forgotten? Is the fondness and regard we hold for you to go ignored?'

'Peace is a better time for such things, my lady.'

'Though as you confess, you are no soldier.'

There was a stab of frailty in his heart, a moment when he wanted to weep. She would understand. She would embrace him and let him sob as any child. The weakness faded and the opportunity passed.

She watched his face. 'If the young of this orphanage win passage to Cyprus, would you not be minded to join them?'

'I can find no reason to desert.'

'There are those who love you and would wish you safe.'

'It is they who remain in Acre.' Benedict was apologetic in his stubbornness. 'Here is where I live, my lady. I know no other place.'

'A boy like you is fearful of new land and exploit?'

'Forgive me, my lady.'

'You have lost Hazzim as companion and have made

enemies of Spada and his troop. Choose another shore until the danger is past and the Mameluk gone.'

He stood. 'It would be shameful to leave in the face of threat.'

'There is no shame in foresight and no cowardice in escaping what will be. Time is short, Benedict.'

'It was so in Tripoli, my lady.' His chin was set and his mouth determined. 'And there I remained until the last.'

The memory still disturbed. It tripped him with visions of St Thomas Island and its screaming huddled refugees, of swimming Mameluk cavalry and the thrust and fall of blades. Lady Charlotte detected the haunting in his eyes.

'I wish that you still remained longer and carefree as a boy.' Sadness and pity brushed her voice. 'Fate and the likes of Beaujeu have set you on a pathway to perdition.'

'Where once I was a fool I am now twice of him.'

Amethyst could be forgiven his complaint. Stationed in a basket soon to be lowered by line to the floor of the moat, the dwarf showed greater unhappiness as his descent grew near. De Flor could be a persuasive negotiator. He had cajoled and bullied, begged and eventually bribed the little jester into the swaying transport. Personal enrichment depended on it. Heaped at the base of the wall were the Saracen dead, hundreds of corpses burnt and putrefying and spoiling the ground. They were there for the taking, many emirs and officers among them, important men with wealth and influence, Mohammedans in possession of amulets and jewels. Their loss might prove the gain of enterprising others.

De Flor offered final instructions as he tightened a knot. 'Make not a sound, dwarf. Crawl fast and do not be diverted.'

'By pleasure? By wine and song and wenches? How may your charnel hound be diverted?'

'A veritable treasury lies down there.'

'I have no wish to lie among it.'

'Think only on the reward.' The adventurer tested the strength of the fastenings. 'Fill the basket well and I shall be minded to return you here.'

'What loyalty and compassion from my fellow thief.' There was angry resignation to the voice.

'We are liberators not thieves, dwarf.' De Flor eased out the basket and began to feed the rope. 'It would be cruel and mean to leave the slain to the rats.'

'Rats?'

The plaintive whisper trailed and faded as Amethyst was dropped on his platform into the darkness. Above him, de Flor would act the fisherman and play the line and stand ready for his catch. Robbing the dead could be explained as a sacred pastime.

Amethyst hit the ground and clambered free, cursing and praying in silent fervour. The secret portal through which the Templars and Hospitallers had mounted their audacious raids had tonight deposited a dwarf beyond the confines of the city. If a defending firepot did not fall on him from on high, to the fore a Saracen arrow might yet strike him. It was the most unnerving of situations.

He retched at the stench and pulled himself forwards, shying to the initial touch and coldness of a hand and steeling himself to climb the damp and piled dead. Maybe it was easier to commit without the complication of light or vision, without the intrusion of blackened faces and maggot-blown eyes. Conscience and a weak stomach belonged elsewhere. Another pause, another oath, another miasmic release from the soft underbelly of the unidentifiable. Never again would he be persuaded into so foul an undertaking.

Something gave and he slipped into a pocket of viscous

remains from which he wriggled in effort and horror. Hell must stink this way, he thought. Yet reward in pilfering required perseverance. His fingers working, he trawled the cadavers, selecting and discarding and inching forwards in fresh search. One could grow accustomed if not immune to the overall grimness. The forage bag started to fill. Bracelets and necklaces, charms and gem-set daggers, the precious objects were given up and expertly scavenged. Occasionally, the receptacle snagged and progress was slowed; intermittently, the bodies wheezed or ruptured. The dwarf swallowed his revulsion and crawled onward. Some night and quite some trade.

A groan from nearby caused him almost to yelp. *Sweet Mother of Jesus*, he swore in his mind. The Saracen was dying, was panting and whispering in the heathen tongue to himself or to his God. His burial mound was the loneliest of sites. Amethyst listened, interrupting his toil, somehow comforted by the presence of another living spirit. Out here, choice was limited and judgement could become a little skewed. Eventually he withdrew, catching his foot on a ribcage and rolling in untidy cascade down a makeshift scree of bones. *Think only on the reward*, de Flor had said. Easy for one who was not lowered by basket into Hades or forced to eavesdrop on the damned or pushed nose first into rotting flesh. There was much to commend performing acrobatic flips for Amalric and his jaded court.

Voices muttered close and the dwarf shrank from the direction of the sound. Others too must be scavenging in the night. So much for the Mohammedan brotherhood. He slithered away, hauling his load, hoping he would be mistaken for nothing more than a prying rodent. At least his enemy were as blind as he was; they could not risk employing lanterns or burning rushes for fear of being targets for Christian archers or their own.

Three tugs on the rope, a fourth and fifth more desperate and finally a yell.

'Lift me, you knave!'

His cry coincided with the crash of firepots and a bursting pulse of flame, the heat and light swelling to bathe all in their sunlike glow. Through it, the basket and its contents rose. Amethyst clung fast, his face scorched and his canvas jacket blackened, his hands gripping a blistered cord that at any moment might burn through. As his platform swung and turned and arrows broke on the stone around, he caught a glimpse of the threat behind. The foe was massed for a further assault.

'You near killed me! You near killed me!'

Almost speechless and yet repeating the accusation in wild-eyed fright, the dwarf danced and shook with trauma. The symptoms did not prevent him catching a jewel that de Flor threw him from the surrendered bag.

'Our medicines will cure you, dwarf.' The adventurer rummaged with the deftness of a connoisseur. 'It appears from the noise that your greed gives rise to fresh attack.'

Amethyst was uncharacteristically unready to share in the jest.

In daylight and beside a different rampart, the Italians also found little to cheer them. Sprawled with their backs to the inner wall, the peasants had been offered temporary respite and chose to gather in sullen throng along the eastern edge. They were in a dangerous mood. This was not the easy victory and quick spoils for which they had prayed and travelled on Crusade. It did not help that the citizens of Acre now blamed them for their woes, claiming that their attack on the heathen traders had prompted the sultan to avenge. The accusation rankled and mutual distrust grew.

Spada sat and stropped a knife and listened to the mutterings and disquiet. He was shrewd enough to understand that the fervent were often the first to be disheartened, that the disappointed could always devour their own. It was why he kept his lieutenants close and his bodyguards closer. There might come a day when his authority diminished and his aura faded and the disgruntled sought him out with blades and clubs. For the moment, he would watch and be careful.

He glanced at two henchmen crouched and playing dice. 'What are you playing for?'

'The first ring or trinket we cut from a Saracen hand.'

'It shall be the second.' The Umbrian rasped his knife hard across the whetstone. 'You owe me tribute from your takings.'

'We have not forgotten.'

Spada tested the steel on his thumb. 'Nor do I forget it is at the northern wall the greatest riches will be found. Rumour spreads it is the jackal de Flor who profits by his boldness.'

'He has a talent for such things.'

'And all the good fortune.' The second player cast the dice.

His leader closed his eyes and rested against a low stone block. 'While we are condemned to sit in the dirt and peddle our lives for the haughty and proud.'

He lapsed to silent reflection, an embittered commander studying possibilities and crafting a plan. There was always a way to plot a more lucrative course. Offering up his life in a futile gesture was scarcely his priority.

Eyelids slid open. 'There is a bauble the adventurer holds dear. A possession he does not guard or stow aboard his ship.'

'We have made great efforts to kill the boy, Spada.'

'Yet he still runs and laughs and breathes.' The peasant leader scratched ruminatively at the scar on his cheek. 'No pleasure exists while he remains.'

267

'If he dies, there will be consequences.'

'Be assured if he lives the consequences will be harsher.' It was a reminder delivered with a threat. 'His face and being affront me.'

'At the Hospital it is Theobald of Alzey and the Knights of St John who protect him. On the walls, he is within the domain of the Templars.'

'Could he not stray or fall into our grasp? Could not an accident or fate persuade him our way?'

The blade tapped in his palm, measuring the seconds and beating out the rhythm to his thoughts. Spada hated leaving insults unanswered. A fourteen-year-old boy had cut him with a knife and yelled obscenities in his face; a fourteen-year-old boy had caused him further injury at the hands and feet of a mute Chin monk; a fourteen-year-old boy paraded himself as though impervious to repercussion. Spada's honour and position were at stake.

The dice players had paused in their game, uneasy.

Spada appreciated their attentiveness. 'Our task in this siege and city is nearly done and the ships of King Henry of Cyprus will soon appear.'

'They bring fresh troops rather than offer us passage homeward.'

'One provides the other.' The Umbrian grasped a stone and flung it at a scurrying dog. 'Empty holds will ferry us for a price.'

'Amalric forbids such flight on pain of death.'

'He does not reckon with Spada. He does not count on the power of gold and silver and the monies we took from the Arab traders we slew.'

A lieutenant cocked his head. 'You would save the lives of all your men?'

'Those who show me obedience and do not disappoint

and those who bring me the severed ears from a corpse of the
boy named Benedict.'

He placed fingers in his mouth to give a strident whistle.
His men came running.

~

Human beings forever grasp at hope. The cheering broke out
in every quarter, climbing from the rooftops and vibrating
through the streets. Relief had arrived. The sails that first
teased the horizon and then appeared as galleys and transports
and the armed men that tramped ashore were a show of
strength and an answer to prayer. The denizens of Acre knelt
and wept and cried out in joy, embracing the newcomers in
frenzied delight. This was their salvation. Henry of Cyprus
himself was here, a sign of commitment and of forces to
come, a Crusader with true swagger and a presence befitting
a warrior-king. After all, he was born of the bloodline of the
former Frankish rulers of Jerusalem and was present to defend
his birthright. Things would change. It was in the stars and in
the runes, in the royal pennants that fluttered and the trumpets that sounded loud. No more was the city leaderless and
Amalric in charge. The fourth of May 1291, a month into
siege, was a day the Saracens would doubtless rue.

Alone on the roof of the Fonda, Benedict did not share in
the jubilation. Certainly, he had witnessed the pageant, had
marvelled at the grand display of the king and his retinue of
knights and bishops. It would lift the spirits of the most
dejected. But he had observed what they had yet to see, for
weeks past he had studied the vast encampments of the
heathen. There would be no change in the outcome. What
trooped ashore in such majesty and style were little more
than two thousand infantry; the one hundred horses that
pranced and reared upon their landing were pleasing to the

crowd and useless in a siege. Although the people roared and the drums beat and the banners waved, from high above the harbour front the youngster discerned the cheerlessness behind the colour and felt sickened by the lie. Europe had turned its back, the princes would not come, the era of Acre and all Outremer was collapsing to its finish. Benedict wondered if the name he had scratched in the hall of the Hospitallers would ever be found in the ruins.

From a distant window of the Venetian Tower, a trusty of Spada watched the boy and prepared to withdraw and make report.

✝

Chapter 16

They came for him before dawn, four Italians armed with cleavers and falchions and intent on doing murder. It should prove a lucrative pursuit. Spada had offered a high reward. This mission was a test of loyalty. With a clandestine departure planned aboard the emptied ships from Cyprus, this was an opportunity to sift the faithful from the idle and the deserving from the contemptible. The boy must die. He had been tracked for some time, his course plotted as he roamed from Patriarchate to Hospitaller compound, and his final resting place had been chosen. Fortunately he had opted to sleep neither at the orphanage nor hospital and was seen to make his berth on a vacant rooftop. Benedict was alone and undefended. Word went out.

On canvas soles they moved towards the target, a quartet unnoticed in a city whose inhabitants had no interest but siege and their own survival. The internal gates had been left open and their guards consigned to the front; roving patrols had been abandoned and their manpower redirected; meanwhile the citizens snatched sleep from the darkness and the hours of desperate fear. Conditions were perfect. One more butchered corpse on a flat roof would scarcely merit investigation. The men closed in on the building. They climbed the stone flight of steps, casting a backwards glance and listening for pursuit or breath or challenge. In every vendetta there were losers. Had time not been pressing, they would have preferred to play awhile, but the situation demanded a quick strike and then retreat. If the youth screamed, he would be smothered; if he fought, he would be held. There were plenty of ways to skin a child.

A whispered command was passed back. The boy lay curled in a blanket, oblivious to the approaching danger. Without Roger de Flor at his side or Theobald of Alzey as his nursemaid, he was no more than a mischievous louse whose life had run its course. The first Italians scurried low and drove in hard, their blades thrusting to the hilt and sinking through skin and flesh and muscle. It was an untidy business.

'*Madre di Dio! E il Lucifero stesso!*'

It was an oath delivered as a cry, the man recoiling in instant fright to the touch of the head of his victim. These were not human ears he had reached to sever; these bristles did not belong to the face of any man. The killers had just encountered the carcass of a pig. It boded ill and would doubtless provoke in Spada a paroxysm of spiteful rage. If the boy had played a trick, it meant he was forewarned. And if he was forewarned, it implied he had set a trap.

'Shame that you would treat me no better than a pig.' Benedict laughed as he taunted them from another corner of the roof. 'It seems Italians are no match for a boy.'

As the youngster dropped lightly on a rope, his assailants were already making their clumsy descent of the stairs. They could not return to their leader without the entrails of the boy carried in a pail. He would regret his prank. They glimpsed his shadow and gave pursuit, running hard and gaining ground. That the little turd might dodge into a cellar or tunnel made no difference; he was wrong to assume he alone knew the secret byways of the city.

'I shall take your balls, *scarafaccio*.' The lead Italian scraped his knife along a wall.

His seconder was close behind. 'And I your tongue and eyes.'

'Come out to greet us, *scarafaccio*. Do not be timid or delay.'

'We implore you, Benedict.'

'Beg you, *scarafaccio*.'

'You should never have angered Spada.' The murmured threat carried to the interior of a courtyard. 'We are here and you are cornered.'

'It was cruel to deceive us, *scarafaccio*. Now it is our turn to show you a merry trick.'

The Italians edged forwards, tapping their knives on the brickwork and heightening the menace. Maybe the boy would bolt, would throw himself at their feet and gibber in the dust for mercy. His effort would be wasted. Creeping through to the inner compound, the leader of the squad called softly to his prey. 'We are not patient men, *scarafaccio*. Let us talk and reason and resolve this matter.'

'*It is right we should.*'

His words ringing clear, Theobald of Alzey gave his reply. From behind the Italians and to their front, armed Hospitallers slid wraith-like to position. Drawing his troops from among the injured of the hospital, the young knight was capable of confronting any threat. Four peasants carrying blades were no match.

Theobald rested a longsword sloped across his shoulder, his mail hood pulled back to reveal his shock of white-blonde hair.

'Understand what confronts you, peasants. You are no match for my soldiers.'

'Give us the boy.'

'You would make demands of me? You would offer a fight in which you will be vanquished?'

'This is not your argument.'

'Nor is it your victory.' Theobald lowered his sword and held it before him. 'Choose whether to drop your weapons or be returned in quartered pieces to your master.'

'All we wish for is the boy.'

'He is protected by the order. Your wish shall not be granted.'

'We will pay you, knight.'

'Neither my conscience nor the boy is for trade.'

Desperation echoed in the hollow bravado of the peasant. 'What authority have you to challenge us? What lends you the right to interrupt our task?'

'Our steel outmatches yours.' The sword twitched.

Resolve broke and a knife clattered earthward. A second joined it, a third and reluctantly a fourth and the surrender was complete. Disarmed, the Italians were bound and led away and the ad hoc band of patients could finally disperse. Left behind were Theobald and Benedict.

'Our plan was well accomplished, Ben.'

'I am blessed in my friends.' The youngster was strangely subdued in the aftermath. 'What will happen to them, Theo?'

'There is room for them on the forward rampart and much battle for them ahead.'

'Will Spada send more against me?'

'One *Schweinerei* for this night I trust is enough.' With mention of a pig, Theobald drew a laugh from the boy. 'Have no fear, Ben. Even a small cockroach may put Italians to flight.'

The youngster was reassured. He had enjoyed the challenge and the chase. For the remaining hours of darkness he could sleep undisturbed. No peasant would upset the balance of things or penetrate the Hospitaller and Templar shield thrown up about him. He had lived through another night and that was reason enough to be grateful. Whether knight or humble infantryman, all relied on him, on the little cockroach, on the one they called Benedict of Acre.

'I am thankful to you, monsieur.'

Cowled against the night breeze, Lady Charlotte stood with Roger de Flor as his crew ushered or carried the orphans to a waiting vessel. The exodus had been arranged, the payment made and the adventurer was well satisfied. His investment would have both earthly and heavenly reward. The good lady was content; the good lady stood beside him; the good lady exerted an influence on him he had never before encountered. It was always disconcerting to be in the presence of the virtuous.

Her voice was soft in the darkness. 'By the will of God and with your help, we have saved a few of the innocents in Acre tonight.'

'Innocents in Acre are rare, my lady. But I am glad for this brood.'

'There is one who does not join them.' She paused to lean and kiss a sleeping baby nestled in the arms of a wetnurse. 'Benedict resists all persuasion.'

'It is his way, my lady. He is stubborn and brave and a creature of the city.'

'He is only a boy.'

'A boy raised here. A boy who is intent on becoming a man. A boy bent on glory.'

'Wherever we seek glory, we find our own destruction.'

De Flor murmured an order to a crewman and returned to Lady Charlotte. 'You are fond of my young charge.'

'It weighs heavy on my heart that he should be so endangered. Oblivion lies here, monsieur.'

'I do not see you stepping to a ship, my lady.'

'Abandon the place to which I came on holy pilgrimage?' She might have been teasing him in the blue-black twilight. 'We each of us have fates left to run, monsieur.'

'They seem to meet and cross, my lady.'

'Perhaps they will do so again.' She embraced a gaggle of children and comforted them onward with soft speech and the sign of the cross. 'There is work yet to do in Acre.'

'Our city will survive or fall without you.'

'I cannot abandon it while a boy and an adventurer cling to its bitter end.'

'You are as immovable as he is, my lady.'

She laughed lightly in retort. 'So I am fortunate to have a galley and its master ready for my flight.'

The last of the children crossed to the deck and the lines were slipped for the ship to depart. She would make fast progress for Cyprus and later return with supplies for the siege. De Flor listened to the creak of timbers and the slap of waves, to the unfurling snap of canvas as the wind took and filled the sails. It was pleasurably disorientating to have thought of others and done right. He would remember the sensation and now direct himself to war.

～

Some were not as fortunate as the orphans bound for Cyprus. To the solitary beat of a drum, prisoners were led out to a scaffold before the palace, deserters captured while attempting escape aboard the transports of King Henry. An example would have to be made. In grand array on a stone elevation, the monarch and his retinue stood in solemn witness, a party garbed in mail and carrying swords and eager to proclaim the cause. Weakness could not be tolerated; cowardice would be punished.

Stepping forwards on his podium, Henry paused to survey the expectant crowd. They might not know him well or have ever seen his face, but they would listen and they would heed.

'I am your King. King of Cyprus and of Acre, a King born to the royal line of those who ruled Jerusalem.' He glared defiant above the scene. 'Ours is a time of war and stuggle, our lot is to resist. What say you?'

'We shall! We shall! We shall!'

'Thus do we stand at the frontier between good and evil and civilisation and darkness, and at the threatened reaches of Christendom. Are you with us?'

'We are! We are! We are!' Their words tumbled upwards.

'There are those not so engaged, those who falter in the face of danger and side with the forces of Satan.'

'Shame on them! Destroy them!'

Henry stood silent until the uproar had abated. 'Where we demand fealty, these fiends betray. Whilst we require bravery, they skulk and seek escape.'

'Bring justice upon them! Send them to hell!'

Hades was close. The king nodded and the ritual of forcing seven bound and struggling captives to mount the steps commenced. They would scarcely be missed; they would be a useful conductor of popular blame and fear. The mob yelled abuse as the ropes were tugged tight about the necks. Seconds passed, shoulders heaved, intended victims shook and fidgeted.

Henry provided the valediction. 'Let them pay for their crimes. Let them taste the vengeful wrath of the Crusader.'

One by one the stanchions were kicked from beneath the planks. Legs thrashed and bodies gyrated as the prisoners fought for purchase and air and life. The mast laid horizontal and from which their ropes hung was the nearest any of the condemned would come in finding passage to a different land. *Long live the King*, the people cried. Seven of his subjects had not much longer left to go.

Motioning to the spectacle, Henry turned to his brother at his side. 'Am I too harsh, Amalric?'

'You are King and I a mere Constable.' The resentment was only thinly disguised. 'You will do as your conscience and calling dictate.'

'And you, Beaujeu?' Henry slewed the question to the Templar on his right.

'Give a man the chance and he will run. Remove that chance and he will fight.'

'Our dancers below forfeited such opportunity.'

'Few will weep.' Beaujeu was sanguine in his assessment. 'A coward on the rampart is more deadly than a thousand Saracen poised armed at the gate.'

'So the coward must die. Thus speaks the warrior I trust, the one who stands firm and undaunted against the foe.'

'You honour me, majesty.' With a dip of his head, the grand master acknowledged the praise for himself and the intended slight to Amalric.

He bridled. 'We all of us here defend these walls, brother.'

'Some with more vigour and prowess.' The elder sibling reviewed the events below. 'Yet I fear, however determined our struggle, we shall not prevail upon the outcome.'

'We hang men for thoughts of defeat, brother.'

'Hypocrisy is the right of a king.' Henry addressed himself to the Templar. 'Speak without flattery or embellishment, Beaujeu.'

'Time and weight of numbers oppose us, majesty. You

come with two thousand men when twenty thousand would scarcely alter our position. By the day our towers are undermined and our annihilation draws closer.'

'You fight with the tenacity of a victor.'

'It is the way of the Temple and the sacred duty of its knights. We will neither surrender nor retreat.'

'The moment may come when we shall count on such sacrifice.'

'We shall give it gladly.'

On the gallows, the frantic movement had subsided to the gentle flicker and fade of men at last gasp. The crowd was silent. The deed was nearly done and the reinforcement of the message had been made. King Henry would not tolerate feebleness and timidity.

The king muttered to no one in particular. 'It seems the noose tightens and brings us all to the throes of death.'

'We shall face whatever is ordained.' Beaujeu glanced at the monarch. 'God alone is our judge.'

'As you alone shall be my counsel. What would you have me do with the Sultan now, Beaujeu?'

'Parley.'

Walking among his handiwork, the hangman pulled at the dangling feet of the departed to ensure there could be no resuscitation or reprieve. The corpses would hang awhile as warning and for the benefit of the scavenging birds. In the hushed throng of onlookers, Spada watched without comment or emotion. He had lost several of his men to this public display, been stripped of authority and his capos through blunder and misjudgement. Another four loyalists had been squandered in his fruitless quest to kill the boy. His position was exposed and that made him angry. Negotiation was far from his mind.

*

'Be silent . . .'

They paused in their tasks, crouching in their scrapes and recesses. The King Hugh barbican was no place for either the fearful or the brave. It was simply a holding pen before death, crumpling before the heavy blows rained on it, a start line and staging post for the impending fall of Acre. Those who crept out by night to reinforce the depleted garrison were quickly disabused of any hope and were often carried back the following morn. Every minute the shot and arrows flew and battle raged. Debris and casualties littered the ground. The forward defence was fading.

Now from its depths they heard a different sound, the rasp and tap of the enemy mining for their foundations. Few underestimated the danger. The prowess of Saracen tunnellers had entered legend, the fall of many a Frankish town and castle owed to the collapse of the walls and the fires set beneath. Stone edifices presented a formidable front, yet their vulnerability lay below in the arches and wooden piles on which they sat. Create a space filled with kindling and brushwood, ignite its timber supports, and the tallest structure would come crashing down. Saladin himself had employed the device. His Mameluk successor in holy war too appreciated its effect.

'As burrowing demons, they come for us.'

In a cellar of the barbican, the sergeant kept his ear to a flagstone and listened to the vibration. His commentary did little to improve the gloom. About him, his men sat in bowed stillness, some praying and others frozen in bewilderment and fear. Volunteer or drafted, each waited for the inevitable and unseen.

'It is as though they dig our graves.'

'No truer word is spoken, brother.'

An infantryman stood and paced fretfully. 'At any instant a thousand stones may bury us.'

'Despair will not aid you.' The sergeant sat upright to deliver his rebuke. 'You would rather a Saracen quarrel in your throat? A heathen lance through your gut?'

'I ask for a chance to live.'

The sergeant scoffed. 'You surrendered it when you came to this barbican. We are soldiers and it is our reason to die.'

'Like rats?'

An Italian with mean eyes and a sour face spat the query from an alcove. He was unhappy to be anywhere near the front, disgusted at his lot in being captured by Hospitallers during the mission to kill a worthless boy and condemned to serve at a doomed post.

He scowled at the group and pulled resentfully on a flask of liquor. 'I did not ask for such commission.'

'Yet you received it.' The sergeant leapt to his feet and dragged the man resisting to the fold. 'No Spada is here to protect you. So be of cheer you are with brave men who shall meet their maker with a roar.'

'I mean no complaint.'

'Nor do I mean to kick you down the shaft.' The sergeant shook the man and gestured to the heaped excavation at the far corner of the room.

Order was restored and the waiting continued. Some began to converse, the better to quell the hollow fear and to mask the echoing resonance. They talked of loved ones, of wives and whores and girls left behind, of towns passed and foreign sights pillaged. King Henry of Cyprus might claim Acre sat at the frontier of civilisation. Only these Christian soldiers were deployed beyond the border.

A filth-caked head emerged above the earth spoil, the eyes alone visible through the grime. The chief counter-miner had returned to make report.

'We are ready.'

It was a voice resigned and aged by dust, conveying horrors seen and acts to come. The shaft dug by the Franks was complete. There was no alternative but to offer battle below ground, to consign men in blind and narrow struggle to hold the line and preserve a while longer the integrity of the fort. Doomed souls could perform heroic feats. They would descend the wooden rungs into the darkness, worm and scrabble their way to an airless and constricted tomb. When the first Mohammedan chisel broke through, then would they strike.

No speech was necessary. Three men rose and walked to join the miner, their course set. There would be no tears and sentiment or long farewell. Theirs was a calculation that, where on the ramparts they were wasted, in the bowels of the earth their effort might achieve something. With a nod to their comrades, they checked their knives and readied for the climb.

At the tunnel entrance, their guide waited. The Assassin was glad for the extra company.

It took either courage or foolhardiness to ride out to the enemy under flag of truce, unarmed on two chargers. The Saracens stood mute and lowered their weapons as the pair of mounted Templars paraded by. The cursed Franks were certainly bold. They had slaughtered many among the faithful, had sallied forth with steel and fire, had ceded not one inch of ground. Yet now they clopped by as though in royal review, proud and imperious knights still with the blood cross upon their surcoats and the manner of victors in their bearing. Ashraf would soon educate and put them to the sword. They continued, oblivious.

Attended by his emirs and bodyguards, the sultan watched their approach. He faulted the judgement of these Latins rather than their pluck. For centuries they had been the hated symbol of invasion; for years, he had dreamt of sowing the fields with their perfidious bones. And here were two of their infidel kind serenely walking their steeds in his direction.

At some distance they dismounted and were funnelled through the ranks of Saracen as they trod the last few hundred paces. Crossbows were cocked and trained and spears bounded their slow advance. There was no predicting what fiendish trickery the zealot knights might try. The javelins lowered and they were forced to halt.

Ashraf was chill in his greeting. 'You bait the lion and yet would place your head in his jaws.'

'We are messengers and no more.' One of the duo answered in Arabic. 'King Henry bids us come to parley.'

'Has he not heard how I treat all Templars? Does he not know I engage in war?'

'As one ruler to another, he seeks fraternal bond and extends the hand of peace.'

'I would as soon strike it from his wrist.'

The Templar was undeterred. 'We commit no wrong that gives you cause for siege. For many years past we enjoyed tranquillity and trade and the bounty of our common understanding.'

'Such understanding is vanished.'

'Though we stand on a plain of war, concord may yet be devised.' The knight gestured to the pressing crowd about him. 'So many will die for so little consequence.'

'Martyrdom is its own reward.'

'Truce too has its merit.'

The sultan almost sneered. 'For the glory of Allah, I would sacrifice ten hundred thousand men and ten hundred thousand more.'

'You broke our binding treaty, Ashraf.'

'Where was that treaty when you butchered our brothers in Acre and laid waste to their villages about? Where was this dignity and shared position when your Grand Master sought alliance with the Mongol and entreated your Roman pope to send Crusade?'

'Mistrust begets mistrust, Ashraf.' The Templar maintained his steady gaze. 'Reconciliation is what we ask.'

'I offer battle.'

'King Henry will make calm redress.'

'It is for Acre that I come.'

Reconciliation and calm redress. Absurd notions, the sultan mused. Yet he admired the fearlessness of the Templar breed. How Beaujeu had manoeuvred and fought. If he were not high priest of the Unbelievers his antics would almost be commendable. Frankish brinkmanship was reaching its natural conclusion.

Ashraf picked distractedly at the gilt thread on his robe. 'Previous envoys sent to me in Cairo had their heads devoured by wild dogs and their bodies fed to crocodiles.'

'Mercy would speak more eloquently of your greatness.' It was the second Templar who chose to speak.

'It would?' The Mameluk ruler eyed him. 'I nailed your brethren to crosses and you presume to offer counsel?'

'I address you as a humble bearer of words.'

'Humility does not become a Templar. Speak of your demands.'

'King Henry desires for terms.'

'And I shall grant them. Lay down your arms and surrender the fight and award me the key to the city.'

Consternation glimmered in the faces of the knights as the first responded. 'If we relayed such things to Acre, we would be deemed traitors.'

'To refuse is to misjudge.'

'We cannot accept your offer, Ashraf.'

'Or is it that you will not?' The eyes were dark and dangerous. 'I propose to spare Henry and Amalric, the grand masters of the military orders, the infidel inhabitants of your besieged domain. My conditions are generous.'

'They give us nothing.'

Ashraf would have replied, but the sudden fall of a catapult shot intervened in a blur of dirt and blood. A long throw and a close landing, an insult and a breach of trust. Men screamed or rolled misshapen and dead and emirs and officers shied. Their sultan wiped a fleck of matter from his beard. Slowly, he drew his scimitar. Plainly the Pisans atop their tower operated to their own particular rules; certainly, they had added range to their engine of war; undoubtedly, there would be consequence. He stepped towards the Templars.

'My Sultan, why stain your blade on such worthless dogs?' An aged scholar bowed low. 'They remain beneath a flag of parley.'

'We stand in the shadow of their deceit.'

Yet vengeance could wait. He would let them live for the while, permit them to leave their mounts and stumble on foot the way they came. There was no further need for talk or prospect of settlement without recourse to massacre. It was only a matter of days.

~

Amethyst was a demanding teacher. As the handstand collapsed and Benedict again fell sprawling in the straw, the dwarf idled against a barrel and demanded a repeat. It had been a bruising afternoon. Yet the youngster welcomed the chance to shed his recent memories of the hospital and the walls and the surrounding vistas of ruin. The cheery tyranny of an undersized jester was the antidote to all ills.

'You must be light on your feet and not heavy on your arse.' Amethyst delivered another sigh. 'Clumsiness is no skill for a tumbler.'

'I'm trying, Amethyst.'

'Endeavour will not win you praise.'

'A dwarf thrown from a roof may raise a smile.' The boy laid flat his palms and tucked in his chin to hoist himself in the lift. 'I have it, Amethyst. I have it.'

'Hold your stance and return with a flourish.'

For half a minute Benedict maintained his inversion, balancing like an acrobat and delighting in success. It could be added to the conjury and illusion, the flips and rolls and the notes of a lute he had carefully mastered. Flushed with exertion he recovered to standing and proffered a bow to his tutor.

'What say you, Amethyst?'

'I say you are a stubborn and ingrate student. I say this dwarf is threatened in his sinecure.'

The youngster beamed. 'You may keep your court and all its lords and ladies.'

'A pity. Their company begins to vex and bore me.'

Benedict eased himself against a neighbouring cask and selected a piece of straw to chew. There were few more observant than his diminutive friend. Where the Patriarch was wise, Amethyst was canny; where de Flor could submit to a rush of blood, Amethyst would appraise from a different vantage. He was a valuable ally.

The youngster gazed skyward and tracked a smudge of haze. 'I wonder where Selim may be.'

'A safer place than you or I. You should have gone with his camels or sailed for Cyprus, Ben.'

'And leave you without your pupil? Desert the Patriarch and Roger and Theo?'

'We are old enough to meet our fate.'

'I too am ready.'

'No one doubts it.' Amethyst folded his arms and joined the boy in staring at the puffs of smoke. 'Still I would favour you resting far from here.'

He was on his feet, at the scarring rumble of sound had bounded forwards in a single leap. To the north-east, pluming high above the city, a volcanic shadow of dust and debris curled heavy in the air. The barbican of King Hugh had just tottered and collapsed.

†

✝

Chapter 17

'Back! Back! Return to the walls!'

In a scattering rush, the royal troops and militiamen retreated pell-mell from the barbican. As its defences avalanched, the garrison set fire to the platforms and floors and fled behind a screen of flame. They had no choice. Around them, the enemy were closing, the clamour of war and cacophony of beating drums and wailing horns driving the Christians back. It was a perilous moment.

For the Assassin amidst the scrambling chaos, the occasion provided cover and a quiet sense of fulfilment. He had worked diligently to speed the final collapse and killed many infidels in the cause. They never suspected. Indeed, he had been lauded for the long and selfless hours he had spent counter-mining in the subterranean gloom. The Franks were not the most perceptive. So here he was, clambering over rubble and blackened planks to escape. It marked the end of the beginning and the beginning of the bloody obliteration of Acre.

'Help me, brother.'

The words were weak with pain and faint against the background roar. The Assassin turned. Pinned by tumbled stone and timber, a soldier lay panting and dying and in a semi-conscious state. What a shame he had ever left Cyprus. Now he was trapped. The Assassin paused to crouch beside him.

There was dull hope in the eyes of the man. 'You come for me, brother.'

'I do.'

'May God bless you.' The man murmured his gratitude through clenched teeth. 'Will you free me?'

'In every regard.'

'My wife and child will thank you.'

'I doubt they will ever know.'

He bent and applied his blade to the proffered neck. The man did not fade without a struggle. Another one down. A mercy killing of sorts, a solitary betrayal among a host of others.

Flames leapt and the King Hugh barbican sank. From the heights of the Accursed Tower, King Henry and his brother Amalric regarded the events with grim acceptance. The cindered ruin of the barbican, the withdrawal across the moat, the colonisation of the captured ground, all were portents of the future.

Amalric coughed the bitter taste of ash from his mouth. 'We bear witness to the funeral of Acre.'

'There is fight yet left in us.' The hand of the king clenched tight on the pommel of his sword. 'Though I concede the prospect is bleak and the enceinte threatened.'

'It is a matter of days, brother.'

'So let those days be counted and our swords be keen.'

The Constable shook his head. 'Your loyalty to this city is wasted.'

'Would you have me quit as soon as I arrive? You would have me mocked and taunted in every court of Europe?'

'Christian princes are in no condition to be your judge.'

'Yet they will still agitate and condemn.' Henry stared

morose at the Saracen banners visible through the billowing haze. 'I must at least make a semblance of a stand.'

His brother scoffed. 'To satisfy your pride? So that minstrels may sing of your endeavour?'

'Though walls may crumble, name and honour and repute may last.'

'Honour will die as the rest and lie mouldering in the ditch.'

Their exchange was disturbed by the eddying blast of Saracen trumpets carrying notes high above the castellations. It was an assertion of creeping victory.

'There is no harsher sound.' Amalric appeared lost to his musings.

'A King running in full cry from his city I vouch would match it.'

'All will run with you, brother.'

'Not the Templars. Nor the Hospitallers. Nor indeed the Teutons.'

'Leave them to their chosen ends.' The Constable gave a bloodless smile. 'Beaujeu offers his order as a willing sacrifice because for him there is no other way. The Crusade is over and the priestly knights finished.'

'I hanged men for cowardice and you now would have me embrace it.'

Amalric squinted at his brother. 'Acre has no worth and rests already on the pyre. It is reason and not weakness that directs us.'

His brow creased in brooding thought and his red beard jutting downwards, the king pondered his dilemma. He was content to waste lives where circumstance demanded it, but Acre was condemned and that was a fact. When the hour came and the towers began to fall, when the outer skin was shed and the Mameluks had their salient, then would he take ship as fast as he was able. It was best to be prepared.

He glanced at his sibling. 'Send word to the royal galley. Inform its master to be ready in stealth and haste for our leaving.'

The throwing arms of the mangonels dipped and swung and the giant shot plunged into the walls in showers of dust and shedding stone. The King Henry Tower faced the brunt of the assault. What had once been battlements now resembled shapeless mounds; what had once seemed impregnable now was scarred with fissured wounds. Remorselessly the feared black oxen worked and patiently the Saracens waited. Already the siege towers had inched forwards in readiness for the end and the orders of the sultan. Daily he would visit from his tent to confer with his generals and engineers in refining the attack. A reckoning was close.

Armed with a sword and embossed shield and with his keffiyeh wound tight about his head, Hazzim sat calmly among his fellows. He prostrated himself and prayed as they did, chanted as they did, rehearsed as they did. In his soul, he no longer yearned for his family or hankered for the village life erased by Spada and his peasant throng. The present and the future were what mattered. It brought joy to see the slow disintegration of the enemy, to think upon the slaughter that would follow. Any day or hour the command might come.

Another volley of rock struck and pitted the defence in a meteor storm of spill and debris. How the Latins must despair. Hazzim thought briefly of his former friend without regret, wondering if Benedict still sat on the roof of the Fonda and looked out across the Bay of Acre. In the final hours that vista would alter to bloody chaos. The Christian boy had once spared his life, had allowed him to slip unharmed from the marauding rage of the Templars. He felt contempt instead of gratitude. All infidels were foolhardy and weak and destined to be crushed under foot.

'No sound is sweeter or sight more beautiful, my brother.' An Arab infantryman gripped his shoulder and pointed to the view. 'Their moat fills with rubble and dead and we are poised to cross it.'

'I am honoured to serve with my brethren.'

'Are you willing to die?'

'As a soldier and a martyr.' A rare smile trespassed on the solemn countenance. 'I will slay the Unbelievers and seek out death for myself.'

'You shall be blessed and rewarded in paradise.'

'It is why I answered the call of the Sultan.'

His response earned a nod of approval. There was no denying the fervour of the youngster or the scope of his commitment. After all, he had tortured the crucified Templars with alacrity and burnt off their screaming faces without a flicker of a conscience. He could be relied upon.

A cheer went up and blades were raised in salute to the bombardment. The white-turbanned emirs were finding it difficult to restrain their men and prevent an early onrush for the foe. Discipline must be maintained until Ashraf decreed. Both pulse and pace were quickening.

'See, it is the emir Shujai.' The Arab directed his gaze at a martial figure seated astride a horse. 'He sends hourly reports to the Sultan and makes calculations for the attack.'

Hazzim studied the distant Mameluk, admiring the gilded armour catching on the sunlight. 'The infidel commanders will also be making their calculation.'

'They have little time remaining. Once their towers fall,

we shall take their outer walls. From there, we will seize the city.'

'I know their knights. They will not go meekly to their graves.'

'Yet they shall go nevertheless.' The infantryman was convincing in his assertion. 'What are they defending but false beliefs and a pile of stone, a nest of whores and foul corruption? What do we seek but salvation and the purity of faith?'

'We are fortunate to bear witness.'

'Remember it, my brother. Ashraf commands that every one of them must die.' The eyes of the Arab soldier glistened with eagerness. 'To the last man, woman and child.'

~

An artificial calm hung over the harbour, the hours of darkness bringing the sea breeze and the wash and lap of waves to replace the tension of the day. Yet few of the citizens slept any more. Benedict was among them. He strolled with easy tread out along the breakwater for the Tower of Flies. The beacon glimmered at the furthest point, radiating defiance and beckoning assistance that would not come. It was like a mourning candle for the dead, the youngster thought. He had walked this way so many times, had dodged the salt spray and raced Hazzim to the end. When Acre fell, it would act as the final outcrop.

He stared back towards the darkened quays, overlaying the invisible with invented scenes of his own. They were of Tripoli at the downfall. Occasionally, the remote sky flickered to an incendiary and the growl of combat rasping faint to his ear. He savoured the isolation, the pause before impending horror. There would be an evening or dawn when the Saracens broke through and the waterfront heaved to the thrashing panic of escape, when skiffs and lighters pulled away and children sobbed and women shrieked and men brawled and clambered to reach the safety of a galley deck. But not yet.

Softly, the charmed notes of a lute stirred melodic in the air and drew him from his reverie. He stood entranced. It was music that belonged elsewhere, to courtly ritual and mannered ways and the peaceful disport of nobles. Captain or troubadour, mercenary or poet, Roger de Flor was a master of contradiction and surprise.

'It seems that both of us seek solace in isolation.' The adventurer plucked at a string and did not look up. 'You are welcome to be my audience.'

'What do you sing?'

'Of love, boy. Old love and lost love and squandered love, love regained and love new.'

'Lady Charlotte?'

The music ceased. 'My sentimental musing will not prevent a strap across your impudent hide.' It was an unconvincing bluff.

'Your words do not frighten me.'

'My song no doubt shall.' De Flor tightened and tested a string on the instrument. 'What brings you here at such hour, boy?'

'I would ask you the same.'

'Where else may a man find peace to play his 'ud or a tower that is not yet undermined?'

Benedict sat in Arab fashion on his haunches. 'I know the barbican is taken.'

'Others will follow, redoubt by redoubt, until we reach the end.'

'Will you fight?'

'Tonight I choose music.' The adventurer ran his fingers in

a sliding scale. 'In a trial of strength, there must always be a final victor. At Acre it is the heathen.'

'You are bound to the Templars, Roger.'

'I am bound to no one save myself. Yet I am torn. My allegiance is both to profit and to war.'

'We cannot flee.'

'Even the aged Patriarch has prepared his oak and cedar caskets for his journey on from here. Even the dauntless King Henry and his timid brother Amalric. Even the Venetians and the Pisans.'

'But not the knights of the Temple or the Hospital.'

'They have their destinies as we have ours.' De Flor ceased plucking absent-mindedly on the instrument. 'Acre is an anchorage condemned, a jetty from which to board our galleys.'

'It is my home.' Benedict found his voice constricting on the words.

'No, boy. It is a way point in your life and mine, a city enjoyed and now to be engulfed. Your true home lies in the heart and spirit.'

'I was born here. Raised here. Forged here.'

'Things are changed as we all must change.' Softening his statement, de Flor reached and patted the arm of the boy. 'We shall yet have plenty of adventures.'

Worry scarcely touched de Flor. He was an immortal in perpetual motion, happiest when cast adrift or seated cross-legged in the eye of a siege with a lute across his knees and a Persian bow and quiver close to hand. As he played, Benedict crouched silent and transported. There was the splash and creak of feathering oars as rowing boats patrolled the harbour chain, the shuttered light of lanterns as guards patrolled the capstan on the landward side. Enemy swimmers or raiders in small boats were an ever-present danger. Yet the thoughts of the youngster ranged to the past, to the camel master Selim and the bandit chief Marzouca, to the slave market of Damascus and the meeting with the Mongol. Still the song caressed the dark. *We shall yet have plenty of adventures.* He was in the desert and the stars shone and the possibilities were endless. His warrior-guardian was right. Things indeed were changed.

A noise and discordant cry, the faint suggestion of a struggle, and de Flor was on his feet with the youngster at his side. His tune forgotten, the adventurer peered towards the city.

'What has happened, Roger?'

'An affray of some kind.' De Flor strained to extract the detail from the gloom. 'No general alarm is raised.'

'Then it is of small concern.'

'If you should be of small mind; but commotion means a fight, and a fight demands de Flor.'

'Why, Roger?'

'It is my nature and my vocation.' The adventurer roughly tousled the hair of the boy. 'Man our craft. We will go together to the battle.'

A waterfront dispute had escalated to a full brawl as the pair steered their commandeered vessel for the seat of the trouble. Where there were broken teeth and argument or the fears and demons unleashed by siege, the enterprising could find opportunity. De Flor might act as fixer or thief, as ally or enemy, as partisan friend or disinterested party. He was less than fastidious in his inclinations. Benedict accompanied him as he so often did, pulling on the oars and lost to the excitement. The fragile moment of tranquillity was broken.

What had once seemed impregnable had now decayed to a crumbled ruin. In hurried succession the English Tower, the Tower of the Countess of Blois and the St Nicholas Tower had ruptured and the walls about them had sunk. Without their frontal bastions, the Latins no longer had platforms for their catapults; without their lofty ramparts, they could not present an unbroken defence. The St Anthony Gate was vulnerable and the King Henry Tower held out forlorn. About them, the banners of the Mameluk crowded and the Crusaders knelt in their rubble redoubts and waited for the onslaught.

With its outer skin flayed away, Acre was a wounded beast staggering towards a brutal end. There would be no relief or change of fortune. So men deserted and men hid, men killed each other and settled scores. Among the peasant Italians, the original quest for salvation and plunder was reduced to argument and bitter reproach. They had no wish to fight or to stay, no reason to obey the command of any king or Constable or bishop. Rebellion was afoot.

'We come for you, Spada.'

Threats ricocheted in the underground passageways, the hunters bearing torches and searching through the labyrinth. Fortune had turned for the Umbrian. His minions blamed him for their setback and his surviving lieutenants fuelled their resentment. Besides, he had promised much and delivered little, had caused some to hang and others to be consigned to the now vanished barbican of King Hugh. Embittered and seeking vengeance, they prowled after him in the depths. He would be forced to suffer and atone.

'Do you see him?'

'Not a single glimpse. It is as dark as Hades.'

'Where Spada belongs.'

'I find a further tunnel.'

'More light this way. He hides close, I know it.'

In truth, they knew almost nothing and saw even less. Pressed into the shadows, Spada listened to their voices and identified the renegades. It smarted that he should have led them so far and been rewarded with pursuit. The ingrate fools. Perhaps he should have expected their dedication to wane, for they were hewn of the same earth clods as he and were quite as venal and cruel. If he did not respect them, then at least he understood. Their mistakes, their weakness and their blundering ways were there to be exploited.

Instinctively he shrank from the encroaching light. For the moment they had no direction or scent. It was moot who was in most danger. Spada flexed the cord in his hands and thought of how his men once searched to butcher a slumbering boy. Peasants could be undiscerning with their targets.

'He is here. I have found his shoe.'

'There shall be no escape.'

'Hush now, brothers.' A more authoritative voice. 'Creep silent and keep your wits and hearing sharp.'

'We outnumber him.'

'Yet he is Spada.'

It was true, the Umbrian mused. He was the sword, the natural leader, the bringer of vengeance to the Holy Land. These creatures were of no consequence without him at their head. But they were making progress and were keen to spill his blood. He backed further into a recess and swore beneath his breath. At any second they might stumble blind on his lair.

Steel connected with rock, the brief sound betraying the presence of a blade. One of the aggressors was on a foray of his own. Most unwise, thought Spada. Things could have been so different. Had his latest attempt to escape by ship not been thwarted by vigilant harbour guards and abandoned in the ensuing scuffle, he would be whoring and drinking the tavern trail home to Italy. A shame it should end this way.

He struck as the lantern swung past, embracing the throat

of his victim into the noose and angling the back hard to his knee. The man struggled and released his lamp and made a vain attempt to slip the trap, but the garrotte tightened and the hands fluttered aimless and absurd.

'You would seek to outwit Spada? To slay him as a cellar rat?' He hissed his contempt in the ear of the dying and expected no response. 'Now who is the cornered rat?'

The reply was inaudible as the ligature crushed the trachea. With care, Spada lowered the body and waited for the reprisal. He was ready for the imbeciles, equal to their force, prepared to gouge out eyes and tear out hearts in order to preserve the natural order.

Yet someone else was at work, uninvited company that had caused screams and ragged grunts of pain to filter through the chambers. The assailants had been ambushed. Scarcely believing his luck, Spada snuffed the lantern and insinuated himself deeper into the murk. From there he would bide and watch and plan.

Above a fresh cluster of kills, the Assassin wiped his blade and looked about the cavern. He was still alive and at large and ahead of the pursuit.

'From dust we are come and to dust we shall return.'

William of Beaujeu was sparing in his comment, for it was indeed to dust the King Henry Tower was consigned as its ravaged front sheared away. Another piece in the defence of Acre was gone and the inner bastions left exposed. Through the unnatural dusk and uproar the enemy advanced, laying plank bridges and casting grapnels and swarming over the wreckage of fortification past, taking ground and cutting away at the pockets of resistance. The crossing had been made. Valiantly, the royal troops fought. Yet outnumbered and exhausted by the weeks of pounding siege, they could not stay the flow. All the while, the Saracen banners crested and fell back and pushed forwards and held. Ashraf was committing more troops into the breach.

With a sanguine eye, the grand master of the Templars assessed the situation with his marshal. 'The heathen has gained a salient from which he will not be forced. Our hour at last is come.'

'It may wait, your grace. The Hospitallers even now charge in to give battle.'

'John of Villiers is a redoubtable and practised soldier. Yet his knights are few and the foe determined.'

'Are we not determined, your grace? Have our swords not winnowed the foe before?'

'We are attempting to crush a locust plague that infests a field of wheat.' Beaujeu studied the arrowhead of knights plunging to the fray and blunting on impact. 'That was a defiant act. A brave and noble act. An act which alters nothing.'

'Should we retreat to the inner wall, your grace?'

'And be seen as cowards and deserters from our post?' The grand master frowned beneath his chain mail hood. 'I have not slept in armour these weeks past to cede honour to the Hospital or ramparts to the Saracen.'

'None may question the valour of the Templars.'

'Yet all suspect and envy us. At every turn I endeavoured to deflect the blow with prayer and parley and manoeuvre and subterfuge. It has all lead to this.' There was resignation in the words, but no rancour.

'God will thank us where mortals demur.'

Beaujeu stared ahead. 'The sun is bright and we find our Calvary.'

Arrayed behind him, his knights stood ready with their longswords and shields, disciplined warriors waiting on command. They would do as their grand master demanded, go forwards to slaughter or stand fast to present arms where they were. They formed a barrier of steel less yielding than the failed walls of stone. Before them, the ringing clash of conflict rose volcanic and spilled along the tortured front. And at the remnants of the King Henry Tower, the Hospitallers regrouped and again threw themselves into attack.

Roger de Flor pushed his way through to Beaujeu. The grand master acknowledged his intrusion. 'You are not one to heed command or to miss the call, de Flor.'

'My nature is blessed with contradiction.'

'As ours is forged with a single purpose. The Hospitallers assail the heathen and soften them for our blow.'

'It is just as well I came to Acre for adventure.'

'You will have it now in bountiful measure.' Beaujeu indicated the combat raging at the tower.

They observed the theatre and felt its shockwave, the cries of men and the ceaseless snap and clatter of weapons relayed in tuneless din. Discipline had given way to the joy and terror and full-throated madness of indiscriminate savagery. The Knights of St John were thrown back and returned, were slowly retaking surrendered terrain. In the Templar ward, their fellow Christians willed them on and awaited their chance. Beaujeu and his men formed up, their pennants flying, the adventurer de Flor a giant in attendance with a Danish axe lofted on his shoulder. No chivalry would be shown or quarter given. There was one aim: to fight and to die in defence or attack.

Beaujeu shaded his eyes to study the next shuddering change. 'The Saracens are reinforcing. Villiers will have to commit his reserve.'

Closer to the embattled remains of the King Henry Tower,

the grand master of the Hospital knew exactly what must be done. Indefatigable and undaunted he strode the confines of his post, roaring orders and defiance and relishing the moment. He could be proud of his brethren in their hour of trial. This was how a military order should behave, with daring and a love of God and in accordance with its sacred vows. His knights would not be found wanting.

'Drive hard, my brothers.' John of Villiers yelled into the storm and waved his sword. 'With faith and fire, we will throw back the demons to the very gates of Cairo.'

'They are too strong, sir.' The words flurried, more lip-read than heard.

'I will countenance no defeat. With steel and fury we shall prevail.'

'Their dervishes are upon us.'

'Then we have more of the heathen in which to dip our swords.' The grand master again raised high his longsword. 'Is St John the Baptist not with us? Are we not ordained to die?'

The reply was desperate. 'The Marshal is outnumbered and hard pressed, sir.'

'So rally to me! We will show the Templars how to fight, shall turn the hour or find eternity.'

Escorted by his senior knights and the grand crosses of the Hospital, Villiers led the countercharge. Around them the battle had unravelled to a hundred separate threads, a dissolving skein of colour and barbarism and changing form. A knight was on his knees and pierced by many spears before sprawling on his face; another hacked valiantly at a host of jabbing Saracen before he too succumbed; a group of wild-eyed dervish cut a savage swathe until crossbows brought them down. A man could lose his mind or his head to such intensity, when the heartbeat rushed and the seconds slowed, when confusion was everywhere, when unnamed figures gouged and cursed and scrabbled through a mist of fury.

Into the fray charged the Hospitaller grand master. Fiery in his hatred, Villiers carved his way fearlessly through the foe. With him, the momentum turned and fortune tipped. The ground was being reclaimed.

'*His grace is down!*'

For every move there was an opposite and a consequence. The Saracens replied with a volley of arrows, the darts puncturing mail and causing fearful loss. John of Villiers staggered and sank, a steel barb embedded in his shoulder and a second in his thigh. Yet he tried to wave aside his officers, protesting as they guarded him with their shields and dragged him to the rear.

'Unhand me and let me to the battle!' The old soldier angrily resisted as a canvas litter was brought.

It was Theobald of Alzey who pushed him back. 'A Grand Master bleeding on the rampart will do no service to our cause.'

'I am needed.'

'Your death is not.' The younger knight felt a Saracen dart strike and rebound from his shield.

'Who are you to countermand me?' Pain seeped through the grimacing lips.

'A loyal knight and a friend to you. I am instructed by the Marshal to take you to your galley.'

The grand master attempted to sit upright, nearly fainting with the effort. He groaned. 'My place is here. I cannot go.'

'You must, sir. For the order and yourself.' Theobald and his men gently eased the wounded veteran on to the waiting stretcher.

A mittened hand gripped his shoulder tightly. 'I command the brethren.'

'Fate commands you. We have evacuated the hospital and are carrying the injured to the ships. With or without assent, you shall join them.'

They bore him away, crossing to the inner wall and descending through a tunnel to emerge in their compound. It was a temporary way point, providing a chance to remove hauberk and chausses and to examine the wounds. The grand master had lapsed to a state of semi-consciousness by the time Theobald carried him to the harbour. With his face covered with a sheet to avoid spreading rumour and collapse, he was quickly taken aboard.

'Is it water or my grave beneath me?' John of Villiers stared upwards at the awning on the poop deck.

'You are tended on your galley and will rest here for the while.'

'And you, my rescuer and brother knight, my young mutineer?' There was still humour in the weak belligerence.

Theobald took and kissed the limp hand. 'My duty remains at the wall, sir.'

'We have no wall and little chance. But I should still be there.' The pale and sweat-smeared face turned towards the younger man. 'I know you, you are the grandson of Otto of Alzey, virtuous knight and hero of the children.'

'Like much else he dwells in legend.'

'He would salute you as I must offer thanks.' Villiers braced his back at the surging pain. 'You are the best of our kind, Theobald of Alzey.'

'Honour and plaudit may wait, sir. And you must rest until next we meet.'

'Pray God we shall.' The breath was fragile and the eyelids heavy.

Villiers slipped into silence and Theobald departed. Though the battle was engaged and soon to be lost, there were loose ends and countless matters to which to attend.

On the outer ramparts, a Templar grand master lingered patient for his moment. And stationed on a rear bastion, Benedict crouched ready for his call.

✝

✝

Chapter 18

Unlike John of Villiers, the Sultan of Egypt was less concerned for the welfare of the people of Acre. Mounted on his horse, he toured the front in a travelling cavalcade of generals and bodyguards, pausing to survey the ruin of the walls and privately exult in the progress of destruction. It had been two days since the mighty King Henry Tower had ceased to stand and its stunted relic was taken. Further attacks had consolidated the gains, pushed back the Latins to the innermost ramparts and carried his forces to the brink of success. From every point, the banners and standards of his regiments could be spied crowning the shattered battlements and marking the line of their advance. A noble and heroic scene. Kurds, Turcomans, Arabs and Africans, all were present to bear witness and heed his call. He would savour and forever remember the moment.

'All hail to the Sultan! Praise be the conqueror Ashraf!'

They announced his arrival at the forward post with clamorous acclamation. He was the one who had led them from Egypt, had promised them victory and revenge upon the Franks. From Bedouin irregular to senior *hajib*, they had good reason to abase themselves and to cheer.

He peered at the youth led out to greet him and now prostrate before the stamping hooves of his parade. The youngster had laid down his sword and shield and in supplication pressed his forehead to the pitted earth.

'Arise before your ruler.'

Obediently, the boy clambered to his feet and kept his eyes averted in trembling respect. A tall and slim youth with reserved ways and thoughtful countenance, one not born to soldiering and yet possessed of the tenacity of a growing lion. Ashraf nodded in approval. Of such a breed were triumphs made.

'Your name, boy?'

'Hazzim.' The youngster spoke at the ground. 'I am your loyal servant and a humble warrior of God.'

'We hear of how loyal. It was you in the midst of the fray when the Grand Master of the Hospital fell. You again who fought so well when we assailed the Templars at the Gate of St Anthony. And it was you who saved the life of my favoured emir in the hot furnace of the breach.'

'My task and desire is to obey my Sultan.'

'As ours is to reward and to lift you up as example to the whole.' Ashraf appraised Hazzim with chill benevolence. 'Tomorrow shall witness the end of Acre and the annihilation of the Unbeliever.'

'If it is the will of Allah, my Sultan.'

'He ordains it and I shall execute. You will stay with me among my trusted. When the deed is done and the Christians vanquished, you will take the bridle of my horse and lead me through the wasteland.'

No higher honour could be bestowed. Hazzim bowed low, a boy once broken by misfortune and loss and since raised up by the brute hand of war. He had found a home more lasting than the village left destroyed, had shed the blood of foreigners and won the regard of those about him. It was a life he could never abandon.

'I am unworthy of your benevolence, my Sultan.'

'Worth is earned.' The sultan gestured to the sword and shield discarded on the earth. 'This battle changes you from boy into man, from a mere Arab soldier to the groom and guide of his master. Our siege may yet transform the history of the world.'

He elevated his gaze to the walls beyond, a commander ready to gamble and sure of his cause and the result. To go too early would be to squander progress; to prolong the combat was to tempt obstruction and provide hope to the infidels besieged. Their situation would not improve. When prayers were through and his formations assembled, then would he commit. By the close of the following day, the harbour front of Acre would be washed red.

Amongst his retinue, Hazzim slapped the filth from his battle-torn robe and stood in proud attendance. The sultan himself had told him that his worth was earned. He would not betray that trust.

'Such meagre fare for a final repast.'

The Templar sergeant dipped the bread in the proffered cup of wine and gratefully took a mouthful. Rapture spread on his haggard features. In these blighted hours before the end, there was little to do save wait and pray, bind wounds and salve bruises, sharpen swords blunted in action and conserve strength for the coming ordeal. Some still managed to smile or murmur comment as Benedict scurried the length of the position bearing a bag of loaves. The knights had received a battering and yet sat contented and ready for the next. Death held no terror for those who embraced it. Faith and resignation brought them peace and their eyes glowed resolutely through the grime and the fatigue. The morning of Friday, 18 May 1291 had dawned. Everything depended on this day.

'Blessings be upon your merciful soul.' Another Templar received his ration. 'This wall is no place for a boy.'

Benedict grinned. 'Nor for a Templar.'

'You are wrong, boy. It is our calling and our creed, our reason and our hour.'

'You may die, uncle.'

'All men must.' The knight betrayed no nervousness as he chewed and spoke.'While we live and breathe we break bread and offer up thanks.'

'Thanks?' Benedict cast a doubtful glance about him.

'Not one of our brethren would forgo this chance to test himself in mortal combat or perish in the service of Christ.'

'Yet they overwhelm us in number and we are forced to the inner rampart.'

'Here we shall rally again to meet them and drench these stones in their blood.' He reached and tapped a fallen boulder with his sword point. 'This is all that is left of Outremer, all that remains of our victories in Palestine. We are pledged to defend to the last each Christian within these bounds.'

A shock of arrows gusted past and fell into the city. It was a random act that drew no comment. Benedict studied the measured preparations of the men and wondered at their courage. They had fallen back only a short distance from their forward strongholds, yet this had changed them from noble praetorians to a ragged and wearied band of scarecrow diehards. Their sacrifice had inflicted a cruel toll.

He watched as Beaujeu moved among his knights, pausing to encourage and talk and give his opinion. Already gaunt, the warrior-statesman seemed almost cadaverous in his torn surcoat and streaked and rusted mail. His order would not fail him. His men greeted him as much as bade a whispered farewell, knights and men-at-arms kissing his hand and renewing their vow of obedience and giving and receiving benediction. Benedict choked back the pang of anguish. These were the righteous and the condemned, the kind he wished to be.

'Listen to the silence, boy.' The Templar interrupted his thoughts. 'The heathen have gone to prayer or ground. It is a portent of the trial ahead.'

'Then I must carry my provisions and share them with the hungry.'

'I know it will bring comfort.'

'We will meet again, uncle.'

'May the Lord preserve and keep you.' There was tenderness in the hardened countenance. 'I know you faced Mouton the baker to bring me this bread. Little else shall daunt you.'

With a jest and a nod, the brief meeting was concluded. Benedict hurried on, vaulting obstacles or scampering low as he had done so many times. No Saracen would impede his progress. He was faster than any on the rampart and he would take food or cheer or a message wherever he was sent.

'*They come! They come! They come!*'

'*To your front and to the flanks, present!*'

'*Stand firm and do not yield! The saints are with us!*'

'*Rejoice! Judgement is at hand!*'

He halted in the shivering stillness, aware of the quickening pulse and the beat of drums before the noise and the shouts of men reached his ears. The percussion rolled in constant thunder, joined by horns and cymbals and the battle-cries of thousands. It seemed to draw the breath from lungs and the colour from every face, setting a sympathetic tremor in torsos and limbs. Dulled by the intensity, walking in slow confusion for the source, Benedict stared out at the shifting terrain. The general assault was underway.

'Down, boy! You are more madman than fool!'

Roger de Flor seized him and propelled him away, his words mouthed and his hurtling form shattering Benedict's trance. Around him, war curled in on a cloud of feathered bolts and raking steel, closing against the quaking front from the St Anthony Gate to the Tower of the Patriarch.

De Flor shook the youngster and shouted to his ear. 'Get to the city and be quick! Gather the noblewomen in the Temple and await me there.'

'What about you, Roger?'

'There is no time to question or complain.' The adventurer cuffed him on. 'You have your path as I have mine. They shall again collide.'

With that he disappeared into the clash and confusion and Benedict was left alone, a dark-haired boy small against the blurred immensity of the scene. He felt the carnage breathe warm at his back and he started to run.

~

For some, departure was the better part of valour. There was no reason to lose everything for the sake of a doomed enclave and its witless inhabitants. Kings were born to rule and their Constables to find more comfortable tenure and the city in which both Henry and his brother Amalric had lodged no longer seemed inviting. In the rich apartments of the palace, shouts bellowed and minions scuttled as royalty prepared its exit. There was no reason for a brave last stand; others better trained and more fervent had volunteered to stay behind.

Amalric scooped an armful of gold plate into the chest and slammed and locked its lid. He did not intend to leave a single bauble for the heathen. Even now the clamour of the Saracen invaded the keep. He wiped sweat from his brow and yelled for his attendants.

'Carry these chattels fast for the tunnel. Delay and I shall have you killed.' He turned to his chamberlain. 'My brother stands ready?'

'He is with his nobles and possessions, your highness.'

'Then we are done here.' He snatched at a gem-set ring and deposited it in the purse at his belt. 'My knights will keep close and guard the train. I want no citizen near us, not one panicked malcontent snapping at our heels.'

'As you command, highness.'

The Constable sneered, his own weakness transferred to contempt for those about him. 'Command? What do I now command save a rabble, an unruly mob that serves me ill?'

'You have our obedience to the last.'

'Indeed so. Your deference until you betray and desert or choose to strike me down.'

His tirade was interrupted by the clatter of a raised coffer dropped and spilling its contents wide across the flagstones. A servant had fumbled. Craven at the feet of his master, he sought desperately to retrieve the situation and return the scattered objects to their case. Drawing his sword, Amalric set about the whimpering wrongdoer with the flat of his blade, hurling invective and raining blows until the man bled.

'You cursed dog! You foul betrayer and base fiend!'

The victim raised a protective arm, only to have his wrist broken in the following strike. 'I beg you, master . . . I mean you no wrong.'

'Spare your pleading for the heathen! They shall have more mercy!'

Another sweep of the arm and a further shriek. Amalric was already feeling so much better. If he was to be denied an opportunity to slay the Mohammedans, at least he could brutalise a substitute.

'Sir, we must leave.' The anxious intervention of the

chamberlain checked his flow and saved a life. 'Waste no more precious moment on this creature.'

Breathing heavily, Amalric turned wordless on his heel. Meek and cowed, burdened with their loads, his retainers followed. There was a steep descent to make.

'My brother is content to idle in the face of a beating storm.' Stationed at the cellar steps, Henry was acidly impatient in his greeting. 'I trust you bring your feathered bed.'

'Would you have me abandon our riches? Allow predators and Mameluks to plunder our treasure?'

'They will rip out our hearts should we tarry any longer.'

'It is unseemly for a ruler to show fear or haste.'

'And it is unwise in flight to be slowed by our baggage.' The king thrust the robe of a mendicant at his sibling. 'We are abandoning our fellow Christians as much as we are escaping the Saracen. Put on this disguise and complete our shame.'

It might give them precious minutes. A disintegrating city was a hostile and unpredictable place. There were plenty who might seize the chance to blame a retreating king and his court. Not everyone had galleys and transports arranged for a swift departure. Matters were ugly enough and might yet evolve to a fighting retreat.

Amalric shrugged on the garb. 'I am ready.'

'I am, too, your highness and beggar-friar.' The dwarf Amethyst had emerged on the summit of the piled sacks and chests. 'While rulers flee their castle, I have become a King of another.'

'This is not the time for jape and merriment.'

'Yet you dress as for a play or masque.'

'Get away from our possessions, dwarf.'

'Your possessions?' Amethyst knelt and prodded a bag of gold. 'You wear the sackcloth of the penitent and pious,

Amalric. To have wealth is a sin against the spirit of your new calling.'

'Whilst to cut you to pieces would accord to my humour.'

The dwarf pulled a face and tutted. 'Have you and your brother not condemned sufficient in Acre? Would you kill me to blood your sword at last?'

'Our court is disbanded and you are dismissed.'

'Then I am free to speak my mind.'

Henry stepped forwards. 'Beware how you address me, dwarf.'

'As Henry or Harry or Hal? As gracious lord and sovereign master? As late-comer or early leaver?'

'Words are finished here.' The king nodded and his servants began to dismantle and ferry the load.

Swaying unsteady on his perch, Amethyst maintained his balance. 'Though my kingdom crumbles, I shall have my say.'

'Your position is perilous, dwarf.'

'What of your own, Henry?' The dwarf cocked his head as he sank lower on the heap. 'I was born with no stature and yet you throw yours away.'

'I need no Amethyst to teach me my worth.'

'You have no Amethyst and you have lost your worth. You came as a saviour and you go as a thief. There was a time when I did tricks and you had a conscience.'

Henry was pale. 'Would my conscience save Acre or its people? Will my remaining here alter destiny?'

'It might stifle future talk of ignominy.'

'Come now, brother. Discourse is for later.' The Constable liberated a box and held it tightly beneath his arm. 'The clamour of the Saracen is more deadly than any gossip.'

That clamour was ever louder and harsh to the ear. Hastily, the baggage was gathered up and the royal party took its leave. Holding a lantern, the king paused at the apex to the narrow stairway and regarded the former court pet.

'Perhaps in discarding you, we squander all reason, dwarf.'

Amethyst replied with a dignified bow. 'And though I lose my patron, I may regain my soul.'

Some minutes later, in a discreet corner of a warehouse close to the western edge, the rulers and their coterie re-appeared in daylight. They might have been merchants and pilgrims, another sorry cluster of humanity in futile wander-ing in the closing stages of the battle. Yet they had more purpose and direction than most. They travelled in a clumsy parade, smuggling through the narrow streets and passing by the quarters, heading for the Cantena. With luck they might be under sail or oar stroke before the doomed inhabitants looked up from their weeping prayers. The masters of the ships already had their orders.

'Is this how you would leave us?'

A boy was pushing by when he happened to glance up and recognise the face. He stood in shock, his easy temperament fading and his features colouring to indignant rage.

Benedict shouted at Amalric. 'You cannot abandon us and flee.'

'Away from us, boy.'

'I will not move.' The youngster had stepped square into their path. 'There are men who die for you and make their stand. Can you not hear the Templars and Hospitallers fight?'

'These are the affairs of men and not of youth.'

Benedict had identified the king. 'Did you not make a speech and promise? You hanged men for their desertion. You pronounced on the need to stay true to our calling!'

'Such calling is over.'

'Not for me. Not for William of Beaujeu or Roger de

Flor. Not for my friend, the Hospitaller knight Theobald of Alzey.'

'To each of them I give my thanks.' Henry looked at his challenger, irritation replacing his mild embarrassment. 'First I am counselled by a dwarf and then chastised by a rude and callow boy.'

'It is not I who is dressed as a monk and hastening for the harbour.'

'Would you contradict a King?'

'I would condemn you.'

The back of a mailed hand took Benedict across the face and swept him to the side. Slumped dazed against a wall and with blood coursing on his cheek, the youngster saw the group pass. He could not face them down; he could scarce articulate the betrayal that he felt. He had scampered the alleyways to round up and ready the ladies, damsels and wealthy maids listed for embarkation on the galley of de Flor, but they were not monarchs or soldiers and had no grounds to place themselves in danger. Henry and his brother Amalric were, by contrast, traitors and deceivers, the lowest of kinds wrapped in high titles and precious silks. It did not take kingship to behave as a man; it did not require an army or adulthood to discover steadfastness and courage. He would abandon no one.

'When Acre is guarded by a dwarf and boy, we are truly deep-mired in the shit.'

With a bound and a forward roll, Amethyst arrived to staunch the wounds with his kerchief. Benedict lay quiet. There was still much left to do.

'I should kill you, infidel.'

Spada considered the remark and dismissed it as an observation rather than a statement of intent. He and the fellow could have fought earlier far from the epic struggle on the ramparts, yet for the present it suited both of them to hold back. By strange circumstance they shared a common terrain and together ate a humble meal, resting up in the underground tunnels as others died and a city fell. An Assassin and an ousted leader of Italian peasants. It was an alliance of sorts.

'You slew my pursuers, friend.' Spada took and chewed on a morsel of bread. 'I should be thankful.'

'Gratitude is of no consequence. It is my calling to destroy and to slaughter.'

'An Assassin?'

The stranger nodded. 'That is who I am, infidel. A *hash-shash*, a hashish-eater, one bidden to bring terror and wreak holy war.'

'I know your kind and I have seen what you did.'

'Those who trailed you died easily.'

The Umbrian believed him; he could scarcely remove the image from his mind. A group of malcontents that had started with the advantage and a keen desire to murder had ended as bleeding cuts of meat strewn about the place. He liked the man.

'You speak my tongue, friend.'

'How else could we infiltrate the Frank?'

'Yet you, as I, are now reduced to common fugitive.'

'At any hour I may return to the world above and resume my duties to the Mameluk.' The Assassin took a mouthful of bread. 'Allah desires it otherwise.'

'You accept death?'

'I reach for martyrdom.'

'Why do you share food with me?'

In the brooding lamplight, the expression of the Assassin was hidden in shadow. Maybe he would strike when the oil diminished and the flame guttered out; perhaps he was simply toying with his prey. Spada was uncomfortable with the subtleties.

'Be of ease, infidel.' His acquaintance studied him in the gloom. 'Your end shall not be at my hands or instigation.'

Spada shrugged. 'I chose my life and even now will choose my fate.'

'You will never leave Acre.'

'Is this so?' The Umbrian gave a primal grin. 'Spada has survived where others have surrendered.'

'Brute strength will not save you.'

'Cunning and savagery may.'

The Assassin glanced about him. 'I see no ships or followers or any plan that could spirit you away.'

'An opportunity may come.'

He would ensure it did. To sit passively and await butchery was hardly to his taste. If the Assassin opted for death, it was entirely his choice. Peasants were made of stronger clay. He would dodge and run, slink and hide until he was free or cornered and slain. He owed this to himself and to the memory of the Crusade on which he had once embarked.

Defiance and not defence was all that could be offered. It ended the same, with ground being given and corpses strewn, with the inexorable press of Saracens cutting their way through. Cracks were exploited and breaches widened and all the while the reinforcements came. The sultan would not rest until he had seized what he journeyed for. Bereft of their grand master and diminished in number, the Hospitallers closed ranks with their Templar brothers, their knights and sergeants fighting as one and forming in united resolve around the figure of Beaujeu. The battle was going against them.

'*The heathen takes the Accursed Tower!*'

'*Drive them back! We must hold them!*'

'*We are lost if they spread along the walls!*'

Yet spread was precisely what they did. In a howling mass the Mohammedans clawed west on the tottering inner ramparts, pushing the ousted guardians before them, aiming for the St Anthony Gate and direct access to the city. It was unlikely to take long.

The rolling impact of the military orders temporarily held the onward rush. The Saracens recoiled, then pushed forwards, scimitar meeting longsword and battle-axe countering Arab spear and Turkish mace.

'Keep your heads low!' Men ducked at the command and a flight of crossbow bolts flurried to their mark. Another strike for the Christians.

In the narrow confines of the front, de Flor had found his rhythm. He was a natural at such brute show, could converse and laugh, sidestep, lunge and kill with deftness and aplomb. No heathen would ruin his enjoyment of the day.

'It is like crushing a louse or a beetle, Alzey.' He slammed his shield in the face of a Turcoman and divided the head with a single blow from his axe. 'They sound much alike.'

Alongside, Theobald parried the thrust of a javelin. 'No louse or beetle is so numerous.'

'Look.' The adventurer pivoted and expertly buried the axe-head deep through the lamellar breastplate of a Mameluk.

'There are yet more.'

'All the better for my peace of mind and state of grace.' De Flor sparred a while and swept an adversary into an untidy descent. 'They do not learn and I do not forgive.'

Impervious to the threat, de Flor was the essence of ferocious contentedness. With a practised hand he dispatched one and turned on the next, the enemy bludgeoned and hewn in bloodied strokes. Still their regiments crowded.

De Flor called to his companion. 'You fight well for a Hospitaller, Alzey.'

'And you for a mercenary hireling.'

'I believed you too kind and gentle for the black art of the sword.'

'And I thought you too mercantile and avaricious for this rampart.'

'It cuts me deep, Alzey.'

'Save your grievance for the foe.'

'I shall.' De Flor lopped off a head.

A trumpet sounded and the knights swelled forwards, wrestling and scrapping on the precipitous edge. In places, the wall folded beneath the weight and sent combatants sliding in the rockfall. Many were buried. Those who remained clung on, consumed by exhilaration and the urge to kill.

Theobald panted a question to de Flor. 'Where is Benedict?'

'Away from here, thank God.'

'He should be stowed aboard a ship.'

'Tell it to the boy.' The adventurer rammed the axe hard into a face. 'He is as stubborn as I.' Theobald reached and blocked an arcing blade while de Flor stamped to disengage the limp body from the weapon. Behind them, William of Beaujeu was urging his men on and pushing for the van.

'Exult in this hour and resolve to die!' The grand master grappled with a Saracen and flung him to the side. 'Do you stand with me?'

The reply was shouted loud. 'We do!'

'So be true to the faith and falter not! There is nothing more noble or glorious!'

Such commitment had sown a thick blanket of casualties. Among them was the Patriarch. Come to preach and give spiritual succour, the old man had been creased by a fragment of shot and was carried bleeding along the line. It provoked a rippled pause in the defence and an emboldening of the onslaught. Now was the turn of Beaujeu.

He stepped back a pace and dropped his sword, appearing to lose his impetus. Few noticed. They were fighting in every direction, sweating and bleeding and trading blows. The battle had lost all order and disintegrated into shapeless mayhem.

Yet de Flor glimpsed the shadow of a change. The grand master stood and stared. There was no rallying cry or prayer, no exhortation or call to God, just a disarmed Crusader without expression, a tall figure and symbol of resistance standing alone and mute and almost overlooked.

'You would give up the fight, your grace?' De Flor bellowed his enquiry above the tumult. 'You would throw down your sword and turn from your brothers?'

'It is my life I throw down.'

'We wait on your command.'

'You must wait awhile for my position is forfeit.' The words were whispered.

De Flor backed towards him in an aggressive retreat, gouging out a space for others to hold. Theobald was with him. They closed on Beaujeu, the grand master patient and watchful as the men drew near. Opaque to the last, he was reluctant to show complaint or pain, to spread consternation in the ranks.

De Flor lowered the haft of his axe. 'Have you an explanation, your grace?'

'Of a kind.'

'You are wounded?'

'No, monsieur.' Beaujeu still had not shifted. 'I am dead.'

Slowly he raised his left arm and the gaping injury was revealed. It seeped blood of bright crimson in a stain that welled and crept across the front. From a distance, it might have seemed the Latin cross that leaked. Beaujeu regarded the pattern forming on his mantle and looked up.

'Is this the adventure you crave?'

As he stumbled into a faint, de Flor lifted him in his arms and bore him away. The Templar grand master had become a casualty. Acre would shortly follow.

✝

Chapter 19

'What news?'

The Templar marshal paused before offering a reply to Beaujeu. The image of the dying grand master and the grim nature of the surrounding events would have caused most to hesitate. Yet he would not lie or hide the truth from the fading gaze of his leader. He knelt close to the bier and spoke softly to the man who more than any had sought to save the order and the rump kingdom of Outremer.

He cleared his throat. 'The Saracens have breached the salient and are pushing through into the city.'

'Is any ground held?'

'John of Grailly and the English give battle on the eastern wall. Yet even they are falling back in search of ships.'

'Our knights?'

'They continue to contest each street and dwelling and to delay the advance.'

'Henry and his brother Amalric are gone, no doubt.'

'As thieves in the night, your grace.'

'The air is more sweet without them.' Parched lips murmured their response. 'None may say that we of the Temple have shown feeble heart or spirit.'

'We shall endure to the end, your grace.'

'Yet I will die as so many of us must. It may save the

323

Templars for a while, stay the jealousy and prowling avarice of those who hate us.'

'There are sufficient enemies crowding in the city, your grace.'

Beaujeu was silent, his face wax-pale and his breath fluttering shallow in his throat. The blood still pooled and the candlelight sputtered cold and faint. At the side of his grand master, Peter of Sevrey bowed his head and muttered a prayer for the souls of the departing. These chambers had once been a crucible of intrigue, a place in which plots were born and from where spies and secret envoys were dispatched. Now it had become a mausoleum.

Again, the soft and breathless voice. 'You should be with our men, my Marshal.'

'My duty calls me here, your grace.'

'And you, Clermont?' Beaujeu's clouded sight drifted to the marshal of the Hospital attending soundless in the background. 'Have the Hospitallers come to bury me?'

'To offer tribute and respect, my lord.'

'Reserve your energies, my brothers. I am with the dead and you are still with the living. Go to where you are most required.'

Sevrey shook his head. 'Forgive my disobedience, but I will keep vigil with you here.'

'A good man, yet a stubborn one.' Beaujeu rasped a cough and recovered from his effort. 'How fares my Chin mystic in his tower?'

'Our strange monk still labours, your grace, but I fear his fire and magic will not alter the ending.'

A twitch of the head. 'It may yet offer a grand display. Hold fast this Lion Fortress. Do not let a single stone be defiled by the heathen.'

'You have my oath, your grace.'

324

'If we are to have a future, it will be forged in the days you stand here.'

'Each one of our brethren is ready.'

'Then I find hope in the shadow of darkness and despair.' The grand master sighed in recognition of what neared. 'Bring me my sword.'

With reverential care, the marshal fetched the scarred weapon he had recovered from the rampart and placed it gently in Beaujeu's grasp. Like a knightly effigy, the grand master lay and stared upwards to the ceiling. He had been the arch-manipulator of events, the grand designer of countless subterfuge. He had negotiated alliances and schemed against his foes with a ruthless dexterity unmatched by others. All for the cause of Christendom and the Temple. In death, he would meet his Maker as priest and as a soldier.

'*Domine Jesu . . . Domine Jesu . . . Domine Jesu.*'

The words caught and the breath held and the chest sank in final exhalation. It was done. Respectfully, the marshal shuttered the eyes with his hand and stooped to kiss the pommel of the sword and the forehead of his chief. Then he made the sign of the cross and with Matthew of Clermont at his side turned on his heel to leave. There was more battle ahead and defence to organise and their own personal sacrifice to arrange.

De Flor was waiting for them. 'You forgot your hauberk, Clermont.'

The Hospitaller was already on the staircase. 'Where I am headed, chain mail will make no difference.' Without further valediction, he was gone.

Remote from the unfolding disaster, Benedict sat cross-legged with the Shaolin monk and cut another length of fuse. About them was the litter of their trade, the clay pots and pitch-steeped twists of rag that would rain fire on the Saracen. The Chin was unhurried in his industry, as if time had no meaning and urgency no place. Yet he cared enough to labour in his usual methodical way. And the youngster was happy to attend, to find comfort without talk and observe sorcery at close quarter.

De Flor sauntered into view and called to his charge. 'Lay down your tools, boy. Beaujeu is dead and the Mameluk are within the city.'

'We are making ordnance for the fight.' Benedict did not look up.

'The Templars may save themselves. Our task is elsewhere.'

'Your galley is loaded?'

'All is set and the crew awaits.' De Flor hesitated. 'There are those who depend on us, womenfolk who have not yet been gathered to the sanctuary of the Temple.'

'I brought any I could find.'

'Some still cower in their homes, paralysed by fear.'

'How can we help them now?'

'By reaching them before the Saracen.' By relieving them of every gold and silver piece. 'I too will search, boy.'

Benedict understood his task. He would be heading into flame and fury, racing through an erupting streetscape of frenzy and destruction. Maybe he would find no one alive and return to the Templar fortress empty-handed; maybe he himself would fall victim to the encroaching foe. But born to the role, he would try.

He stood and bowed to the fighting monk as he had seen him do. Then he turned to the adventurer. 'We have not much time.'

~

Horror was everywhere. Every street and every building seemed to carry lapping flame and the lowing screams of fear and torment. Knights and soldiers fought desperately, standing and falling as their barricades were toppled and their positions overrun. Nothing would stop the Mameluk. Citizens jumped from windows or crawled for cover, driven in frantic chase until they weakened and were submerged. Crusade and Crusaders were dying on this spot. In a vast and bellowing tumult one front crumpled as the other swept in, weapons were flung aside or raised in conquest, bodies mutilated and left behind. And always the exultant cries. *Allah! Allah! Allah! Allah!*

Benedict hunkered down and covered his ears. He recognised the sound, remembered the past and felt the tortured din invade his soul and bones. Acre had ceased to resemble a city. Even its churches were now ablaze, spewing timbers and the animal shrieks of those trapped inside. On the roof of one, a cleric had emerged wreathed in fire, his arms outstretched in macabre entreaty. He vanished as the roof caved in. Few noticed, for the feverish dash for the waterfront had begun, men and women and children tripping over themselves and throwing each other aside as they raced dogs and rats and maddened livestock through the shuddering streets. Behind them the tips of spears jabbed at the sky. Some glinted in the sunlight, while others paraded severed heads.

A hand plucked at the arm of the youngster. 'Come away, boy. It is no place to stay.'

The boy ignored him and the man departed terrified on his way. Benedict too was moving, travelling against the flow, negotiating the churning ferment. He stopped and stared. Beyond an eroding line of Syrian knights, the Saracens had reached a corner house and were butchering its inhabitants. A body was pitched windmilling from a window and was followed by another. Strange shapes and oddly beautiful sights. Yet the youngster was peering at something else, at the small body mass in motley garb pierced through and born aloft upon a hunting lance. Only the cross-guards prevented the torso sliding on the shaft. Amethyst, the dwarf, had been caught. Somewhere, a church bell crashed from its station in apocalyptic descent.

A knight called out to his comrades. 'We are lost, yet our dignity is won! Be strong, my brothers!'

'*Kill as many heathen as you may!*'

'*Give praise to God and ask forgiveness! We are numbered and are blessed!*'

'*We shall die where we stand . . .*'

And they did, in varied ways and in rapid sequence as their kind had done at Tripoli. *Hosanna! Hosanna! Hosanna!* they cried. It displaced the fear and gave them meaning and filled the seconds before oblivion. The choke point was ripped wide. Moslems occupied the void, their chattering battle-chants and beating tread flooding the space before them. Benedict hurtled himself on to a flat roof, sprinting to a different axis while the enemy swept by below. He vaulted a narrow chasm and slithered to the ground again, waiting and counting and panting as the battle raged about him. There was no longer any chance of discovering the missing persons for the ship. He should return to the Lion Fortress, but first, he must survive.

A figure pushed towards him, a brute form armed with a stabbing-sword, its face scarred beneath a requisitioned helmet. Spada was loosed. The Italian peasant and orphan boy gazed at each other, their history and hatred cold. For Benedict, it was almost a relief. He had wondered when the Umbrian might strike. Spada, the pilgrim and murderer; Spada, the frustrated tyrant; Spada, the deposed chief with little left to lose. Vengeance was in play. It was no surprise that the man approached with a swagger that presaged a cull. Not if Benedict was quick.

Spada advanced. 'Did you think I would forget? Forgive?'

'There is no point in this.'

'I shall decide that.'

The youngster danced from the presented blade. 'Your work is finished, Spada.'

'It is scarcely begun.' Blank contentment had settled on the coarse features. 'Providence frowns on you, little dog. You have been brought to me for a reason.'

'What purpose is there in this?' Benedict accelerated his retreat.

'The sound of your scream is its own reward.'

There was to be no negotiation. The boy took flight, weaving and dashing between unfolding scenes of misery. Refugees could provide either obstacle or opportunity. A handcart was toppled and its contents strewn and a hoard of timber fell; citizens jostled and cursed while pots clattered and earthernware broke. The personal contest ran parallel and barely noticed in the general plight.

Still Spada came on, sure-footed and determined in the chaos. He would neither retreat from his mission nor lose sight of his target. Too much pride rested on the result and too much of his face had been lacerated by this taunting youth. That grin would not outlast a close encounter. He should never have relied upon his henchmen or expected any but himself to complete work of such meaning. Nothing else mattered, for all were doomed and everything lost. Yet somehow, a mean and impish boy managed to endure.

They were near the Patriarchate when a priest stumbled in their path. He did no wrong, but his action irked Spada and the sword went in deep and quick. The gutting over, the peasant threw aside the corpse and continued in pursuit. There were many crowding the alleyways on their desperate way to the harbour. Benedict had slowed. He tripped and the hunter was almost on him; but a manoeuvre and a roll as Amethyst had taught him, and once more he was away.

'Height will not save you. Nothing shall.'

There was a certain glee in the shout. The boy had committed a fatal mistake. Ladders had been set at the base of the Venetian Tower. Benedict chose to climb. Instinct rather than reason had propelled him, the illusion of sanctuary and the urge to ascend committing him to a precipitous course. Along the four hundred paces to the Lion Fortress, the harbour esplanade bulged with the groaning weight of the populace. The city was imploding and its fragments congregated here.

'Such stairways are for the guards and they are since gone.' Words floated up insistent. 'How fast you climb, little child.'

Benedict did not look down. 'I am no child.'

'Then I have no guilt in pricking you with steel.'

'Why do you act like this, Spada?' It was a question delivered as a yell.

'Because I can. Because I made a vow to myself. Because you showed me low regard.'

'I have no regard at all.'

'Thus will you suffer.' Spada sheathed his sword and placed his hand on a rung. 'You now wage war with me and not my men.'

His menace encouraged the youngster ever upwards. He was clambering for height, reaching for the window and throwing himself through.

Spada had not slowed. 'You prolong your agony, boy.'

Without thought or pause, Benedict darted through the

deserted interior. Another floor, another landing, another spiral staircase. The Venetians had been proud of their magnificent tower, which proclaimed in stone their mastery of commerce and aspirations in the Holy Land. Things had changed. Those who were still alive would be with the rest fighting for repatriation at the harbour edge.

'I am at your heels, boy.'

Gasping for breath and with Spada's threats rising muffled behind, Benedict burst through to the sunlight. He had made it to the roof. Below him a panorama laid out the final throes of empire. To one side, the deep and azure calm; on the other, the streaming colours of the Mameluk melding to an unsightly grey where they poured into the Christians. For a single moment, Benedict was transfixed.

'We meet.' Spada was looping a cord about his fingers. 'You gave me some coursing, boy.'

'Acre dies and you would kill me?'

'Our battle is separate to the fight below. I have waited for this and thought of little else.'

'You waste your precious time.'

'Waste?' The cord tightened. 'I will recall each step and savour every memory.'

The boy had lost his fear, had trodden too close to death to find it so disturbing. God would provide. Templars had been crucified and friends ripped asunder, familiar faces burnt or shredded beyond his recognition. Even Amethyst had ended as nothing more than a lump of meat pinioned on a spear. To be confronted by Spada was to be treated as a man. That counted for something.

The Umbrian charged with bullish delight. He was not fleet of foot. Benedict dodged and circled, coaxing and goading, drawing away and creating diversion. His adversary persevered. With a howl the Italian was upon him, dragging him to the low parapet and applying the knotted twine. Pressure increased.

'This city is gone and you will go with it.' The words were hissed guttural with the effort. 'I am Spada, the sword, the man from Norcia, the place of slaughter.'

'*No!* . . .' Resistance was fading and wasted.

'Listen to your final breath. Feel your last heartbeat.'

In crossing the roof, Benedict had scouted for purchase and weapons; in allowing the peasant close, he had established the framework for his conjury. Everything was a risk. Yet he had been taught well by the tricks of a court jester and the skills of a Chin monk. His aptitude for learning was strong.

Twisting with speed and directed fury, he drove the piece of basalt hard into Spada's temple. The eyes trembled and the hold slackened and puzzlement spread across the man's face. Before he could recover, Benedict leapt upright and put his shoulder to the swaying form, launching Spada into free fall.

For long seconds, Benedict surveyed the puff of dust and point of impact and the widening stain in which the distant figure lay. It was the first human life he had taken. Once, he had been content to swim and fish and roam, to laugh and jest and befriend the heathen. That was all in the past. Fourteen years old, he had come of age as a common murderer.

'They are breaking down the door! Greet them well, my brothers!'

Inside the Hospitaller compound, a gaggle of knights readied for the end. They were fortunate to have survived so long, had only sought refuge as last resort and when the environs were in enemy hands. None expected to outlive the day. Now the foe was come for them. Wood cracked and hinges buckled to each strike of a battering ram and beyond the enclave walls flame cast its eerie light and cries and screams billowed. The Knights of St John of Jerusalem, symbolic of Christian resolve, were a priority for the Mameluk.

From the small and waiting group, the words of a psalm reverberated calm as though sung in the peaceful solitude of a chapel. *Though a host should encamp against me, my heart shall not fear; though war should rise against me, in this will I be confident.* And confident they were. It mattered not that they would die, for obedience and sacrifice were to be celebrated. The inhabitants of Acre might run screeching in undignified pandemonium to be hunted and quartered as frightened beasts. In the square formed by the four great buildings of the order, a separate narrative unfurled.

'Steady, my brothers. Let every one of your blows be true.'

Swords and battle-axes were raised. Some of the knights leant on hastily fashioned crutches while others sat on stools and pews arranged for the occasion. Not all the wounded had accepted places aboard a departing galley. For them, it was more honourable to face the demons at the gate. No doubt the Templars and Teutons would be similarly engaged; no doubt there were countless surrounded pockets resisting with aplomb.

Composed, they watched the splinters fly and the last bolt give. Perhaps the magnitude of the instant forced the Saracens to pause. Then they were through. The initial wave staggered and dropped to the aimed impact of crossbow quarrels and the next took its place. More were behind. Javelins and arrows pelted into the knights and the angry flood engulfed them. They fought as they had vowed and intended, answering the onslaught with frenzied commitment. It took some time to subdue them. Christ was with them even as they chanted and tore into the multitude, even as they were hewn apart and trampled.

Almost dead, his jupon jacket a ragged sponge of blood, a man crawled dogged from the brawl. He was spotted. A Mameluk infantryman sat astride his back and pinned him to the ground, pulling back his head and applying a long knife to saw through his throat. Another trophy won; an intimacy of violence within the general slaughter. The limbs and torso stilled.

Surging from the epicentre, the Saracens roamed the complex to pillage and eviscerate. Any organised defence had long since collapsed. In grain stores and dormitories, in the great hall and refectory, the residue of the order was quickly cut to pieces. Swathed in bandages, a senior knight stumbled down the outer steps to the courtyard. He loosed off a quarrel from his crossbow and was reloading when a javelin took him in the chest. His foot still in the cocking stirrup of the weapon, he plunged. A few paces distant, comrades were being thrown down the well. Fresh victims plummeted, thrown from windows and the towering height of the donjon to kick and scream and join the ritual. To the Saracen they were manna.

At last the clearance was complete and the sacred banner of the Hospital flung down. A flag that had once fluttered so proud was now shredded and dipped in the blood of its followers. Souvenir gatherers would treasure such keepsakes. In the aftermath participants enjoyed their own pursuits, some creating patterns of heads and some donning Hospitaller robes, some hefting sacks of sugar and some squabbling over weapons and trinkets. Others wandered through the chambers of their enemy, wondering at the cloistered secrets of a warrior caste thrown wide.

At least they were distracted. Deep in the bowels, in the sewer system of the order, Theobald of Alzey led civilians down the sluice tunnel. Wading through filth and nearly overcome by fumes, his charges were in no state to express their thanks. Yet he had given solemn word to his wounded grand master that he would save as many as he was able. They were pilgrims and innocents, women and children, all inching through the stinking darkness and trusting on his instinct. The Mohammedans would not follow them here or dare imagine any Frank might voluntarily submit to the perils and asphyxiating gloom.

'Make no sound and maintain your pace.' Drawing the cloth from his mouth, Theobald whispered back instructions. 'We have not much time.'

Ahead, the fetid channel widened to a hollowed cavern illuminated by shafts of light glancing faint from above. It was the pit below the public latrine, its canopy pitted with the stone lavatories once occupied by the backsides of the masses. On a slope, the excreta would be carried to the sea; on a slope, the refugees were paddling the same route. All had changed.

As they approached, Theobald held up his hand and forced his retinue to a stumbling halt. There was danger enough in passing beneath. But a torch falling sputtering from the ceiling had lit up a scene of unsparing grimness. At random, the holes were filling and objects dropping to patter and sink into the carrying stream. The sitting benches had been turned to makeshift execution blocks. Below them, the hidden exiles received the heads, heard the prayers and pleading shrieks garbled into the blackness. Then the blade and the silence, the cheer and the descent.

'It is more hellish than Hades itself.' Fear and hesitation were loaded in the murmuring complaint. 'We cannot go on.'

Theobald answered. 'Would you rather be lain on a plank above than stand with us below?'

'This is no place for a mortal.'

'It is the perfect retreat for us.' The young knight was calm and insistent. 'I made my vow to my Grand Master and I will not break it.'

'A promise is futile when mortal remains rain upon us.'

'I will guide you safely, brother.'

'Where is shelter? Where is hope?' Panic and despair added to the volume.

'Step forwards and you have a chance. Withdraw and I will kill you.' Theobald had identified the dissenter and reached to grip the quivering face. 'No more argument.'

The party trod onwards through the human drizzle. The blood-letting pursued them. They would have known many of those who now arrived as chuck meat and slopped about their knees. It was sensible not to think, wise to bend low and hold tight to the person in front and keep moving downstream. Rats too were on the journey, slithering fast and showing the way. Everyone wished to escape the wreckage of Acre.

Theobald marshalled them, counting them past and encouraging them on. If his grandfather Otto had escorted children to the Holy Land, then he, Theobald, would ensure a few survivors made it out.

'Be of heart, brother. There are but three hundred more paces to go.'

Three hundred paces of cheerless splashing and gagging through the dripping murk. The noise of murder receded and the line wound on, its sodden tramp interrupted only by occasional retch and stumble and oath. Blind faith carried them forwards.

'*Allahu Akbar! Allahu Akbar!*'

Faith of a different kind intruded. From a side cavity the attack arrived, the ambusher lying in wait to launch himself on the rear of the column. He must have anticipated they would use the route. The refugees cowered or were chased on. Yet in a swift and fluid move Theobald responded with his sword, shattering the assault and cutting short the sacred Koranic shout. Steel sparked and a methane pocket flared and the enemy slid as flotsam to the cess. The young Hospitaller followed his charges. He was grateful to have escaped without so much as a scratch. In these conditions a graze would prove fatal.

Before them, freedom shone through the dark in a single point of light. To their backs, the corpse of the third and last Assassin was being reconnoitred by a questing pack of rodents.

The realisation of calamity had replaced the illusion of defence. As streets were taken and buildings sacked and death and flame lanced through every quarter, the condemned clung to prayer or to each other. Only their numbers slowed the Saracen, for looting and butchery could hinder the flow. There were many barriers to tear down and inhabitants to enjoy. From all directions the regiments descended, their blades and spear tips working. By the minute, hope was fading and refuge diminished; with each pulse, citizens flocked and floundered in the approaches to the waterfront. Chivalry was gone and Arthurian myth abandoned. The revelry of carnage was sweeping in.

'Stay back or I will kill you!'

It was a threat that had lost its resonance and caused its speaker himself to be slain. His longboat was quickly commandeered. Beside jetties and landings humanity fought for berth and purchase, for any means to flee. The vision was one of beseeching faces and callous eyes, of flailing arms and oars and brutish terror. At a wharfside, beating back the fray, a group of monks and guards lowered the wounded Patriarch to the deck of a waiting skiff and readied to cast off.

'Who am I alone to be saved?' the old man called feebly to his men. 'Let others accompany me to the ship. We must ferry as many as we may.'

'Holy Father, there is no time.'

'Nor is there excuse to turn our backs on those who suffer.'

Reluctantly, they obeyed and the sentinels parted to permit the citizens through. They responded in a rush, filling the vessel in a tumbling throng and ignoring the protests of the loyal praetorians. The result was inevitable. Anxious to remove his master and small craft from the pressing hazard ashore, the tillerman pushed away and steered passage for a transport. He did not travel far. Overburdened and off-balanced by its clinging load, the skiff capsized to a whirlpool of thrashing limbs and drowning faces. Among them was the Patriarch. Few noticed and none truly cared; the waters closed and the incident was forgotten.

In a guardroom beneath the Lion Fortress, Roger de Flor was more systematic in his preparation and limited with his charity. After all, the women in his care had paid in gold or carnality for the privilege of escape. He would allow no Mameluk to rip apart his contract or interrupt his plans. He was all confidence as he mingled with his guests, quelling their doubts and allaying their fears, a charming host and amoral chancer exuberantly at home in the moment and enriched by his enterprise. Benedict and the crewmen looked on.

Raising his hand for silence, de Flor addressed his gathering. 'No further word is needed. Do not dwell on the past or what you lose, for you have your future and a ship awaits. Come now and follow.'

They did, allowing themselves to be escorted to the winding depths of the Temple and the entrance that led by candlelit passageway to the waterfront redoubt of the Cantena. It was a route through which the Templars had conducted much of their clandestine business. For a while, it would remain secure and undiscovered; in the final hours of Acre, it afforded a parallel world of order and calm. The heavy portcullis was already hoisted and would close on their departure.

'Onward, my ladies. There is no cause to tarry.'

Insistent and cajoling, the words of de Flor pursued his flock. He would not permit his women to think or pause or argue or hinder; he was not about to let his investment slip. His revenue and reputation depended on it. Rapidly he counted them through, ensuring smooth progress and performing the calculation. By God, he was rich. With a shout, he called to the guards, and the chains moved and the portcullis slid and fate and departure were sealed with a thud.

Taking a candle from its recess, the adventurer waved on the last of the stragglers. As they receded into the distance, something caused de Flor to halt and glance back to the iron gate. Almost hidden on the other side stood Benedict.

Returning the candle, the giant swung to stare. 'What sort of prank is this?'

'It is no prank.'

'Then it is a blunder of the deadliest kind.' De Flor approached the grille and searched out the shadowed eyes. 'Explain it, boy.'

'What explanation may I give?'

'One that could prevent me scolding or berating or cursing you.'

'That is no way for friends to bid farewell.'

The silence lengthened.

'The guards above have orders never to raise the gate to outside command. You are trapped, boy.'

'Maybe I am saved.'

'Your head is inhabited by fanciful dreams and this city with corpses.'

'I am staying.'

'For what? Futile gesture? Sacrifice without meaning?' De Flor gripped the bars. 'I have guarded you as my son, taken you on adventure, kept you at my side.'

'Acre is my home.'

'It is vanished and your mind gone with it.' The adventurer shook his head as though attempting to slough off a headache. 'There is no cause for your madness.'

'Everything is mad.'

'You would choose death over life?'

'I will stand as the Templars stand, fight as they fight.'

'You are no knight or man-at-arms. You are a boy of fourteen years.'

'Those fourteen years have carried me as a messenger and spy, as a battlefield scout and a runner on these walls.' The youngster was calm in his conviction. 'Beyond this gate, I am no one. Here I am something.'

'Indeed you are. A discarded cadaver, another mutilated body left to swell and blacken in the sun.'

'Would you forget me? Will you not bless me?'

'I will sooner box your ears and drag you to my ship.' De Flor pressed his face hard to the portal. 'You have done your duty.'

'It is yet to be done. I left the people of Tripoli to die. I watched as the Saracen cavalry swam out and butchered them to the last.'

'Who remains to be saved in Acre? Beaujeu is dead and Amethyst too, Theobald is lost and his Grand Master departed.'

'We each have our calling.'

De Flor's eyes bulged. 'Find sanity and reason, boy.'

'They are found. Leave me to my course.'

'Never.'

Roaring in anguished fury, the adventurer shook and pummelled the bars and shouted for the portcullis to be lifted. The barrier remained in place. Still the assault continued, the soldier kicking and throwing punches in fruitless exertion. Eventually he calmed and leant his frame against the iron.

'You have hurt me, boy.'

'I did not intend to.'

'Would you have me weep? Plead? Climb in trembling supplication to my knees?'

'You must go.'

Reaching through, de Flor held out his hand for the youngster to grasp. 'Permit me to embrace the one I love and cherish as my own.'

Benedict smiled and stepped back a pace, aware his mentor was not averse to any low device in order to gain advantage. The adventurer nodded, approval breaking through his frown. He had taught the boy well.

There was no need for gesture and weeping, for confirmation of their bond. De Flor studied the boy to imprint the lasting image and abruptly turned to make his exit.

'I killed Spada.' The confession travelled sotto voce to his ear.

He did not look back. 'Then you are a greater man than I.'

Lady Charlotte remained patient and waiting for him in the tunnel. He thrust his head forwards and marched on, a galley master in search of a different shore.

*

Few left in Acre enjoyed pleasant or pain-free endings. In every quarter and in all manner of ways, the citizenry was flushed out and harried, chased down and finished. Ruthlessness permeated every act. Even the bakery was invaded by a host of enemy that found diversion in stabbing the irascible Mouton and burying him in his kneading trough and throwing the oven-boys alive into the furnace. They were the last items to be cooked in the Christian enclave. It seemed almost an afterthought.

By the evening of Friday, 18 May 1291 the royal city of Acre lay in Saracen hands.

†

Chapter 20

Triumph was rarely without cost. Yet the scale of devastation caused even the sultan to avert his eyes. Too many heads on spikes, a surfeit of entrails adorning the buildings, could tarnish the allure of a jewel he had coveted. He would not show the disappointment in his heart or the flatness in his soul, would betray nothing in his countenance save an expression of imperious duty. It was expected of a leader.

Proudly holding the bridle and guiding the royal steed, Hazzim walked exultant. Acre had become a different place to the one he once knew. Those familiar streets, those courtyards and alleyways, those belfries and rooftops were all transformed to blistered ruin and infested with the maggot-like forms of the dead. He peered about, mesmerised by the result, attempting to remember how things had been. A younger self had roamed these parts. Now he was returned, an agent of the destruction. It was good to see the churches burn.

'All hail to Ashraf, conqueror of Acre and destroyer of the Frank!'

Spears dipped in salute and exhausted men hailed the slow progress of the cavalcade. There was much still to be done, hidden plunder to find and cowering women and children to flush with torches from the underground caverns. Hazzim

343

was sure he could be of service. He steadied the horse and negotiated a fly-blown heap of the dead. Retreat and advance and the shattering impact of the Mameluk incursion could be read in the clustered patterns of the reaped. Their numbers grew in the access to the harbour front. The Arab boy led his master on, never wavering in his task.

Close by the Venetian Tower, the royal party halted. Stretched to its fore was confirmation of the final moments, the wash of bodies in the reddened water or sprawled on the wharves and loading steps. Victory was qualified. At the opposing end of the esplanade, the restless energy of battle continued and the edifice of the Temple loomed unbroken. It was a slight and a challenge to the sultan; a further insult perpetrated by that most defiant of military orders. Ashraf leant forwards in his saddle and studied the walls as he had the ramparts of Acre, searching for weakness and assessing the throw and fall of shot. Already his feared black-oxen mangonels directed their fire on the curtain defences and the stonework crumbled and slid; already his sappers dug beneath the foundations and readied the way for collapse. Then would he mete out his justice. But the Templars appeared unconvinced, rained pitch and wildfire and bursting fireworks on his force. It would not do to test his patience.

His chief engineer approached and abased himself before him. Reputation and longevity might be at stake.

'Acre is yours, my Sultan.'

'It is not mine until every stone is taken.'

'That shall soon be, al-Ashraf.' The man clasped his hands in obsequious supplication. 'A cornered band of infidel knights will not delay us long.'

'I trust it is so. Yet I have no doubt of their ferocity and zeal.'

'Their garrison is small and their Grand Master cut down.'

'They will grow another head, offer up their pagan oaths and taunt us from the furnace.' Lifting his gaze to the scene beyond, the sultan observed the tumult. 'How long until we undermine them?'

'Within days, my Sultan.'

'In the meantime, their ships will supply them and their faith provide succour.'

'None will stand when our fire-troops are through.'

'Let us hope it is no idle boast.'

Impatience pricked at the mood of the Mameluk ruler. He did not appreciate delay or impediment and once more being forced to stay the assault. His tent would be erected on this site and he would sit out the closing drama as though it mattered not at all. Perhaps events could be accelerated and the Templars persuaded; a chance existed that sheer inevitability might encourage the knights in their besieged redoubt to consider terms. Whatever the path to conclusion, the end days spoken of by the chief engineer were fully in train.

Wearing a jerkin and helmet and clutching a spear, Benedict mounted guard on the roof of the Temple keep. He shook a little, not through fear or regret or anticipation of event, but with the cumulative fatigue of exertion and the immensity of his calling. On a pillar in the great hall of the Hospitallers he had as epitaph carved his name; here at the Lion Fortress, he built his grave.

His childhood had finished long ago. It belonged to an age when the stench of ash and putrefaction did not clog his nostrils, Spada had not come ashore, and the command tent of a foreign sultan did not rise at the eastern edge of the waterfront.

Another shot from a catapult struck and carried away part of the outer wall, but there was no Patriarch nearby to pass a wry comment. After a week of bombardment, the Temple and its inhabitants were not faring well. By day, the ships of the order roved offshore and by night the small boats slunk in to send supply by hook and line to the garrison. None were fooled that the stronghold could endure. It was a near miracle to have resisted at all. Yet every assault was met and beaten back and every breach filled with an unyielding line of armoured knights. They would show the heathen how to die.

The youngster glanced seaward and for a moment watched the rise and dip and glinting oars of the galley belonging to de Flor. He must have delivered his passengers to Cyprus and returned for the climactic performance. There might be profit in it, a commission for scrap and loose stone or an attempt to purloin abandoned weapons. In spite of the pang of sorrow, Benedict smiled to himself behind the mask of dust.

'There remains levity in your heart, boy?' A Templar approached. 'It is a rare thing in this realm.'

'What else is left to us?'

The knight cocked his head. 'Our boy is grown into a wise soldier and one called to meeting with the Marshal.'

'Sevrey wishes to speak?'

'With every man, woman and child who takes refuge here. Events are apace and he shall explain.'

Such explanation would be delivered without embellishment or artifice. Little time existed for mannered courtesy. Besides, the marshal was a fighter rather than a diplomat, a man less attuned to the subtle arts of Beaujeu. Attended by senior knights, he regarded the ragged gathering of survivors in his care. Maybe they were fortunate to have outlasted the rest; maybe they already cursed their luck. Benedict too surveyed them, noted the strained and pallid faces and the hope-famished eyes. A woman cried and fed a baby on her breast as another tried to comfort children squatting wretched on the flagstones. Around them, former burghers and worthies muttered or sat stoic, stared bemused or clung to each other for support. They had lost everything.

Sevrey began to speak. 'I gave a vow to our Grand Master that I would permit no Saracen to defile the territory of our Temple. And as a Templar I have made a solemn oath to guard each living Christian soul.'

'Then defend us now.' A challenge issued almost as a whimper from a merchant slumped disconsolately in a corner.

'It is our vocation and desire. Yet should you stay in this condemned place, you choose certain death.'

'There are high walls to shield us and armed knights beside us.'

'An illusion.' Sevrey dismissed the argument with a wave of his hand. 'Our walls are buckling and our foundations are undercut. Our military brethren are reduced to but a few.'

'How long may we hold?'

A pause before the reply. 'Two nights at most.'

'So we are doomed?' A voice rose querulous towards hysteria.

'Not quite.' The marshal disguised his irritation with gruff civility. 'We have received a message from the sultan, an offer of terms for our surrender.'

'You would abandon us? Throw us on the cruel mercies of the heathen? Cast us to their blades or to enslavement?'

'Ashraf offers safe passage to you all.'

'He lies.'

'Is there such need? Does he not already have us by the throat?' Sevrey sighed in fierce resignation. 'Heed well what I say. You have no other offer.'

Dispute was loud and fuelled by powerlessness. Anger and anxiety spilled through the room, men standing up and shouted down and women and children clinging the tighter. Benedict was frozen in his uncertainty. He believed and disbelieved, had made his peace and found it trampled, was both glad and resentful that a decision had been reached for him.

'Silence amongst you!' The marshal emphatically thrust the point of his longsword on the ground. 'Deliberation and debate are through.'

A bishop rose from his seat, a prelate shorn of position and rich vestments. 'What of the Knights Templar?'

'Our duty is clear. We defend our post.'

'We are grateful for your sacrifice and shall remember you in our prayers.'

'It is all we ask.'

Persuaded by reality and Templar resolve, the assembled bowed grudgingly to the will of Sevrey. They departed the meeting in subdued voice, some hopeful and others despairing and all afraid, a few cheered by thought of a plan. Better to accept a fleeting proposal than submit to the cutting edge of a Mameluk blade. Benedict followed, tentative in his expectation. There was much to go awry. To his ear came the sound of treadmills and whetstones and of knights resharpening their swords.

~

Ceasefire brought an emir and an unarmed escort of one hundred Saracen through the gates of the Temple. They had arrived to administer the handover of civilians under flag of safe conduct, but they came with swagger and contempt. Ashraf would not pass up an opportunity to display his primacy. He was the sultan who had erased Acre and sent its leaders scurrying, who had fought an infamous military order to a trapped standstill and stripped it of all pride and possibility. His emir could be forgiven a certain degree of arrogant self-satisfaction.

Peter of Sevrey met him with a scowl and fluent Arabic. 'We have what you have come for.'

'Perchance it will sharpen our appetite for the rest.' The emir glanced approvingly about him. 'How many citizens are gathered for us here?'

'Over two hundred and thirty, all told.'

'They will be counted and taken back with us.'

'We shall signal to our galleys to send small boats for their recovery. Only when they are away and safe from this shore will we release you and countenance further discourse.'

The Mameluk gazed smugly on the Templar. 'For a wounded beast, you show misplaced spirit.'

'As an agent of Satan caught behind our walls, you have an excess of conceit.' A terse note of warning infected the words.

They went ignored by the emir. 'I see you have arranged the goods. Let us inspect them.'

He proceeded in the direction of the inner ward, his attention diverted to the rows of dispossessed humanity arrayed forlorn for the count. His eagerness increased. It was pleasing to examine the haul and spread terror in the wretches.

On occasion he paused to stroke his chin, peering into eyes or reaching to prod.

Benedict thrust aside the hand that pinched his cheek and stared furious at the stranger. 'I am no serf or slave of yours.'

'A boy who speaks our tongue and his mind.' The emir viewed the youngster through idle lids. 'It would be a pity to waste you by granting you freedom.'

'I expect no Mameluk to keep his word.'

'Such bravado, dog.'

'My friends have died in defence of Acre. I will not shame their memory.'

'You may yet join them.'

'It holds no fear for me, heathen.'

'Does it not?' The face moved close, in search of the truth. 'Does it not?'

In spite of himself and because of the instant, Benedict proffered a grin. He had remembered Amethyst parodying the ways of important men and the disrespectfulness of de Flor. They would cheer him now, offer their counsel, whip the hide of this hateful intruder. The intruder failed to recognise the joke.

'What is your name, infidel?'

'Benedict.'

'Reflect upon this hour, Benedict. Regard the mounds of dead and breathe the stinking air. It is the end of the Christian invader.'

He turned and gestured and a lieutenant climbed a flight of steps for the flagstaff atop the gateway. Carried by the man was the banner of the sultan. It would replace the Templar standard, signify that accord was reached and matters were in hand for the imminent departure of civilians.

It also marked an escalation in the brutish manner of the Mameluks. They were dividing the crowd, pushing and beating them with their fists, separating the women from the men and dragging children from their guardians. There was sport in what they did, a vengeful glee in provoking the cries and groans.

Sevrey strode to remonstrate. 'Be advised to be more respectful and restrained.'

'We take what is ours and behave as we may.'

'They are not prisoners, but citizens charged to your care.'

The emir laughed. 'We shall give them care enough.'

'You stand before armed knights, Saracen.'

'Whilst you face an entire army.'

At the flagstaff, the Mameluk officer grabbed to rip down the Templar *Beauséant*. It would be the final misjudgement of his life. The banner was sacred, invested with the blood and sacrifice of the Crusade, symbolised the honour and prowess of the order over almost two centuries of campaign. No heathen should touch it and no Templar stay immune to obvious humiliation. As his fingers grasped the silk totem, the skull of the man splintered to the downward blow from a flanged mace.

A cue for carnage had been given. Everywhere knights attacked their opposites, the iron-clads moving through the screaming and coursing throng to deliver their reprisal. In many ways it was a release, a return to sanity and the methods they knew. They hunted and slew, hacked with abandon at Mohammedans who attempted to flee or hide in a space that gave no cover. Caught between the encroaching ranks or flushed from their shallow nooks, they stumbled and bellowed and pleaded and sank. Templars were methodical in their killing.

Clutching to hide in his shadow, a young Mameluk dodged behind Benedict and pushed the boy forwards. It did not deter a sergeant-at-arms from bringing him down with a strike to the legs. For a while, the Christian let the Moslem wallow and roll before pressing his blade straight through his ribs.

It was the turn of the emir. He still stood in the midst of the bloodshed, his expression fixed by shock and suddenness and his confidence shredded by encircling murder.

Sevrey faced him. 'Fortune switches, does it not?'

'Nothing is changed.'

'I vouch you are wrong.'

'What are one hundred of us slain? Two hundred?' The Mameluk official quivered with fright and the effort of speech. 'You shall all be consumed.'

'Not before we salve our conscience and our name. The Lion Fortress will forever belong to the Templars.'

'How long may you last?'

'In the minds of men, perchance until eternity. No Saracen will dictate the conduct of this order.'

'Yet we shall determine your fate.' The emir attempted to convince himself as much as Sevrey. 'Ashraf will raze every aspect of the city.'

'A corner of it holds true.'

'See reason, infidel.'

The marshal shook his head. 'I see instead the Saviour. I see my brothers resolved to lay down their lives. I see angels and saints awaiting us.'

'There remain the innocents you are sworn to protect.'

The remark provoked a silence as each man regarded the other. Only one was in a position to offer reprieve. Pondering his move, the marshal flexed his fingers on the sword-grip and seemed weighted by his decision. Man to man, it was never easy to snatch a life in cold blood.

Resolution was found. 'I will send communication to your Sultan.'

'Tell me in what manner I may serve.' Hope had sprung in the voice and eyes. 'We have concerns to address and fresh agreement to reach.'

'With regret, such accord is broken.'

A violent sweep of the blade and the marshal concluded his negotiation. The message was dispatched.

'You are troubled, monsieur?'

'I am condemned.'

Stalking the area of the poop deck, de Flor again paused to stare moodily at the grey seaward ramparts of the Temple. It was a place from which he had escaped, a tomb from which he had plucked the rich and the grateful and deposited them for gain on the safer shores of Cyprus. Yet he had returned. There was little he could do and no rescue he might perform, for the swell was high and the rocks jagged. Frightened by the rumoured approach of Saracen war galleys heading north from Alexandria, the Frankish masters of other ships had steered their vessels away. Not this Catalan fighter. He would wait and watch and bid farewell and attempt to expunge from his heart the stain of guilt and bitter sadness.

He let his gaze travel the length of the castellations, hopeful for a sighting. There had been a moment when he spied a figure alone and knew it to be the boy, had raised his arm in fond salutation and received a shy wave by reply. Agony rarely came deeper. So he walked at a loss and commanded the slaves to backstroke their oars so that he might keep on station. Someone must record the dying hours of the fortress.

Lady Charlotte spoke softly from behind. 'Fretfulness will save neither the knights nor the boy.'

'I know it to be true.' He summoned a weak smile for her benefit. 'Yet even a dog will return to the post he has left.'

'You saved many souls, monsieur.'

'Not his.' He motioned to the rampart with his eyes. 'And not before I lost my own.'

'It was his freedom that you granted and his decision that he made.'

'I moulded him and put such notions in his head. I imbued in him foolish stubbornness and pride.'

'His gallantry and courage are his own.'

She moved to stand with him, a woman of grace and understanding who had elected to stay aboard when the vessel turned south. It had both comforted and unsettled him. At every stage she had outplayed him, had set the terms and seized advantage; on every occasion he had bowed to her quiet charm and never regretted his surrender.

'Angels will defend them where we cannot, monsieur.'

'I have found them wanting in the past.'

'Then we must commit our brothers and sisters to God and trust in His great mercy.'

'There will be less pity from the Saracen.' He braced himself against the rising deck and placed a hand to steady and draw her close. 'The old Patriarch spoke of a time of judgement and the end of days.'

'You believed him?'

'From where I stand now, I surely do.' De Flor glanced towards the enemy grouped distant on the breakwater and the Tower of Flies. 'Few moments will ever be like this, few matters touch our present and future with such consequence.'

'Have you become a seer as well as soldier?'

He laughed. 'I am made thoughtful by a burdened spirit.'

'And tomorrow you will be a mariner once more, a restless soul on quest for exploit and renown.'

Leave me to my course, the youngster had said. In that dark Temple passageway, he had remained behind because he had his calling and no alternative. It took the medium of a tousle-haired juvenile to enlighten and explain. The adventurer was grateful to the Lady Charlotte. She had understood long before he ever had.

There was a tearing sound from the Lion Fortress, the crumpling of a landward wall that was hidden by the keep. De Flor felt the fingers of his companion seek out and tighten on his own. Frantically, he scanned the roof line for the boy, wondering if he had retreated there, but there was no sign of him. A pall of dust coloured the air, signalling a breach and

354

the approaching end. The Templars could not endure forever.

Lady Charlotte whispered a prayer and gave thanks for the life of Benedict.

They visited the chapel for their last sacrament and absolution, confessing their sins and offering praise to the Lord. It was the only foundation on which they placed their hope, for the very floors on which they trod appeared to shift and quake beneath them. The Mameluk tunnellers must be hard at work. Shorn of any outer defence and with the twin lions of the fortress now lying shattered in the ditch, it might be hours or minutes before the next assault came.

Yet the Mameluks were masters of tactics and control. Even as the stones slid, the sultan had renewed his offer of talks and invited the marshal to parley. It would be ill judged to squander the remotest chance of negotiating for the welfare of the refugees. On this bleak evening, Peter of Sevrey conferred with his senior knights and readied for the dawn.

'The treasury is stowed?'

Its chosen guardian nodded. 'I have ensured all is secure and our crew attends.'

'We should trust in a fair wind and thank God for small mercies.' The marshal rested a hand on the shoulder of his brother knight. 'Sail fast for our redoubt in Sidon and build defences there. Tell them of our deeds and valour and remind us to our friends.'

'What of you, brother Marshal?'

'It matters not.' Sevrey gave a tired shrug. 'In the morning, I shall walk with our fellow brethren to bargain with Ashraf. I am in no doubt that he will treat us with the civil pleasantries we accorded to his emir.'

'Must you go?'

'As surely as you must take leave this night and flee north for safer climes.'

'I salute you, brother. I commit you to my heart and commend you to the hands of the Almighty.'

The two military men embraced, aware the meeting was their last. At the south-western boundary of the fortress, a skiff sat poised on a rock ledge ready to be launched. It was a transport of final resort, a means to conjure away the most sacred of prizes from beneath the catapults and noses of the Saracen. Only when the Temple itself faced annihilation would the rope ladder drop and the elected descend. That moment had come.

Striding to the far end of the chamber, the marshal returned with a small chest bound in a hessian sack. No explanation was required of the gem-set reliquary and its precious content held within. The humble appearance was designed to mislead. The holy grail was passing beyond the clutches of the heathen.

'For nearly ten days we have held the Temple, slaughtered the Mameluk and made good our vows. Now we bid farewell.'

The knight bowed his head. 'It will be but a temporary parting.'

'Our most precious of things is in your care.' Sevrey kissed the sackcloth and delivered the object. 'Use it well, brother.'

'None shall divert us in our aim.'

They heard the footfall and noticed the shadow of a presence entering the room. Benedict had been summoned. He stood in his soldierly garb, uncertain, and yet with the confidence of youth. In spite of everything, there might still be an opportunity for a concluding flourish.

'Are you afraid, boy?'

'Not so much I could not fight.'

The marshal considered him with narrowed eyes. 'Our Grand Master held you in fondness and regard. You served him and the order well.'

'You speak as though all is finished.'

'Have you not seen the walls tumble?'

'It changes nothing, uncle.'

'Though our destinies may wane.' Sevrey lowered his voice to solemn murmur. 'Beyond these confines rests a small boat bound for Sidon. There is room left on it for you.'

'What makes me so deserving?'

'You are lighter than many and worthier than most. You are trusted and loved and charged with vital duty.'

'I have already my task.'

'If I should command you?'

'Your command would go ignored.'

The marshal frowned, unaccustomed to slightest mutiny. 'You will die here, boy.'

'It seems you will also, uncle.'

'Let us hope our effort is rewarded.' Bowing to rebellion and bestowing respect with a dip of his head, Sevrey glanced at his companions. 'Each to his quarters and everyone to war.'

It was the night of Sunday, 27 May 1291.

~

They stepped over the rubble and corpses and crossed to enemy territory, Peter of Sevrey and three lieutenants walking purposefully to do business with the sultan. On their mantles were adorned the Latin crosses of their faith and in their bearing was the spirit of men undaunted by adversity. Once, they had strolled this path as though by birthright, as haughty guardians of Outremer; now they journeyed as

357

hostages to fate and the last Crusaders of the Holy Land. Two hundred years summarised in a few hundred paces.

Glimpsing back, the marshal perceived the fallen towers and exposed foundations, the jutting paw of a stone lion raised in ironic farewell. He could not fault his brother knights or the defiant stand that they had made. Everything had been done in the name of God and yet a heathen deity prevailed. He turned to his front and stared towards the Venetian Tower and the imperial tent set below. Not far to march. Around them, Mameluk soldiers were falling in as escort, drawing them to the appointed close. The eyes of the knights were raised and their faces unflinching. Their passage, their exit, their Via Dolorosa.

'We are transformed to objects of study and fascination.' The veteran Sevrey strode on without a care. 'Whether we are bound for negotiation or the blade, I cannot guess.'

'We have little left with which to bargain.'

'Be content we give them theatre.'

Another Templar kept step beside them. 'I am glad our tread bears us closer to God and His presence quiets our hearts.'

'Embrace Him, my brothers.' Sevrey breathed the air deep through his nostrils. 'We stand now at the door.'

Without warning or request, the four were seized and their wrists tied. The Franks submitted with grace, stoic and upright as the spear points of their captors pressed them forwards.

Ashraf received them outside his tent. 'Your priesthood is as a serpents' nest, many-headed and truly venomous.'

'Is this how you would welcome an ambassador?'

'I see before me only prisoners.'

'Prisoners who have held at bay your army and inflicted grievous wounds. Prisoners who come in trust to consult and settle issue.'

'All matters are decided.'

Sevrey did not shrink. 'There is talk yet to make, Ashraf.'

'Words have lost their power.' The sultan drew his blade and held it at his side. 'Kneel as you would before your cross. Stretch high your necks and offer them up for justice.'

'You may destroy the Temple, but shall never vanquish the Faith.' The marshal threw off the hands that held him and climbed with studied dignity to his knees. 'While I have voice, I curse you loud and sing praises to the Lord.'

It was Hazzim who dealt the blow and with a borrowed sword brought similar fate to the three remaining. He was living proof that all True Believers were equal to their calling and the most feared of Christian knights. Although he was inexpert, none could question the result. The sultan had chosen him with care.

Ashraf indicated to a trumpeter and the call went up, relayed and repeated in echoing refrain. Allah decreed and His servants obeyed. In thundering formation, two thousand men charged for the Temple, covering the broken ground and sweeping aside the defence. At the feet of the Mameluk leader were the draining corpses of the Templar hierarchs; before his eyes was the scarred shell of their former fiefdom. Everything was for the taking.

The final piece began to fall, the keep at first appearing to shudder and sway and then with random majesty decline into itself. Noise followed in hollow roar, chasing the tower down, belching from the clouded debris as the crenellated bulk folded and lost height and shape and slumped from general view. Undermined by fire-troops and bombarded by artillery, the structure had been no match for the weight of the storming infantry. Somewhere within, the body of William of Beaujeu had lain in state. And on the summit, as the edifice teetered and commenced its plunge, a boy of fourteen years had calmly held others close and bade the fearful to be strong.

Several hundred yards offshore, de Flor witnessed the event. He leant on a wooden rail, motionless and without speech, a soldier and mariner unable to intervene and scarcely able to believe. Slowly, the adventurer reached for his 'ud and in a gesture of loss and as an offering to the memory of a youth who had once listened to him play, flung the instrument far into the waves. Then he blew thrice on a whistle. The galley swung and the beat increased and the prow thrust northward to the matched dip and pulse of oars.

Some months later, a laden camel train trekked south across the plain of Acre. It had far to go and would not stay long. Already the men muttered of curses and bad luck and fretted at remaining where the air still tasted of horror and destruction. But the old caravaneer Selim was unpersuaded and stood awhile to gaze contemplatively upon the scene. Here there had once been trade and a host of Franks who welcomed his arrival. Only crows and buzzards and the odd sly fox greeted him today. He scanned the distant ruins and sighed at the waste and pity of it all, and murmured a prayer for the souls of the departed. Whatever had occurred, of one thing he was certain. His beloved *Waladii*, the youngster who had sat with him beside a spreading mulberry to engage in duels of backgammon, had finally made his choice between life and death, departure and remaining, boyhood and becoming a man.

Far to the east, a Chin monk from Shaolin continued to stride onward for his homeland.

✝

End

Few visitors bothered to divert there or had reason to cast a glance in the direction of the vanished city. Acre became a place not for pilgrimage or remembrance, but a site to avoid, a wasteland picked over by scavenging peasants. The ghosts kept most away. Yet twenty years after the siege and fall, a governor from Egypt was travelling that way. He was journeying north to quell revolt and impose punitive taxes, to bring the force of the Mameluk against those who opposed. With him were his retinue and bodyguards and regiments of royal troops and three sons he had brought for the purpose of their education. At the edge of the sunken traces of a former village he called a halt and continued west to the abandoned ruins accompanied only by his youthful heirs.

The boys appreciated the excursion, using the freedom to roam among the strewn foundations and stumps of buildings and to play hide-and-seek through deserted shadows. Their father listened to them clamber and call, almost smiled at the reverberation of their voices. They awoke many spirits. In a previous time he had done the same as they, had run and laughed in these parts where people lived and dwellings stood. Both he and the area had changed. So much battle, so much death, so much razed to blackened emptiness. His sons would not see the past or future as he, were not transported down alleyways inhabited by spectres and screams and lurking memory. Perhaps they were fortunate.

He wandered on, guided by instinct and recall, an Arab whose family had once made eau de vie. Occasionally he halted, jolted by a random sighting or distracted by sudden thought. There, the Venetian Tower, derelict and forlorn; there, the subsided remnants of the Fonda on which he had sat to watch the ships; there, the skeletal remains of the Church of St Andrew, its portal removed to Cairo to provide the grand entrance for a victory mosque. In the background, Hazzim heard the chattering argument and mirth of his sons. There were some who had never reached an age for the reward of progeny.

He climbed over a rock spill to gain entry to the great hall, the battered relic of a compound in which the Hospitallers had once held sway. It was in this corner that he had found shelter when the Italian peasants destroyed his world and down that well the corpses of valiant knights had eventually been thrown. But he explored the interior for a more specific reason. Treading with care, he negotiated a passage through fallen beams, smelled the charred particles thrown up underfoot and tracked the fluttering path of birds through the open roof. Desolation rarely came greater. Slowly he counted the pillars, examining each one and moving to the next, deliberate in his approach. None would hurry him in his funeral observance. His fingers slid to the rear of the column and crept upwards to the name. There it was, indented in the stone, letters etched by a young hand as statement and farewell. Hazzim pressed his forehead to the surface. The Latin who had befriended and protected him, who had shared with him this territory of the Holy Land, came alive vivid and cheerful in his mind. *Benedict*.

With his emotions controlled and countenance restored,

he emerged to take the air and stroll in meditative solitude to what had ceased to be the harbour front. Wreckage lay everywhere. Yet he knew where he had beheaded the marshal of the Templars, remembered where he stood when the mighty Lion Fortress had collapsed. The light and darkness of the past were not so easy to ignore. Before him, the Tower of Flies tilted at an angle from the tip of the flooded breakwater, its lamp extinguished and its sides despoiled. Still strangely defiant.

'Father . . .'

One of his sons ventured to approach, his tone hesitant and questioning. A tall and intelligent boy. Hazzim beckoned him near and placed an arm about his shoulders to steer his gaze across the bay.

'What happened here, Father?'

'Countless things, both good and ill. The triumph of our faith and the end of the Crusader.'

'Many must have died.'

'Thousand upon thousand. Soldiers and citizens, believer and infidel, slain atop walls and in streets that are long since vanished and along this waterfront once busy with craft.'

'I cannot imagine such a scene.'

'Nor could the Franks.' Hazzim felt the sea breeze warm on his face. 'They believed themselves our masters, invincible and chosen, divine messengers of their God.'

'Yet they are destroyed and we stand here.'

'Absorb it well, for it was a prize hard won.'

The boy observed with detachment the encircling view. 'The battle is far distant, Father. It is so peaceful now.'

His parent did not respond. He was staring to the west above the blasted ruin of the Temple, was projecting the brute experience of his youth to invisible lands and generations to be born. The boy was wrong. Other cities would fall and further towers crumble in a sacred war that was eternal.

✝

Historical Note

In the weeks following the demise of Acre, the sultan al-Ashraf marched his forces up and down the coast, mopping up resistance and capturing the weakened Latin enclaves of Tyre, Sidon and Beirut and forcing the surviving Templars from their castles at Tortosa and Athlit. Fortifications were levelled and churches razed and the monasteries on Mount Carmel were burnt to the ground. There would be no possibility of a beachhead left for a future Crusade.

Ejected from their strongholds, the Templars retreated to their small fortress island of Ruad (modern-day Arwad), some two miles off Tortosa. Here they stayed, maintaining a token presence near the Holy Land for twelve more years until adverse conditions in Europe forced their withdrawal in 1303. The order eventually fell victim to the greed and jealousy of the French king and was brutally suppressed from November 1313.

Faring better than their rival military order, the Hospitaller Knights of St John made their home on the island of Rhodes. For over two centuries they thrived at this location until, besieged in 1522 by the Ottoman Sultan Suleiman the Magnificent, they took to their galleys and settled finally on Malta. Chafing at unfinished business, Suleiman once more deployed a vast armada against the order in an action of 1565 that would enter legend as the Great Siege of Malta (the backdrop for the author's thriller *Blood Rock*). Many of the most precious artefacts and relics of the order were later seized by Napoleon and lost aboard the French warship *L'Orient* when she exploded during the Battle of the Nile (Aboukir Bay) in August 1798.

After retreating from Acre, King Henry and his dynasty consolidated the powers of a nominal Kingdom of Jerusalem on the island of Cyprus. His descendants were to rule there for several hundred years until they were ousted by the Ottomans. There were numerous schemes to reinvade the coastal lands of Palestine and build anew the Frankish empire of Outremer. Yet the will, funds and manpower were lacking and no interest was shown by the feuding princes of Europe. In 1365 a Latin force sent from Cyprus landed at Alexandria and sacked the Egyptian city. It did not stay long and was engaged in a mission to pillage rather than to occupy. The age of the Crusade had ended.

Enriched by his venture in smuggling to safety the wealthy women of Acre, Roger de Flor used the windfall to capitalise his later enterprises as pirate and mercenary. So notorious was the adventurer (also known as Rutger von Blum), he was even denounced by the Pope as an 'apostate and thief'. Born in Brindisi (*circa* 1267), the second son of a German falconer in the employ of the Hohenshaufen rulers of southern Italy, de Flor became one of the most effective military leaders of the age. Post-Acre, he raised and commanded a mercenary army on behalf of Frederick, King of Sicily, and was appointed Vice-Admiral of the Fleet; he also led campaigns against the Ottoman Turks laying waste to the Byzantine Empire and broke their siege of Constantinople in 1303. Marrying the daughter of King Ivan Asen III of Bulgaria, de Flor was awarded the title of Grand Duke and made commander-in-chief of the army. His old habits persisted, however. Having led his vicious *almogavers* in further successful raids upon the Turk, he became embroiled in a palace coup attempt in Constantinople and fell foul of powerful Genoese trading interests. In May 1305 he was assassinated and his Catalan mounted troops massacred. Revered by his men, he was avenged by an army that launched itself upon a sustained and bloody war. He would doubtless have approved.

Some five hundred years after the fall of royal Acre, the city was again at the strategic epicentre of historic event. In 1799, following the destruction of the French fleet at the Battle of the Nile, Napoleon found himself stranded with his army in Egypt. Deciding to turn the situation to advantage, he began to march north with the intent of occupying Syria and seizing Constantinople. The Ottoman Empire and ultimately British interests in India were under threat. Yet at Acre the ambitions of the French were thwarted by a spirited defence undertaken by the flamboyant British spy and Royal Navy captain Sir Sydney Smith and his small garrison. After two months of siege, having endured heavy bombardment and the undermining and capture of key positions such as the Accursed Tower, the motley Anglo-Turkish force of defenders successfully drove off the attack. Eventually Napoleon was able to slip away from Egypt and return to France, where he soon became emperor-dictator. Not until 1815 and the Battle of Waterloo did he once more suffer defeat on land at the hands of a British commander.

Acknowledgements

My profound thanks are owed to the following for contributing in so many ways to the writing of this book: Nick, Lizzy, Ram and Inga for turning a research trip into a vacation; Ram Seeger for his tactical knowledge and vast military experience; Eliezer Stern of Israel Antiquities and Chief Archaeologist at Acre for his extraordinary insights and expert opinion; Zivit Cohen Aviram for scouting the ground and guiding our expedition; Eugenie Furniss, my agent, and Kate Parkin, my editor, for their friendship, judgement and sound advice; and the American Colony in Jerusalem for providing the deepest of bathtubs and a myriad reasons to return.

The character of Benedict draws to some extent on that of Rudyard Kipling's Kim. But his spirit also owes much to Freddie Brind, the fourteen-year-old boy soldier captured with the British forces in Singapore during the Second World War. He survived the brutality and appalling conditions of the jungle prisoner-of-war camps established by the Japanese – harrowingly described in Alistair Urquhart's *The Forgotten Highlander* – yet died young having never fully escaped the mental burden. This book is essentially about Freddie and other youngsters caught up in war throughout the ages. They should be remembered.

Read more ...

James Jackson

REALM

England's hour of peril . . .

1588. In Lisbon the great Spanish Armada stands ready. In the Low
Countries the forces of the Duke of Parma prepare for war. And in
the shadows an even greater game is underway – a game of espionage
and murder, treachery and deceit, played with the stiletto-blade, the
poisoned chalice, the torturer's rack . . .

Faced with such deadly foes, legendary spymaster Sir Francis
Walsingham sends young Christian Hardy to discover the truth. But
as one by one his agents vanish, time is running out – for Hardy, for
England, and for its sovereign Queen Elizabeth.

*Order your copy now by calling Bookpoint on 01235 827716 or
visit your local bookshop quoting ISBN 978-1-84854-003-3
www.johnmurray.co.uk*

Read more . . .

Jack Hight

EAGLE

Book One of the Saladin Trilogy – A warrior is born

When the Crusader army is routed beneath the walls of Damascus, a young Saxon named John is capture and enslaved. He is bought by a Kurdish boy, Yusuf, for the price of a pair of sandals.

Timid Yusuf will grow up to become the warrior Saladin; John will teach his young master the art of war. And so begins the story of two enemies brought together by fate, and of a friendship that will change the face of the Holy Land.

'This is an ambitious book . . . a fascinating picture of momentous events' *Daily Mail*

'Excellent . . . a trip to a distant and dangerous era' Barry Forshaw

Order your copy now by calling Bookpoint on 01235 827716 or visit your local bookshop quoting ISBN 978-1-84854-299-0 www.johnmurray.co.uk

Read more . . .

Jack Hight

KINGDOM

Book Two of the Saladin Trilogy – A warrior comes of age

1164. The young warrior Saladin joins a Saracen army headed for Egypt – a land of wonders yet also of unparalleled danger. No one can be trusted. Saladin is surrounded by enemies and haunted by a deadly secret.

Meanwhile, in Jerusalem, Saladin's closest friend, the former crusader John of Tatewic, has been branded traitor. Spared execution on condition that he serves King Amalric, he becomes embroiled in court intrigue. Dark forces conspire to seize the throne. The battle for Egypt and for the Holy Land begins; Saladin and John will meet as enemies.

'Action, politics and drama are the hallmarks of this excellent series which gives a fascinating and balanced insight into one of the most turbulent periods in world history' *Lancashire Evening Post*

Order your copy now by calling Bookpoint on 01235 827716 or visit your local bookshop quoting ISBN 978-1-84854-533-5 www.johnmurray.co.uk

From Byron, Austen and Darwin
to some of the most acclaimed and original
contemporary writing, John Murray takes pride in
bringing you powerful, prizewinning, absorbing
and provocative books that will entertain you
today and become the classics of tomorrow.

We put a lot of time and passion into what we
publish and how we publish it, and we'd like to
hear what you think.

Be part of John Murray – share your views with us at:

www.johnmurray.co.uk
▶ johnmurraybooks
🐦 @johnmurrays
f johnmurraybooks